RUNNER
SAPPHIRE DUET BK 1

KAY RILEY

RUNNER

SAPPHIRE DUET BOOK 1

KAY RILEY

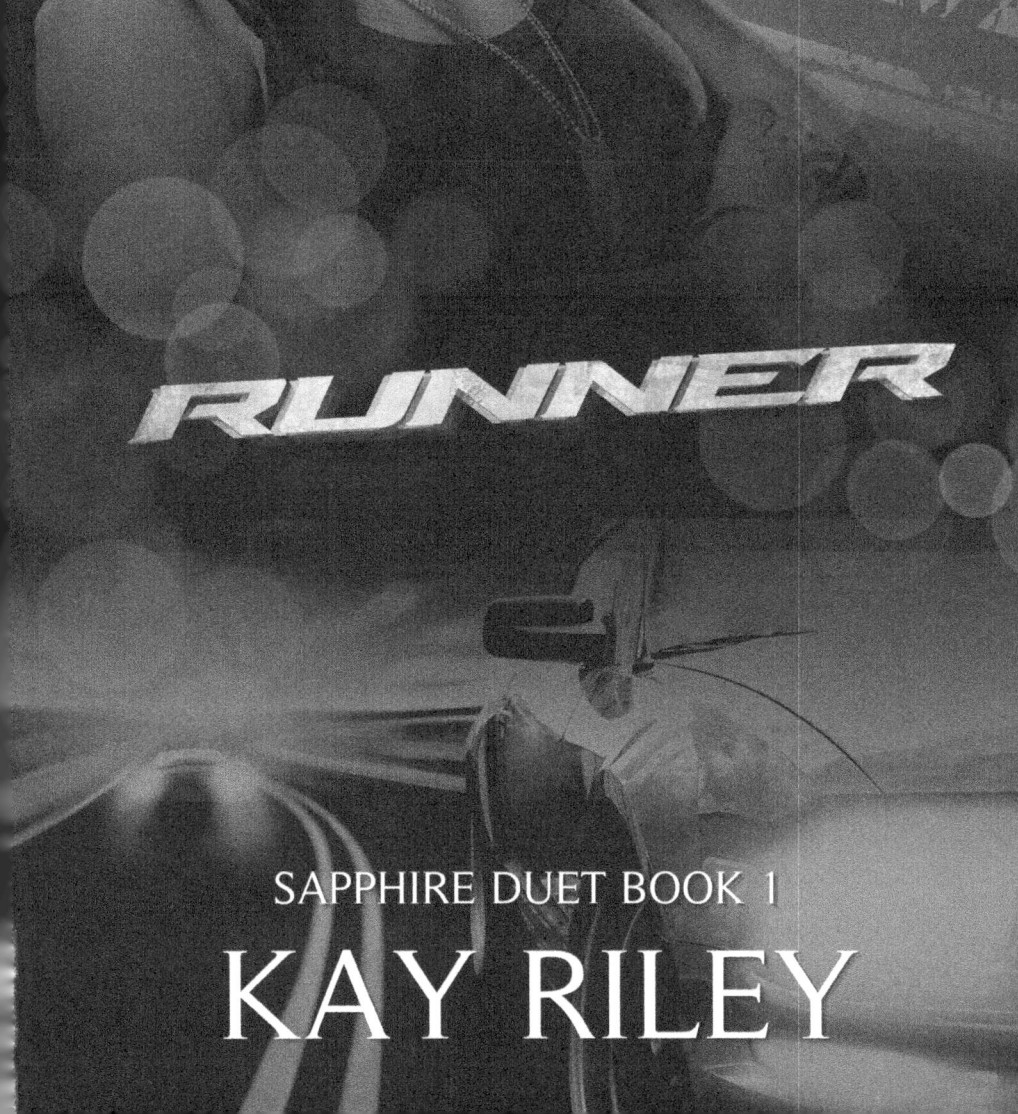

Copyright © 2022 Kay Riley

All rights reserved. No part of this book may be reproduced in any form or by any electronic or mechanical means, including information storage and retrieval systems, without permission in writing from the publisher, except by reviewers, who may quote brief passages in a review.

Names, characters, businesses, places, events, locales, and incidents are either the products of the author's imagination or used in a fictitious manner. And any resemblance to actual persons, living or dead, businesses, companies, locales, or actual events is purely coincidental.

Designations used by companies to distinguish their products are often claimed as trademarks. All brand names and product names used in this book and on its cover are trade names, service marks, trademarks and registered trademarks of their respective owners. The publishers and the book are not associated with any product or vendor mentioned in this book. None of the companies referenced within the book have endorsed the book.

Cover Design by: Dark Ink Designs

Edited by: Editing by Gray

Proofread by: VB Proofreads

Formatting: Dark Ink Designs

NOTE TO READERS

Runner is an enemies to lovers dark romance. It is why choose which means the female main character will have more than one love interest. There are dark themes and content throughout the book. If you'd like more information about content, please visit the author's website.
This duet is interconnected to my Suncrest Bay series. Both can be read independently, but there are crossover characters.

https://www.kayrileyauthor.com/

For all my readers who love the tension fueled spice between enemies before they become lovers, I hope you enjoy!

PLAYLIST
THEME SONGS:

"Get My Way" by RIELL & Vosai
And
"All Alone" by SkyDxddy

Full Playlist:
https://open.spotify.com/playlist/0yC8RQLi9f7lIgaLB5LPzx?si=dc737477e2d9473f

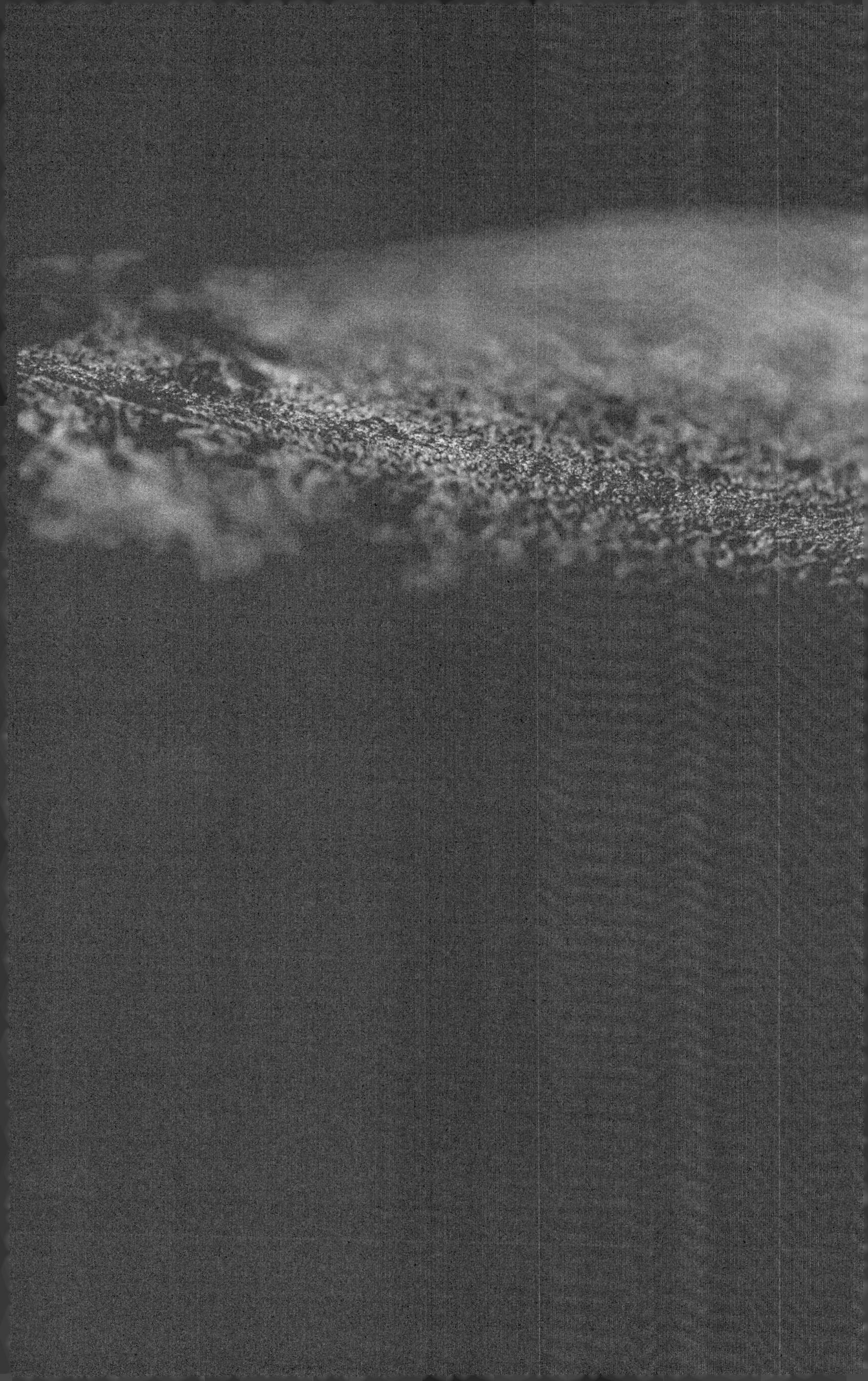

PROLOGUE

Kade

"Don't forget your lip ring," I muttered as I slipped on gloves to cover my tattoos.

"I know, Kade," my best friend, Grayson, grumbled, pulling his long dirty-blond hair behind his head. "Have I ever forgotten to take it off during a job before?"

"I don't like changing the plan." I tucked my gun into the holster under my suit jacket. "Maybe we should wait for another opportunity."

After taking out his lip ring, Grayson glared at me as if my words personally insulted him. "If we don't come back with that car, we'll be laughed right out of the next meeting. We told the bosses we could get it no problem."

"That was before the prick decided to go back to his car for a quick fuck in the middle of dinner," I snapped as we strode around the mansion to the back where the cars were. "We plan for a reason. So nothing goes wrong."

"We've been at this for years." Gray slung his arm around my shoulder. "We look the part. The guy won't have any idea."

"Fucking Orange County," I mumbled, tugging at my tie that was as suffocating as a length of rope. "Full of rich assholes and plastic women."

Gray snickered. "True. But the assholes also have the best cars."

"That's the only reason I'd be caught dead in this outfit."

"Be careful with your collar." He jerked my dress shirt higher up my neck before I shoved him away. "Your tattoos are almost showing."

"You think the other valets at this party don't have any tattoos?"

"Doubtful. This is one of the biggest parties of the year. They don't want anyone thinking thugs with ink work for them." Gray rolled his eyes as we started walking down the first row of cars. "Where did the valet park his car?"

"Fifth row," I answered, glad the sun was still going down. There weren't any lights this far from the house, but we wouldn't need them. We'd be long gone by the time the moon rose.

We grew quiet as we got closer, my pulse strumming with excitement like it did during every job. I lived for the adrenaline. Cars were my life. And I was a pro at stealing them. Gray and I both were. We didn't just take random cars off the street. We were the ones people called when they wanted the rare vehicles. Like the one we were getting tonight.

"There it is," Gray murmured in a low voice. "Damn, she's beautiful."

I followed his gaze and stared at the shiny black exterior of the Rolls-Royce Sweptail. In the ten years we'd been doing this, I hadn't been behind the wheel of one of those. But I would be tonight. A smile played on my lips as we walked closer.

We froze when a hand slapped on the inside of the rear window. Ducking behind the Cadillac we were near, I raised my head just high enough to keep my eye on our prize car. But what I saw through the window was what kept my attention.

"I can see why he chose to skip dinner." Gray knocked his shoulder into mine. "She's fucking hot."

I nodded grudgingly as we stared at the woman facing us. Her hand rested near her head on the glass, her red hair framing her face. Her eyes weren't focusing on anything as she stared at the sky.

A thick hand came from behind her and wrapped around her throat before a man started kissing her neck. Even though she tilted her head to give him better access, her pouty lips turned down with disgust.

"Just like every other woman in this city," I muttered. "Using him for his money."

"I mean, he has to know," Gray said with a shake of his head. "He's like sixty-five, and she looks our age. I don't think he cares as long as he has somewhere to put his dick."

"Let's get this over with. We need to be gone before the guests start leaving," I said, my gaze not leaving the couple in the car. "You got the key?"

Gray pulled a silver key out of his pocket. "Yeah. Everything's in place."

I nodded, standing up and rounding the Cadillac. The woman noticed me first. A hint of what looked like annoyance flashed through her eyes before her mouth fell open in surprise. She said something to the man, and he stopped kissing her to look at us. My muscles tensed as the rear door swung open and the man stumbled out, zipping up his slacks. His stomach strained against his wrinkled dress shirt, and stray gray hairs littered his nearly bald head.

"We're sorry for interrupting, sir," I said smoothly, wearing a fake smile. "We have to start moving the cars for guests who are leaving—"

"And why are you interrupting me when I have nothing to do with other guests?" Mr. Hughes spat out, not hiding how angry he was.

"Charles, these men are just doing their job." The woman stepped out of the car and gently laid her hand on his arm. "It's not their fault they ruined our fun."

Gray loudly cleared his throat as I tried remembering what I was about to say. Her voice was soft, but at the same time powerful. It was the kind of voice someone could listen to all day and not tire of. She pulled the straps of her black cocktail dress back over her shoulders and fluffed her hair as Charles glared at us before turning his attention back on her.

"Clarissa, I'm tired of waiting," Charles nearly whined as he faced the woman. "This is our third date, and you told me my waiting would end tonight."

I dug my elbow into Gray's ribs, knowing it would be almost impossible for him to stay silent at that. This poor fucker was getting strung along for his money, and she hadn't even fucked him yet. I didn't feel bad for either of them. Both were using each other for different purposes.

"It will end," she soothed, giving him a warm smile. "Maybe we can park the car somewhere else and continue what we were doing—"

"I'm sorry," Gray spoke up. "We can't allow anyone out here. There are rules in place to make sure nothing is disturbed during the party."

Charles's face grew red. "You think I'm a threat?"

"Of course not," I said quickly, trying to calm him. "Our boss made us come out here. It's the owners of the house who want to make sure no one is out here with everyone's vehicles. I'm sorry we have to be the messengers."

"Don't apologize." She turned her gaze on me, her amber eyes making me uneasy as she studied me. "It's not your fault. You're just following orders like good boys."

Her condescending tone had me clenching my fists. Anger scorched my veins as she smiled at me. Her eyes darted to my hands, curiosity flaring. Flexing my fingers, I reined in my emotions, reminding myself this was a job. And one shallow little girl wasn't going to fuck it up.

"If you two just make your way up to the house, I'm sure you can find a place to continue your fun." Gray winked, distracting her and giving me a chance to calm down.

"Watch yourself," Charles snapped. "She has no interest in the help."

Gray's grin didn't falter, even though I knew Charles's words pissed him off. "Of course, sir. Sorry. It's not often I'm in the company of such a beautiful woman."

"Come on, Clarissa. We'll go find an empty bedroom." Charles gripped her elbow, and I raised an eyebrow when she seemed hesitant to leave.

"I left my clutch in the back seat. Let me grab it." She turned toward the car, but Charles pushed her away.

"Stay here," he ordered. "I'll get it."

He moved toward the car, and when his back was turned, Clarissa stepped in front of me. I went still, not sure what the hell she was doing when she trailed her hand down my chest. Gray exchanged a look with me over the top of her head as he shrugged, not understanding what was happening either.

"You two don't belong here," she purred, her eyes sparking with a sinister fire that hadn't been there before.

"Do you always talk to *the help* like this?" I ground out, not liking how my dick was reacting to her light touch.

She was a fucking siren. The name Clarissa didn't match the gorgeous creature touching me. She had the voice of an angel and a body men would drown in sin for. It was easy to see why men like Charles would give her anything she desired just to get a taste of her. I knew exactly the type of woman she was, and yet keeping my head clear while she spoke to me was nearly impossible.

I bit my tongue when she raised on her tiptoes and pulled my collar until her lips were near my ear. Her coconut scent hit me, and my body leaned toward her before I could stop myself.

"I know you're not valet," she whispered, making me go rigid. "I hope your crew isn't too upset when you come back without the car."

I lurched back as her hand slid under my jacket. My heart stuttered when I felt my gun slip from the holster as she got a grip on it. Before I could even reach for it, I went to my knees when she kicked me straight in the balls.

"Motherfuck," I groaned out as pain ricocheted through my body. Shooting my arm up, I snatched her wrist, realizing my mistake a second later. As I kept a grip on her arm, she slammed the gun that was in her other hand into my temple.

"What the fuck?" I heard Gray bellow as I hit the ground. My vision went black, and I rolled onto my back as nausea swirled in my stomach. If she had hit me any harder, I would have been unconscious.

"Back off." Her voice sounded far away, and I flinched when a loud bang rattled my skull. A thud alerted me that someone else had hit the ground, and I hoped to God it wasn't my best friend. I blinked, trying to focus through the pounding in my head.

"Clarissa," Charles spluttered out from somewhere behind me. "What did you do?"

"My name isn't Clarissa," she informed him. "And I'm just fixing the problem these two were creating for me."

"Problem?"

"They're trying to take what I already worked for."

My blood ran cold when I focused and saw Gray slumped beside me, blood seeping from his shirt. Pushing myself off the ground, I scooted over to him as a lump grew in my throat.

"Fuck," I muttered, trying to control my growing panic. "Where are you hit?"

His head snapped up, his green eyes dark with pure rage. "I'm fine. The bullet didn't hit anything important."

"We need to stop the bleeding—"

"I will." He pulled his gun out and tossed it to me. "Go get her and show her why no one fucking messes with us."

I nodded, jumping to my feet, trying to ignore the extra heartbeat in my head. Charles was staring at Clarissa—or whatever the fuck her name was—with his hands in the air as she pointed my gun at him.

Aiming the pistol at her, I stepped closer, and she turned her head toward me but kept the gun on Charles.

"You shot my friend," I growled, my finger hovering on the trigger.

She grinned wickedly. "Only once."

"The only reason you're still alive is because you missed his heart." I kept my voice low as it shook with rage. "But killing you might be a mercy compared to what my crew will do to you for shooting him."

"I didn't miss. If I wanted him dead, fucking believe me when I say he wouldn't be breathing right now."

Her confidence had me convinced her words rang true. I had underestimated her because she looked nothing like a threat. That's what I got for letting my guard down. And it wasn't fucking happening again.

"Who are you?" Charles stammered, drops of sweat falling from his forehead. "I thought we were having a good time together—"

"You really should be thanking these men," she cut him off. "The death I had planned for you was slow and painful. But these two just sped up your timeline."

As she focused on Charles, I glanced at Gray. He was sitting up, pressing his hand against his bullet wound near his shoulder above his heart. His face was pale, but his eyes were alert, and that gave me a slice of relief that he would survive until I got him to a doctor.

"I don't understand." Charles took a step forward, but the second his foot touched the ground, another shot pierced the air. Charles went down screaming, his knee buckling where the bullet hit. I clenched my jaw, hoping no one heard that. We needed to get the car and get the fuck out of here.

"Tell me, Charles," she spat his name as if it were acid on her tongue. "After you were finished with me, what was the plan?"

He was barely coherent as he held his leg, staring at her pleadingly, tears pooling behind his lashes. "I don't know what you're talking about."

"Were you going to sell me?" she asked, making ice drip down my spine. "Like you do with all the other girls you get into your bed? Or is twenty-six too old for the men who buy women?"

I had known this guy was in some shady shit from the research we'd done on him, but somehow, we'd missed this piece of information. She had dug deeper than we did. Charles looked at me, shaking his head profusely.

"She's fucking crazy," he screamed at me. "Kill her before she—"

This time, she shot him in the head. He fell forward, dead before his face smashed into the dirt. Without wasting a second, she swung her gun toward me, keeping her aim level with my chest. Her eyes danced with amusement as we stared at each other.

"Drop the gun," I ordered coldly. "And maybe you'll survive this."

She laughed. "You made a mistake."

I raised an eyebrow. "How's that?"

"You came here with someone you care about." Shifting her stance, she aimed the gun behind me to where Gray was. "In this life, that's an easy way for someone to take advantage of you."

"You shoot him, and you'll be dead a second later," I grated out, my heart racing.

"Yes, but your friend would be dead right along with me." She cocked her head. "Could you live with that?"

"Fuck her," Gray shouted hoarsely. "Take the shot, Kade."

I wanted to. But as she backed away, I hesitated. She'd already proved she could aim, and the chance of her shooting Gray before I shot was fifty-fifty. There was no way I would be the reason my best friend went home in a casket.

"Good choice," she praised me, her voice smothered with faked sweetness. "I'll get out of your way. Good luck finding your way home."

"How are you going to do that when we have the key?" I asked, realizing she planned on taking the car.

"You really think I would have let that asshole lay a finger on me if I didn't have a way to take the prize I'd planned this entire thing for?" She grinned. "He gave the valet a spare key."

She kept the gun pointed at Gray until she ducked behind the open rear door of the Rolls-Royce. It dawned on me why she had wanted to get her clutch earlier. That was where the fucking key was. Once she reached inside the car, I bolted forward. I didn't want to shoot at her and risk damaging the car.

By the time I got to the open door, the purse was in her hand, and she was trying to climb into the front seat. The gun wasn't in her hand anymore, and I took advantage of that. Lunging forward, I grabbed her ankle, yanking her toward me. She might be able to fight, but she couldn't overpower me on strength alone.

"You should have killed me when you had the chance," I told her, dragging her closer. "When we take you back, it's not going to be pleasant for you."

"I could have. But I know who you work for." She didn't seem fazed as my grip tightened on her ankle. "And I don't feel like having a target on my back."

"Too late for that."

"After tonight, you'll never see me again," she promised. "Unless, of course, you get in the way of a job again."

"Who do you work for?" I asked, wondering how the fuck our paths had never crossed before this.

She wasn't struggling to get out of my hold. "I don't answer to anyone. A freedom I'll never take for granted again."

I had her halfway out of the car when she leaned forward. I didn't see the blade until she sliced my hand. I hissed out a breath, not letting her go. Her other leg shot toward me, her heel stabbing me in the ribs. She crawled farther onto the seat, and I jumped on top of her. Her fist collided with my cheek hard enough for my head to snap to the side. She reached for the gun on the seat, and I raised my arm and got a fistful of her hair.

"What the fuck?" I muttered when her hair slid off, doing nothing to stop her. I dropped the wig, but the wasted second was all she needed. The cold metal of the barrel of the gun pressed to my forehead as she lay under me. Her real hair was black and pulled into a tight bun. I stilled, not moving a muscle, as her chest heaved with each breath beneath me.

"You're going to get the fuck off me and scoot your ass out of this car," she demanded. "Or, unlike your friend, this bullet will fucking drop you."

The fact that she was giving me orders sent rage rippling through me. "I thought you didn't want a target on your back."

"My freedom or your life." She pretended to ponder for a moment before pressing the gun harder into my skull. "I will choose myself every time."

"I'm going to find you," I warned her, knowing her patience was waning as she frowned. "You won't get away with shooting him."

"Good luck. Now get the hell off me."

Deciding she wasn't bluffing about killing me, I slid back and stepped out of the car. She kept the gun on me as she reached into her clutch with her free hand.

"I hope your gun won't connect you to any other crimes," she said as she grasped the keys. "Or you'll be busy running from the law when they investigate Charles's death."

"You think I'd bring a dirty gun to a job?" I snapped. "We're not amateurs."

She licked her lips. "Could have fooled me. Shut the door."

I slammed the rear door, waiting for her to turn her back. When she moved to climb into the driver's seat, I pulled my gun out and shot out the passenger window. I cringed, hating myself for damaging this rare car. But it was clear I wasn't taking it tonight, and hell if I was going to let her have it that easily. The car roared to life as she ducked, trying to get out of my sights.

"Asshole," she snarled through the shattered window. "Do you know how much of a bitch it's going to be to get that fixed?"

"Get out," I yelled at her.

"Fuck you," she shot back, sliding down even more. The car changed gears, and she tore out of the parking spot blindly. I fired two more bullets as she straightened out after turning. Gray scrambled off the ground, diving to safety as she raced past him.

I saw her head pop back up once she felt she was far enough away. With the last bullet, I shot it into the back window, far enough away from her that I knew there was no risk of hitting her. I didn't want to kill her. Not yet. I wanted to know who she was first. It was obvious she ran in the same social circles we did if she pulled jobs like this. We'd find her.

I ran to Gray as the taillights disappeared when she turned out of the parking lot. Blood dripped from where he was pressing his hand. His body was shaking, and I was seriously worried about the amount of blood on the ground. I glanced down the row, looking for the easiest car to hot-wire. Once I spotted one, I helped Gray to his feet, letting him lean on me. I supported nearly all his weight as we moved closer to the car that was going to get us out of here.

"What a shit day." Gray forced out a laugh before grimacing. "Not only did we lose the car, we lost it to a girl. The guys won't let us live this down."

"She'll pay for this," I promised, busting out the window of the car, not taking the time to jimmy the lock. "We'll find her."

"I know."

1

Gray

TWO YEARS LATER

"Happy twenty-ninth, man." Kade slapped me on the back, making me spill my shot. I laughed, motioning for the bartender to get me another one.

"It's too bad we have business tonight." I downed the shot, enjoying the small buzz. "The club is on another level."

"The meeting shouldn't take too long," he replied, glancing at his watch. "We'll be done with plenty of time to still enjoy the night."

I nodded, swiveling on the barstool to face the dance floor. We owned the club and spent the weekend nights here if we weren't working. It had been a while since we'd had a free night. Black lights shone down on the crowd of people dancing. The music was so loud it was nearly deafening, but no one in here cared.

Kade ran a hand through his short brown hair as he turned to chat with a girl who had walked up to us. She traced the tattoos that covered his lower neck while giggling at whatever he'd just said. My gaze drifted to the dance floor, and almost immediately stopped on a girl in the middle.

Her back was turned to me as she danced like no one was watching. And fuck, she could move. Even with how dark the club was, I could see every curve under her tight outfit. A short black skirt hugged her ass, and a shimmery crop top revealed her bare back. Her hair was pulled into a high ponytail and whipped around as she moved. It didn't look like she was dancing with anyone as she moved to the beat of the song.

"Go." Kade nudged me. "We have time before the meeting."

I didn't need to be told twice and hopped off the barstool before making my way to the dance floor. Once people recognized me, they gave me space, making it easy to move behind her. Grasping her hips, I pulled her back until her spine hit my chest. She tensed as I dropped my head until my lips brushed her ear.

"My friend got me a new car for my birthday," I murmured, inhaling her addictive scent. "But I think a dance with you might top that."

She giggled. "Well, I wouldn't want to disappoint you on your birthday."

I could barely hear her over the music, but that didn't matter. I didn't come over here to talk anyway. The song changed, and she pressed herself against me, her grinding instantly causing my dick to stir. I trailed my hands all over her as we moved. The longer we danced, the more I touched, and her reaction had me wanting to pull her into a private room.

Her moves slowed as my fingers grazed her erect nipples through her thin top. I kissed down her neck and slipped my hand under her skirt. I half expected her to push me away since we were on the dance floor, surrounded by people, but she spread her legs wider instead. I groaned, feeling her soaked through her panties.

"Happy birthday to me," I muttered, pushing her panties to the side and finding her clit. I wrapped my other arm around her waist, keeping her close when she started squirming at my touch. Moving my fingers in small circles, I ignored everyone around me except her. If anyone saw what I was doing, they'd look the other way. They knew who I was, and in here, I could do whatever the fuck I wanted.

Her head fell back and rested below my shoulder as I picked up my speed. Raising my hand from her stomach, I wrapped it around her throat. Her pulse was thrashing like crazy, and I squeezed firmly, stopping just before I cut off her air. She didn't seem uneasy about how I took control of her body.

I slid two fingers into her, letting my palm rub against her clit as I moved. The grinding she was doing now was all to get the friction she needed. Her body tensed, giving away how close she was. I continued my movements, my fingers curling every time I plunged them back inside her. I could hear her cry even over the music as she came hard. Pulling my hand out from her skirt, I sucked on the fingers that had been inside her seconds ago.

"Fuck me," I mumbled, wanting to properly taste her. Besides smoking weed, I didn't do drugs. But in this moment, I understood how people became addicted. I would do some dicey shit for a chance to bury my face in her pussy. She tried pulling away, and my hand tightened around her throat. "Where do you think you're going? We're nowhere near done."

She laughed. "I have somewhere to be. But thanks. I wasn't expecting to have that much fun tonight. Raincheck?"

"I promise the things I'll do to you will make being late more than worth it." I lightly bit her neck, feeling a shudder run through her body.

"I'm sure that's true, Grayson."

My name fell from her lips as if she'd known me forever. With a frown, I released her neck before grabbing her arm and spinning her around. She was smiling, but her eyes were filled with warning. Her light brown eyes. The same amber eyes I stared into when I'd taken a fucking bullet to the shoulder.

"You," I hissed, keeping my hold on her arm.

"Oh no, you found me. Just like your little friend promised two years ago." She sounded bored, and when she dramatically yawned, my self-control snapped. Grabbing her other arm, I kept her in front of me as my anger rose.

"I don't know what the fuck you're playing at, but coming here was the worst mistake you could make," I growled, scanning her body again, looking for hidden weapons. There was no way she had anything on her. I'd touched nearly every inch of her, and her outfit didn't leave room to stash even a small knife.

She pretended to pout. "Just a few seconds ago, you were promising me amazing sex. You mean that option isn't still on the table?"

"It's really too bad," I murmured, letting my face go cold. "We could have had some fun if you hadn't tried to kill me."

Her smile grew bigger. "I didn't try to kill you."

"Bullshit."

"It was a graze."

"I needed surgery and was in a sling for months."

"But you're not dead. You should feel lucky. I usually don't leave witnesses when I do a job."

I studied her, knowing her words were true. She was as cutthroat as we were. And probably even more dangerous since she was a threat no one saw coming. Keeping a tight hold on her upper arms, I glanced over my shoulder at Kade. He was watching us in confusion, and I realized he hadn't seen her face yet. I jerked a nod, making him slide off the stool before striding over to the dance floor.

"You never should have come here. Or you should have killed us," I told her, turning my attention back to her. "Because now you won't be leaving this city."

"Like I told you before, I'm late for something." She peered around me, a frown forming on her face. "Tell your friend I said hi."

"Tell him yourself. I'm sure he has a lot to say to you—"

I yelled out a curse when her thick heel connected with my shin. Then she dropped. It was impossible to keep a hold of her arms when she fell straight down. Hands grasped my ankles and yanked. It was enough to make me stumble but not fall.

"Too late to run now," I said loud enough for her to hear as I bent down to grab her.

"Who says I'm leaving?"

She ducked around my hand and crouched lower, swinging her leg out. Pain shot up my calf, and this time when her fingers wrapped around my ankle and tugged, I went down. I hissed out a breath as I landed on my tailbone. The dance floor cleared around me, and I shot back up, watching as she shoved through the crowd to get to the back of the club. The music quieted as I raced to catch up to her.

"Lock it down," Kade roared from behind me. "Nobody fucking leaves."

I closed the distance between us as she passed the bar. A waitress with a full tray of drinks pressed against the bar as I reached past her and snagged the girl's wrist. She whirled around, her face a mask of calmness. Her eyes went from my hand and then back to my face.

"Can't keep your hands off me?" she asked, planting her feet when I tried pulling her closer.

"There's nowhere to go," I informed her. "The doors are locked."

"Fine with me." With her free hand, she grabbed the waitress's arm and pulled her between us. The waitress screamed as she was shoved into me. Her tray of drinks tipped forward, drenching me in what smelled like tequila. I clenched my teeth, feeling her twist her wrist from my grip before she pushed the waitress into my chest.

She bounded up the stairs behind the bar, taking two steps at a time. Kade flew past me, hot on her heels. After steadying the waitress, I followed behind him but took my time as I calmed my nerves. The only thing up there was our private room. And there was no way out unless she had a key.

I shrugged out of my soaked black leather jacket, shaking off the alcohol that was dripping from it. I grumbled under my breath as I climbed the steps. If she'd ruined my favorite jacket, I was going to be more pissed than I was when she shot me.

Kade had left the door open, and I closed it behind me, being sure to lock it. I could hear her screams of frustration, but as I scanned the room, I couldn't see them anywhere. In front of me were four couches surrounding a round glass table. A table for meetings was on the side of the room that held ten people. The entire front of the room was one-way glass that gave us a view of the club below. A few plush chairs were scattered in front of the mirror, and they were all empty at the moment. I threw my jacket on one of the chairs as I continued to look for them. In the back of the room was a black velvet pool table next to a small bar. Another door was on the side of the room that led to a smaller room and the exit.

I rounded one of the couches and stopped short when I saw them. Kade was sitting on top of her. He had one of her hands trapped under him and her other wrist pressed to the wood floor near her head. She was deathly still. It probably had something to do with the knife Kade was holding against her throat.

I bit my tongue, trying to ignore how her skirt had risen far enough to get a peek of her red lace panties. Shaking my head, I walked forward until I saw her face. Kade glanced at me for a moment before looking back at her. I frowned, not seeing any panic or fear on her face.

"Give me one reason I shouldn't kill you now," Kade murmured, his voice venomous.

Her gaze flicked to me and then back to Kade as her lips curled into a devilish smile before she answered.

"Hellfire."

2

Milina

"What did you say?" Kade asked in a low voice.

"Hellfire," I repeated, resisting the urge to flinch when the blade against my neck pressed nearly hard enough to draw blood.

"Where the fuck did you hear that?" Grayson snapped, crossing his arms.

"Is that not the word you've been waiting to hear?" I raised a brow, my eyes darting between the two of them. "Or was I told the wrong time for our meeting?"

"You're not the one we're supposed to meet with. Somehow, you found out and are using it to save your skin." Kade's hold didn't lessen as he spoke.

"No one knows that word unless I want them to know," I snarled, losing my patience. "You're about to fuck up your only chance. No one gets a second meeting."

"Why the hell would they send you as a messenger?" Grayson asked, eyeing me with suspicion.

My anger burned red hot, and for the first time since Kade tackled me, I struggled against his hold. The knife he had against my throat put me at a disadvantage. When I'd walked into their club tonight, I had every intention of explaining who I was in a calm, rational conversation. Until I had a couple of drinks and somehow Grayson's hand ended up under my skirt.

I wasn't complaining. This way was much more fun anyway. But the fact that they thought I was some lowly worker was insulting. I worked too hard to be mistaken for nothing more than a fucking messenger.

"Would you like me to prove that I'm supposed to be here?" I asked sweetly, covering my other emotions. Revealing true feelings was the quickest way to lose the advantage in any situation. I'd been trained years ago on how to twist my features to portray what I wanted others to see. It had been more than five years since anyone had been able to draw out my real reactions, and it had almost killed me. It wouldn't ever happen again.

"Show me," Kade demanded, his eyes still burning with fury.

"First, let's look at the facts." I spoke as if we were having a friendly chat. "I walked into your club completely unarmed. Knowing the two of you probably still held some resentment for what happened in the past."

"Some resentment," Grayson repeated in disbelief. "You shot me and then left us there with a dead body."

"Yet I still came here." I shifted my body, testing how serious Kade was with his threat. When the knife nicked my skin, I let out a sigh, knowing I'd have to show them who I really was before we could get down to business. "I'm going to need my hands if you want me to show you."

"Tell me, and I'll get it for you," Kade replied, not backing off.

I chuckled. "It's not something I can just pull out. It's a tattoo."

Kade's eyes narrowed in suspicion. "Where?"

"Lift up my shirt."

Silence filled the room as Kade exchanged a look with Grayson. After a few moments, Grayson kneeled near my head. He grabbed the wrist Kade had been holding before reaching down and grabbing my other arm, pulling it until he had both my wrists in his grip. His hold was as tight as Kade's had been. Kade pulled the knife away but stayed on top of me. Stretching my neck, I looked at Grayson upside down as he peered at me.

"This whole meeting is a waste if you two can't trust me enough to have a civil conversation." My words made Kade glare at me, but he didn't say a word as he grabbed the hem of my shirt.

Besides my heavy breathing, I didn't move a muscle as he raised my top, revealing the tattoo I wanted them to see. Kade's eyes widened, and Grayson leaned over me to get a better look. The ink covering my upper stomach defined who I was. Light blue flames spanned across my ribs just under my breasts, but I was sure it was the object in the flames that had them both in shock. Right in the middle was a vibrant blue sapphire stone.

"There's no fucking way," Kade ground out, his eyes glued to my body.

"Why?" I snarked, relishing in their disbelief. "Because I'm a woman? You think I can't succeed in this world because of that? Let me tell you a little secret. It actually makes it easier. Because men think with their dicks. Making it simple to get whatever the fuck I want from them."

"You're Sapphire?" Grayson asked, as if waiting for me to laugh it off as a joke.

"Yes," I snapped. "This business deal is huge. I wanted to handle it myself."

"The Sapphire is a ghost," Kade muttered to himself.

"That's the whole point." I rolled my eyes. "It makes it hard to get jobs done if people know who I am. Usually, I send others in my place for business that has to be dealt with in person. A faceless ghost is the perfect criminal, wouldn't you agree?"

"What's different about this job?" Grayson asked, glancing at my tattoo again.

"Get the hell off me and I'll tell you."

"I don't give a shit who you are," Kade threatened as he climbed off me. "If you try anything, you won't leave this room alive."

Annoyance flared, and I bit my tongue, keeping my words to myself. I didn't deal with disrespect very well. But I was here for a reason. This business deal needed to happen. Because fuck me, it was one job I couldn't do myself. And even though they were dicks, the two guys staring at me with pure hate were some of the best car thieves in the country. As much as I didn't want to admit it, I needed them.

I let Grayson grab my arm and pull me around to the front of the couch. I fell onto the cushions myself before he forced me to sit. Crossing my legs, I gave them a wide smile when they both sat on the couch across from me. The space they gave me proved what I already knew. The doors in this room were locked, and I could bet there was no unlocking them without a key.

An unwanted tightness smothered my chest when I realized getting out of here wouldn't be easy if this meeting went south. Everything I did, I planned meticulously. I never left anything to chance. That was how I survived this long. My gaze traveled to the bar in the back of the room and then to the pool table with a couple of pool sticks scattered on top of it. Even though I wasn't armed, there were enough things to use as weapons if it came down to it. That thought eased my nerves a fraction.

I promised myself I'd never be trapped again. Living years in a life that was a prison was a hellish nightmare, and I would rather die than lose my freedom again. I'd do this job and get out of this city.

"Are we going to get down to business, or are we waiting for more members of your Riot Crew to get here?" I asked through the tense silence. "I was under the impression that your boss wanted to meet me."

"You expect us to believe that one girl is Sapphire?" Kade obviously wasn't coming to terms with who I was.

I cocked my head to the side. "Did you forget I stole a Rolls-Royce right out from under you two?"

"A damaged Rolls-Royce." Grayson smirked. "I'm sure it wasn't fun having to replace the windows that were shot out."

So their new tactic was to get under my skin. I could play that too. Letting my gaze drop to his chest, I bit my lip. "It was probably more fun than dealing with a bullet wound. But after tonight, I almost regret shooting you."

Both of them stared at me until Grayson couldn't help but speak up. "Why?"

"Because it would have been an atrocity for the women in this world if you lost the use of your arm." I pretended to inspect my nails. "You got me off in almost record time. There aren't enough men in this world who know the right way to touch a woman."

My unexpected compliment shook them, and I slowly uncrossed my legs, making Grayson's eyes drop from my face. A muscle in his jaw flexed when he got a peek under my short skirt as I readjusted.

"At least you can say you're good at something." I waited to continue until he met my stare. "Because if we go by our one and only previous interaction, it's clear you may need to up your game when it comes to stealing cars."

Grayson didn't say a word as he moved his lip ring around with his tongue. Even though they were staying quiet, their simmering rage saturated the room. Falling back into the cushions, I made myself comfortable on the couch. They were far enough away from me that I'd have time to defend myself if I pissed them off again.

"At least we keep our clothes on when we do jobs," Kade murmured, leaning forward and resting his elbows on his knees. "You're right. I'm sure boosting cars is easier for you."

The back of my neck flushed with heat. Not from embarrassment, but from surging anger. Keeping the smile on my face, I looked at him questioningly. "Was I not wearing clothes when you saw me last? It really is amazing what men will do with the promise of seeing a woman naked. Though I always finish the job before they realize they'll never get what I promise."

"I don't know. You seemed pretty easy on the dance floor." Grayson stole my attention as he tried to shake me.

"If we work together, you'll learn quick that no one touches me unless I want them to." The threat was clear in my voice. "I let you believe you had control over my body, Grayson. But you did exactly what I wanted. I'm the one who got the orgasm. While you got blue balls—with the added bonus of pleasuring the woman who shot you. If anything, you were easy."

"It's Gray," Grayson snapped. "Don't call me Grayson."

Interesting. I'd found something that bothered him without meaning to. Filing that little fact away for later, I glanced around the room again.

"We won't be working together," Kade said with certainty. "We need to trust everyone on our team. That won't ever happen with you."

"Thanks for clarifying that." I stood, and they both bolted to their feet, already on the defensive. "If this deal isn't happening, then there's no reason for me to be here."

Kade's cruel laugh shot a shiver down my spine. "You don't think you're just going to leave, do you?"

"That's exactly what I'm doing."

I strode to the door, only to freeze when Grayson slipped in front of me, close enough for our chests to touch. I didn't need to turn around to know Kade was right behind me. I could smell the alcohol that was still soaking Gray's black V-neck shirt. Even in my wedges, I had to tilt my chin up to meet his eyes.

"Move," I ordered, letting venom sink into my voice. "Or that warehouse you have on Fifth Street will go up in flames."

Gray's hazel eyes darkened while he leaned closer, as if trying to intimidate me. "How do you know about that place? That's Riot business."

"You think I didn't do my homework before I came here? If I don't walk out of this club in the next hour, then someone who works for me will light that warehouse up." I tapped my chin. "How many cars do you have there right now? As of yesterday, it was ten. I can't imagine the cost of losing all that merchandise."

Before either of them could respond, the door swung open. Gray spun around as two men walked in. I smiled, knowing these were the men who would decide whether to do business with me. Kade and Grayson owned this city. But the Riot Crew was much larger than the city of Ridgewood. And the men who were staring at me with interest were the big bosses.

Maybe this job would happen after all.

3

Milina

"I'll have a gin and tonic, sweetheart." One of the men nodded at me dismissively before starting a conversation with Gray. I laughed under my breath, spinning around to face Kade.

"Gin and tonic sounds good." I trailed my fingers down Kade's arm, making him scowl, before I headed back toward the couches. "I'll take one too."

The men stopped talking as I sat back down, staring at them intently. The guy who had mistaken me for a waitress was glaring at me with his mouth hanging open. He was a large man who was in great shape, and was wearing jeans with a crisp buttoned black shirt. The sleeves were rolled just below his elbows, and tattoos covered his exposed mahogany skin. His black hair was styled just as perfectly as his short beard.

I knew exactly who he was. I'd researched every person in the Riot

Crew that was worth knowing about. This man was Victor Stiles. Most call him Vic. He wasn't married, and he was in his early forties. He lived for the Riot Crew, and there was a reason they were as large as they were. Because the bosses didn't take any bullshit.

The man who walked in with him was Juan Lopez. He was shorter than Vic. Maybe a couple of inches taller than my five-foot-six frame. His black hair was bone straight and came down past his ears when it wasn't slicked back. He kept his face clean shaven, showing off his sharp jawline.

He was just as ruthless as Vic. The two of them ruled the Riot Crew together. Their origin story made waves in the criminal world. Having two bosses on top was almost unheard of. From what I was able to learn, Juan was from Mexico, and years ago, he ran a gang down there. The two of them had always been friends and decided to merge their criminal enterprises. Juan lived here in California but still did lots of business south of the border.

From everything I could uncover, the two of them had never had a falling out or betrayed each other. They weren't blood, but they were as close as brothers. I was sure there was more to their story, but even with my extensive research, I knew I didn't get all the facts.

"Who are you?" Juan asked, his eyes narrowing on me.

"She claims she's Sapphire," Kade spat out.

"She knew the codeword for the meeting," Gray spoke up as his eyes trailed down my body. "And she has a tattoo."

Vic glanced at Juan before he crossed the room until he was standing in front of me. I rose from the couch, an electric current of adrenaline buzzing under my skin. This was the riskiest move I'd made in a long time. I could handle myself in almost any situation, but four against one wasn't good odds, especially when I didn't have a weapon.

"I don't see a tattoo," he said, his gaze trailing my body.

"We did," Kade replied. "It's a sapphire surrounded by blue flames."

"Hmm," Vic hummed out before moving away from me and walking to the bar.

"You wouldn't have the symbol for Sapphire inked on your skin unless you have a death wish," Juan said, pulling the toothpick from his mouth.

"Unless I am Sapphire," I snapped, losing my calm. I didn't come here to be questioned about my identity. "If you aren't serious about doing business, I'll go to the next person on my list."

"How old are you?" Juan asked as Vic handed him a glass of whiskey.

"How is that any of your business?"

My question had both of them frowning at me. Being rude to the bosses of Riot wasn't something anyone did unless they wanted to die. But they hadn't earned my respect, and I wasn't one to give it away freely.

"She's twenty-eight," Gray answered, shooting me a smug grin.

I chewed on the inside of my cheek as I stayed quiet. Telling Charles my age before I killed him two years ago was a mistake. However, I never expected to see Kade or Gray again, so I hadn't cared if that detail about me had slipped out. I was regretting that now.

"She's the one who took the Rolls-Royce," Kade admitted grudgingly, glaring daggers at me.

Vic and Juan looked surprised at that. They inspected me again, but this time in a new light. I doubted anyone got the drop on their guys often, so what I'd done to Kade and Gray must have been a big deal.

"Excuse us a minute." Vic nodded at me before the four of them went to the back of the room near the bar. They spoke quietly enough that I couldn't pick up any part of their conversation. I kept my eyes on them, not hiding the fact that I was watching. If they wanted privacy, they could have left the room. For the first time since I entered the club, I was able to really look at Kade and Gray. I had researched everything I could about them too when I decided to make this deal.

Kade Jacobs and Grayson Scott had been friends for as long as they'd been alive. They grew up here in Ridgewood and had been associated with the Riot Crew since they were fourteen. They were also in line to take over the crew when Vic and Juan stepped down. I guessed they wanted to keep the tradition of two bosses alive. I still didn't understand it. There wasn't room on top for two. That's why I worked alone.

Kade glanced at me, looking more than a little heated, before turning back to Vic and arguing about something. Even when he was angry, he was still hypnotizing to look at. His hair was a dark brown, almost black, and he kept it cut shorter on the side with the top a bit longer. Both his arms were covered in tattoos, and I could bet he had just as many under his shirt. His light brown skin was flawless, and though he wasn't stocky, his ripped muscles were impossible to miss.

I was almost positive he was related to Juan. The two didn't share the same features, but Kade did more business on the south side of the border with Juan and was immersed in Juan's family. Kade had been raised by his single mother, and no matter how much I dug, it was impossible to find anything out about Kade's father. It made sense. Even though they wanted two bosses at the top when Juan and Vic retired, they wouldn't trust just anyone. With an empire as large as this, they'd want at least one family member leading it.

My gaze drifted to Gray. He was as breathtakingly hot as Kade, but in his own way. His dirty blond hair was almost as long as mine, resting just past his shoulders. He usually had it pulled back like it was now. His green eyes were usually light with amusement unless he was angry. Then they were a few shades darker, and when he met my eyes, I could tell he was more than a little agitated about me being here. I shot him a little grin before he turned his attention back to Vic and Juan.

If he didn't have his lip ring or tattoos, he'd be the perfect picture of a surfer. But from what I'd learned about him, he had no interest in sports or the ocean. Like Kade, cars and the crew were his life. He almost always wore a black leather jacket that he seemed unhealthily attached to. It was a mystery to me on how he'd gotten so deep with the gang. His parents, by all accounts, were the picture-perfect family. His father had a respectable job, and his mother stayed at home to raise him and his younger sister. I guessed he got involved because of his friendship with Kade.

Vic cleared his throat, ending their conversation as they all made their way back to where I was on the couch. I met Juan's stare, keeping my face emotionless. I understood their shock. In all the years of the rumors and stories of Sapphire, I doubted anyone ever suspected a woman could fill the shoes of the infamous name.

"You contacted us to work together on a job," Vic stated, his voice full of authority. "Why did you choose us?"

"Because you have bad blood with the Panthers. Which means we have a common enemy." Standing up, I took my time smoothing out my skirt before continuing. "This is a three-person job. Your boys here can help get what I need. And, of course, we'll split the profits."

"Stealing from the Panthers is a good way to get killed if you get caught," Kade said, distrust lacing his voice.

"We won't get caught. We have six months to plan to make sure everything goes perfectly." I didn't add that the Panthers had stolen from me first. All they needed to know about were the cars we were going to steal. "Between the three of us, we'll be in and out before they even realize what's happening."

Juan flipped the toothpick with his tongue. "My boys don't trust you. And for good reason. They could have ended up dead or in prison with how you left them two years ago."

"If that were the case, then they wouldn't be worth my time. They got out of that predicament with ease, proving they're worthy to work by my side."

Gray grumbled under his breath, glaring at me as I spoke. Kade crossed his arms, suspicion scrawled across his face. I rolled my eyes, preparing to make my exit.

"It's clear they don't want to work with me. This was a waste of time." I moved toward the door until Vic stepped in front of me. My muscles tensed, and I prepared to fight my way out if I had to. He must have noticed my change because he raised his hands and stepped back a couple of feet.

"We would love a chance to work with the notorious Sapphire," he said, trying his hardest to keep his voice light. "If you want to work with Kade and Gray, we will make that happen."

Raising an eyebrow, I glanced over my shoulder, expecting the two of them to argue. But they stayed silent, their eyes focused on Vic.

"But we can all agree that there needs to be trust to work a job together. Especially a job as large as the one you're suggesting." I turned my attention back to Vic as he spoke. "We'd like you to work with them on smaller jobs while we plan. That way, you three can get comfortable working with each other."

I hesitated, considering his idea. That wasn't what I wanted. I planned to only be in Ridgewood when we met to plan, and that was it. I worked alone and had no desire to change that. However, out of everyone on my list, I wanted to work with Kade and Gray the most. They were nearly as good as I was, and with them, this heist had the best chance at succeeding.

"All right," I agreed slowly. "I'll stay here so we can work while we plan. But I do not follow anyone's rules. Including your gang's. I'll respect your city while here, but do not expect me to do fall in line like your soldiers."

Juan tensed, not liking my words. But they needed to know I wouldn't do jobs for their crew while I was here. Car jobs were fine, but anything else wasn't my problem. Vic nodded, accepting my deal.

"What's your name?" Gray asked stiffly.

I smiled. "For now, you can call me Sapphire. No offense, but I don't think we've built up enough trust to spill my personal life to you."

"Why do I have a feeling you know everything about us?" Kade muttered under his breath, not looking happy about the arrangement at all.

I ignored him, facing Vic and Juan again. "As you already know, I like to stay under the radar. No one outside this room is to know who I am. If I find out you're telling people who I am, I'll be gone without so much as a goodbye. I'll call to set up our next meeting."

"You don't have our numbers," Gray interjected.

I had reached out to them via email to set this meeting up, but they had no idea that I had both Kade's and Gray's personal numbers. It would come in handy in the future.

"We have many properties in the city you can stay at—"

I cut Juan off. "Thank you, but I can find my own place."

They all frowned at me, not liking that I wasn't giving them an inch about anything. With a nod of my head, I strode to the door and let myself out. Bounding down the stairs, I moved faster than usual, not wanting Kade or Gray to catch up to me while I was still weaponless. Vic and Juan obviously wanted to work with me, but I had a feeling Kade and Gray were still very skeptical.

A few curious stares met me as I stepped back into the club. No one bothered me as I jogged to the exit, the silence of the outside street hitting me once the door closed behind me. Their club was on the north side of Ridgewood and wasn't usually a place a woman wanted to be walking around alone. Especially at night. The north side was the poorest area of this massive city. And was also where most of the Riot Crew lived and had their businesses. Cars lined the narrow street, and even though it was nearly eleven at night, many people were still milling around on the sidewalks.

I passed a small garage, which I knew was also an illegal chop shop. I had researched everything about this city before I came here, focusing mostly on where the crew was. This street was filled with locally owned businesses. I got swallowed by shadows as I turned the corner. Apparently, working streetlights weren't a priority here.

My ears pricked up, hearing someone behind me. I continued to walk, listening as the person's footsteps got closer. Once I guessed they were within hitting distance, I whirled around, my arms already raised. I slammed my forearm into the man's neck, shoving him into a parked car on the street. To my surprise, it wasn't Kade or Gray.

"I'm sorry. I didn't mean to startle you," the man said, staying still as I pressed my arm into his throat. Unease flowed through me, noticing that my sudden attack didn't seem like a surprise to him.

"Who are you?" I asked coldly.

He flashed me a sheepish grin, keeping his hands at his sides. He was wearing an expensive suit and looked very out of place on this side of town. He looked to be my age or maybe a little older, and although he wasn't my usual type, I couldn't help but admire him. It took a lot to scare me, and this man was nowhere near the type of predator I was used to playing with.

"I was in the club when I saw Jacobs and Scott going after you," he explained, and I swore I heard amusement in his voice. "I wanted to make sure you were okay."

The moonlight was my only light as I inspected him. His smile was easygoing and friendly—which made my guard rise. His hair was either dark brown or black and was styled perfectly. Between the suit and his hair, I guessed he was a businessman. The question was whether he was legit or on the dark side of the law. For some reason, I had a feeling he didn't belong in my world.

"As you can see, I'm fine." I reluctantly removed my arm from his neck and stepped away from him. "And for future reference, following a woman at night looks bad, even if you had good intentions."

I was still watching him closely, not sure if he was really just a concerned citizen. He chuckled, adjusting his suit jacket as he kept his eyes on mine.

"You know Kade and Gray?" I asked, referencing how he used their last names.

"Almost everyone in this city knows who they are," he answered, looking at me curiously. "That crew makes this city chaos."

The bitterness in his voice wasn't lost on me. "I thought the crew did good for this town. They give to the people who need it. Money, food, jobs."

"Yes, by their illegal doings," he said with a frown. "They aren't the type you want to get mixed up with."

I laughed. "I can take care of myself. And if you don't like them, why were you in their club?"

"What's the saying? Keep your friends close and enemies closer."

I stiffened a little at that, wondering who this guy was. After a moment, I gave him one of my best smiles, offering him my hand. "I'm Mili. It's nice to meet a man who is concerned about a woman's well-being. Especially when I'm new to town and don't know anyone."

"Nice to meet you, Mili." He shook my hand firmly. "I'm Rylan. And you seemed well acquainted with Grayson. Although he didn't seem happy with you."

I bit my tongue, not happy that he didn't tell me his last name. I wanted to see what I could find out about him. If he was an enemy of the crew, then I wanted to know everything about him. I giggled, waving my hand dismissively.

"He was someone I was dancing with. He got angry when I didn't want to take it farther. I had no idea who he was until they shut down the entire club. We worked it out though."

"Just be careful around them," Rylan said, and it was driving me crazy that I couldn't tell if his concern was real or not. "Those two are some of the most bloodthirsty and dangerous people in this city."

"Thanks for the warning," I said lightly, beginning to walk away from him. "Have a good night, Rylan."

"Do you need me to walk you home?"

"No offense, but you could be dangerous too," I said, only half teasing. "I don't make it a habit to walk with strange men."

"Smart girl," he muttered, sliding his hands in his pockets. "You need smarts like that to survive in this city."

I didn't answer him as I strode away, making sure he wasn't following me. I wasn't sure what to make of him. I doubted he was as innocent as he portrayed himself to be. At the same time, he didn't emit danger like Gray and Kade did. Hopefully, I'd be able to find out more about him once I got to my laptop.

The salty air was a reminder of how close I was to the ocean. It was a far cry from New York City, which was where I'd spent the majority of the last five years unless I was working jobs. The air was warm but not oversaturated with humidity, and I decided I could get used to this. I wouldn't miss the cold winters of the East Coast while I was here.

Not that I would have much time to enjoy California now that I had agreed to work jobs with the Riot Crew. It would be worth it to pull off the Panthers' job. But I needed to watch my back. Even with Vic and Juan wanting to work with me, I saw revenge in Gray's eyes. They weren't over what I'd done to them, and I wouldn't put it past them to try and get even.

It would be fun to see them try.

4

Kade

"Have you found anything?" Vic's voice was almost deafening through the car speakers, and I flicked down the volume while Gray answered him.

"There's nothing to find," Gray grumbled. "There's nothing online about her at all. Whoever helps keep her invisible does a damn good job."

"Do we know when she started working jobs?" Juan asked.

I gripped my steering wheel, wishing we could have found more about her before Vic and Juan called. "No. There was no obvious shift when the last Sapphire stepped down."

"I want you to keep us updated on everything when it comes to her," Vic ordered. "Having her in your city can hurt or benefit us, and I'd rather it be the latter. Do not let what happened in the past cloud your judgment."

"You mean when she shot me?" Gray mumbled.

"She could bring good business if she likes working with you," Juan said. "Keep it professional."

"We will," I grated out, not enjoying being told what to do. Vic and Juan were technically our bosses, but we'd been running this city for years.

"Is the meeting still happening?"

I glanced at the café through my window. "Yeah. In ten minutes."

"Let us know how it goes." With those last words, Vic hung up. I grabbed my phone from the center console and slid it into my jeans pocket.

"It would be nice to know how the hell she got our phone numbers," Gray said, shaking his head. "I wasn't expecting a text from her."

I nodded in agreement. It had been three days since she had shown up at our club, and we hadn't heard from her at all. Until we both got a text last night, telling us to meet her here for lunch to discuss the job.

"Are we really going to do this?" Gray asked, giving me a pointed look. "I don't trust her. If things go bad, she wouldn't think twice about leaving us behind on a job."

"Let's just see what she has to say. If we don't like it, we'll find a way to get her out of our city without Vic and Juan knowing. They want her connections."

"Or we could make her disappear," Gray muttered.

"We need to find out more about her first." I'd had that thought too, but it was too early to act on it. "If she really is Sapphire, killing her could be a bad move."

If she really was Sapphire. Even with her tattoo, I had doubts. That name had been known in the car world for decades. The original Sapphire was a legend. Street racing became huge in the sixties in Detroit with the Big Three car companies. No one knew his real name, but Sapphire was the best. People came from everywhere to see him race. Then he disappeared without anyone knowing what happened to him.

Until a new face showed up, claiming to be Sapphire. He told a story of how the original Sapphire chose him to carry on the name. Sapphire gave the guy his prized racing car and all his knowledge with the promise that he'd pass it all on to someone else who was worthy. Over the years, every time Sapphire disappeared, someone would take his place. And as time went on, it went from just street racing to stealing cars and becoming powerful in the criminal world.

As technology improved, the more Sapphire went underground. The symbol of that name was exactly what the girl's tattoo was. A dark blue sapphire sitting in light blue flames. Most people who held the title had stayed anonymous in the last few decades. The name was infamous, and people wanted to know who was behind the mask. Especially when Sapphire started doing big-time jobs. Enemies wanted to destroy the empire built around the name. Others wanted the rumored fortune. Some were just curious.

A few times, we had known who Sapphire was, but those usually didn't last long. They either ended up dead or in prison. But there was always someone to take their place that the Sapphire had chosen. For the last fifteen years, no one had set eyes on Sapphire. But everyone knew he or she still existed.

Jobs were still happening. Sometimes they'd show up for large street races, with their face covered and not letting anyone know until the race ended that it had been Sapphire racing. When Gray and I were eighteen, we watched a race, not even realizing we'd witnessed Sapphire winning the last race until they threw a calling card out the window with the flaming sapphire symbol on it before speeding away.

Seeing as she was our age, there was no way that had been her. But if she really was Sapphire now, then she knew who we'd seen over ten years ago at that race. If she was staying in town, then I wanted to find out all I could about her.

"Ready?" Gray asked, opening his door.

"Let's get this over with." I tucked my gun in the waistband of my jeans after stepping out of the car. My phone went off, and I looked at the text that popped up on the screen.

Unknown number: I'm sitting outside. Don't be late.

I gritted my teeth, showing Gray the text really quick. If she thought she was going to order us around, this little peace we had wasn't going to last long. We turned the corner, and I scanned the outside eating area for her.

"If she expects us to be on time, she should be too," I said, scanning the busy tables again.

"She is." Gray pointed toward the back, where a couple of tables were right near a glass wall. "The only reason I recognized her was because I caught her eye."

I looked at her table again, wondering how I'd missed her. Until I saw her appearance. Unease made my pulse thud as we made our way over to her. She was wearing a pink sundress with flip-flops. Her black hair was braided and hung over her left shoulder. A paperback book sat on the table in front of her. The way she could blend into any crowd was unnerving. When she was in our club the other night, she was dressed like the ultimate party girl. The night she stole the Rolls-Royce, her role of a rich socialite was perfection.

"Hi," she greeted us in a bubbly voice. "I ordered crepes for all of us. I hear this café has the best in town."

I sat down stiffly, realizing it wasn't just her clothes. It was everything. The pitch of her voice. The look in her eyes. Even her posture. Like right now, if anyone was watching her, they'd see a cheery young woman who looked like she attended church every Sunday. Taking a moment to study her bare arms, I wondered if she had any other tattoos besides the one she'd shown us. As far as I could tell, she had no identifying marks at all. That probably made jobs easier.

Gray sat down between her and me. The round table was small, and if she was nervous about Gray sitting so close to her, she didn't show it. Unlike the night at the club, I could guarantee she came here armed.

"Is there a reason you didn't want to meet at our club again?" I asked.

"I thought a public place was better. Until I know you aren't planning my demise." She giggled as if she'd told a joke, catching the eye of the server who was setting down the food she ordered. She shot him a flirty grin, and he returned it before quickly averting his eyes when he met my glare. He quickly shuffled away, and she cast a disapproving look at me.

"You two attract too much attention," she stated, her gaze drifting to my tatted arms.

"You're the one who wanted to meet here." Gray snagged a crepe from the plate. "We have no reason to hide. This is our city, and everyone knows who we are."

"Why'd you want to meet?" I asked, wanting to get down to business.

Her smile changed, going from bubbly to lethal in an instant. "Your bosses wanted us to work together. I have a job tonight and decided to extend an invite."

"Tonight?" I repeated. "That gives no time to plan."

"I already have it worked out." She sipped her iced coffee. "But it's two cars, so having you both with me will make it go faster."

"We don't even know your name," Gray muttered. "We're not doing a job when we don't know who we're doing it with."

"You can call me Mili," she told us without hesitation.

I raised an eyebrow. "That's your real name?"

Her grin widened. "It's my real nickname."

Since she gave it up so easily, I doubted we'd find anything with that name if we tried searching it.

"How long have you been Sapphire?" Gray asked.

"Long enough to know how to survive without people catching on."

"Who was Sapphire before you?"

Her smile stayed, but her eyes went cold. "Sorry, we don't talk about our predecessors. I was chosen, and I've had the keys to the kingdom for a long time."

"Is he dead?" I pushed, trying to get one straight answer from her.

"Why are you convinced it was a guy?"

"No one has laid eyes on Sapphire in over ten years." Gray cocked his head to the side, studying her. "Why is this job against the Panthers important enough for you to come to us?"

"They have a car I've wanted for a long time." Setting her coffee down, she pulled keys out from her designer purse. "I didn't call you here to be interrogated. If you don't want to help me on this job, then I'm leaving."

"Wait." Gray grabbed her arm when she tried standing. The façade of the innocent woman dissolved, and her frigid glare went from Gray's hand to his face.

"You have three seconds to get your fucking hand off me," she warned, her free hand moving for her purse.

"Well, if it isn't the two most upstanding citizens in the city," a voice said from behind me.

Mili's eyes flashed with surprised recognition as she looked behind me. I groaned, not having to look at him to know who it was. Gray tensed, letting go of her arm. A shadow came over me before the empty chair next to me was pulled out.

Forcing a smile, I faced him. "And what can we do for the great mayor today?"

5

Milina

Shock coursed through me as I stared at Rylan. He was the fucking mayor? That's what I got for procrastinating when it came to researching him. I'd been busy the last couple of days, trying to find a place to stay where no one would find me. If I had taken five seconds to search his name with the city's name, that would have come up immediately. I made a mental note to look into him the second I had a free moment.

"Nice to see you again, Mili," Rylan greeted me with a warm smile.

Gray's and Kade's heads snapped toward me when Rylan said my name. If I thought their prior suspicion was bad, it wasn't anything compared to how they were looking at me now.

"Are you keeping tabs on me?" I asked with a giggle, pretending that seeing him again hadn't shaken me. What were the odds of seeing him twice in three days? It could be purely innocent, but I didn't believe in coincidences like that.

"It's not you he's keeping tabs on," Kade grated out, his dislike for Rylan very apparent to everyone at the table.

"You all know each other?" I asked, acting curious.

"Unfortunately," Gray muttered under his breath.

"I try to know all business owners in my city," Rylan said, eyeing the crepes in the middle of the table.

My gaze trailed over him, taking in the small details I had missed the night I met him. His hair was a deep brown with lighter natural highlights throughout. His face was clean shaven, and I noticed a small scar running along his jawline on the left side of his face. His hazel eyes met my brown ones, and he grinned before taking a bite of a strawberry crepe. I watched a crumb fall onto his navy-blue suit until Kade stole my attention.

"Did you need something, Rylan?" he asked, crossing his inked arms. I bit my tongue, realizing our table was attracting stares. Nerves skated through my veins, not liking the eyes on me. I always stayed under the radar, never gaining attention unless I wanted it. I'd have to remember to keep my future meetings with them more private.

"I just wanted to make sure you weren't giving her any problems." Rylan tossed the half-eaten crepe back on the plate. "I would hate for you two to catch harassment charges."

"Says the man who followed me the other night," I interjected.

Rylan looked surprised at my words. "I guess my warning about them fell on deaf ears."

I bristled. "I heard you. I like to judge people on my own."

"They might want people to believe they're good people, but they're not," Rylan tried convincing me. "You make them mad, and I'll be finding your body in a field."

Gray snorted. "Who the hell is dumb enough to dump a body in a field?"

"We own multiple companies throughout town," Kade said, shooting a look at Gray.

"They're criminals," Rylan forced out through clenched teeth. "Criminals rich enough to keep themselves out of prison."

Kade smirked. "Careful, Mayor. You don't want slander charges brought against you."

The way they interacted had me believing there was a history between the three of them that wasn't pleasant. The fact that Rylan was so blatant about voicing his hate for them and the way Kade and Gray acted like his accusations were a joke made me uneasy. I wasn't used to being thrown into situations that took me by surprise.

Rylan took a deep breath and looked at me. "I'm only trying to do my job as mayor and tell you the type of men you're spending time with."

I let my eyes trail down his crisp suit. "So I should be spending time with men like you?"

His eyes widened in surprise before he cleared his throat. "No, I'm not saying that. But I'm more trustworthy than them."

I scoffed. "Politicians are just criminals wearing expensive masks."

Gray barked out a laugh when Rylan frowned at my response. "I don't think you're getting her vote in the next election. Why don't you cut your losses and leave us the fuck alone?"

"Actually, I'm leaving." I snatched my purse off the table and stood, catching Rylan's eye. "And just so you don't worry about me, I'm not hanging out with these so-called criminals. Grayson wanted to apologize for how he acted the other night."

I didn't need the mayor of this city thinking I ran in the same circles as the Riot Crew. Catching his attention this much was already a mistake. I could feel Gray's glare, making me wonder why he hated his name so much. But knowing I found an easy way to get under his skin had me smiling. I moved to leave, and Kade caught my wrist. His small grin dared me to threaten him like I had with Gray earlier. I scowled, not saying a word. There were too many eyes on me at the moment to make a scene.

"I hope you enjoy your time in Ridgewood," Kade said in a low voice. "I'm sure we'll run into you again."

"This city is huge, so that's doubtful," I replied, pretending to be uncomfortable that he was touching me. I shook out of his grip and strode away. Before I made it halfway to my car, my burner phone dinged, and I glanced at the message.

Kade: We're in for tonight. Send us the details.

I grinned and pulled out my other phone, pressing the only number on speed dial. He answered as soon as I slipped into my car—well, not my car. The one I borrowed for the day. Somewhere in the suburbs, a poor guy was searching for his cherry red Jeep that was taken from his driveway in the early hours of the morning. Tonight, once the car was wiped of my fingerprints, I'd return it.

"It's good to know you're still alive," Caleb said the second he answered my call. "I've been worried about you all morning."

"I told you I'd be fine."

"I still think it was a mistake telling them who you are." Worry smothered his voice.

I sighed, starting the Jeep. "They wouldn't have worked with me otherwise. We've been working toward this for the last four years. It's our best chance to get that car."

"It won't be worth it if it costs you your life."

"But if we do this, we'll be free," I said softly. "We can have our lives again."

"I have a bad feeling about this, Mili."

A rare warmth filled my chest at his concern. I didn't care about many things in this world, but I'd fucking kill for Caleb. He was the reason I'd survived this long. He was the brains behind Sapphire. All my jobs and contacts went through him. Computers were his life, and he could hack into nearly anything. Thanks to him, my identity had been wiped. If anyone tried finding me by my real name, all they'd find is a death certificate.

Milina Porter died in a fire five years ago with no surviving family. I was a ghost in the world, and that's how I planned to stay.

"I'll come visit at the end of the month," I promised him. He lived in Florida, and we were careful when we were together. But if I pulled this job off, we'd never have to watch our backs again. "But I need you to email Kade and Gray the layout of the job I'm doing tonight."

"You asked them to help you?" It took a lot to shock Caleb, and I laughed at his reaction.

"Yes. Vic and Juan don't trust me. I need to prove we can work together before the Panther job," I explained, driving to my new apartment.

"You told me they were assholes to you the other night."

"They were. I don't think they believe I'm Sapphire."

"You're going to end up killing them before they have a chance to help you with what we need," he said bluntly.

"I have more patience than that—"

"Not when people piss you off."

"Caleb. Believe me when I say I have it under control," I soothed him. "I want this job to happen more than anything. If I have to make nice until their use runs out, then I'm perfectly capable of it."

"I have the plan in place in case they try anything."

"And if they do end up killing me?"

Caleb sucked in a breath. "Can you not be so morbid?"

"Come on. In this life, every breath I take is one more than I thought I'd have."

I could just imagine him pinching the bridge of his nose. Sometimes I felt guilty that he worried about me so much. But it would all be in the past once we finished the Panther job.

"If you die, they do too," Caleb finally muttered. "Let's hope it doesn't come to that."

"I don't think it will," I said, sounding more confident than I was. Kade and Gray were dangerous. And they didn't trust me. It was a bomb waiting to go off.

"Make sure to call me every three days like we agreed," he reminded me.

"I will. I have to go. Once the job is done tonight, I'll let you know.

The last time I got a car for this buyer, he tried skimping me on my pay. That won't be happening again."

"I'll make sure it's in the account," Caleb said. "Be careful."

"Always."

I hung up, tossing my phone onto the passenger seat. Tall buildings were on both sides of the road, letting me know I was on the south side of Ridgewood. It was as far away as I could get from crew business. This was where the wealthy and privileged lived. The type who would turn their noses up at me if they knew who I really was. But for now, I fit in perfectly because I was playing the part of a recently divorced young woman who came from old money.

Parking in the underground parking structure, I got out and quickly changed the plates on the Jeep after making sure I was alone. I'd already done it once today but wanted to be careful. This was one of the few spots in the garage that was a blind spot for the cameras.

I'd bought an apartment in the nicest building in town. I wanted the penthouse but figured that would be too obvious if Kade and Gray tried finding me. Plus, the ground floor was better, in case I needed to leave in a hurry. The apartment was under a fake name. My driver's license had another fake name with a different address in town. There was nothing connecting me to anything.

Unlocking my front door, I threw my purse on the island in the kitchen before stripping off my dress. I needed to wear something more comfortable when I did the job tonight. I walked into my bedroom and opened the walk-in closet. The apartment was brand new and had state-of-the-art everything. It was a small one-bedroom but had all I needed. I bought it furnished, not caring that everything was in white and gray. I couldn't remember the last time I lived somewhere that I actually cared enough to decorate. I was never in one place long enough to worry about it.

My phone went off again, and I went back into the kitchen to grab it. I frowned, staring at the new text. Shuffling backward, I fell on the white leather couch as I debated what to do.

Kade: We have some questions about tonight. Meet us.

Along with the text was a link for a city park on the north side near their club. This was most likely a ploy or a trap of some kind. Caleb would have sent them every detail they needed for tonight. I decided not to text back, even though I was going to meet them. I'd make it clear if they did something to me, their deaths wouldn't be far behind.

I went back into my closet and picked out a pair of leggings that had a pocket for my pistol in the waistband. I slid a pocketknife into my sock before pulling on a baggy T-shirt that would hide the outline of the gun easier.

I was more curious than anything to see what they'd try to do. It was clear Vic and Juan wanted to work with me, which meant they were most likely doing this behind their bosses' backs. Kade and Gray were definitely men to be wary of. They could potentially put fear in me like they did everyone else if I hadn't faced worse demons in my past.

But they were nice to look at. And I had no plans for the afternoon. Ignoring the small nagging voice of Caleb telling me to be careful, I grabbed my keys and walked out the door again.

6

Gray

"You think she'll show up?" I asked, looking out the window as the sun began to set.

"Hopefully. If it all works out, she won't be a problem anymore," Kade answered as he parked the car.

I turned on the radio, ignoring Kade's overdramatic groan when I chose my favorite playlist.

"I can only take so much eighties music before my ears bleed," he grumbled, not making a move to turn off my music.

"Vic and Juan won't be happy when they find out," I told him, ignoring his jab at my comfort music.

"I'd rather them be pissed at us than get killed because of her."

I agreed, which was why I was sitting here with him. But I knew Vic and Juan were going to chew us out for it. I'd still rather deal with them than trust Mili. I narrowed my eyes, seeing a woman jogging alone. It wasn't until she got closer that I recognized her.

"You owe me a hundred bucks," Kade stated with a grin. "I knew she'd show up."

"Lucky guess," I grumbled.

"You ready?" he asked, turning serious.

I nodded, swinging open my door right before she ran past the car. She skidded to a halt, not looking surprised when she met my gaze.

"This park is huge," she told me as she stretched her legs. "You could have given me a better idea of where you'd be so I didn't need to go searching for you."

Her baggy shirt hid the toned body I knew she had, and although I couldn't see any, I was positive she had at least one weapon on her. She trusted us as much as we did her—which wasn't at all. Hopefully, she didn't put another fucking bullet in me tonight.

"Get in." I shot her a charming smile.

She raised an eyebrow, surveying Kade's most precious possession. The Jaguar E-type we were sitting in was a sleek black, with black leather interior. Kade had gotten it years ago, which was a record for him. Usually, he went through cars like they were snacks. He loved this fucking car.

"There's only two seats," she finally said.

"There's more than enough room." I patted my lap, and she let out a boisterous laugh.

"Fuck off. This isn't worth it. If my email wasn't enough for you, I'll do the job myself."

I waited for her to turn her back on me, but instead she backed away, making sure to watch me. She was already defensive, which was going to make this much fucking harder. Before she could guess my next move, I lunged halfway out of the car, just catching the hem of her shirt when she attempted to duck away from me. I yanked her closer, grabbing her wrist.

"You really don't want to do this," she snarled, her eyes bright with fury.

She clocked me in the face, making my ears ring, but I didn't let go, pulling her into the car. She was on my lap, facing me, and she immediately put her free arm behind her back. My heart lurched, knowing exactly what she was going for. Kade leaned over the middle console, grabbing her other arm and wrestling away the gun she already had in her hand. In a quick move, he slid the chamber out, tossing the gun and bullets onto the floor near my seat.

I jerked my head to the side when she tried headbutting me. She had to lean over to keep from hitting her head on the roof of the car and her breasts were pressing into my chest as she fought to free herself. This car was tiny, and she just barely fit on my lap. I heard the click of the handcuff when he locked it around her wrist. Her struggles instantly intensified while Kade and I worked together to lock the handcuff around her other wrist.

"You fucking assholes," she spat out, trying to slide out of the cuffs. I tightened them before shutting my door, and Kade started driving the second my door was closed. "If you're going to kill me, you better do it before you take me out of this car."

"And what happens to us if you die?" I asked, knowing if she really was Sapphire, killing her would have consequences.

Her smile held nothing but hatred. "Why don't you do it and find out?"

"We're not going to kill you," Kade said, turning out of the park. "If we were, I wouldn't have driven my car."

Mili didn't relax at all from his words. Her heart was beating wildly against my chest, and she was shifting slightly. I was worried she was trying to get out of the cuffs, and I hoped Kade was keeping an eye on them, since I couldn't see them behind her back.

"If you're not going to try and kill me, then what the fuck are you doing?" she asked, her glare shifting from me to Kade.

"We wanted to show you the city," I answered, feeling her thighs squeezing my legs together. She was trying to act calm, but being trapped in here was clearly aggravating her.

"If I was going to take a tour of the city, I'd choose a better car than this piece of shit."

She stared at Kade, as if waiting for his reaction, like she knew how much he loved this car. I gave him credit for not rising to her bait. His grip on the steering wheel tightened a fraction, but he kept his eyes on the road.

"And where's your leather jacket, Grayson?" she purred, focusing back on me. "You're always wearing it."

A muscle in my jaw ticked, and I gripped her hips tighter when Kade took a curve faster than usual. She was trying to get under our skin and show that she knew about the things we loved. Her coming to our city to work with us must have been a long plan in the making.

"I didn't want it to get stained with blood in case things got messy," I said, giving her a grin of my own.

"Good thing you weren't wearing it the night I shot you."

Kade was weaving in and out of traffic, going twice the speed limit. It didn't seem to bother Mili at all. She hadn't looked out the window once since I'd gotten her in the car. I was usually the only person who could handle Kade's driving, but he might have met his match with her. If she wasn't such a pain in the ass, I would have loved to see what she did when she was behind the wheel.

"I'm guessing this means you don't want in on my job tonight?" she asked, glancing over her shoulder at the clock on the radio. "That's fine. You two would have only gotten in my way."

"We're doing the job," Kade said, his stare lingering on her instead of the road. "But I think you'll be too busy to join us."

If his words scared her, she didn't show it. She leaned back, pushing her legs off the seat a bit. It was barely noticeable, but having her on my lap had her every move going straight to my dick, so it was easy to pick up on it. Her calmness made me pause for a moment before I realized I should have fucking searched her the second I got her in the car.

"I think your mayor friend was right about you two," she said with a pout. "You're nothing but criminals who kidnapped an innocent girl who was out jogging."

"Why do I have a feeling your body count is larger than both of ours?" Kade mumbled, turning down the main street in the city.

She opened her mouth to answer but went rigid when I ran my hands down her thighs. She bucked against me, her move useless because she was already stuck between me and the dashboard.

"You better move your hands," she growled, her voice deadlier than ever. "Or I'll fucking rip that cute little lip ring out with my teeth."

"Calm down. I am moving my hands," I taunted, moving farther down her leg until I touched her ankles. "I'm just looking for—here it is."

I pulled out the knife she'd been hiding in her sock. It was already halfway out, which meant she'd almost gotten a hold of it. Her amber eyes were promising my death as I tossed the knife on the floor next to her gun. I quickly patted her down, satisfied she didn't have anything else on her.

"I don't know if I believe you're really Sapphire," Kade said. "For someone who is supposed to be feared, we got you in this car pretty easy."

"You really think I came here not knowing you two were up to something?" she asked with a roll of her eyes.

"And if we had killed you?" I asked, trying to figure her out.

She shrugged. "Then I had a good run."

Kade laughed sarcastically. "You're exactly the type of person we want to do jobs with. Someone who has a death wish."

"If I had a death wish, I would have let myself succumb to it years ago," she snapped. "I just know that if I die, so do you. And it will be much less pleasant for you. I've been Sapphire for years and have many who work for me without ever having seen my face. If I was easy to kill, someone would have done it already."

"Why is this Panther job so important?" I asked, wanting to know why this one was so different.

"It's a rare car."

Before I could question her further, blue lights lit up behind us. They reflected her eyes when she looked out the back window. Instead of panic or fear, true excitement filled her gaze. She glanced at Kade expectantly.

"Let's see how fast this car goes," she demanded with a grin. "It's not as good as mine, but even this should outrun a cop car."

"You think I'm going to run?" Kade asked.

"Please." She scoffed. "You two aren't the type to pull over."

"True," I mused. "But I think this time we're making an exception."

Her guard came back up when Kade slowed the car, pulling onto the shoulder. Two police cruisers came up behind us and stopped.

"What the fuck are you doing?" she hissed, twisting her body to try and open the door even with her hands behind her back. She tried to slam her head into mine again, and I wrapped my hand around her throat, keeping her back.

"I can't believe you tried to steal my car," Kade murmured, taking the keys out of the ignition. "I wonder how long of a sentence car theft carries. And with a loaded gun and knife? We won't be seeing you for a while."

Her shock wore off, and her mask slipped back on as she laughed. "You think this will ever hold up in a court?"

I kept my hold on her throat. "We don't need it to hold up in court. Did you forget whose city you're in? We own half the police force. They'll keep you in jail for as long as we line their pockets."

"I have to say, I didn't see this coming." Her eyes went back to the window. "Using cops to do your dirty work. How boring."

She was calmer than I expected, not even flinching when the passenger door was ripped open. Two cops stood there, and after giving us a respectful nod, they looked at Mili. One of the men's stares went straight to her chest, and anger ripped through me. I wanted nothing to do with her—she'd probably kill me in my sleep. But thinking of others touching her pissed me off in ways I didn't understand. Which pissed me off even more.

"She's not to be touched," Kade ordered before I could. His eyes were clouded with warning as he stared at the cops. "If I find out someone did, there'll be problems. Got it?"

They both nodded quickly, fear blatant on their faces. I released Mili's neck, lifting her off me so they could get her out of the car. They only grabbed her arms, being careful not to even brush another part of her body.

"I want daily reports," I said, catching her eye. She stared back at me blankly, not showing an inch of emotion.

"She doesn't get a phone call. Put her in a cell by herself." Kade started the car back up. "Enjoy your vacation, Mili."

She suddenly grinned, her eyes burning with vengeance. "Oh, don't worry. I'll see both of you soon."

My heart thudded unevenly, and I stared at her while they dragged her to the closest police car. She didn't try to get away or fight when they pushed her into the back seat. I glanced at Kade to see him watching through the rearview mirror.

"I really hope that was the right thing to do," I muttered. "She seemed too calm."

"They'll put her in a cell and leave her there. Even if she is Sapphire, I doubt she's an escape artist. It'll work for now." He didn't sound as sure as he usually did, but he started driving anyway.

"If she gets out, we better watch our backs." I had no doubts that she wouldn't blink at killing us.

"I think she needs us alive more. She risked a lot coming here."

"Let's fucking hope so."

"We'll worry about it later," Kade said with a small grin. "Let's go do this job."

7

Milina

"Motherfucking assholes," I mumbled under my breath, watching the Jaguar drive away. "Fucking good for nothing bastards. Can't even do their own damn dirty work."

"Did you say something?" The cop sitting in the passenger seat turned to look at me. He was the same one who couldn't keep his eyes off me when they'd taken me out of Kade's car. I could play with that. I let my face crumple, working myself up to real tears when the other cop spoke up.

"Don't talk to her, Randy," the driver snapped. "She belongs to the crew."

Red hot anger shot up my spine, and I went rigid, glaring at the back of the driver's head. Hell fucking no. I belonged to no one. I had promised Vic and Juan I'd respect their city. But that was before Kade and Gray had fucked up. I didn't care where the hell I was. I didn't want a soul in this world thinking I was owned by someone. I'd gotten out of a life like that, and it would never happen again.

Instead of playing the sobbing, terrified girl I had planned, I decided on a different tactic. Leaning forward, I rested my forehead against the bars that separated the front of the car and the back seat.

"What can we do to come to some type of deal?" I asked, keeping my voice sweet.

The man named Randy jumped, startled that I was so close. He whipped his head around to stare, and I bit my lip, giving him a small grin.

"No." The driver barked without looking away from the road. "Shut up. We're doing exactly what Mr. Scott and Mr. Jacobs told us to do."

I still had Randy's attention, and I licked my lips, telling him exactly what I'd do if he helped me—or what he thought he would get.

"What did you do to them?" he asked curiously.

"Said the wrong thing." I shrugged. "They couldn't care less if I died. They'll forget they even had me arrested by tomorrow. So how about I give you some attention and you let me go?"

"I said to shut the fuck up," the driver snarled before looking at his partner. "Randy, don't even think about it. You do not want to get on the bad side of the Riot Crew."

"We could just say she escaped," Randy said, looking toward the front again. "They'd never have to know."

"And what happens when they want to take it out on you that she's gone?" the driver retorted.

Randy paused. "Accidents happen. I'll give you my half of what they paid us."

As they argued, I lifted myself up and slid my cuffed hands under my ass. It had been a while since I'd escaped handcuffs, but it was ingrained in me to always be prepared. I bit back a groan when I bent my leg as tight as it would go, and I lowered my arms until my leg slipped through. Fuck, I needed to stretch more often. After a bit of a struggle, I bent my other leg far enough to slip through it.

With my hands now in front of me, I slid them under my shirt, keeping my eyes on the men in the front. I fumbled with my bra until I felt what I was looking for. Pulling the thin wire out, I bent it in half and pushed it into the keyhole of the handcuffs. Every single bra I owned had a wire I could slip out and use to pick a lock. And even if I was searched, it would pass as the underwire of my bra.

Anticipation bubbled through me, and I coughed to cover the sound of the cuffs unlocking. I slipped the wire under my leg, knowing I wouldn't have time to put it back in my bra. I quickly put my hands behind my back, keeping a tight grip on the cuffs.

"No. We're not fucking doing it," the driver said. "She's going to the station like they wanted."

I was as disappointed as Randy. It would have made my escape much easier if we were going anywhere but to a police station. I could still make it work. I just needed to get away before they got me inside. I'd been careful over the years to never get fingerprinted. As cautious as I was, I was sure my fingerprints were at a couple of crime scenes, and I had no plans to get them put in a police database. Even if this was under the table and they took me straight to a cell, I wasn't fucking chancing it.

A few minutes later, we pulled into the police station, parking a few spots away from the front doors. I closed the handcuffs and placed them over my knuckles before wrapping my fingers around them as makeshift brass knuckles. Not as good, but still better than nothing.

Randy was still sulking when he got out and opened my door. He roughly grabbed my arm, yanking me out of the car harder than I was expecting, breaking the light hold I had on my own wrist to make it look like I was still cuffed. He pulled my arm in front of me, his eyes bulging when he saw I wasn't restrained.

"How about you let me go and no one gets hurt?" I tightened my grip around the metal when he frowned.

"Come on," he said gruffly, tugging me toward the police station.

I planted my feet, twisting out of his grip. He spun around, lunging for me. I swung the cuffs into his ribs, and he grunted, stopping in his tracks. The cuffs ripped into my knuckles, but I barely felt it. Lifting my leg, I kicked him in the center of his chest, knocking the wind out of him. As he staggered back, an arm wrapped around my throat from behind me.

"Don't make this worse," the driver warned me. "I don't want to have to explain to the crew that you got hurt."

"I'm not the one who's going to get hurt," I replied, throwing my elbow into his gut. He was stockier than Randy and was squeezing tight enough that I only had seconds before I passed out. I threw my fist up, smashing the cuffs against his nose.

"Shit," he bellowed in pain, his arm leaving my neck. Drops of his blood fell on my shirt as I grabbed his arm and twisted until he was facing away from me. I ripped his arm upward, keeping him immobile, slamming him against the side of his patrol car. I released my hold on the cuffs and locked his wrist before leaning into the car and snapping the other cuff to the bars inside.

"You crazy bitch," he spat out, swatting at me with his free hand. Blood covered his mouth while a steady flow continued to come out of his nose. "I hope you enjoy misery. Because that's what you're getting when we lock you up."

"I'm crazy? You were going to take me to jail for something I didn't do." I paused, pondering for a moment. "I think this is the first time I've ever been set up to take the fall for something I'm actually innocent of."

He reached for me again, and I jabbed him in the throat, needing him distracted. He made a choking sound, and I used that free time to wrangle his gun from his belt. I slid it free, spinning around right as Randy was sneaking up behind me. He froze, raising his hands in the air. Nervous sweat covered his bald head when I aimed the weapon at his face.

Stepping away from the car, I kept the gun on him. "I'm going to walk away now. And you're not going to follow. Not unless you want a bullet in your brain."

"You can't kill a cop and get away with it," he said, not looking very sure.

I shrugged, not telling him I'd done it before. Granted, the two cops I had shot were corrupt as fuck, but that probably wouldn't help my case.

"What the hell is going on?"

Shock coursed through me, seeing Rylan stepping out of the station. What was worse was the five cops who followed him. After one look at what I was doing, half of them raised their weapons. Fuck me. This wasn't something I could just walk away from. Not without witnesses. I'd have to leave the damn state.

Let's hope they all believed the show I was about to put on.

8

Rylan

"Lower your weapons," I snapped, looking at the police chief to back me up. He hesitated for a moment before ordering his men to stand down.

Mili burst into tears, the gun in her hand shaking. She had blood all over her shirt, and the knuckles on her hand were cut to shit. The cop in front of her charged at her, knocking her against the car while prying the weapon from her hand. She let out a pained cry, her spine hitting the trunk of the cruiser.

"Stand down," I repeated, my pulse thumping like crazy. I barely knew this girl, but something about her had me fascinated. And I didn't want to see her hurt.

"She attacked us," the other cop screamed, trying to unlock his cuffed hand.

"Only because you arrested me for no reason," Mili said, her voice cracking. Fear swam in her eyes when the cop who'd shoved her grabbed her arm, dragging her closer to me and the police chief. "I didn't do anything wrong. They were going to throw me in a cell and not tell another soul. I was scared for my life."

A couple of the policemen murmured under their breath as they took in her words. Her face was now streaked with tears, and she slumped toward the ground when the cop let her go. I was closest, and I reached forward to keep her upright. She clung to me, burying her face in my chest. The scent of coconut drifted over me, and my hold on her tightened without even thinking about it.

"She attacked us—"

"Randy," the police chief cut him off. "No need to scream. Explain what happened."

"We caught her stealing a car," Randy said gruffly. "Got back here, and when I opened the door to get her out, she had slipped her cuffs and attacked me."

"Rylan," she whispered, her voice trembling. "You were right. I should have listened to you. The crew—they're bad news. They did this. I wanted nothing to do with them, but they grabbed me at the park, and then, suddenly, I was being arrested for stealing Kade's car."

I stared down at her, my mouth dropping in surprise. "They wanted you to get arrested? Why?"

"I don't know." New tears formed in her eyes, her hands grasping my suit tightly. "They don't like me. I never should have moved here."

"Calm down," I said softly. "We'll figure this out."

I didn't know how the hell Kade and Gray were still walking free. They pulled shit like this all the time without thinking. One of these days, it was going to catch up to them. I doubted it would happen tonight. Not without proof. But if her story is true, then the least I could do was get her out of it.

"Where's the car?" I asked, looking at the cop named Randy.

He rubbed his head nervously. "What?"

"The car you say she stole." I spoke slowly. "Is it at the impound?"

Randy glanced back at his partner for help, but the guy was still acting like his broken nose was the end of the world.

"Randy," the police chief barked. "Answer Mayor Hunt."

"No, sir. It's not at the impound."

"Where is it?" I asked tightly.

"Um, you see—"

"Whose car is it?" I cut him off, asking another question.

"I haven't made a report yet. I don't remember the names," Randy mumbled.

"Did you call dispatch when you responded to the call?" This time it was the police chief asking questions, and he looked pissed.

"No, sir."

"Why the fuck not?"

"It was the Riot Crew," Randy sputtered out, glaring daggers at Mili.

Silence settled over everyone, and the police chief glanced at me. I raised an eyebrow, knowing what was going to happen.

Absolutely fucking nothing.

"They kidnapped me," Mili squeaked out, pushing away from me. "I was only trying to protect myself."

"You broke my partner's nose," Randy ground out.

"Enough," the police chief said. "You were really going to take an innocent woman to jail?"

"It was either me or her," Randy shouted. He looked around, waving an arm. "Let's not pretend half of us here wouldn't have done the same thing. They would have killed me if I told them no."

He was right. The only difference was he got caught. The crew had half the police force in their pocket. Mili stood next to me, hugging herself as she stared at Randy.

"She assaulted two officers," Randy's partner spat out. "We can arrest her for that."

"Not happening," I said stiffly.

The police chief nodded in agreement. "Ma'am, you are in no

danger of being arrested. But if you're willing to testify against the men who kidnapped you—"

"Are you crazy?" she asked shrilly, her panicked filled eyes finding me. "The police are scared of them, and you want me to speak against them?"

"No, you don't have to," I told her, trying to keep her calm.

"You two," the police chief pointed to Randy and his partner, "in my office. Now."

The chief nodded at me and then strode inside the station. The rest of the cops scattered, leaving me alone with Mili. She sniffed, wiping the last of her tears away. She wasn't shaking anymore but still looked terrified.

"Are you okay?" I asked, studying her for any other injuries.

"Fine," she mumbled, giving me a hint of a smile. "Thank you."

"I didn't do anything. It's not like you really broke the law."

"I can honestly say I didn't. Kade and Gray are fucking dicks."

I blew out a surprised laugh. "Yeah, you could say that. Did they hurt you?"

She raised an eyebrow. "Are you worried about me?"

"I worry about anyone who crosses the crew."

"And how do I know you're not paid off by them like those cops were?"

Her accusation didn't faze me, especially after what she had just been through. Half of this town was corrupt.

"If I were, do you think I would have defended you?"

She studied me with quizzical eyes. "I guess not."

"You really messed the guy's nose up," I said, suppressing a grin. "Remind me to never make you mad."

"I'm a single woman who lives alone. Self-defense is important."

I noticed how her fear and panic had completely disappeared. She was still being cautious with me, but her subtle change was interesting. I had a feeling there was much more to her than she was letting people see.

"What time is it?"

Her question threw me for a moment, and I glanced at my watch. "Nine."

"I have to go."

She turned to leave, and I rushed forward, cutting her off. "Go where?"

"Home."

"Let me drive you."

"No, thank you."

My frustration with her bullshit politeness grew when she tried darting around me. She was acting completely different from when I saw her at the club or at the café. She darted around me, and I raced to get in front of her again. Her eyes flashed with annoyance for a split second before she frowned.

"Look, I appreciate you standing up for me, but I need to go," she said, keeping her voice soft.

"There's nothing but businesses around here. No matter where you live, it's going to take you forever to walk. Let me drive you," I told her.

"No. I like walking."

"Or do you just not want me to know where you live?"

Her gaze trailed down my face. "Is that a problem? That I don't want to give a stranger my address?"

"You don't trust me," I stated, wondering why the fuck I cared if she trusted me or not.

"No offense, but I don't trust anyone."

I tilted my head. "Someone hurt you."

She laughed, but it sounded hollow. "Everyone has a past, Rylan."

Wanting to shake her and see if I could get some truth out of her, I changed the subject. "How'd you get out of the handcuffs?"

She shrugged. "Slipped out of them. They didn't put them on very tight."

Realizing I wasn't getting anywhere with her, I pulled out my wallet and took out one of my business cards. She stared at it as I held it out to her for a few seconds, then she grabbed it.

"If you need anything, you can call," I said, curious about whether I would hear from her again.

"Thanks," she muttered, turning on her heel and nearly jogging away. "Have a good night, Mayor."

I watched her disappear into the darkness. If she was on the crew's radar, I had a feeling this wouldn't be the last time I saw her. Hopefully, she was smart enough to leave before she ended up dead. I ran a hand down my face, making my way to the doors of the police station until I noticed the rear door of the police car was still open.

I moved to shut the door and saw something on the seat. Reaching inside, I grabbed the bent wire, holding it up in the light. I quickly stood up to see if Mili was still within sight, but she was gone. Letting out a small chuckle, I strode to the dumpster and tossed the wire in. She didn't slip out of the cuffs; she picked the damn lock.

There was a lot more to her than she showed everyone. Excitement churned in my gut at the thought of seeing her again, and I tried pushing it away. She was involved with the Riot Crew, which meant she most likely wasn't the innocent bystander she portrayed herself to be. As mayor, I did everything to keep my life clean. Getting mixed up with her would be the exact opposite of everything I'd worked so hard for.

But I still couldn't get her out of my damn head.

9

Kade

"I can't believe we're doing a job that we're not getting paid for," Gray grumbled as I cut the chain on the warehouse doors.

"Aren't you curious to see what kind of jobs the famous Sapphire gets?" I asked, slipping the bolt cutters back into my backpack. "This is easier than jobs we do."

"We do all the work, and the payment goes into her account." Gray shook his head. "Too bad the email didn't include that."

I scoffed. "It's not like she can use the money while she's stuck in a cell."

It had been about five hours since we'd left Mili with the cops. We were an hour out of Ridgewood, and after parking our car a few blocks away, we'd come to the warehouse. We had scoped it out first, making sure it seemed like a legit job.

"We have two hours to get the cars to the dock." I set my watch. "I want to be in and out within twenty minutes."

He nodded, slipping on black leather gloves. He pulled the warehouse door open, and I followed him inside. It was pitch-black, and I flicked on a small flashlight to search for the lockbox that had the car keys. The email had said the box should be on the wall near the door. Gray nudged me, pointing a little farther down the wall to where a black box was.

Gray took out his lock picking kit before sliding it into the keyhole while I held the flashlight. I stared out into the dark, listening to make sure there were no unusual noises. All I could hear were the small clicks when Gray got the box open. He tossed me a set of keys, keeping one for himself.

We stepped lightly on the concrete floor, moving quickly to the back where the cars should be. I halted, shining the light in front of us. Spinning around, I scanned the entire warehouse. The empty fucking warehouse.

"Where the hell are the cars?" Gray hissed.

"Not here," I muttered.

"Was there even a job?" he asked, thinking out loud. "Or was she just messing with us? The email was detailed."

"Maybe she planned a trap for us." We jogged to the exit, tossing the keys onto the ground. "Probably a good thing she didn't come with us, if that's the case."

"Let's get the hell out of here," Gray muttered.

We walked down the street, going slow so we didn't attract attention. Gray pulled off his gloves, shoving them back in his bag. My heart was hammering, my mind racing with scenarios about what this job really was. We turned the corner, and Gray stumbled a step before grabbing my hoodie to stop me.

"Shit." His eyes were focused straight ahead, and when I followed his gaze, my stomach dropped.

Mili was leaning against the small white sedan we had brought for the job. We never took our own cars when we worked. She was wearing the same clothes as earlier, and as we slowly moved closer, I could make out dark stains all over her shirt. If I had to bet, I'd guess the stains were blood.

Once we were about fifteen feet away, she raised her head, meeting our stares. A wicked grin spread across her face, her eyes dancing with a dangerous fire. Her arms were at her sides, and in one hand, she was holding a handgun.

"Did you kill those poor cops?" Gray asked, stepping in front of me so I could get my gun out without her seeing. "They were just following orders."

"If you wanted to get rid of me, you should have killed me while I was still in your car," she responded, her voice light, which was completely contradicting the look in her eyes like she wanted to bury us alive. "I warned you."

My grip on my gun tightened. "We'll remember that for next time."

"There won't be a next time. You two are adorable." She chuckled, tapping her gun on the outside of her thigh. "You really think you forced me into that car against my will? That Gray grabbing my shirt was enough to overpower me? I got in the car because I wanted to sate my curiosity. And your grand plan to fuck me over was very underwhelming."

I spied a car parked behind ours, and my eyes widened. It was one of the cars that was supposed to be in the warehouse. She noticed what I was looking at, and her grin grew.

"I already did the job. A little earlier than scheduled, but it all worked out. I just need to deliver this one and collect my cash. Too bad for you both, you won't be seeing a fucking dime of that."

"How'd you get away from the cops?" Gray asked gruffly. "By taking your clothes off?"

Her gaze cut to him. "You two have no idea who the fuck you're messing with. I'm Sapphire. The name known by everyone in our world. You want to play games with me? Go for it. I love competition.

But you better up your game before trying something again. If you don't—it'll all blow up in your faces."

She giggled as if she'd told a joke and pushed off the sedan. She raised her gun when I aimed mine at her. Her finger curled around the trigger without hesitation.

"I'm not going to shoot you," she said, looking between us. "I have a feeling you'll light the fuse, killing yourself before I do."

I tried processing what the hell she meant by that as she backed away. I kept my gun aimed at her but slid the safety back on when she lowered her weapon.

"Leaving town?" I called to her as she opened her car door.

"Nope. I'll text you about the next meeting. We still have a lot to plan." She glanced at our car before shooting us a smirk. "Enjoy the rest of your night…I'm sure it'll be a blast."

With those words, she got in and slammed the door. Putting the car in reverse, she did a U-turn in the street and sped away from us.

"There's no way she still wants to work with us after what we did," Gray said, staring uneasily at our car.

"I think that Panthers job is more than just a car," I replied. "There's something about it she's not saying."

"There's a lot she's not saying."

"What are the odds she really isn't doing anything to get us back for what we did to her?" I asked, replaying her words in my head. Something wasn't right.

"Zero," Gray answered. "I'm honestly shocked she didn't try to kill us."

"Or she is," I mumbled, her words echoing in my head. *It'll blow up in your faces…light the fuse…it'll be a blast.*

Gray cursed under his breath, coming to the same conclusion as me. We backed up while he pulled out the car key. I braced myself when he hit the engine start button. The car hummed as the engine started, and we waited for a few moments before I began to relax.

"I guess we were wrong—"

A loud explosion ripped through the car as it burst into flames, causing both of us to hit the ground. A second blast had my ears ringing, and I covered my head as metal pieces rained down on the road.

"Jesus Christ," Gray hissed, grabbing his bag from beside him. "We need to get the fuck out of here."

We jumped up, bolting to the closest alley. I glanced over my shoulder, seeing the entire car engulfed in flames. I followed Gray to another street, where we both slowed down. I spotted a car we could boost easily enough, and we made sure we were alone before I broke the window. By the time Gray hot-wired the car, sirens were already getting close. Gray stayed under the speed limit until we got on the expressway.

"That was way too close," I grumbled, my heart still racing.

"I don't care how much money she's promising us. I want her fucking gone." Gray glanced in the rearview mirror to make sure we weren't being followed. "We already know we can't kill her. The next best thing is to get her out of our town."

"What? Piss her off enough that she wants to leave?"

He nodded slowly, keeping his eyes on the road. "But we also risk the chance of getting her mad enough to actually try and kill us."

"I think we're already there. If she wanted us dead, she easily could have done it already. For some fucking reason, she needs us."

He frowned at me. "You want to take that gamble with your life—and mine?"

I shrugged. "You heard her. She practically told us to try again. She thinks it's a game."

"I'd rather not play a game where we have a chance of getting blown up."

I sighed. "She apparently doesn't want to leave. So either we make her, or we're stuck with her."

"Fine," Gray grumbled. "But we both have to agree with what to do with her. No going off by yourself."

"I know." I ran a hand through my hair, calming down more as we got closer to Ridgewood. "We have a meeting with Vic and Juan tomorrow. We tell them the job went fine. They still want us to work with her. They don't need to know all the shit that went down tonight."

Gray nodded in agreement, turning on the radio and finding the classic rock channel. We drove in silence, and like me, I was sure he was thinking of Mili. This one fucking girl was flipping our world upside down, and I hated it. This was our city. And if she didn't want to leave, then she'd learn the hard way.

10

Milina

"Another drink, Mili?" Vic asked, looking at my empty glass.

I gave him a sweet smile. "I'd love one, thank you."

I was back in the club where I'd first introduced myself to Kade and Gray. Vic and Juan had invited me back upstairs into the private room when they noticed me sitting at the bar, just like I hoped they would. Swiveling slowly in the plush chair, I stared through the one-way glass, watching people dance. It wasn't a weekend, but the club was still busy. The music vibrated the floor, and I turned my attention back to the Riot bosses when Vic handed me another gin and tonic.

"How are you liking Ridgewood?" Juan asked, studying me. I had a feeling he didn't like me as much as Vic did but wanted my business anyway.

"It's fine. I haven't had much time to explore."

Vic nodded. "Kade and Gray told us the job last night went smoothly. We appreciate you working with us."

"The job was easy," I replied lightly.

Of course they fucking told them that. I kept the smile on my face, waiting for the right moment to start the conversation I came here to discuss. I looked out over the crowd below me, and my heart jumped when I saw them. Kade and Gray were talking to the bouncer and didn't look in a hurry to come up here yet. If they thought the bombs I had planted last night were the last of my revenge, they were going to be in for a surprise.

"It's too bad that you two aren't the ones in this city," I said coolly. "I bet you'd be easier to deal with than Kade and Gray."

Juan frowned, glancing at Vic. "They're giving you trouble?"

"I don't think they believe I am who I say I am." I made eye contact with both of them before continuing. "You believe I'm Sapphire, right?"

After a bit of hesitation, Vic spoke up. "Yes, we do."

"When I first met you, I said I'd respect your city and your gang. But if I don't receive respect back, then I'm taking my business to someone else. I do not appreciate being belittled because I'm a fucking woman. Do you understand?"

The door opened, and with perfect timing, Kade and Gray strode in. They stopped short when they saw me as I spun the chair to face them. Kade's gaze traveled down my body, a muscle ticking in his jaw. I was wearing tight black leather pants with a matching leather crop top that just covered my tattoo. It was odd that I was wearing the clothes I wanted. Usually, I dressed to get a job done or to blend in. But there was no need for that since the men in this room knew who I was.

"What are you doing here?" Gray snapped, crossing his arms.

"I was just informing your bosses of how last night went," I said, raising my eyebrow.

"You told us everything went great," Juan said, focusing on Gray and Kade. There was a touch of annoyance in his tone. I kept my glee to myself when Kade opened his mouth to respond.

"We realize what we did was a mistake," Kade grated out. "We didn't trust her to do the job with us. We were going to have the police let her go once the night was over."

"Liar," I muttered under my breath, watching shock fall on Vic's and Juan's faces.

"You did *what*?" Vic bit out, his eyes flashing in anger.

Gray's eyes snapped to mine in confusion, and I pressed my lips together to keep from grinning.

"What did you tell them?" Kade said, advancing toward me.

I stayed sitting, not the least bit nervous that he was coming closer. "Just that the job went fine."

"Why don't you tell us what exactly happened?" Juan demanded, glaring at Kade and Gray.

"It doesn't matter," I cut in, looking at Juan. "The job was done. And I can have your half deposited into whichever account you'd like."

Suspicion seared in Kade's eyes. "What are you playing at?"

I blinked innocently at him. "Nothing. I want to make sure my partners are happy."

"We can't do this," Gray growled. "We don't want to work with her. We want her gone."

"No." Vic's voice oozed with dangerous power, pulling his rank on them. "She's giving us new business. More money than we make in months. And she promised to give us any jobs that she's too busy for, even after she leaves. I'm not turning that down because you two can't accept that a woman can do your job as well as you."

"What?" Kade sputtered out. "This isn't because she's a fucking woman—"

"Better," I interjected, standing from my chair. "I can do their job better."

Juan pinched the bridge of his nose. "It's less than six months. Can you three get along for that long?"

"We have other men you can work with," Vic offered.

Kade and Gray went rigid at the idea of being demoted. If looks could kill, I'd be in my grave by now. I leaned against the glass, staring above their heads as if I were actually considering Vic's words.

"No. I want them. Even if they are assholes, they're better than anyone else I've looked into."

"Did she happen to tell you how she planted not one, but two fucking bombs in our car?" Gray grated out, rage swimming in his gaze.

Vic whirled toward me. "Did you?"

"That was the end of the night," I said dismissively. "And I told them I did it. It was just a warning."

"You did not fucking tell us," Kade shot back.

"If you didn't pick up on my hints, then that's on you." I shrugged. "Seeing as you're here, you obviously did."

"We need to leave." Vic nodded to Juan. "I want you two to talk to her and figure out a way to work this out."

"I have no issue working with them," I said sweetly.

Vic muttered something in Kade's ear before he and Juan disappeared through the doorway, closing the door behind them. Kade was on me in a second, his chest bumping against mine. My fingers tightened around my glass, but I stayed where I was.

"Why'd you come here tonight?" he asked, his voice low and steeped in anger.

"I was having a drink, and Vic invited me up here."

"Bullshit. You wanted them to know what we did last night."

I laughed, patting him on the shoulder. "You did that all by yourself. I didn't say anything."

"Just like you planned, I'm sure," Gray muttered from behind Kade.

"It must be a punch in the gut to know Vic and Juan have lost their confidence in you." I clicked my tongue disapprovingly. "They don't even want you working with me anymore. But don't forget what they chose—which was me. Over what you wanted."

I slid to the side, keeping my guard up as I went to the bar and poured myself another drink. I could hear one of them coming up behind me, but I still took my time refilling my glass with gin. Deciding

I wanted both my hands free, I kept my drink on the counter and turned around. They were both right in front of me, and they caged me in the second I was facing them.

"This is not talking it out like Vic wants," I murmured, my tone filled with warning. "Did you not learn your lesson last night?"

"What do you want?" Gray asked.

"You already know that. I want help with the Panther job."

"Leave town," Kade demanded. "We'll do the job with you, but you don't need to be here for the next five months to plan it."

"No." My answer slipped out, surprising even me. I cursed silently for letting myself get carried away. I never spoke without thinking about it first.

"Why not?" Gray ground out.

For once, I decided to be honest. "Because I'm having fun."

"Fun?" Kade repeated in disbelief.

I attempted to push past them, but neither moved an inch. They only moved forward, pressing my spine against the bar counter. Hot excitement burned through my veins when I realized they weren't going to back down, even after I nearly blew them up last night.

"I'll admit, when I first came to Ridgewood, I didn't want to stay." I trailed my fingers up Kade's shirt, feeling his hard abs underneath it. "But you two changed my mind. I'm usually alone. And I've never met men who think they can go up against me and win. So...you two can try your hardest to get me to leave. But just remember that payback's a bitch."

"You want us to make you leave?" Kade asked, tensing when my fingers reached his chest.

"I want you to try." I grinned, dragging my nails back down to his stomach. "And when you don't succeed, then you'll agree to do this Panther job with me—how I want to do it. I'm in charge when it comes to the planning and the execution. Got it?"

"And if we do get you to leave?" Gray asked, his eyes glued to my hand.

"You won't. But if you do, then I'll give you the entire payout for the job." Shock lined their features, and I knew exactly what they were thinking. I continued before they could question me. "This isn't about money for me. It's personal."

Kade snatched my wrist when my fingers grazed the zipper of his jeans. "What are your rules?"

I tugged out of his grip, only for Gray to grab my wrist and twist my arm behind me while grabbing my other arm and holding both of them at the base of my spine. He stood behind me, his body pressing against me to help keep me in place. Kade was in front of me, and I stared at him curiously, not fighting to get out of Gray's hold. Once again, they were trying to intimidate me. It seemed they hadn't learned much from last night.

"Rules," Kade murmured, his fingers grasping my chin, forcing my head back until I met his gaze. "Or are you so confident you'll start a war with us without restraints?"

Unease constricted my chest from being sandwiched between them. It wasn't that I couldn't get myself free—that wouldn't be too difficult. It was that I wasn't hating their hands on me. During some jobs, men would touch me and I'd have to take hour-long showers and scrub my skin raw until I felt clean again. But with these two, my body was buzzing with excitement. Which was why I stayed still, even when Kade leaned so close his lips were inches from mine.

"Rules?" I questioned, biting my lip. "Where would the fun be if we had rules?"

Kade's eyes fell to my mouth, not missing the sexual intention bleeding from my voice. Gray's hold tightened while he shifted behind me. I knew he could feel the gun in my waistband, but he didn't make a move to take it.

"I guess we should make one thing clear," I continued. "Whatever you do can't interfere with the jobs we do. Because that would fuck us all over, and seeing as that's my livelihood, I can't let that happen. Oh—no telling people who I am. If I find out you're doing that, you're not going to like what I do."

"And what's stopping you from trying to kill us if we do something to piss you off?" Gray asked gruffly, his mouth closer to my ear than I had thought. Goose bumps skated down my spine as I let out a laugh.

"Nothing."

Kade's eyes darkened as he kept his grip on my jaw. "But I'm sure something happens to us if you end up dead."

I smiled. "I haven't stayed on top for this long without protecting myself."

"How long have you been Sapphire?" Gray asked.

I paused. "Not as long as the person who held the name before me. But I plan on outliving him."

"Who was he—"

Kade's question was cut off when I lunged forward, smashing my lips to his. He went still, not reacting at all, even when I pushed my tongue into his mouth. Our eyes were open, and his suspicion-filled gaze was locked on mine. He tasted like tequila, and the scent of new car with a hint of cigarettes engulfed me as I leaned against him. I nipped at his bottom lip, making him snap. Heat smothered his gaze, and his hand moved from my jaw to the back of my neck, pulling me closer to him. Gray's hold loosened around my wrists, but I didn't move, enjoying this too much. It had been way too long since someone could make my pussy pulse from a kiss alone.

Wanting to be the one to stay in control of this situation, I broke the kiss while ripping out of Gray's grip at the same time. I knocked Kade's hand away when he tried wrapping his fingers around the back of my neck. Bracing my arms, I pulled myself onto the bar counter and slid off to the other side. I picked up my forgotten drink and downed it in one gulp while they both stared at me from across the glossy wood counter.

"I can't decide which was better." I twisted a lock of hair around my finger. "When Gray fingered me or that kiss. Now, if you boys will excuse me, I need to go find someone to finish me off. Do you know how good an orgasm a day is for your health?"

I had no plans to seek someone out to sleep with, but their glares proved I'd hit a nerve like I wanted. The best way to get under the skin of men was to bring sex into the equation. A sudden knock at the door interrupted the growing tension in the room, and I glanced over to see a young guy poking his head in. He stared at me with interest until Gray cleared his throat.

"What do you want?" Kade snapped.

"Sorry to interrupt," the guy sputtered out. "There's someone at the bar saying they had a meeting with you two—"

"We'll be there in a minute," Gray cut him off without looking away from me.

"Oh, don't let me keep you. I'm leaving anyway." I rounded the bar, heading toward the door. I glanced over my shoulder and shot them a grin. "See you two later."

Before they could respond, I slipped past the guy in the doorway and bounded down the stairs. I brushed my fingers to my lips, still tasting Kade. My stomach twisted at the thought of what was going to happen with them next. They were smart and didn't want me here. But I was confident I could stay one step in front of them.

For a half moment, I second-guessed it all. Caleb would not be happy with me playing around with these guys. He'd tell me I was being reckless. There was a reason I'd perfected blending into the background for the last five years. But my problems were half a world away from Ridgewood. And as long as the crew kept their mouths shut that Sapphire was in town, I'd be fine. If that changed, I'd be gone in a heartbeat. Messing with Kade and Gray was fun, but nothing was going to destroy my chance of finishing the Panther job.

11

Gray

Music blasted as we walked through the crowd of people admiring the cars. The dust had settled from the last race, and people were enjoying themselves before the next one started. Kade lit a cigarette, inhaling the smoke as a calm washed over him. He smoked whenever we went to races or if he was stressed. Which seemed to be a lot since Mili came to town. But tonight, we were in the middle of the desert, hours from Ridgewood and the girl who had been on our minds more than both of us wanted to admit.

There were a couple hundred people here, and we came to the desert a few times a year for big races like this. The races rotated places, and the last time we were in this exact spot was ten years ago. We hadn't raced that night, but tonight we were. Kade had already won a race, and I was up next.

My sky-blue Mazda GT-R was parked next to Kade's red Camaro, and a few people were surrounding them. They nodded at us, stepping back as we got closer. Over the years, we'd made names for ourselves at the desert races. We didn't always win, but our records were good enough for people to take notice.

"Gray." An arm went around my shoulder. "Good to see you two."

"Hey, Andy," Kade greeted the guy who had me in a bear hug.

"We missed you guys at the last race," Andy said, letting me go.

"We were dealing with crew business," I answered.

Andy nodded. "Life happens. Glad you're here tonight."

Kade asked him how the last race went as I snagged the cigarette from his hand and took a long drag. Anticipation for my race had my body buzzing. I loved racing, and it had been way too long. Andy didn't race. He was the man in charge. He organized the races and made sure all the bets and cash stayed clean. He'd been in the game for a long time, and we'd known him since Vic and Juan took us to the races as kids.

Hardened wrinkles surrounded Andy's eyes, and scars covered his hands from working on cars his entire life. He owned his own garage and lived a few hours from Ridgewood. I didn't think I'd ever seen him wear anything other than worn out blue jeans and a black T-shirt. Even though he was in his sixties, he could easily pass for much younger. His blond hair had turned a light gray years ago, and he kept it buzzed short.

A horn blasted through the air, signaling the next race was about to start. I nodded to Kade and Andy before getting into my Mazda. Kade leaned through the window once I rolled it down.

"I bet five hundred on you. Don't fuck it up," he told me, his tone playful. I hadn't lost one race since buying this car. "Be careful."

I chuckled, putting the car in gear and slowly driving through the crowd to get to the start line. I settled into the leather seat, switching on my favorite playlist. A pure white Corvette C6 was already at the line, and I peered through the windows, seeing nothing. The windows were tinted, making it impossible to see the driver.

A woman dressed in clothes that barely covered everything stood in front of the cars, a red handkerchief in her hand. She looked at the Corvette, and the driver pressed on the gas, showing he was ready. I did the same when the woman looked at me. I turned the volume of my music up as she raised the red cloth above her. My hand hovered over the gearshift, my foot already on the gas pedal.

The woman waved the flag, and the Corvette matched my speed as we flew forward. I kept my window down, feeling the wind hit my face. This track wasn't straight, there were curves and turns, and it took us around the outskirts of where the cars and crowd were. There were cones spaced wide apart to show where the track was. I downshifted, taking the first curve with ease while taking a slight lead. I glanced in the rearview mirror, barely seeing the headlights of the Corvette through the dust my tires were kicking up. My gut knotted with the excitement of the competition as we both slowed down, taking a sharp turn.

"I don't think so," I muttered, jerking the steering wheel to the left when the Corvette tried passing me. My move kept me in the lead, and I glanced in the side mirror, frowning when the Corvette weaved around the cones, leaving the makeshift track. I cursed under my breath when my Mazda suddenly slowed down, even though my foot was still on the gas.

My excitement fizzled to anger when the Corvette quickly passed me, slipping back inside the cones before gunning the engine. I had hit a soft patch of sand, slowing me down enough that there was no way I was going to fucking win. Whoever I was racing against knew that. I turned sharply, hitting a cone as I got back on the hard sand. My eyes were glued to the Corvette's taillights as I pushed my engine to catch up.

I passed the finish line not even five seconds after the Corvette, and my grip on the steering wheel was tight enough that my knuckles were white. I cruised around the crowd, pulling into the spot next to Kade's car. To my surprise, the Corvette took the empty spot next to me. I hurried to get out of my seat, wanting to see who the fuck had beaten me because they knew the track better.

"What happened?" Kade asked when I slammed my door shut. "You were winning—"

"I hit soft sand," I gritted out, keeping my eyes on the Corvette.

"Shit," Andy said with a frown. "I thought we kept the tracks away from those spots. Sorry, man."

My response died in my throat when the door of the Corvette opened, and the spiked heel of a black boot hit the ground. The woman stepped out, shaking out her black hair before she caught my eye. My heart stuttered as she grinned, not having to say a word as she gloated over her win.

"Son of a bitch," Kade muttered. "She's fucking everywhere."

Mili was wearing tight white jeans that were tucked into knee-high boots. Her black shirt was tucked into her jeans and had such a low-cut V that her breasts looked fucking incredible. She was turning almost every head in her vicinity. If she was trying to keep a low profile, she was doing a shit job.

Andy stepped forward, studying her before his eyes widened with recognition. "Mili? Is that really you? Shit, it's been years."

She had already been heading toward us, and Andy met her halfway, wrapping her in a hug. After a few seconds, she slipped out of his arms, a smile on her face.

"You know her?" Kade asked Andy once they got closer.

"Oh, yeah. She's been around cars for years," Andy answered, glancing at her questioningly. "But it's been a long time since you've been to a race. We thought something happened."

"No," she said smoothly, "life just got busy."

I wondered if Andy knew she was Sapphire. It didn't sound like he did. But it made me wonder what her past was in the car world. She had to have been in California before if she knew Andy, and I was shocked we'd never run into her before this.

"You still with your old man?" Andy asked, making Mili's eyes flash dangerously before she reined it in. "You two seemed head over heels in love."

His words had me flexing my fingers as something pretty fucking close to rage seared through my veins. She was with someone? And why the hell did that bother me so much? Kade's jaw was clenched so tight, I thought he was going to crack a tooth.

"He died. Years ago," she said curtly.

Kade glanced between Andy and Mili, looking thoughtful, and I knew immediately what he was thinking. Even if Andy didn't know she was Sapphire, he knew of her past. Maybe he could tell us things she wouldn't.

"Sorry to hear that," Andy said, gazing at her with sympathy. "What happened?"

"I heard you sell bikes," she said, completely changing the subject.

Andy nodded. "Yeah, I do. A lot of the biker clubs in California go through me."

"I'm in the market. I'll call you to set up a time to look at what you have if that works."

"Hey, Andy," someone called. "A guy over here doesn't want to pay up on his bet."

"Sure, Mili, anytime. Excuse me," Andy muttered, looking annoyed. "I need to handle this."

He strode away, and Mili leaned against my car, crossing her arms. Most of the crowd was heading toward the start line to watch the next race, leaving the three of us alone.

"Nice race," Mili told me, looking at my car. "You almost won."

"How'd you know the sand was soft?" I asked stiffly.

"I've raced here before."

"When?" Kade asked.

She shrugged. "In the past."

"Can you give us one honest answer?" I grated out.

"Sure. If you want to win a race, don't use a foreign car." She grinned at Kade. "At least he has taste. Nothing can beat the Big Three when it comes to cars."

I scoffed. "This isn't the sixties. Some of the best race cars are foreign."

"Obviously, yours isn't on that list."

"Stop trying to get under his skin," Kade snapped. "Did you know we were going to be here tonight?"

"Yes. But that's not why I came. I wanted to race."

"Does Andy know who you are?" I asked in a low voice.

Her gaze cut to me. "No. No one here does. Except you two. And that's how it'll stay. Understand?"

"But you've been around these races," Kade murmured. "How did we not see you before?"

She waved an arm around. "Look at this crowd. Very easy to blend in. But tonight, I don't have to. Andy knows me as a girlfriend who hung around because my asshole boyfriend used to race. I never come to things like this and announce my other name. I do that work in the shadows. Makes everything easier."

It didn't seem like she was especially sad that her boyfriend was dead. And for some reason, that made my anger ease.

"And you might not have seen me, but I've seen you here before." She was looking through us, as if reliving a memory. "You were here with Vic and Juan."

"What? When?" I asked, knowing if I had seen her, she wouldn't have been easy to forget.

"A long time ago," she muttered, as if she hadn't meant to tell us. She glanced at the phone in her hand, and something close to fear crossed her face before she pushed off my car. "I have to go."

She rushed toward her car until Kade stepped in her way. "Go where?"

She had a gun pressed to his chest faster than I had time to see where the hell she pulled it from. "Get the fuck out of my way. I'm not in the mood to play right now."

Her voice was ruthless, leaving no room for argument. Her eyes bored into Kade's as if daring him to say a word. It was easy to see how she'd held on to her power for however long she'd been Sapphire. Every inch of her screamed that she was a force to be reckoned with.

Kade looked down at the gun jabbed into his chest before slowly backing away. She bolted to her car, starting it before the door was closed. We watched as she raced off into the night as Andy stepped up beside me.

"She's leaving?" Andy asked. "Without collecting her winnings?"

I shrugged. "She looked at her phone and said she had to go."

"How long have you known her?" Kade questioned as her taillights disappeared.

"A long time." Andy counted a wad of cash as he spoke. "Her boyfriend used to bring her with him. But she never raced before. He was a dick and liked keeping her out of sight."

"Who was her boyfriend?" Kade asked before I could.

"He went by Chris, but that wasn't his real name."

"When did she stop showing up to the races?" I asked.

"Hmm, maybe about five years ago."

I wondered if that was when she'd taken over the Sapphire name. Or when her boyfriend died. I suddenly wanted to find everything out about her but had a feeling we wouldn't find out much unless she shared it.

"The last time you had a race here was ten years ago," Kade stated. "Unless you had a race we didn't know about."

"No, ten years ago sounds about right."

"She was here," I muttered, looking at Kade.

We were at that race too—with Vic and Juan. That must have been when she'd seen us.

"I can't remember if she was there," Andy interjected, his gaze darting between us. "But I know for a fact she didn't race then."

"Then she knew someone who raced," I said.

"Why all the questions?" Andy grinned. "One of you have a crush?"

Kade scoffed. "No. Just curious about the girl who beat Gray's ass."

"She barely won," I grumbled. "And if she'd stayed on the track, I would have fucking won."

Andy chuckled. "You've always been a sore loser, Gray. Guess it's a good thing you usually win."

With those words, he walked away to chat with other people. Kade and I moved toward the start line to watch the next race. My mind was racing, trying to connect the dots with what we'd learned about Mili tonight. It wasn't much. She'd been in our world for as long as we had, but we'd already figured that. People didn't become Sapphire out of luck.

"Juan wants us to do one of our usual jobs with her next week," Kade said, lighting up another cigarette. "They're still pissed about what we did a few nights ago."

"They want the money and connections." I rubbed the back of my neck. "They'll get it. She doesn't need to do jobs with us for that to happen."

"We'll just make sure she's busy that night." His eyes gleamed with mischief as he got an idea.

"If she stays in town. She seemed panicked by whatever she saw on her phone."

Kade shook his head. "I doubt it. I'm sure when we get back, we'll run into her within a few hours. She has a knack for knowing where the fuck we are at all times."

"I guess we'll see."

12

Milina

My muscles ached, and I pushed myself harder, running on the treadmill as fast as I could. I'd already pushed myself to my limit during my workout, and I shouldn't have even considered cardio. But I'd rather feel my body screaming with exhaustion than focus on the terror that had sunk into my bones when I got that email.

After a few more minutes, I slowed to a walk, sucking in air before I took a sip of water. I was at a local gym on the south side, and I ignored the stares from women who were here just to scope out the single men instead of working out. There was a gym inside my apartment building, but there were cameras, and I didn't want anyone connecting me to living there. I'd been moving to different gyms throughout the city. So far, this was my favorite one.

Turning off the machine, I jumped off, grabbing my towel and wiping my face. I'd been working out way too much in the last few days, but I needed something to keep my mind from wandering to the past. As I walked out of the gym, I pulled my phone out and opened the email for the thousandth time, fear washing through me like it did every time I read it.

Unknown: You've been a bad girl, Lina. Making everyone believe you died. Don't forget who you belong to. I'll see you soon.

No one had called me Lina in five years. I detested that nickname more than fucking anything. It brought back memories of the life I'd barely survived. A life I'd escaped from and would kill myself before ever going back to.

I collapsed onto the bench outside the building, ignoring the mist of rain hitting me. I hit Caleb's number, bringing the phone to my ear.

"You okay, Mili?"

"No," I muttered, making sure no one was within earshot. "I haven't been okay for a week. Ever since I got this fucking email."

"I tracked it," he said quickly.

My heart sank. "Who sent it?"

"He did."

Fear cemented me to the bench, and my grip on the phone turned painful as I stared at the cars driving past me. That wasn't fucking possible.

"He's exactly where he's been for five years," Caleb said softly. "I don't know how he got access to the internet, but he's not free. You're still safe."

"No, I'm not," I hissed. "I was safe when he thought I was dead."

"Mili, I warned you this could happen." He paused, as if trying to think of what to say. "I told you not to take the Sapphire name. Even with how careful we've been, it was only a matter of time before his people realized it was you."

"How'd he get my email?"

"I have no idea."

"Maybe I should leave Ridgewood," I mumbled. "What if they know I'm here—"

"They don't," Caleb cut me off. "I've been keeping an eye on everyone he used to be in contact with, and they all still think you're out of the country like we wanted."

I sighed. "I can't leave anyway. I need to do this Panther job, Caleb. Especially now that he knows I'm alive. It's the only way to get rid of him for good."

"I know. Just make sure those guys you're working with aren't blabbing your name."

"They haven't so far."

"I don't like that you're working with them. We can't trust anyone—"

"I can't do this job by myself. You know that."

"Just be careful," he urged me. "Don't take any unnecessary risks."

I chuckled humorlessly. "Like going to the desert to race? I'm regretting that now."

"No one in California has any contact with them. That wasn't the reason they found out you're alive. Don't feel guilty for wanting to have fun. Just be careful, okay?"

I didn't tell him I'd been having more fun than I had in years. Messing with Kade and Gray had been giving me a feeling of joy that I hadn't had in years.

"Mili?"

I looked up to see Rylan striding toward me. I muttered a goodbye to Caleb and hung up. Tingles of suspicion ran down my spine as he approached. I didn't run into someone this many times unless I planned it. He seemed to pop up wherever I was, and I was getting sick of it.

"Long time no see," he said with a warm smile. "Have you been staying out of trouble this week?"

"How'd you know I was here?" I asked, my gaze stone cold.

Confusion swept across his face, and his eyes flashed with hurt as he raised his arms, acting like he came in peace. "I didn't know you were here. This is the gym I go to."

I glanced at his outfit, realizing this was the first time I'd seen him in something other than a suit. He was wearing black track pants with a baggy white shirt. All designer, of course, but he looked like a normal guy now instead of a politician. A fucking hot normal guy. Not that it changed anything.

"My office is in the next building." He pointed to the large skyscraper. "I come here almost every day."

Sounded plausible. But after the email, I wasn't taking anything to chance anymore. I grabbed my bag, sliding the strap over my shoulder as I stood up.

"I have to go," I told him curtly, walking away.

He hurried to catch up with me, making my guard rise. "Did I do something wrong?"

I scoffed, shaking my head. "Not that I'm aware of. But I can see how you look at me. And let me break it to you early—I'm not the kind of woman you want. So cut your losses and go find some blonde whose goal in life is to look pretty on your arm."

He darted in front of me, making me stop my quick strides. "You have no idea what kind of women I like."

"I can promise you won't like me."

"You crying at the police station was an act, wasn't it?"

The only reason I was able to rein in my shock at his blunt question was because of years of practice. Raising my eyes, I met his gaze. There was no anger or suspicion. He looked honestly curious about me.

"Tell me, Mayor," I tilted my head to the side, "are you as strait-laced as you claim to be? Or are you in someone's dirty pocket?"

He frowned at my accusation. "I don't work for anyone. No one pays me off. I've been in city politics since I was twenty-one. I work my ass off to make sure everything that comes out of my office is honest."

"And I really believe that," I said softly, watching his eyes widen. "You are a gentleman. Someone who seems like he wants to do good and get rid of crime. I researched you after we met. You haven't had one scandal. You respect women, and you seem to really care about those who need help. I am not part of that world. I don't need a big, strong man to help me. I take what I need and leave everything else burning. You don't want someone like me being associated with you."

Being honest usually wasn't how I went about things. But with him, this was the best way to go. He saw me as someone he could help, and until he realized that would never happen, he wasn't going to leave me alone. He could even believe I worked with the crew. I didn't care anymore. There would never be evidence tying me to anything. If he couldn't take down Kade and Gray, he'd never be able to touch me.

"I don't believe that," he said slowly. "I can read people pretty well. And you don't come off as someone dangerous at all."

Raising my arm, I gently patted his cheek. "And that's why I'm so good at it."

He looked taken aback but didn't move, letting me trail my nails down his cheek. I waited for fear or suspicion to cross his features, but he still seemed stuck on curiosity. I sighed, giving up. That's all I was sharing with him. I wasn't going to come out and say that my list of crimes was longer than his impressive resume.

"Bye, Rylan."

I spun around, not waiting for a response. Hurrying down the street, I pulled my hoodie out of my bag and slipped it on, pulling the hood over my hair as it started raining harder. A hand wrapped around my arm, and I reached for my knife until I realized it was Rylan.

"Wait," he said gruffly. "You didn't let me answer you."

I laughed. "You really can't take a hint, can you?"

He tugged me off the sidewalk, onto a small side street between two stores. I let him push me against the wall, knowing I could handle myself if he tried something. He planted his palm on the bricks next to my head, leaning down until his eyes bored into mine.

"Everything you said about me is true," he murmured, heat entering his gaze as he glanced at my lips. "Except one thing."

"And what would that be?"

"I am not always a fucking gentleman."

He captured my lips in a bruising kiss, and I jerked back in surprise. He only leaned closer, trapping me against the wall as he dominated the kiss, pushing his tongue in and sweeping it inside my mouth. He tasted like a delicious forbidden secret—two worlds colliding that would never survive together. He was probably the most innocent thing that had ever touched my lips.

And he kissed like he was sinning.

He jostled my bag out of the way so he could press his body against mine. His growing erection hit my stomach as I pushed off the wall, wrapping my arms around his neck before I realized what I was doing. His hand slid under my shirt, gripping my hip as if making sure I wouldn't try to leave.

He groaned into my mouth, and I snapped my eyes open. What the hell were the men in this city doing to me? I was always in control. But when I was with one of them, my strict rules seemed to fly out the damn window. I slammed my palm on his chest, giving myself much needed space as I broke the kiss.

"You're exactly the type of woman I like," he said, his voice husky.

"That was a mistake," I muttered as I ran a hand through my hair.

"Didn't feel like a mistake. You wanted it as much as I did."

"Forget about me, Rylan." I stepped back onto the busy sidewalk. "I won't be here much longer anyway."

"I want to see you again." Determination gleamed in his gaze, making my stomach flip.

"No."

This time, I nearly ran to make sure he couldn't catch up with me again. I didn't go straight back to my apartment. Instead, I walked down some random streets until I was positive I was alone. I rubbed my temples as I walked into my building.

I loved sex as much as the next person. And there were three men in this city that I wouldn't hesitate to fall into bed with. Even if two of them would probably rather see me dead. But it was becoming a problem. I was getting so caught up in the fun that I was forgetting why I'd come here in the first place.

No more thinking about them. From now on, the Panther job was the only thing that mattered.

13

Milina

"Come in."

I pushed the door open, instantly wary when I met Gray's amused gaze. I should have done this over the damn phone. But I couldn't deny I was curious when they invited me to meet at their house. I already knew where they lived, but learning more about their personal lives was smart if I wanted to stay one step ahead of them. They lived on the north side, a couple of blocks from their club, and their house was huge. I'd only seen the foyer before one of their men pointed me to the study. I wondered if I could sneak away after the meeting to explore more.

I greeted Vic and Juan, relaxing a bit since they were here. Kade and Gray wouldn't pull any bullshit with their bosses here. I quickly scanned the study, noting that the only exit was the door I'd just walked through. The room was large and different from other offices

I'd been in. Two large desks spanned the back wall, proving that this odd arrangement worked for their crew. I wondered if they ever disagreed on decisions—and if they did, how did they come up with a solution if neither of them could pull rank?

It didn't make any sense to me at all. I guessed that was why I enjoyed working solo. I could never deal with waiting for someone else's approval to do what I wanted.

Besides the two desks, there were two black leather couches facing each other, with a small table between them. A couple of bookcases were on the left wall, but it was the right wall that caught my attention. It was bare except for four eyehooks screwed into the drywall.

Usually, there was a special room—like a basement—where torture happened, but it seemed Kade and Gray did their dirty business right here. It wasn't a shock, and didn't bother me, but those circle bolts had my gut twisting with a reminder that these men were as ruthless as I was.

"What did you want to talk about?" Juan asked, offering me a drink. "I thought the plan was to meet with Kade and Gray to help them with their job tonight."

Vic glanced at his watch. "Yes, in a half hour. We want to make sure it happens on schedule."

I smiled. "This won't take more than a few minutes. I wanted to tell you in person that I'm not working with them tonight. Or on any of their other jobs. They're more than capable without me."

A tense silence covered the room as they all stared at me. Kade and Gray were frowning, trying to figure out what I was doing, while Vic and Juan looked downright annoyed that I was changing the script.

"Why?" Juan finally asked. "I thought we came to an agreement. You three would work together until the Panther job."

"And we will." I took a sip of my drink. "When I have a big job, I'll include an invitation to them to join me. And we'll continue to plan the Panther job. But I like doing things my way. Being a third wheel on jobs that I don't plan doesn't interest me."

"I don't think it's possible for you to be part of a team," Kade grated out.

"When it's something I want, I can." I shrugged. "This job isn't something I want."

My words weren't the truth. I lived for any job that included stealing a car. Any job that made my adrenaline pump so I'd forget about life, I'd take in a heartbeat. It was them I didn't want to work with. They were a distraction I didn't need, and after Rylan's kiss yesterday, I promised myself that I'd make my time in this city all about business.

"We'll discuss this more in the future," Vic said, clearly not happy with my decision. "You two go collect the car, and we'll see you tomorrow."

Kade nodded as Gray kept his eyes on me. I set my glass down, getting ready to make my exit. Juan and Vic left, and I moved to follow until Kade stepped in front of me. I straightened my spine, not missing the mischief dancing in his eyes.

"There has to be another reason you're backing out last minute," Gray said from behind me.

"Nope," I said, keeping my smile while my muscles tensed. They were up to something and had the advantage of being in their home. "Your little job is beneath my skill set. I don't deal well with boring, so I decided to skip it."

"Or you're going to run the job by yourself and fuck us over again." Kade moved with me when I tried going around him. I didn't blame them for thinking that, but for once, I wasn't planning anything behind their backs.

"Not this time," I answered, losing my patience when Kade darted in front of me for the third time when I went for the door. "This is the only time I'm going to ask nicely. Move. I'm leaving."

"That wasn't asking nicely. How about you stay here while we get the car so we know you aren't going to stab us in the back?" Kade murmured.

"Fuck you. I don't listen to anyone—especially you two," I sneered.

Gray was being silent, which meant he was most likely sneaking up behind me. But I refused to look away from Kade, knowing the second I did, he would attack. I feigned a move to the left, and when Kade followed, I ducked under his arm, darting to the right. Gray must have been closer than I thought because when I pulled open the door, a hand slammed onto the wood next to my head.

I didn't even try to open the door again. I twisted around, hitting Gray inside the elbow to weaken his hold on the door. He was facing me, and his smug grin disappeared when I kneed him in the balls. He went to the ground with a pained groan as a hand tangled in my hair, yanking me back against a chest.

"You wanted to have fun with us," Kade muttered in my ear. "Let's see how long it lasts until you choose to leave our city."

I giggled. "But the fun is just starting."

His hold on my hair was tight, but I still managed to turn and wrap an arm around his waist. Hooking my leg around his knee, I shoved at the same time, bringing us both to the floor. I landed on my shoulder and hissed out a breath as I scrambled to get on top of him. He refused to let go of my hair, and I took note that he was smart enough to know not to give up his one leverage over me. If only I were wearing a wig again.

He pulled my other arm out from under me, causing me to fall back onto the floor. Bending my knees, I kicked his stomach, stopping his attempt to climb on top of me. When it came to fighting, I was better than most, but having a man who had more than fifty pounds on me pin me down would put me at a disadvantage. Reaching into my boot, I slipped my knife from its holder and swung at his wrist. I sliced enough for him to finally let go of my hair but not deep enough to do any real damage.

I rolled away from him, keeping a tight grip on my blade. I was nearly standing again when someone slammed into me, taking me back to the floor. The scent of leather surrounded me, and I grinned wickedly when I caught Gray's eyes. He was practically sitting on my arm as he squeezed a pressure point in my wrist, giving me no choice but to drop my weapon. Too bad for him, that wasn't my only one.

"I must be losing my touch," I taunted as I reached behind my back with my free arm. "Men are usually down for much longer than that when I kick them there. Unless you have nothing between your legs to hurt."

"What can I say," Gray shot back through clenched teeth, "getting you on your ass is good motivation to push past the pain."

I pulled my gun out, sliding the safety off and pressing it to his head. "Game's over. Get off me."

Gray's eyes widened, and I smiled smugly. They were scared to kill me—with good reason. I didn't have to show the same restraint. Although I had no plans to kill them in their own home. This place was crawling with men from their crew, and a gunshot would bring them all to me before I had a chance to escape. But these two didn't know I wouldn't pull the trigger.

"Can't win against us without a weapon?" Kade ground out as Gray slowly slid off my arm and scooted away.

"No, I could. I just don't feel like getting blood all over my new outfit." I jumped to my feet, keeping the gun aimed at both of them. "That was a good try though."

"Who says we're done?" Gray asked, his gaze focused on my weapon.

I backed up to the door, and they both slowly crept toward me, making me frown. Kade darted forward, and I pulled the trigger, aiming right in front of his feet. While I was focused on him, Gray lunged at me. I swung the gun toward him, but he was close enough to grab my wrist. He raised both our arms up, and another shot went off, hitting the ceiling.

"Give it up," Gray huffed out, backing us up until my spine hit the door. He pressed my arm above me, trying to pry the gun out of my hand.

I laughed wildly. "If I surrendered that easily, I wouldn't be alive today."

Kade shot toward us, grabbing my free arm and smashing it against the wall. I kicked at him, but he turned, and I got his thigh instead of his groin. My heart beat rapidly when I felt my hold on the gun slipping. I hated to admit it, but between the two of them, I wasn't getting out of this room unless I went for the kill. Which I didn't want to do. For one, someone was already banging on the door, which meant their men had heard the shots and I was drastically outnumbered.

Gray yanked the gun from my grasp and clicked the safety on before tossing it across the room. I fought against their hold, but neither of them relented as they dragged me away from the door. I sucked in a breath when my chest hit the wall. Kade captured both my wrists, using his entire body to keep me from moving, as Gray moved away from us. Ice ran through my veins when, a few moments later, the distinct noise of clanking chains filled the air. I tried craning my neck to see what Gray was doing, but Kade was blocking my view.

"That was a good try," Kade mocked my words, and my jaw clenched in annoyance. One of them wrapped something cold around my wrist that was much thicker than a handcuff. It clicked when it locked, and then they did the same to my other wrist.

"You think you can keep me here?" I snapped. "You're going to regret this when I'm free."

"I don't think we will," Gray murmured as they spun me around.

Kade kicked the backs of my legs hard enough that I fell to my knees, and before I could do anything, they were both padlocking chains to the eyehooks mounted on the wall. The chains that were connected to the cuffs on my wrists. I tugged against them, knowing it was useless. The chains were short, making it impossible to get off my knees.

"Let's see if you can slip out of those as easily as you did handcuffs," Kade told me, satisfaction glistening in his eyes. "Our friends on the force told us how you really did a number on the two cops who picked you up."

"That will be nothing compared to what I do to you," I said

sweetly, refusing to show them how being trapped was making my anxiety skyrocket. No one has gotten me into a situation like this in five years. This was what fucking happened when I took my eye off the mission. Gray moved to the desk and grabbed something before sauntering back to me. Heat swarmed his gaze when he crouched in front of me.

"I know how important your health is to you," he stated, opening his hand. "I wouldn't want you to miss your one orgasm a day."

In his hand was a vibrating toy. I didn't own one like that, but I'd seen them before. They created a suction, staying on the clit until it was turned off. Shock coursed through me as I shot them a flirty grin.

"Who says I haven't gotten one already today?"

They both faltered for a moment and glanced at each other, and I laughed. They weren't going to let me go, so I might as well make it enjoyable for myself. I sat as high as I could on my knees, straightening my back.

"Don't threaten me with a good time," I goaded them. "You do know how to use that, don't you?"

Gray's eyes darkened, and he held my stare while pulling the waistband of my leggings. Heat swirled in my lower stomach when his hand grazed my pussy as he placed the toy where it needed to go. The second he pushed the toy on, it suctioned to my clit, and it took everything in me to stay still. I was going to enjoy the toy, but I wouldn't give them the satisfaction of seeing my pleasure. Gray pulled his hand out and readjusted his jeans.

"Need a release?" I purred. "You should make use of my mouth while you have me on my knees. Because I can fucking promise this won't happen again."

"Yeah, so you can bite it off," Gray muttered, standing back up.

I swiped my tongue over my teeth and grinned. "Why don't you try it and find out?"

"Next time." Kade gripped my chin, tilting my face up. "The job shouldn't take more than an hour. Enjoy yourself."

I scoffed. "I'm sure I'll have more fun than you two."

Neither answered me as they strode to the door. Gray messed with his phone for a minute before rock music started playing through the speakers that were around the room. I tested the chains again, my chest tightening when they didn't budge. My arms were pulled tight enough that I couldn't reach for anything. I studied the room when the door slammed shut and spotted a camera in the corner that was pointed at me. I shifted on my knees, my anger bubbling that they'd gotten the upper hand.

I had egged them on last week about trying to run me out of town. That was before I had decided to stop playing around with them. Too late now. I wasn't backing down. And as pissed as I was that I was here, I couldn't help but imagine how I was going to payback this favor.

It was going to be fun.

14

Kade

"Forty minutes." Gray checked his watch. "That has to be a record."

"We do this job every two weeks," I muttered. "Picking up a car from the docks and dropping it to the buyer is simple. We could probably pawn it off to someone else in the crew."

"We could," Gray mused, his eyes glued to his phone. "But you have to admit that some of the cars we pick up are fucking sweet."

I rolled my eyes. "I don't think anything's changed in the two minutes since you last looked at her."

"I think the toy is broken," he grumbled. "She's barely moved a muscle since we left the room."

"Or she spotted the camera and knows we're watching."

"Vic wants us at the club. Right now." Gray glanced at me. "Maybe one of us should go back to the house—"

"No," I cut him off. "She'll be fine a little longer. Especially since you decided to give her something to focus on."

He snorted. "Oh, come on. It was worth it. Did you see her surprise when I showed her the toy? It was the most emotion she's let slip since we met her."

"Didn't we say that when it comes to her, we agree on everything? Actually, you're the one who told me that," I said, trying to keep my patience in check. "That's how we deal with every decision."

He frowned at me as we walked in through the back door of our club. "I'm sorry. I didn't think I needed your permission for every little fucking thing I do."

"You can fuck any woman in this city," I said in a low voice as we climbed the stairs. "She's a wild card. We can't trust her. She'll fuck you, and then probably shoot you again for the fun of it."

"She's a rebel," he mumbled, playing with his lip ring. "You can't deny that she's like us."

"Unlike us, she doesn't seem to have anyone she cares about." I paused at the top of the stairs. "That makes her dangerous. It gives us no leverage to make sure she doesn't screw us over."

"Maybe she does have someone, and we just haven't found out who it is."

"We need to dig up more of her past."

He nodded. "I'll call Andy. Maybe he can give us more info on her ex-boyfriend."

The door in front of us opened, and I swallowed my response as we greeted Vic.

"Where's Juan?" Gray asked as he poured us both a glass of whiskey.

"Out for the night," Vic sank into the couch cushions and lit a joint.

Gray and I exchanged looks, knowing Vic only smoked weed when he was stressed. Even knowing that I wasn't going to enjoy whatever conversation Vic was going to start, it was still nearly impossible to get the image of Mili on her knees out of my head. My words to Gray were as much for me as they were for him.

Mili was a fucking force of nature—in every damn way. She dripped sex appeal when she was in our presence, and she knew exactly what she was doing. But it wasn't just her body. It was her strength. She took complete control of every situation she was in—and if she lost it, it didn't take her long to steal it back. She was smart and was born for the world she'd risen up in. And I fucking hated that she had crawled into my head and refused to leave.

"What's up, Vic?" I sat on the couch across from him. "Why the rush to meet?"

He hesitated. "Juan and I have discussed this over the last week. We want her."

Gray nearly choked on his whiskey. "Want who?"

"Sapphire," he answered gruffly. "After the Panther job. We want her to stay in Ridgewood."

"Seriously?" I asked in disbelief. "She's not going to do that."

"We want you to convince her," Vic said slowly. "I want her connections. Her jobs. Do you realize how much we could expand the crew if she worked for us?"

"*For* us?" I repeated before huffing out a curt laugh. "I know you haven't spent as much time with her as we have, but I can tell you right now, that girl will never fucking work for anyone."

The night we set her up with the police, and again tonight when we finally managed to cuff her to the wall, I saw it in her eyes. The tiny flash of raw panic when her freedom was cut off proved what I'd already guessed. She would never give that up for anyone.

"I think we all believe now that she is Sapphire," Gray said, resting his arms on his knees as he leaned forward on the couch. "And she's not going to downgrade what she does now to work with us. Our crew might be large, but her name is infamous."

"And that's exactly why we want her," Vic said, taking a long drag from the joint. "To have her name connected to ours could help us expand to the East Coast."

"She won't do it," I stated gruffly. "And if we try, she'll try to kill us. Again. She doesn't like being told what to do."

"Then find something we can use against her," Vic snapped, getting annoyed that we weren't agreeing with him. "This is going to be your empire soon. We want to grow it as much as we can. Your Uncle wants the best for you, Kade."

"Juan agreed to this?" I asked with a frown.

Juan was my uncle. Not that I ever acknowledged that in public. No one except our family, Vic, and Gray knew I was related to him. Juan's brother—my dad—died when I was a baby, and Juan took care of my mom and me. She never wanted me mixed up with the crew when I got older. But that obviously didn't fucking happen.

"Yes, he agreed," Vic answered, pulling me back into the conversation. "Find out what she's done in the past and see if there's anything we can use to hold it over her head."

"Blackmail her," Gray muttered. "This won't end well."

"If you two can't do it—"

"We will," I cut Vic off. "Andy knew her. We'll talk to him and see what he knows."

Vic nodded. "Good. I want to know everything we can about her before the Panther job."

Vic smashed the rest of his joint in the ashtray before getting up and striding out of the room. Gray was on his feet in a second, giving me a look of impatience as he headed to the door. Nerves knotted my stomach as I got up from the couch and followed Gray out of the club. This situation with Mili was already crazy, and now it was only going to get worse.

"There was no trouble," Jay told us as we stopped in front of the study door.

We already knew that, seeing as Gray had been watching the camera nearly nonstop since we had left her a little over an hour ago. But we still had Jay stand outside the door the whole time, just to make sure no one tried walking in.

I didn't care much for Jay, but he did what he was told, no matter what it was. He was newer to the crew and wanted to climb the ranks quickly. His shaved head was covered with tattoos, and he loved wearing tight muscle shirts to show off the work he did in the gym. He was cocky, always acting like he was hot shit.

"Stay here," I told him. "We'll be out in a few minutes."

Jay looked curious but was smart enough not to question me as Gray opened the door. I closed it behind me, my eyes immediately seeking out Mili. She was exactly where we left her, and she shifted on her knees when the door clicked shut. Her head had been bowed toward the floor, but as we got closer, she looked up, her gaze locking with mine.

"How'd the job go?" she asked casually, as if we hadn't kept her in here for over an hour.

Gray frowned, shooting me a quick glance. She seemed relaxed, but her fists were clenched tight as we stopped in front of her.

"I owe you a thank you," she purred, focusing on Gray. "Now that I got a free sample of that toy, I know not to waste my money."

I grinned in amusement. "You didn't like it?"

"The thing died before I even got off." Her eyes went cold. "I've been stuck here, bored out of my damn mind. So fuck you very much."

I held in my groan, already knowing what Gray was going to do next. And it made my dick twitch before I could help myself. Gray dropped to his knees in front of her, making her straighten up as she stared at him warily.

"I would hate for you to leave here unhappy," Gray murmured.

"Why?" she tossed back. "Worried my revenge on you two will be worse than blowing up your car?"

I bit my tongue, knowing when we did this that we ran the risk of her doing something to get back at us. Now I was wondering if being more cautious would be enough to make sure we didn't fall for whatever she tried doing.

"If I remember correctly, you said I was in the small group of men who knew how to pleasure a woman." Gray ran his hand up her thigh, stopping at the waistband of her leggings. "I want to see if I can get you off as fast as I did in the club."

Mili's stare cut to me, as if she was trying to figure out what I thought about it. I kept my face blank, refusing to give her any reaction. She didn't say a word when Gray slipped his hand into her pants. She did spread her legs wider, and he took that as a yes, quickly grabbing the useless toy and tossing it to the floor. His hand disappeared again, and I could tell when his fingers found her pussy because she sucked in a small breath.

"You are fucking soaked. Either the toy did its job before it died"—he slid his other hand to the back of her neck, getting a grip of her hair and tilting her face up—"or you have a thing for being chained up. Which one is it?"

"Neither," she nearly panted as Gray continued to finger her. "Sitting here and planning how I'm going to fuck with both of you after this is what got me all hot and bothered."

By now, my cock was rock hard and pressing uncomfortably against my jeans. I flexed my fingers, refusing to act on it as I watched her. I didn't want her to know how much she affected my dick. She'd only use it against me.

I stepped closer, and her eyes found mine. "How about we call the night even once Gray gets you off?"

Her laugh was cut short from whatever Gray was doing to her. "*If* he gets me off. I think he's a one-trick pony. Because this doesn't feel nearly as good as it did at the club."

"The way your pussy is holding my fingers hostage proves that's a lie," Gray responded gruffly.

She didn't answer, staring past us as she attempted to not react to what Gray was doing to her. My cock ached, and it was taking everything in me to keep it in my fucking jeans. Her kiss played over and over in my head, and I gritted my teeth, not giving in to my desires. Gray let out a frustrated noise.

"Stop fighting it." He tugged on her hair, making her scowl. "I can feel how much you want it. Fucking come for me."

"It won't be for you." Her chest heaved with every breath. "It'll be for me. My pleasure—not yours."

"As long as you remember who gave you that pleasure," Gray said, his voice smothered with satisfaction as her body went rigid. Her lips were pressed tightly together, but a small cry still escaped when she climaxed. I watched, transfixed, as her face flushed, her hips rocking while Gray continued to finger her.

Her head sagged when Gray released her head, and her hair fell around her, hiding her face from us. Gray climbed to his feet, licking his fingers, dramatically sucking as if he couldn't get enough of her taste.

"Jay, get in here," I called loud enough for him to hear me through the door.

Mili's head snapped up, her defenses instantly going up when Jay stepped into the room. He glanced at her with interest before turning his attention to me.

"What do you need, boss?" he asked.

"We want you to make sure she gets off the property," Gray answered, digging through a drawer in his desk.

"Sure," Jay replied, looking uncertain. "Who is she?"

"Someone we don't want snooping around." My words had Mili glaring at me. But I knew she wouldn't say anything. She was the one who didn't want anyone to know she was Sapphire.

Gray sauntered back toward her, and I pulled the cuff keys from my pocket as I moved beside him. I unlocked the cuff, pulling it from her wrist, and Gray locked a handcuff in its place. I freed her other arm, and Gray snapped the other cuff on her, locking her arms behind her back. We didn't want her to chance doing anything else tonight. I was sure we'd deal with her backlash when she decided to strike back. But I wanted her out of our house before she found anything important.

She stayed silent when we pulled her to her feet. She stumbled a few steps, unbalanced from being on her knees for so long. The anger brewing in her eyes had my heart thudding, but we walked her to the door where Jay was waiting.

I handed Jay the handcuff key. "Once she's off our property, let her go. Then come and tell us when she's gone."

Jay nodded, putting the key in his pocket before grabbing Mili's arm. She didn't fight him as he led her out of the room. We stayed silent, listening to their footsteps getting quieter as they moved toward the front door. I turned to Gray, but my words died in my throat when we heard Jay talking.

"You're a hot piece of ass." Jay's voice echoed through the foyer. "How much would it cost me to have you for a night?"

The next noise was an unmistakable slap that most likely landed on her ass. My shoulder collided with Gray's as we rushed to get through the doorway. A pained groan filled the air, and we halted in the foyer, seeing Jay on the floor. Mili was lying on her back, already slipping her legs between her arms to get her cuffed hands in front of her. Once she did, she jumped to her feet, sneaking up behind Jay as he stood up. She threw her arms around his neck, the chain of the handcuffs pressing against his throat.

"If I did charge, you could never afford me," she told him calmly as he struggled to breathe.

He whipped his body around, attempting to knock her off. She held on tight until he reached down and pulled a knife from his pocket. When she spotted the blade, she kicked his feet until he staggered and fell to the floor. She went down with him, finally moving the chain off his throat. Her foot connected with his cheek, and he cried out. His head snapped to the side, and he stared at us in a daze. Neither Gray nor I moved a muscle to help him. He shouldn't have fucking touched her.

She got to her feet, taking advantage of him not moving. She stepped on his wrist, pressing harder until his grip on the knife loosened. Bending down, she pried it from his hand. He snapped out of it, realizing he had lost his weapon. Grabbing her ankle with his free hand, he twisted, knocking her off balance. He shakily stood up before lunging at her. He wrapped his arms around her waist and slammed her into the wall. She had kept her cuffed hands above her head, but she brought them down and stabbed the knife into his neck.

His hold on her body went lax, and he choked on his own blood as he tried breathing. She pulled the blade out before shoving him away. He collapsed on the floor, writhing as he fought to stay conscious. It didn't last long, and a puddle of his blood spread across the marble floor as he went still.

We watched as she wiped his blood off the knife before flicking it shut. She leaned over his body, fishing her hand in his pocket until she pulled out the key. I rubbed the small cut she had given me earlier as she unlocked the handcuffs.

"We're not going to have a problem because I killed a member of your crew, are we?" she asked, finally meeting our gazes.

"Nope," I said with a shrug. "Looked like self-defense to us. And that's what we'll tell Vic and Juan."

"Good." She grinned, not looking the least bit bothered that she was covered in Jay's blood. "See you boys later."

She strode out the front door, leaving Gray and me standing there in shock. The entire fight had lasted less than two minutes. She had overpowered a man twice her size—while handcuffed. I knew she could fight, but fuck. It was painfully obvious she had been holding out on us when we fought with her in the study. She could have easily stabbed me in the neck instead of slicing my hand.

"I think we need to make sure neither of us ever gets caught alone with her when she's pissed," Gray muttered. "Whoever taught her how to fight created a fucking monster."

I agreed with him. It didn't matter if she was a woman. It would be stupid of us to think we could take her just because she was smaller than us.

"We need to call Andy and find out what we can about her before she retaliates for this," I said, turning to go back into the study.

"You agree with Vic and Juan?" Gray asked in surprise.

I shook my head. "I don't think we could ever force her to stay. But finding dirt on her can help keep her in line while we plan the Panther job. If not, I have a feeling she's going to spill a lot more blood."

"Let's just make sure it's not our blood," Gray mumbled.

I pulled a bottle of whiskey out of the cabinet. She was going to make the next few months very interesting.

15

Milina

Andy's garage came into view, and I pressed down on the gas, making my Corvette fly forward. I didn't usually drive this car during daylight, but I couldn't resist. The four-hour drive to Andy's was mostly desert road, meaning I could go as fast as I wanted. Plus, I was in a hurry to get this done. It had been a few days since Kade and Gray had locked me in their study, and I decided they'd sweated enough. I wanted to get even. And tonight was perfect.

I pulled into the garage yard, parking next to a few motorcycles. I studied them, wondering if these were the bikes he was going to show me. Motorcycles were needed for the Panther job, and I trusted Andy to give me ones that were in great condition.

I climbed out, the desert heat already making me sweat. The large roll-down garage doors were shut, but the small side door was open. Reaching back inside my car, I grabbed my gun, putting it in the elastic holder I had under my shirt. I could feel it on my back as I walked toward the door, and it calmed me. There was no reason for me to use it on Andy, but taking a weapon everywhere had become a habit.

I knocked loudly on the door before stepping inside. Cool air greeted me, and I scanned the large garage. A couple of cars were in here being worked on. One was on a lift, about six feet in the air. I walked around it, searching for Andy.

"Andy?" I called, spotting a counter in the back. Someone was sitting behind the counter, facing away from me.

Tingles pricked at my spine, a feeling of unease hitting me. I'd learned long ago to trust my instincts, and I pulled my gun out, slowly walking forward.

"Andy?" I said again.

The chair suddenly spun around, and I gasped when I saw Andy. His face was beaten, and blood was seeping through his shirt.

"I'm sorry," he choked out, regret shining in his eyes.

Before I could make the choice between helping him or getting the fuck out of there, something hard pressed against my spine. My breath caught in my chest, ice flowing in my veins as someone pushed me forward, keeping the gun to my back. A man stepped in front of me, and I didn't move a muscle when he took the gun from my hand.

"Who are you?" I let my voice tremble, deciding fear was my best defense until I figured out who I was dealing with.

The guy didn't answer right away, and I studied him closely, trying to see if I knew who he was. But I was coming up blank. His bleach-blond hair was slicked back, and tattoos covered his arms. I guessed he was a few years older than me. Bringing up his hand, he rested his knuckles under my chin, and I froze from his touch.

"It's been five years, but there's no denying who you are," he murmured, his eyes gleaming with excitement. "You look even better than I remember, Milina."

Panic swarmed me as he spoke the name only a handful of people in this world knew. He was from my past. That name was supposed to have died five years ago. There was no point in pretending now. I tilted my head to the side, letting my gaze wander down his body.

"I wish I could say the same about you," I said in a bored voice. "But you must not have been important because I don't know who the fuck you are."

He scowled, his fingers grabbing my chin roughly. "I'll be important once I tell them that you're still alive."

"You haven't told them yet?" I asked, my small hope of leaving here growing larger.

"We wanted to make sure Andy was talking about the right girl," the guy answered.

I looked past him at Andy, who shook his head. "I didn't know, Mili. I never would have called Mike if—"

The guy in front of me laughed, cutting Andy off. "Andy called me to offer his sympathy. Said Mili came by the races and said her boyfriend died years ago. I couldn't believe my ears. Everyone thought *you* were dead."

I ground my teeth, kicking myself at my mistake. I didn't think Andy had any connection with people from my past. I never should have gone to that damn race. I shifted, and the gun was jammed into my back harder.

"Now why don't you be the good girl I remember and come with us quietly?" Mike withdrew his hand from my face and reached into his back pocket, pulling out a thick zip tie. I breathed in deeply, trying to shake my fear so I could think clearly. There was no way in fuck I was letting him tie my hands. If I left here with them, I'd be wishing I were dead.

I wondered if they knew I'd taken on the Sapphire name. By the way he was acting, I doubted it. He wasn't wary or scared of me—he was looking at me as if expecting me to obey his every word. Six years ago, I would have. Back when I was a shell of nothing. Letting my body shake, I widened my eyes while raising my arms, as if letting him put the zip tie on. He smiled smugly, wrapping the plastic around my wrists.

"But the thing is," my tone started off sweet, getting colder with each word, "that good girl you remember? She doesn't fucking exist anymore."

Mike's gaze cut to mine, trying to tighten the zip tie faster, but I was already pulling my arms away. I threw a punch, hitting him across the jaw, causing him to stagger back. The gun that had been on my spine was now pressed to the back of my head.

"Stop," a deep voice ordered from behind me.

"You won't shoot me," I said, confidence radiating through my voice. "I'm no good to you dead, and we all know it."

"Knock her out," Mike bellowed.

The metal barrel left my head, and I spun around quickly, going for the weapon. He wasn't letting it go, so I wrapped my fingers around his, pulling the trigger as I tried keeping the gun steady. I managed to shoot Mike in the arm, which was a surprise since the guy was attempting to yank the gun from my hold. The pistol Mike had taken from me was on the floor, and he lunged for it. I let go of his partner's hand and stepped forward, bringing my knee up to meet his face before he reached it. He cried out in pain, and I leaped forward, snatching the gun up.

Without a second thought, I shot Mike in the head, not even waiting to see him hit the floor before I spun around, raising the weapon to the other guy. We locked eyes, and my heart stuttered. My aim faltered before I tightened my grip.

"Hey, Mili," he said softly, keeping his gun on me.

"Liam," I choked out, shocked that out of everyone who wanted to come after me, he was the one who'd found me.

"You need to come with me," he said curtly, his bright blue eyes showing none of the empathy he used to have for me.

My mind swirled, memories and present-day colliding as I stared at him. Liam was one of the few who showed me kindness in the years I was trapped in my own personal hell. He was one of the few I had trusted back then. Just like it was all those years ago, his light brown hair was buzzed short. My eyes trailed down to his forearm, dread claiming me as I stared at the tattoo I still had nightmares about.

"I would have thought everyone would have split ways after he went away," I said, trying to stall. I never hesitated to kill when my life depended on it, but with him, I couldn't make myself pull the trigger. His kindness was one of the only reasons I survived as long as I did.

"Don't act like that wasn't your fault," he said bitterly. "Do you know how many people you fucked over when you faked your death?"

"Not you," I said quickly. "I made sure—"

"You disappeared," he snapped, anger clouding his eyes. "You have no idea what happened to me. Now I'm taking you back. I might not be able to bring you to him, but there are others running things now."

I laughed humorlessly. "Better put a bullet in me then, Liam. Because I will never fucking go back."

I nearly flinched when he raised the gun and moved to the side before firing off a shot. I didn't dare take my eyes off him, even when I heard Andy let out a pained scream.

"I know who you are, Mili," he said in a low voice. "You might have started killing, but I can guarantee you still don't take lives of innocents. Not after what happened to you."

I willed myself to fucking shoot him, but I needed to know who else he'd told about finding me first. I hated how he was bringing up my life like he knew everything about me. But he was right. I'd lost count of how many I'd killed over the years, but they were always people who deserved it.

"That shot won't kill him, but the next one will," Liam said, aiming his gun back at me. "Unless you come with me."

There was no way I was willingly going with him, but a tug of guilt pulled at my heart at the thought of Andy. I'd only met him a few times, and he had always been nice to me. Even offering me a way out during one of his races when he saw my ex backhand me across the face because I didn't answer how he wanted. Andy was a good guy. And now he was probably going to die because of me.

"You weren't going to let him live anyway," I accused. "I remember how it works. Can't have witnesses."

"Let's go, Mili," he said, losing patience. "Or I'll shoot you in the leg."

"Why are you doing this?" I screamed, losing it. "You were going to help me get out—"

"I was," he cut me off, "and they found out about it. You know what they did? They fucking killed her."

My stomach plummeted, remembering his wife. He loved her more than anything in this world and would have left the life for her if he was able to. But once someone was in with that crowd, there was no getting away.

"I'm sorry," I said hoarsely. "But I'm not going back."

"They'll let me walk," he said quietly. "If I bring you back, I'll have my freedom again. The price for your head is larger than I've ever seen."

My chest constricted, and I fought my guilt as I kept the gun on him. "You chose that life, Liam. You wanted it. I never did. I didn't have a fucking choice. But I make my own decisions now. And I promise you, I won't go with you unless it's in a body bag."

"Everyone heard the rumor that you were alive." He took a step forward, making my gut knot as I held my ground. "But they're searching in South America. What's so important in California that you're hiding here? I'm guessing Caleb is the reason behind that? You never were good with computers."

I didn't answer, not liking that he'd made the connection between Caleb and me. I debated just shooting him in the knee and running, but I couldn't. He couldn't leave here alive if I wanted to complete the Panther job.

"Who else knows?" I asked. "That I'm here?"

His slight hesitation was all I needed to know that his next words were going to be lies.

"I called someone before coming here."

I chuckled. "Liar. You wanted to make sure it was actually me.

Because if it was a false lead and you came back empty-handed, then you'd pay for it."

A vein twitched above his eye, and he frowned as he crept forward. "Don't make me hurt you."

"You couldn't even if you tried," I snapped. "I've been numb for years."

He was nearly within arm's reach, and I squeezed the trigger, aiming at his shoulder. He must have anticipated my move because he ducked out of the way, lunging at me. I swung my gun toward him, and he easily blocked my hit with his forearm. Panic seized me, knowing my chance at beating him in hand-to-hand combat was slim. He used to be the eliminator—someone who was called when someone needed to die. He was one of the best fighters I knew.

I saw his hit coming too late, and blood filled my mouth when his gun collided with my cheek. Luckily, my arm had been up, deflecting the worst of it, or that would have knocked me out. Blinking through the pain, I fell to the floor, scrambling back so I could get a clear shot.

"I never should have taught you to fight," he said tightly, almost getting a hold of my ankle when I ducked behind a car. "You wouldn't have lasted this long if you were still the same girl I met when you were sixteen."

"Back then, you cared if I survived," I told him. I took a deep breath and glanced around the car to shoot. I frowned, not seeing him anywhere. Jumping to my feet, I peered over the car, seeing him racing for the door. My heart lurched as I chased after him.

"I believe that you won't be taken alive," he yelled without looking behind him. "So, I'll just tell them where you are. They'll bring enough people back to collect you. See you soon, Mili."

He disappeared out the door, and I was seconds behind him. The sound of an engine cut through the air, and I saw him just in time for him to rev his motorcycle before racing away. I ripped open my car door and jumped in, glad I had driven one of my faster cars today. I shifted gears, my pedal to the floor as I raced to catch up. The car fishtailed as I shot onto the road.

I waited for him to veer off the road into the desert, but he was smarter than that. The odds of him crashing on sand were higher than on the concrete. Reaching over and ripping open my glove box, I grabbed a burner phone and flipped it open, keeping my eyes on Liam's bike.

"Nine-one-one. What's your emergency?"

"There was a shooting," I said in a high-pitched voice. "Andy's Garage. Off Breen Road. Hurry, he's bleeding out."

I snapped the phone shut, making sure to power it off before tossing it into the passenger seat. I was slowly gaining on Liam, and I pushed my car harder, my RPMs higher than I was comfortable with, but I didn't slow down. If he told anyone I was here, I was fucked. I couldn't let that happen.

The road suddenly curved, and I knew he was going to crash before his wheels left the road. He was taking it too fast. My emotions were mixed as the bike slid, and he was flipped off. He had been going over a hundred miles an hour. I slammed on my brakes, my relief slightly overpowering my guilt.

He wasn't moving as I came to a stop. I took a couple of deep breaths and dug into the glove box again, pulling out a pair of gloves before I hopped out. My shoes crunched on the sand as I moved toward him, slipping the gloves on. I raised my gun, waiting for him to jump up. It didn't even look like he was breathing. He was on his side, facing away from me, but blood was staining the sand around him. Crouching down, my head snapped up when I heard something.

"Fuck," I muttered, seeing a car far down the road.

I quickly reached over and pressed my gloved hand to his throat. I stilled for a few moments, waiting for a pulse. But there wasn't one. He was gone. A wave of sadness hit me as I stood back up. Liam had been an anchor for me in the past. Even if he was going to betray me, I didn't want to see him dead.

Glancing at the car again, I ran to the road and dragged the bike off. I wanted it to take as long as possible to find Liam's body. Because when they did, more people I didn't want here would come investigating. I was glad I was four hours from Ridgewood, or I'd flee right now.

I rushed to my Corvette and drove onto the sand to turn around and drive back toward Andy's. His garage came into view, and I hesitated, wanting to check on him, but I could already hear sirens. He lived just outside a small town, and they'd be here in minutes. I hoped he survived. Fear slid through me, wondering if he knew who Liam and Mike were. If he survived, what if he told others about it? I doubted Liam had told Andy why they wanted me. But I still didn't like anyone knowing anything about my past. An ambulance raced past me, heading toward the garage. If he did live, I'd have to visit him and convince him to keep it all to himself.

For once, I stayed under the speed limit as I headed back to Ridgewood. The sun was setting, and I kept my eyes on the empty road, letting my mind wander. I brushed my fingers across my lips, feeling the drying blood. My lip was split, and I winced when I pressed on it. My heart was still pumping on straight adrenaline. That was the closest I'd gotten to my past since leaving it five years ago. And now that they knew I was alive, it made this Panther job even more important.

If I was able to pull it off, I'd be free.

16

Rylan

I dropped the stack of papers I'd been reading and picked up my office phone after the fifth ring.

"Hello?"

"Mayor, this is Officer Hill," the guy said nervously. "I'm sorry to bother you so late, but I have information I thought you'd want to hear."

"What is it?"

"There's been talk about how the Riot Crew has had their guys keeping an eye out for a white Corvette, and I know you always want any info on the crew," Officer Hill rambled.

"I appreciate it," I said quickly, the paperwork forgotten. "What's so important about the car?"

"I don't know, but I'm on patrol right now, and there's a white

Corvette parked. I don't know if it's the car they're looking for, but I wanted to let you know."

I leaned back in my chair, processing the information. This was why I made friends on the police force. It helped to stay in front of things happening in my city.

"Where is it parked?" I asked.

"In front of the Chinese takeout, a block from your office. Do you want me to follow it?"

"Did you see the driver?"

"I got a glimpse—it's a young woman."

I nearly bolted off my chair. "Thank you, Officer. I'll handle this."

I hung up and pulled my suit jacket on before rushing out of the office. There was only one woman the crew seemed to be obsessed with, and I'd been looking for her for over a week. Ever since I kissed her, I hadn't been able to get her out of my damn head.

I pressed the elevator button, willing it to hurry the fuck up. I'd been going to the gym twice a day, hoping to run into her, but she must have found a different place to work out because she hadn't been there at all. My life had always revolved around my career, and the fact that one woman had been taking over my mind was driving me crazy. Especially one I knew was not good for me.

Even as these thoughts jumbled around in my mind, I still didn't stop myself from racing outside. I wanted to see if it was Mili. I turned the corner, slowing to a walk when I saw the white Corvette parked on the street. It was a quiet night, and streetlights lit up the sidewalk as I strode toward the car.

I got within a few feet when the door of the Chinese restaurant opened, and someone rushed out. I hesitated, not knowing if it was her. The woman was wearing black sweats and a hoodie that was swallowing her. The hood was up, concealing her face. The night was too warm to be wearing such heavy clothes unless she was trying to hide herself.

"Mili," I called out, acting like I knew it was her.

She whipped around, clutching her bag of food. Annoyance flared in her eyes as she faced me. My stomach clenched, and I stepped closer, wondering if it was just the shadows or if there was something on her face.

"What are you doing here?" she questioned, fishing her key out of her pocket.

I decided to be honest. "Word on the street is the crew has been looking for a white Corvette. I was curious to see who owned it."

"How do you know crew business?"

"It helps to have friends in the city," I said with a shrug. "If I want to stay ahead of crime, I need people who watch for me."

"What do you want, Rylan?" she asked, sounding exhausted.

She moved under the light, and my heart lurched. She backed away when I reached out toward her face.

"What the hell happened?" I asked, staring at her busted lip with a large bruise forming on her cheek. "Did someone attack you?"

"Nope," she stated, her face showing no emotion. "I fell."

I gritted my teeth. "Bullshit."

"Listen, I've had a shit day, and really don't feel like talking." She unlocked her car. "Bye, Mayor."

"Did the crew do this?" I asked, wanting to know who hurt her. Kade and Gray might be dicks, but their long list of crimes never included beating women.

She didn't answer, rounding her car and jumping into the driver's seat. Without thinking about it, I opened the passenger door and slid in. She went rigid, slowly turning her head to look at me.

"Get out of my car," she demanded.

"No. Tell me what happened."

"You know, I have a pile of problems, and I don't need to add a stalker to it." She raised an eyebrow. "You don't want me to make your life difficult, Rylan. Because I promise, I can wipe away your perfect image in a fucking heartbeat."

Her threat didn't faze me at all. "If there's a man in my city going around hitting women, I need to know about it."

"Lucky for you, it didn't happen in your city. So it's none of your concern."

"That means it was a guy that hurt you?"

She sighed. "What do you want?"

"I don't know," I muttered, wondering that myself. "For some reason, I worry about you."

"I'm a big girl. I don't need anyone worrying about me."

"Sounds lonely."

"What about you?" She looked me up and down. "You don't have anyone, do you?"

"I have friends."

"Good. Go worry about them."

I chuckled. "Let me take you to get your face checked out. That cut looks deep."

"I'm fine. It looks worse than it is." She stared at me. "What is it going to take to get you the hell out of my car?"

I thought for a moment. "An honest conversation."

She frowned before her entire demeanor changed. She grinned wickedly, leaning back in her seat. "I think you want something else. That kiss proved you want to do more than just talk."

Her words went straight to my dick. "Tell me, what do I want?"

She leaned closer, placing her hand on my jaw. "You want me naked and screaming your name."

I cleared my throat. "And if I do?"

"Then let's go." She put her car in gear and pulled onto the street. "You want to go to a hotel or your place?"

Confusion had me pausing from her sudden change. "Your place isn't an option?"

"No."

"I feel like you're trying to distract me from something," I mumbled.

"No, I want to distract myself. Sex is an amazing way to do that."

"Mili—"

"You're the one stalking me. I'm giving you what you want."

"I'm not stalking you."

"Whatever you say, Mayor."

I scrubbed a hand down my face. "I'm curious about you."

"Well, here's your pass. One night with me." She looked away from the road and smiled. "But after tonight, I don't want to see you popping up wherever I am."

"Do you work with the crew?"

My question made her smile fade. "Why? Worried you're about to get into bed with someone you should be arresting?"

"That's a dangerous life, Mili. You don't want to be mixed up with them."

She changed the subject. "Your place or a hotel?"

"My house. Take the next right."

"You live on the north side of town?" she asked in surprise.

"It's where I grew up. And living there helps me stay closer to the people who voted me into office."

She nodded. "Hmm. It looks good for the mayor to act like he's one of the common people. Living in a mansion on the south side would have the opposite effect."

"Yes," I grated out. "It helps my image too. But that's not the only reason I chose to live there."

"Sure it's not."

She turned down an alley, taking a shortcut only to slam on her brakes when a car darted in front of her, making it impossible for her to leave the alley. My stomach clenched, recognizing the black Jaguar.

"Looks like you were right about the crew looking for my car," she muttered, throwing it into reverse.

Another car stopped behind her, keeping her trapped in the alley. She cursed, glancing at me. After hesitating, she reached over me and grabbed a gun out of the glove box. Fuck. I knew she was into some sketchy shit, but seeing it was different. I did not need people to see me in a showdown with the crew. Rumors that I was in their pocket would make the damn morning papers.

I debated calling the few I trusted at the police station to come and run them off, but that would only create more witnesses. I didn't want anyone to know if I could help it.

"Stay in the car," she ordered, tucking her gun behind her shirt.

"Are you kidding?" I snapped.

"They won't kill me," she said with a roll of her eyes. "Let me see what they want, and then we'll be on our way."

I pinched the bridge of my nose as she opened her door and got out. After a few seconds, I opened my door and stepped out. Kade was already out of his car, and surprise covered his features when he saw me. Mili was leaning against the hood of her car, facing Kade. I glanced over my shoulder, seeing Gray getting out of the car behind us.

"What the hell are you doing here?" Kade asked me.

"We were on a date," Mili answered. "Until you two decided to crash it."

"A date?" Gray laughed from behind us. "The great mayor doesn't date. He's too busy trying to get us behind bars."

"Is it possible to be in this town without people finding me?" Mili asked in a bored voice. "What do you want?"

"If you're trying to stay under the radar, you should probably keep that car in the garage," Kade answered, anger returning to his gaze. "Your date's over. Why don't you go home, Mayor?"

"I'm not leaving," I said coldly. "Why don't you move your car so we can leave? Before I make a call."

Gray scoffed. "This looks bad for you. Meeting us in an alley so late at night. Looks like something a dirty politician would do. You're not going to call anyone."

I didn't answer, annoyed that he was fucking right. Both Kade and Gray moved closer to Mili, and I rounded the car, stopping beside her. "If you hurt her, I will call someone. I don't give a shit about what rumors start from it."

"We just have to ask her something," Kade said. "It can't wait."

"Where were you today?" Gray asked her.

Mili raised her gaze to him. "I've been with Rylan all day."

My heart hammered, wondering what she was hiding. They both turned their attention to me, questions in their eyes.

"She's been with me," I said, keeping my voice even.

"Her pussy must taste like heaven if she got you to lie for her." Kade glared at me.

Anger rushed through my veins, and I took a step forward. "Watch your fucking mouth."

"What happened to your face?" Gray asked quietly, focusing back on Mili.

"I fell."

Kade lost his patience, lunging at Mili. I moved to intervene, but Gray stepped between us, pressing a gun to my chest. My eyes widened as I looked from the gun to him. This was the first time they'd physically threatened me.

"Don't move, Mayor," Gray said in a low voice. "And you'll survive this."

"You must be stupid," I snapped. "You think I won't press charges?"

Gray chuckled. "Try it. There are no witnesses here. I can promise if you tell anyone about this, it won't end well for you."

"Put the knife down, Kade," Mili said, not looking the least bit worried. Kade had a blade to her throat as she stayed absolutely still.

"One of our friends called," Kade said slowly. "Andy was attacked in his own garage. He's at the hospital. In a coma. You know anything about that?"

"How could I?" she asked. "I've been with Rylan all day."

"Really? Because Andy's friend said that the paramedic recalled seeing a white Corvette driving away from the garage." Kade shook his head in warning when Mili shifted.

"I'm not the only one with this car," she said tightly.

"What's under the hoodie, Mili?" Kade asked, his eyes dropping to her chest. "Are you still covered in blood? Did Andy do that to your face when you attacked him?"

"I didn't fucking attack him," she hissed, her calm act disappearing.

I knew who Andy was, thanks to his affiliation with the crew. But he kept his racing business quiet, making it hard for the law to catch up with him too.

"He's a friend," Kade stated. "We're not going to let you hurt people we care about."

"Let me?" she laughed coldly. "No one lets me do anything. But I didn't hurt him."

"There's dust all over your car. You were in the desert," Gray said, his eyes not leaving me.

She stayed silent for a few moments. "I was there. But it wasn't me who shot him."

"You're lying," Kade accused. "He knows about your past. And you didn't want anyone finding out—"

"He knows nothing about me," she cut him off. "I went there to buy a motorcycle. Two other guys were already there. They were the ones who hurt Andy. I barely fucking got away."

Kade shook his head. "We've seen you fight. Barely getting away doesn't sound right."

"It's true," she insisted. "I tried helping Andy. Who do you think called the paramedics? I did. Don't believe me? Go look at my phone in the glove box."

Kade and Gray exchanged a look before Gray pulled the gun away from me. He moved to the side of the car, opening the door before leaning inside. He came back out with a phone in his hand that he was already looking at.

"It shows she called," Gray muttered.

"Put the knife down, Kade," I told him. "You don't want to do this."

"Oh, I think he does," Mili said with a laugh. "They're learning that having me in their city is a pain in the ass. But he won't. Because he knows better. Don't you, Kade?"

Kade's jaw clenched, but he lowered the knife from her throat and stepped back. "Who attacked him?"

"I don't know." She glanced at me warily. "They weren't able to answer before I left."

I stared at her, wondering if she was hinting that she'd killed them. But she was smart enough not to say it out loud if that's what happened.

"You better hope Andy tells the same story. *If* he wakes up," Gray said, still glaring at her with suspicion.

"He will," she said, pushing off the car now that Kade had given her space.

"Watch yourself with her, Mayor." Gray looked at me. "You try so hard to stay on the right side of the law—she'll drag you to hell if you let her. Sex isn't worth that."

"You didn't seem worried about me dragging you to hell when you were fingering me the other night," she purred, sauntering toward Gray.

He laughed. "Fucking you won't make me burn. I'm already in hell with you, Rebel."

I frowned, my pulse spiking uncomfortably as they spoke. How close were they that Gray had a nickname for her? And knowing he had touched her was bothering me in ways I didn't even want to fucking think about.

"If we find out you're hurting people we consider friends, we're going to have a problem," Kade warned. "You better not be lying about what happened to Andy."

She ran her tongue over her busted lip. "And we're going to have a problem if you keep trying to corner me. I don't do well with threats."

"Let's go," Gray nodded at Kade. "See you next week, Mili."

"Oh, that's right. We had a meeting planned." She paused. "Cancel it. I need a break from this fucking city. And from all of you."

"You're leaving?" I asked.

She ignored me. "Move your car, Kade."

"We have a deal," Kade said stiffly. "You can't just leave."

"I can do whatever the fuck I want. I'm not backing out." She opened her car door. "But this conversation is done. Sorry, Rylan, you'll have to find your own way home."

She slammed her door shut, and I heard the distinct sound of her locking the doors. She cracked her window a bit, staring at Kade with impatience.

Kade glanced at me, frowning. "This stays between us. Or I'll tell every fucking news outlet that you're on our payroll."

I scowled. "Even if I don't say anything about this, I'll still find other evidence against you two."

"Good luck," Gray taunted, walking back to his car. Kade got into his Jaguar, and the second he pulled away, Mili sped off, disappearing around the corner. Gray left last, leaving me alone in the alley. I began walking the mile to my house, hoping I didn't run into anyone. I had been right about her. She was as deep in the criminal world as the crew.

Yet that still didn't stop me from wanting to see her again.

17

Milina

My stomach heaved, and I wrapped my arms around myself while the taste of pennies filled my mouth. I crouched down, trying to hold it in, but lost it when my gaze landed on the puddle of blood in front of me. Bile burned my throat as I threw up everything I'd eaten today. A hand touched my shoulder, and I flinched away. Tears blurred my vision as the hand squeezed my upper arm, pulling me up from the floor.

"Why did you do this?" I choked out, not able to tear my eyes away from the table.

I was spun around until I was facing him. His pale blue eyes studied me while he touched my cheek, as if trying to comfort me. His brown hair was flopped to one side, and the other side was short, revealing tattoos under the buzz cut.

"I had to, Lina," he said softly. "They were in the way."

"No, they weren't," I cried hoarsely. "I could have talked to them—"

"You did. And they called the fucking cops on me." His voice was still quiet, but impatience flashed in his eyes. "They wouldn't have let us be together. Now no one will stop us."

I couldn't breathe as I looked back at the table. A lump grew in my throat, making it impossible for me to respond. This couldn't be real. But even my worst nightmares didn't come close to the scene in front of me. My parents were slumped over the table, their chests ripped open from multiple bullet wounds. One of my older brothers was slouched in his chair with one bullet hole in the center of his forehead. My oldest brother was on the floor with blood surrounding him. I gagged, unable to look away, wishing I could take back the last year of my life.

I jumped when a loud crash came from behind me. I turned to see Liam destroying my childhood memories. He pushed the bookshelf to the floor before sweeping all the picture frames off the wall shelves.

"I would have left with you," I shrieked. "I promised I would."

The man who'd turned my life upside down tugged me into an embrace, and it took everything in me not to shudder with disgust. He pulled away, catching my chin and forcing me to look at him.

"The day I met you, my life changed," Joel told me. "I knew you were meant to be mine."

My thoughts went back to that night a year ago as I stared at him. My friends and I had decided to go to an illegal street race. At sixteen, we knew nothing about that kind of life, and wanted an adventure. We snuck out of our houses and went downtown, where we knew the races were happening. The plan was to stay hidden and just watch. Until Joel saw me.

He invited me into his car during his race, and that was the beginning of the end. I began seeing him in secret, the excitement of dating an older bad boy overshadowing the danger I'd put myself in. The more time I spent with him, the more I realized it was a mistake. I went from an honor roll student to sneaking out every night, partaking in activities I knew could get me arrested. But the thrill of everything was addicting, and the life consumed me.

Until my parents found out about Joel a few weeks ago.

"Your family didn't understand. You're my soulmate, Lina. They were going to take you away." Joel pulled me away from the dining room, and a sob escaped me as I looked at my family one last time. "Age is nothing when it comes to us. They couldn't see that."

I hadn't known he was thirty when I met him. And by the time I found out, it didn't matter. I was infatuated with him. But now he was my personal devil, and he had a hold so tight on me that I was struggling for every breath.

"Go pack a bag," he told me, giving me a push toward the stairs. "We need to leave."

"Joel, I can't leave. At least let me put my family to rest," I pleaded as numbness began climbing through me. If I left with him, I was never getting away.

"No," he snapped. "Pack whatever you want. We won't be coming back here. Ever."

My chest heaved as I raced up the stairs, needing to get away from him. I flung open my bedroom door, letting my tears flow. I sobbed uncontrollably, grabbing my bag and throwing in whatever clothes I could find. Rushing to my window, I silently lifted it like I'd done every night for the past year. I had one leg out before a voice shot terror down my spine.

"You don't want to do that." Liam was standing in my doorway.

I'd met Liam the same night as Joel. It was clear that Joel was the boss, but at the time, I had no idea how deep in the criminal world they were. Liam did whatever Joel asked, but he had always been nice to me.

"I can't do it," I choked out. "I can't be with him."

"You can," Liam said firmly. "You have to."

"Or what? He'll kill me?" I asked in a whisper. "I deserve death after what I did to my family—"

"That wasn't you. That was him," Liam cut me off. "I'm sorry, Mili, but the second Joel laid eyes on you, your life was his. No matter how hard you fight against it. Make it easier on yourself and be agreeable."

"Please, just let me leave," I begged, knowing it was useless.

"I can't do that." He sighed, sympathy covering his face. "But I'll try to make your life easier when I can."

My heart lurched when I heard footsteps on the stairs, and I fell back into *my room, shutting my window and spinning around as Joel strode in. He glanced at my bag on my shoulder and smiled.*

"Ready, baby?" He took my bag from me before leading me back to the hall. "Now that we can leave this town, I can show you the world. It's going to be amazing."

I could feel the strings of my free will being sliced with every step I took. I was trapped with the man I'd thought I loved until I realized what a monster he was.

And he was never going to let me go.

Cold sweat covered my body, and I went rigid, feeling someone pulling my arm. Sliding my other hand under my pillow, I gripped my handgun and whipped it out.

"Mili, it's just me. It's just me," a voice said quickly.

I blinked, trying to make sense of my dark surroundings. Caleb was staying absolutely still, and I pulled the gun from his forehead as my heart beat against my ribs.

"Jesus, I'm sorry," I muttered, tossing the gun onto the mattress. "I forgot where I was."

"I thought the nightmares stopped." He scooted closer to me.

"They did. Until I had a close brush with my past," I mumbled, jumping to my feet.

I paced in front of the window that took up the entire bedroom wall. The full moon illuminated the ocean waves crashing onto the beach. I'd flown to Florida to see Caleb the night after everything happened at Andy's garage. And then passed out before I could tell him why I'd come. His small beach house was outside Miami and was one place I felt truly at home. I ran my hands down my face, sucking in deep breaths. I didn't know what time it was, but there was no way I'd be able to fall back to sleep now.

"Please tell me whoever did that to your face is in the ground." Caleb stood up and caught my arm. "If those fucking guys in Ridgewood are touching you—"

"It wasn't them." I met his gaze. "It was Liam."

His red hair was disheveled from sleep, and tattoos poked out from under the tank top he was wearing. Shock had his jaw dropping, and he stayed quiet while I explained what happened. When I was finished, he wrapped me in a hug. I stiffened but leaned into him, knowing he was trying to comfort me.

"I'm sorry," he murmured. "I know you had a soft spot for Liam."

"He was going to take me back," I said in a choked whisper. "I couldn't let him live."

"You did the right thing," he soothed, brushing hair out of my face.

He pulled out a pack of cigarettes, offering me one before he opened the glass door and we stepped onto the patio. I lit my cigarette and inhaled, not caring that I'd promised I was going to stop smoking when I was stressed. It had been a bad fucking couple of days. The door opened again, and I was instantly on guard until I saw who it was.

Tucker glanced at me before looking at Caleb. "Is everything okay? I heard screaming."

Caleb smiled at him. "We're fine."

Still not looking convinced, Tucker looked back at me. "It's good to see you, Mili. It's been a while."

"I thought it was time to make sure you two weren't getting into any trouble." I managed a small grin, but Tucker took the hint and went back inside. I wasn't in the mood for talking, even with Caleb. But he wasn't about to leave me alone with my thoughts.

"How are you two?" I asked.

"We're good." Caleb chuckled. "Still getting used to living with someone again though."

I giggled, remembering how Caleb and I were at each other's throats when I'd lived with him. I wasn't exactly a slob, but Caleb detested any kind of mess, and it caused a lot of heated arguments. He and Tucker had been dating for the last three years, and they seemed right for each other. At first, I was suspicious of him, and so was Caleb. After the life we came from, trusting anyone was next to impossible.

But Tucker hadn't given up, and Caleb slowly let him in. Tucker knew bits and pieces of our past, but not everything.

Caleb turned serious. "I didn't know Liam—or any of them—were still in the game. I'd been keeping up with their lives online, and there wasn't a hint about it. They must be doing it completely different from how they used to."

Caleb used to be Joel's tech guy, and he was the reason I'd escaped. I owed him my life, and I'd do anything for him. Ever since I became Sapphire, he'd gone above and beyond for me. He was the one who chose my jobs off the dark web. He managed my bank accounts and did research so I could plan each job. A couple of years ago, I offered him an out. To go live a normal life, but he just laughed, saying I couldn't get rid of him that easy.

"What if Joel is free?" The question felt like acid on my tongue, but I had to ask.

He shook his head. "He's not. I promise."

I couldn't kill Joel, so I'd done the next best thing. He's locked away in a third-world prison where I pay to make sure he stays there in isolation. Liam and the rest of his gang thought he was dead, and I needed to keep it that way. Until I did the Panther job, and then I was free to kill him. A moment I couldn't fucking wait for.

"Do you mind if I stay here for a while?" I asked, sinking into the patio chair.

"Mili, you know you can stay here for however long you want." He stared at me curiously. "You don't like Ridgewood?"

I chuckled. "Actually, I do. The two guys I'm working with are… interesting. And the mayor seems to have a thing for me."

His eyes widened. "You like one of them?"

"No," I snapped. "They're nothing. I need them to help me with the job, that's all."

"Not every man is like Joel. You'll find someone again," he said softly.

"I'd rather spend my life with cars than men. At least I know cars won't try to fuck me over."

"You'll change your mind."

"Don't hold your breath." I stood and opened the door. "You care if I raid your fridge? I'm starving."

He waved his hand. "Take whatever you want."

I walked through the guest bedroom and out into the hall, moving slowly through the dark. Once I got to the kitchen, I flicked on the light, surprising both myself and Tucker, who was leaning against the black granite counter. He set his glass of water down as I moved past him to get to the fridge.

"Caleb will do anything for you. Even if it costs him his life." Tucker's words made me freeze. "I love him. So whatever you two are planning, please be careful."

I faced him, giving him a confident grin. "I'm always careful, Tucker. I swear Caleb won't get hurt."

I had every intention of keeping that promise. I was doing the Panther job, or I'd die trying. Because if I failed, there would be no reason to live anyway. At least if something happened to me, I knew Caleb would always have Tucker.

I rummaged through the fridge for food, pushing away the intruding thoughts of the three guys I left back in Ridgewood. It was annoying me that I couldn't get them out of my head, and I wasn't used to it.

I'd almost rather be back there, messing with them, than here in Florida.

18

Kade

I tilted my head back, downing the tequila in one swig before pushing the empty glass toward the bartender. Our club was packed tonight, and Gray and I had just gotten here after meeting with Vic and Juan. They weren't happy that Mili had disappeared. It had been two weeks since we'd accused her of attacking Andy. And since then, she was just gone.

Gray swiveled on the barstool beside me. "I don't think she's coming back."

"That's what we wanted."

He turned, giving me a pointed look. "And that's why you've been searching for her as much as I have."

"Because Vic and Juan are on our asses about it," I grumbled. "I'm glad she's gone. We can get back to normal."

Gray didn't call me out on my lie, even though he knew my words were bullshit. Life seemed painfully boring now that she wasn't around to cause chaos.

"Did you get a hold of Amber?" I asked, changing the subject.

Gray nodded. "Andy is still in a coma but stable."

Amber was Andy's girlfriend, and she'd been keeping us updated on how he was doing. The police had found a body in Andy's garage, but it still hadn't been identified. His tattoos didn't show any gang affiliation that we knew of. It seemed like Mili had been telling the truth that she wasn't the one who attacked Andy. But I was still positive there was more to it than she shared.

I glanced up, looking toward the entrance, hearing yelling that was loud enough to be heard over the music. Another bouncer ran toward the noise, and Gray frowned, jumping off the stool.

"I'll deal with it," he said before shooting me a grin. "Why don't you stay here and enjoy getting back to normal?"

I huffed out a chuckle, watching him disappear into the crowd. Ordering another drink, I leaned against the bar, watching people dance. A guy rushed past me, pulling a woman with him as they headed toward the bathrooms. I rolled my eyes, knowing exactly what they were doing. I stared at the back of her short white dress as they moved farther away, and I narrowed my eyes, realizing there was something familiar about her.

My grip on the glass tightened when she glanced over her shoulder and caught my gaze. My stomach clenched as Mili smirked before giving me a little wave and then flipping me off. The guy tugged on her hand, pulling her focus back to him as he pushed open the door of the men's bathroom. I was on my feet before I knew what I was doing, pushing people out of the way as I stalked toward the bathroom.

Excitement churned with apprehension as I got to the door. When it came to her, I never knew what to expect. I pushed the door open quietly, and what I didn't expect was the blind fucking rage that swallowed me when I saw her pinned against the wall while the guy was kissing her throat. Storming across the bathroom, I grabbed the back of his neck and flung him away from her.

"What the fuck?" the guy hissed, squaring up to me until he saw me. His face paled as he lowered his fist. "I'm sorry. I didn't know it was you."

"Get the fuck out. And I don't want to catch you even looking at her again," I growled, catching Mili's arm when she tried darting around me. "Not you. We need to talk."

She pouted, her eyes vibrant with mischief. "I didn't come here to talk. But if you don't want me here, that's fine. I'll take my friend somewhere else."

Hope filled the guy's eyes until I shot him a death glare. He nearly fell over his own feet, racing out of the room. Letting go of her, I pushed the door shut the rest of the way, flicking the lock before facing her again.

"Where have you been?" I asked, leaning against the door and crossing my arms.

"I told you I needed a break." She jumped up to sit on the long counter. "But I'm back now."

She scooted farther back on the counter, purposefully spreading her legs apart, revealing that she wasn't wearing any panties. My dick twitched, and I had to force myself to raise my eyes from her bare pussy. She twirled a lock of hair between her fingers, giving me a seductive smile when I met her gaze.

I cleared my throat. "What do you want?"

"I think my motive for coming here was clear." Her eyes went to the door behind me. "Until you chased him off."

"Bullshit." I crossed the room, stopping in front of her. "You came to my club, making sure I saw you. You wanted my attention. Why?"

She shrugged. "I came here because I like your club. The DJ knows what he's doing. Believe me, Kade, if I wanted your attention, my actions would be unmistakable."

I leaned over her, gripping the edge of the counter. "Well, you have my complete attention now. So tell me, where the hell have you been for the last two weeks?"

She laughed, my closeness not bothering her at all. "Since you messed up my chance to get laid, I guess you'll be an adequate replacement."

She gripped the hem of my shirt, trying to tug it off. I snatched her wrists, keeping her in place as my heart thudded. Even with the minimal clothing she was wearing, I was positive she had at least one weapon on her. What she'd done to Jay was an image I hadn't forgotten, reminding me that it only took a moment for her to get the upper hand. I'd rather not get stabbed tonight.

She studied me, her grin fading. "I can't remember the last time a guy stopped me when I wanted sex."

"That's not the reason you're here," I muttered, still convinced she was up to something.

She twisted her right arm out of my grip in a quick move and shoved me back far enough that she was able to bring her legs up and use her heels to push me away even farther. I didn't move as she jumped off the counter and messed with her hair before striding to the door.

"If you don't want me, then I'll find someone who does." She reached for the lock, and I ran after her, knocking her arm down before she could unlock it. She whirled around, the look in her eyes warning enough without her speaking. Yet I ignored it and grasped her hips, pushing her into the door.

"That guy is going to be running his mouth around the club that I'm being possessive of you," I murmured.

"So?"

"So I don't claim women—ever."

Pure anger clouded her eyes, and for the first time since I came into the bathroom, she looked ready to fight. "No one fucking claims me. I'm not yours. I'm not anyone's."

"Yeah, well, that's not how people are going to see it when we walk out of the bathroom." I watched her closely, waiting for her to react.

"They'll think you're mine. And if you go out there and try to fuck another guy, that's going to be a problem."

Curiosity filled her gaze. "Worried about your reputation?"

"This isn't your city. It's mine and Gray's. If people think you're mine, and you're sleeping around on me, then it won't look good."

"Please," she scoffed. "I bet the guy didn't say shit."

"I can promise all eyes will be on us when we leave. There's only one reason a guy and a girl go into the bathroom together."

She moved forward, pressing her body into mine. "Well, if they're going to talk, then let's give them something to talk about. Make me scream, Kade."

I chuckled, trying to ignore how her soft touch felt when she slipped her hand under my shirt. "What the hell are you up to?"

"You don't want me?" Her hands went lower, brushing my jeans. "It sure feels like you do."

"If you want someone to fuck, then go somewhere else," I gritted out. "Everyone here on the north side is going to think you're mine. I'm not going to be disrespected because of you."

She froze, her gaze locking on mine. It was clear she hated being told what to do. But instead of storming away, she went on her tiptoes and kissed my neck.

"Fine. I'll go to the south side," she muttered before nipping at my earlobe. "I know a certain mayor who wouldn't mind being squeezed by my thighs."

"You just go looking for trouble, don't you?" I growled, not liking how irrationally pissed I was at the thought of her being with someone else. "You should stay away from people who try to put us in prison."

"I think I've been ridiculously fucking patient with you making demands of me," she purred in my ear. "But I've reached my breaking point. Either let me walk out the door so I can find someone else or fucking do something about it—"

I slid my hand up the back of her neck and gripped her hair, tipping her head back before smashing my lips to hers. She responded immediately, opening her mouth, her tongue colliding with mine as I deepened the kiss. I backed her up until she hit the counter. Her hand went for the bottom of my shirt again, and she tugged it up. I scowled when her lips left mine, and I gripped the back collar of my shirt, pulling it over my head with one hand while keeping my other tangled in her hair.

I tossed my shirt on the counter behind her as I leaned down to kiss her, realizing I'd been waiting to taste her again since she kissed me almost a month ago. I went rigid when her nails dragged down my back until she gripped my gun.

"If you shoot me, you won't make it out of this building alive," I mumbled, not taking my lips off hers.

She giggled, pulling my gun out. "If you fuck as good as you kiss, then I'll have no motivation to shoot you. But I do think we should keep weapons out of this, seeing as we can both lose our tempers."

Her words shook some clarity in me, and I snapped out of the sex haze I was in. She'd shot Gray and had no issue trying to blow us up. For all I knew, she could be acting right now and flip the second I let my guard down. But when she kissed me again, I didn't have the fucking self-control to walk out. Instead, I gripped the hem of her short dress and pulled it off her. My gaze raked over her nearly naked body. All she had on was a thin lace bra and her heels. Her tattoo sat right under her bra, and I caught sight of something silver pushing against her breast. She stayed still as I reached forward and plucked the pocketknife from her bra. I tossed it onto the counter next to my gun.

"That's it?" I questioned, raising an eyebrow.

"The dress I wore didn't have room for anything else." With a wide grin, she reached into the other side of her bra and pulled out a condom. "But I made sure to bring what I needed."

I grabbed the condom from her, throwing it onto the counter before reaching behind her and unclipping her bra. Her breasts fell free, and I pushed her against the counter, running my hands all over her body. She unbuttoned my jeans, pulling them down along with my boxers, before she froze.

"Oh my fuck," she muttered after her gaze dropped.

I grinned smugly, enjoying her genuine shock. "Why are you acting like a blushing virgin?"

She laughed in disbelief. "Oh, hell no. I didn't survive this long to die from cock impalement. I'm going to find the guy you scared off."

I glared at her, wrapping my hand around her arm when she reached for her dress. "I don't think so, Little Hellion. You told me to make you scream, and you're not fucking leaving until I do that."

Her hand wrapped around my cock, and I groaned when she stroked it. "Just because you have a big dick doesn't mean you know how to use it. Don't be a disappointment, Kade."

Her attempt to piss me off didn't faze me in the slightest. I ran my fingers down her thigh, slowly trailing up until I reached her pussy. Until she pushed me away. I frowned, my annoyance flaring.

"If I'm naked, then you have to be too," she stated, glancing down at my jeans.

I chuckled. "I don't need to be naked to fuck you."

"That's not what I said." She put her own hand between her legs and began touching herself. "You want me? Then fucking strip."

Her desire to control this only made me want to bend her over the counter even more. Keeping her stare, I kicked off my shoes before sliding my jeans and boxers off. By club standards, this bathroom was pristine, but getting naked in public wasn't something I normally did. My stomach flipped when I realized I was under her spell, just like every other man she set her sights on.

But right now, I didn't fucking care.

I grasped her hips, pushing her back into the counter while I grazed my lips down her neck. The image of the other guy kissing her had heat rushing through my veins, and before I could think about it, my lips were pressed against her throat. With a shriek, she pushed me away. Again.

"Did you just give me a hickey?" she hissed, rage flickering in her gaze.

Grabbing her thighs, I lifted her onto the counter where my shirt was lying. "I told you people are going to think you're mine when we walk out of here. I decided to play up the part."

The glare she gave me made me happy I'd already taken her knife. Before she had another fucking chance to shove me away, I lowered my head between her thighs and swept my tongue over her pussy. Fuck, she tasted delicious. Her legs began to relax the longer my tongue explored her. I flicked it over her clit, causing a shiver to jolt through her. Taking my time, I tried different things, seeing how she reacted to them. When my mouth covered her clit as I sucked, her thighs squeezed my head.

"This isn't a marathon," she said thickly, trying to cover how much I was affecting her.

I nipped at her clit, and she moaned. "Don't interrupt me when I'm eating."

"Then stop playing with your food so I can fucking finish."

Even though I had her on the verge of coming, she was still trying to control this. It wasn't fucking happening. She had flipped every situation with us to her favor—this time it would be on my turn. I shot to my feet, and her guard rose at my sudden move. She lifted herself up, and I wrapped a hand around her throat, pushing her down until her spine hit the counter again.

"What the fuck are you doing?" she snarled, her nails digging into my wrist.

"You want to finish," I murmured, reaching beside her and grabbing the condom. "That's only happening when I'm fucking you."

After seeing what she did to Jay, I knew she could break my hold if she really wanted. Her pulse was thrashing against my palm, and when I met her heated gaze, I couldn't tell whether she wanted to kill me or let me fuck her. My grip tightened on her throat when she tried squirming away. One of her hands was still wrapped around my wrist, while her other was pressed against the counter. Keeping my hold on her, I ripped the condom open with my teeth, tossing the wrapper onto the floor.

Her legs were around my waist, and I backed away from her

enough to slide the condom on. I pressed my cock against her entrance, and she went still as I inched inside her.

"If this is going to take all night—"

Her snarky words were cut off when I thrust inside her, going as deep as I could. She sucked in a breath, her legs tightening around me as she adjusted to my size. I pulled out only to plunge back into her, and she bucked against me.

"Oh my God," she cried out, my hand on her throat the only reason she didn't leap off the table.

"Next time, it better be my name you scream," I muttered as I began moving faster.

She forced out a laugh. "Don't flatter yourself."

I pulled out of her, and she protested when I flipped her over, placing my hand between her shoulder blades to keep her on the counter. I kicked her legs apart, and she tottered on her heels as I slammed my cock back into her.

"Fuck," she whimpered, her back arching. "God, do that again."

I scoffed, knowing she threw in that last part to piss me off. Reaching over her, I fisted her hair, tilting her head back until I could see her face in the mirror. My cock twitched, feeling her pussy throb around me. She pressed her palms against the counter, trying to regain some type of control. But I had her, and she wasn't leaving unless she told me to stop or broke my hold. The way she was rocking her hips had me believe she didn't want to go anywhere.

"You can say that name as much as you want," I murmured, placing my fingers over her clit. "But so help me God, you're not fucking coming until you worship mine."

Her jaw clenched as our gazes were locked on each other through the mirror. I circled her clit as I kept a steady rhythm. I broke our stare down, trailing my eyes down her bare back until something right above her ass caught my attention. Apparently, her Sapphire tattoo wasn't her only one. I brushed my free hand over her tattoo, noticing the skin was raised as if there was a scar or something under the black ink. The tattoo was an open book, with the words *Live Free* in the middle of the pages.

"What the fuck?" I growled when her heel nearly crushed my toes.

"I'm sorry. I thought we were fucking, not you taking the time to inspect my body."

I gripped her hair when she tried pulling out of my hold and placed my other one back over her clit while taking note that she didn't want me touching her tattoo. I began moving again, and her struggles slowed as I fucked her faster. The anger in her eyes faded as she began spiraling with pleasure.

"Yes," she moaned, her body slamming into the edge of the counter each time I thrust. And then I slowed, lazily circling her clit. "No. Don't stop."

"I told you what you had to do to come."

I caught her gaze in the mirror again as shock flared in her eyes. I grinned, pulling my cock out before slowly sliding into her again. She bit her lip, refusing to give me what I wanted. Letting go of her hair, I gripped her hips, upping my speed. Her legs quivered as her head sagged onto the counter.

"Say my name. Scream it so you can come," I demanded, my voice gruff.

"Fuck you."

I chuckled, pinching her clit, causing her to cry out. "Try again."

"If you can't get me off, I was right about you not knowing what you're doing," she choked out between deep breaths.

"That's not going to work," I switched between rubbing her clit and burying myself in her. "You know what I want."

"Please," she forced out through clenched teeth.

Placing my palm on her back, I plunged into her again and again, only to slow down when she got close to her orgasm. There was a knock at the door, and the handle jiggled before someone banged angrily. I didn't give a fuck. We were staying in here until my name fucking fell from her lips.

"Fuck. Fuck. Fuck," she screamed when I slowed down again. "Give it to me, Kade."

She froze, realizing what she'd said. I knew with her that was as good as I was going to get, and I'd take it as a win. Letting go of the control I'd been holding, I rammed into her, pleasure ricocheting through me. I played with her clit, feeling her body go rigid.

Her pussy clenched around my cock as she came. She leaned farther onto the counter, with one palm on the glossed surface as she reached back with her other hand, gripping my wrist and keeping it on her hip as if I was going to let her go. Her moans turned into screams as I plunged deeper into her.

My balls tightened, and I dug my nails into her hips. I was nearly there but got distracted when her hold on my wrist tightened and she yanked my hand away from her body. I didn't stop fucking her, figuring she wanted to readjust. But when she began tugging my hand under the counter, I slowed down.

"What are you doing?" I asked gruffly, my body begging to fucking finish.

"Nothing," she answered. "Just making this a little more interesting."

There was something in her voice that made me pause. Then something cold touched the hand she was holding hostage, and I pulled out of her, suspicion slamming into me. Before I could turn her around, she slipped under my arm, twisting it behind my back as she moved behind me.

"What the fuck?" I grunted in pain when she wrenched my arm higher. Her other hand went to the back of my head, and I flinched when she shoved me forward. My head slammed into the mirror hard enough for the glass to crack. My vision went black, and I slumped onto the counter as pain exploded through my skull. I fought her blindly when she yanked my arm back under the counter.

"Mili," I ground out, feeling something tighten around my wrist. "What the hell are you doing?"

"Payback's a bitch," she murmured smugly.

Forcing my eyes open, I slouched over the counter, looking under it to see my arm cuffed to the pipe under the sink. Gritting my teeth, I attempted to slide out of the cuff, but the metal only bit into my skin. Twisting my body, I was barely able to stand straight up as I faced her. Anger ripped through me as I stretched as far as I could to grab her. She danced away from me, and my stomach lurched when I spied my clothes in her arms.

"Don't you fucking dare," I snarled, watching her drop my clothes on the floor before she slipped back into her dress.

"Don't what?" she mocked. "Chain you up and then leave? That's exactly what you and Gray did to me."

"We didn't do it in public. And you weren't fucking naked." My chest constricted when she flipped the lock. "I fucking swear if you leave me in here—"

"You'll what?" she cut me off. "You can't kill me. And I'm not leaving this city until I want to. So, keep trying to scare me off—I'll come back five times harder. Although right now, it's you who's still hard. It really sucks being left on the edge, doesn't it?"

She looked away from me to grab my clothes, and I took a second to glance under the counter to inspect the pipe that the handcuff was locked to. I pulled, hoping it would move, but it didn't fucking budge.

"I tightened the connectors on that pipe. And I made sure it would be strong enough to hold you," she sang out, her amusement enraging me even more. "But good luck trying."

"You better be long gone before I get free," I threatened.

She tilted her head. "My night isn't over yet. Don't worry, I'll make sure Gray stays busy so you have some time to think about why you two should give up trying to run me out of town."

She pulled open the door, slipping out and taking my damn clothes with her. There was no way to cover myself if someone walked in, and I didn't want to take my eyes off the door. But I needed to bend down to try and free myself. Keeping the door in my sights, I crouched down, yanking as hard as I could. The pipe must have been cemented in place, because it didn't move an inch.

I cursed under my breath, bending farther to kick it. But it was too awkward of an angle for it to help at all. Panic swelled when the door was slowly pushed open.

"Get the fuck out," I bellowed, covering my dick with my free hand. "And go get Grayson Scott. Right fucking now. There's an emergency."

Whoever was at the door let it close, and I hoped to God the person listened and went to get Gray.

19

Gray

I pushed through the crowd, heading for the lone table in the back, near the dance floor. I didn't know where the hell Kade had gone, and I was tired of sitting at the bar by myself. And then I saw someone who usually didn't visit our club. I guessed it would help pass the time. I sat at the high-top table and met Rylan's glare.

"This table is taken," Rylan snapped, his eyes darting around.

I laughed. "This is my club. I can sit wherever the hell I want."

Rylan didn't answer, and my gaze trailed down his suit. He stuck out like a sore thumb in here. That was probably why he was hiding in the shadows.

"You keep coming around, and people are actually going to believe you work for us," I said, shooting him a grin. "Looking for a bigger paycheck?"

"Fuck off. I'm not here for you."

"Why are you here?"

"You know, this is my city too. I can go wherever I want," he responded stiffly, his eyes locked on the dance floor.

"You can go wherever you want," I agreed. "But let's not pretend like you have more pull in this city than I do."

"If I agree with you, will you leave me the hell alone?"

I frowned, wondering why he was trying to get rid of me. He usually came into the club once every couple of months, but everything we did in here was legal, so it never bothered us. But tonight, he seemed to be here for a different reason. I followed his gaze to the dance floor, and my stomach flipped when I realized what he was staring at.

"Where the fuck did she come from?" I muttered, watching Mili dancing with another guy.

"She texted me," Rylan stated. "That she was going to be here tonight."

I managed to keep my surprise to myself, not taking my eyes off Mili. "If you're here to see her, why are you just watching her grind on another guy?"

Rylan scowled. "I'm waiting until she's done dancing."

"Why..." I trailed off and chuckled. "Oh, I get it. It's one thing to come to our club. But what would your supporters think of dancing with people who are most likely with the crew? Especially a woman who looks like that. Definitely not the conservative type."

We both stared at her. She looked fucking stunning in her white minidress. Her hair was down and moving around as she danced. Making up my mind, I jumped from the seat, pushing the rest of my drink toward Rylan.

"Since you won't dance with her, I will. Have fun watching."

A muscle in his jaw flexed, but he didn't say a word as I walked away. I quickly headed onto the dance floor and gripped the guy's shoulder, spinning him away from Mili. Panic lit up his eyes.

"Get lost," I said, loud enough for him to hear me.

"Again?" the guy muttered, rushing away before I could ask him what the hell he meant by that.

Mili completely ignored me, and she attempted to walk away before I hooked an arm around her waist and spun her into my chest. Her heels were tall, but she still needed to lift her head to meet my gaze. Her smile promised all kinds of sin as she began dancing with me. Her moves went straight to my dick, and I held her close.

"I thought you left for good," I said, noticing the bruises on her face had healed in the two weeks she'd been gone. "Where were you?"

"Am I mistaken, or do you sound happy to see me?" She slung her arms around my neck, her hips continuing to sway to the music.

"More like intrigued," I told her, glancing at Rylan. His annoyance was clear even in the dim room, and I grinned, letting my hands roam over her body until I gripped her ass. I noticed people around us were staring at us—more specifically, her. "Why does everyone seem so interested in you?"

Her eyes widened with fake innocence. "I have no idea. I came out of the bathroom and people were just staring."

One of the strobe lights flashed on her neck, and I stopped dancing, running my fingers over a mark. A mark that could only be a fucking hickey.

"Who did this?" I growled.

She giggled. "If it means anything, I think you'd like the guy I fucked."

"I think you're dancing with me, knowing it's getting my dick hard, when another guy's saliva is still on your throat."

I dropped my arms, not enjoying her games anymore. But she tugged me back, keeping me on the dance floor.

"Are you jealous, Grayson?"

I gritted my teeth. "I told you not to call me that."

"Mr. Scott," a young guy rambled as he came up beside me, "there's an issue—"

"I understand not liking your name," Mili cut the guy off. "I don't like mine either. It's why I only go by my nickname."

I stared at her, surprised that she was offering up something personal about herself. "What's your real name?"

"Mr. Scott—"

"Go get the bouncer," I said gruffly. "He can deal with it. Get the fuck out of here."

The guy hesitated before scurrying away, and I grabbed Mili's hips, bringing her close. I wasn't about to waste a chance for her to spill things about herself.

"I'll tell you my name if you tell me why you hate yours," she said, looking curious.

I scoffed. "I know you probably researched all you could about us. Couldn't find that out, could you?"

She shrugged. "I know you came from a middle-class family. Unlike Kade, you don't seem to have any family ties to the crew."

"You think Kade is related to someone in the crew?" I asked, knowing there was no way she knew that Juan was Kade's uncle.

"I have my guesses."

"I don't have a great relationship with my dad," I said slowly. "He calls me by my full name, and I fucking hate it."

"Did he beat you?"

I raised an eyebrow. "Kind of a personal question to ask someone."

"Well, telling you my name is personal. It goes both ways."

I paused. "Yeah, he did. Before I got old enough to fight back. He hasn't touched me since I was thirteen when I got involved with the crew."

"Why didn't you kill him?" she asked bluntly.

"Things aren't always that simple."

"Why?"

I shook my head. "You asked, and I answered. Your turn."

"I think I changed my mind," she muttered.

I locked my arms around her, stopping her escape. "I don't think so, Rebel. You owe me a name."

"Why are you calling me rebel?" she questioned, looking like she wasn't sure how she felt about it.

I grinned. "You like eighties movies?"

"I've never seen one."

"Then you wouldn't understand."

She frowned. "I need a drink."

"Tell me your name first."

She huffed out a breath. "Milina."

"Milina," I repeated. "What's your last name?"

She laughed. "I don't think so, Gray. But even if I did tell you, you'd never find anything out about me. I buried everything years ago."

"Why don't you like your name?" I asked.

She tensed, and pain filled her eyes for a brief moment before it was gone. "Because the girl with that name died a long time ago."

I dropped it, sensing that if I pushed her any more, she was going to leave. Her gaze drifted to the side, and she grinned when she saw Rylan.

"Why are you toying with the mayor?"

She gave me a pointed look. "I'm not toying with him. He's nice."

"Then why are you dancing with me instead of talking to him?"

"Good question."

She slipped out of my hold with ease and rushed to Rylan's table before I could stop her. I didn't move from the dance floor, watching Rylan give her a wide smile. I chuckled under my breath. Whatever she was doing wasn't going to end well for him. Everything she did had an ulterior motive. My gut knotted when I remembered that. There was a reason she'd given up her real name to me. Now I needed to find out why. I crossed the room, settling onto a barstool, and ordered another whiskey. Our regular bartender handed me my drink and lingered longer than necessary.

"Need something?" I asked.

Her eyes darted toward the dance floor and then back to me. "Rumors are flying around here tonight."

I leaned on the bar counter, her words catching my interest. We paid her extra to keep her ears open. People liked to talk more when they were drinking, and it made it easier to know what was happening in our city.

"What rumors?"

"Everyone is saying Kade has a girl," she answered nervously.

I nearly fell off my stool. Kade kept the girls he fucked private. He rarely went out with a woman in public, and when he did, he made it clear it was never anything serious.

"Who said that?" I asked quietly.

She pointed out the guy who had been dancing with Mili. I jumped to my feet, hurrying to him before I lost him in the crowd.

"Dancing with you wasn't enough. Let's get out of here and do something else."

Mili was suddenly in front of me, her voice dripping with sex as she ran her hand down my shirt. I laughed in disbelief, realizing how fucking stupid I was. She'd been distracting me. Not answering her, I strode toward the guy, who looked like he was about to run away screaming.

She got a hold of my leather jacket, trying to stop me. "What's wrong?"

"Why don't you tell me? I have a feeling this is all connected to you."

Mischief danced in her eyes, but she stayed silent as I faced the guy.

"I hear you're talking shit about Kade Jacobs," I said loudly.

"No, I'm not," the guy squeaked out. "I fucking swear."

"Then tell me what happened."

"I was with a chick, and Kade stormed in, telling me not to ever look at her again," the guy stuttered out.

I grabbed Mili's arm, pulling her forward. "This the girl he was with?"

"Yeah. And—"

"This guy doesn't know what the hell he's talking about," Mili cut him off. "He's just mad I didn't want to sleep with him."

"We all heard her screaming," the guy said, trying to prove to me he was telling the truth. "I wasn't the one she fucked."

I whirled toward her and saw the guy run off out of the corner of my eye. "Where's Kade?"

She grinned devilishly. "I have no idea."

Anger bubbled in my chest, knowing she was lying. "Where is he, Mili? If you did anything—"

I stopped talking, realizing another guy had been trying to tell me something while she was distracting me on the dance floor. I scanned the room, seeing him watching me from a small table.

"I guess one out of two isn't bad for one night," she said with a laugh. "You'll get your payback another time. Bye, Gray."

I didn't chase after her as she raced for the exit. She wasn't going to help me find Kade since she was the reason he was fucking missing.

"What did you need to tell me earlier?" I asked the guy once I got close.

He shifted in his seat. "I tried using the restroom, and someone yelled not to come in and to go get you, Mr. Scott. It sounded important…"

I was already running toward the bathroom before he finished talking. I pushed open the men's bathroom door and stopped short.

"Shut the fucking door," Kade hissed, covering his junk.

Stepping forward, I let the door swing shut. I couldn't have stopped the laugh that exploded out of me even if I tried. He was cuffed to the sink, and I'd never seen him so angry. I grabbed my stomach, doubling over and roaring with laughter.

"Yes, it's fucking hilarious," he gritted out, my amusement only pissing him off more. "Can you get me some damn clothes now?"

I wiped tears away, my laughter starting all over again when I realized she had taken his clothes out of the bathroom.

I raised my arms up. "Wait, wait. What was it you told me? Oh yeah. Don't fuck her. I see you went against your own advice."

"Gray, go get me some fucking clothes," he seethed, tugging against the cuff. "And find her. She has my phone and wallet."

"Maybe I should take a picture to remind you not to repeat your mistakes—"

"I will fucking kill you."

Still laughing, I turned and went back out the door. There was a line of guys and they all looked at me as I stepped into the hallway.

"Stand in front of the door and don't let anyone in, got it?" I ordered the guy closest to me. He was in the crew, and he nodded quickly, moving where I told him.

I made my way to our private room upstairs where we kept spare clothes. I sobered up as I climbed the stairs, realizing that if she'd had found me first, I would be right where Kade was. There wasn't a doubt in my mind that she would have been able to convince me to take off my clothes. I probably would have fallen for it faster than Kade. I swallowed, remembering her words before she left. She was repaying us for locking her in our study. She got Kade back, but I was still on her shit list.

Fucking great.

20

Milina

I switched the phone to my other ear as I stepped out of my car.

"This is a mistake," Caleb told me as I walked around the block to the restaurant. "You've had this planned for months—"

"It'll be fine." I sighed. "I need to give something, or they won't help me with the Panther job."

There was only silence, but I waited, knowing he hadn't hung up. The Italian restaurant came into view, and I slowed my steps.

"What did you do?" he finally asked.

I cleared my throat. "We're still working on trust."

"Mili," Caleb chastised me. "You did something to piss them off."

"It was days ago. And I was only getting them back for the shit they pulled on me."

"It's too late to find others to help you with the Panthers," he said carefully. "You need them."

I gritted my teeth, hating that he was right. "I know. That's why I'm extending an olive branch tonight."

"Hmm," he hummed out, and I could hear him clicking the keys on his laptop. "Why are you meeting them an hour outside of Ridgewood?"

"Stop tracking my phone. That's supposed to be for emergencies only."

"You must have really done something bad for you not to want to meet them in their city."

A laugh bubbled up. "It wasn't that bad. I didn't even spill blood."

"Are you scared of them?"

My humor died instantly. "Absolutely not."

"Then why drive an hour to meet them?" he asked, the amusement in his voice shooting annoyance through me.

"They've caught me by surprise a couple of times," I snapped. "And after what I did to Kade, I decided neutral ground is best."

"This isn't just some normal job. I think you should handle it yourself. Let them help you on smaller things," he said, his concern evident.

"I'm not planning many jobs right now, especially after Liam finding me," I told him in a low voice. "If I don't start including them, they aren't going to trust me for the Panther job."

"Just be careful."

"Always. I have to go. I'll call you later."

I hung up and pulled open the restaurant door. It was a fancier restaurant, but with my black cocktail dress, I fit in perfectly. My heels clicked on the hardwood floor as I walked up to the hostess.

"Hello, I have a reservation under Mili. For three."

The lady smiled after looking at her screen. "Your party is already here."

A hint of nerves swirled in my gut as I followed her through the restaurant. It had been three days since I left Kade cuffed in the bathroom, and I hadn't seen them since. I'd left his phone in the club because I figured he could track it. But I'd kept his wallet for the hell of it.

"I requested a table on the balcony," I said as we passed the open patio area.

"Yes, ma'am. Your table is at the end."

I frowned, my guard rising when she opened a door. I peeked around her, seeing the lone table. Technically, it was on the balcony. It had a wall to ceiling window facing the water, but it wasn't an open area like I wanted. Instead, it was a private room. Kade and Gray were already seated, and they both glanced up when the hostess moved to the side so I could step into the room.

"This is the only table available?" I asked quietly. The whole reason I'd chosen this place was to stay in public. This tiny room was the complete opposite.

Gray grinned. "We decided to upgrade your reservation when we got here. We figured privacy would be best for our conversations. Don't you agree, Mili?"

I swallowed my laugh, walking into the room with my head high. Once again, they surprised me, but I was more entertained than anything. It wasn't like they were going to do anything to me in a public restaurant.

"Would you like to hang up your purse?" the hostess asked, motioning to a row of hooks on the wall near the door.

"No, thank you."

Kade's eyes drifted to my purse as I clutched it tighter. The hostess nodded and closed the door behind her. I stared at the guys, waiting for one of them to move. There were four chairs around the table, and they were sitting in the two closest to the door. I wasn't about to crawl over them to get to my seat. After a few strained moments, Gray finally stood up, moving so I could sit. I purposely took his seat, setting my purse on the chair next to me so they both had to sit across from me.

Kade's gaze stayed on me while he slid over, sitting near the window. Gray took the other chair across from me, a grin still on his face even though I could tell he was tense. I leaned back, tapping my fingers on the table as a server came in and set a glass of water in front of me.

"Can I have a gin and tonic, please?" I told the server when he began taking orders. "No food for me. I won't be here long."

The second the server left the room, Kade leaned over the table. "Where the hell is my wallet?"

I blinked innocently. "Did I not leave it with your phone?"

"Cut the shit," Kade hissed. "I already canceled my credit cards."

I let out a laugh. "You think I need your money? I probably have more than both of you combined."

I reached into my purse, pushing my gun to the side, and fished out his wallet. I tossed it to him over the table, and he caught it, immediately opening it to make sure I hadn't taken anything. Sipping my water, I rested against the back of the chair, keeping my posture relaxed.

"Why'd you want to meet here?" Gray asked.

"Italian food is my favorite."

"Yet you didn't order any food." Kade tilted his head. "Didn't want to be alone with us?"

I scoffed. "Please. I think I proved I can handle myself against you when we're alone. Don't you think, Kade?"

His eyes clouded with anger. "That won't happen again."

"Did Gray get to you in time?" I asked tauntingly. "Or did someone see the badass Kade Jacobs in all his naked glory?"

Kade lunged across the table, knocking over my water glass. Gray grabbed his arm, yanking him back as I stared at him with a mocking grin. Water dripped onto the floor, but none of us moved to clean it up.

"I have a job next week. It's out of town, but I could use the help if you're interested," I told them calmly, as if Kade hadn't just tried to attack me.

Gray frowned in suspicion. "You want our help?"

I nodded. "I could do it myself, but having you two there would make it easier."

"Why?" Kade asked through clenched teeth.

"Because this won't be the first car I've stolen from this man. He's seen my face before," I lied smoothly. It was a half-truth, but I had no intention of telling them why I was really doing this job. "We'd be gone a few days."

"Why so long?" Gray studied me.

"I'll tell you the details once you decide if you want to join me."

A muscle ticked in Kade's jaw. "You've been here almost two months, and we still haven't done a job with you. I don't know what the hell you're playing at, but we get the feeling you don't want to work with us."

"That's on you." I shrugged. "I had every intention of working with you, and then you decided to try and have me arrested. I'm giving you a second chance. And believe me, the payout is worth it."

They exchanged a look, staying quiet when the waiter came back with our drinks. I slowly stirred my gin and tonic, waiting for the door to close again.

"Where's the job?" Gray asked.

"About four hours from here," I answered, standing up. "I leave in two days, so tell me your answer by then."

They both shot up from their chairs when I reached into my purse, and I chuckled, pulling out my cash and tossing some on the table for the bill.

"If I was going to do anything, I wouldn't have chosen to meet here." Grabbing my drink, I finished the rest of it.

Gray crept closer when I moved toward the door. Facing him, I raised my arm and trailed my nails down his cheek, making him go still.

"Don't worry about me trying to get you back like I did with Kade," I murmured, keeping my voice sweet. "At least while we're working. I told you before that I take my jobs seriously. No need to be wary until after the job is done."

Gray snagged my wrist, pulling my hand from his face and backing me against the door. He pressed his body into mine, his leather scent surrounding me. He kept a tight hold on my arm as I peered over his shoulder, locking eyes with Kade.

"I have no need to be wary of you," Gray stated, pulling my attention back to him. "I'll know you're up to something the second you start taking your clothes off."

I giggled, letting my stare turn lethal. "I can fuck you just as hard when my clothes are on. Don't forget that, Gray. Now back the fuck up."

Gray slowly released me and stepped away. I moved to grab my bag before opening the door, glancing over my shoulder at them.

"You have my number. If you want to do the job, text me." I didn't wait for their answer as I walked away. The hostess glanced at me in surprise as I passed her. I was sure people usually stayed here longer than fifteen minutes. But I had other things to do tonight and needed to get back to Ridgewood before it got too late.

I knocked on the door, not waiting for a response before pushing it open. Rylan was sitting behind his desk, and his pen fell from his hand when he saw me. I strode inside, glancing around. His large oak desk was in front of the window, and bookshelves lined the left wall. Pictures and framed awards were perfectly organized on floating shelves on the opposite wall. Two oversized chairs faced his desk, and I passed them, rounding the desk.

"Do you always work this late?" I asked as he pushed back his chair, giving me room to stand between him and the desk.

"Politics never sleeps," he muttered, his eyes raking over my black dress. "To what do I owe the pleasure?"

"You keep popping up and surprising me. I thought I'd repay the favor." I perched on his desk, and he didn't make a move to push the paperwork out of the way before I sat on it. "I haven't seen you in a while."

"I thought the crew killed you until you texted me to meet you at the club." He raised an eyebrow. "It was a long two weeks."

A fluttering filled my stomach that had no business being there. Having someone other than Caleb worry about me was unnerving, and

I wasn't enjoying the small amount of guilt clinging to me. I shouldn't fucking feel bad about not telling him that I was okay.

"I appreciate you trying to cover for me." I reached forward and began loosening his tie, catching a flash of confusion on his face. "When I tried making you my alibi when Andy was hurt and you lied for me. Why did you do it?"

He shot me a small smile. "Have I not made it obvious enough that I like you?"

The unwanted flutters grew, and my hands froze on his tie. Using men to get what I needed had never been an issue, but as I locked eyes with Rylan, hesitation stirred inside me. He was an innocent, and using him wasn't sitting right.

"I should go," I muttered, my muscles tensing when he caught my wrists, keeping my hands on his shirt collar. "You don't want to get involved with me, Rylan."

"Too late for that," he stated gruffly. "Why'd you come here, Mili? What do you need?"

I bit my tongue, not liking how quickly he'd picked up that I'd come here for a certain reason. His hands drifted away from my wrists, trailing over my skin until he was grasping my hips.

"Nothing. I can do it myself."

Interest flared in his gaze, and he kept his hold firm when I attempted to get off his desk. "Tell me what you need."

I grinned wickedly. "How about I give you what you need?"

He chuckled, leaning closer. "You really don't like answering questions, do you?"

I brushed my lips against his as I went back to loosening his tie. "I can tell you what I do like."

"You made that sound dirty."

"I know." I bit my lip, keeping my gaze on his as I slowly unbuttoned his shirt.

He stopped me, rolling his chair back to create space between us. Pouting, I leaned back, resting on my palms.

"Tell me why you came here," he said softly.

I sighed. "You're very different from all the other man I deal with."

"Because I'm choosing to talk to you instead of having sex?" He cleared his throat. "Believe me, it's taking a lot of fucking self-control."

"Then stop fighting it," I purred, giving him a seductive smile.

"I will—once you tell me why you're here."

"Fine." I scooted farther onto the desk. "The night you refused to get out of my car, you told me that you heard about how the crew was looking for my Corvette. I'm guessing you have police reporting to you. Probably some civilians too." He didn't say a word, but his shoulders tensed as I kept talking. "Maybe you even have someone from the crew in your pocket. Or not. If you did, then maybe you would have gotten Kade and Gray behind bars by now."

"You still haven't told me what you want," he said, studying me with a slight frown on his lips.

"I need to stay one step ahead of the crew." I paused for a moment. "It would help if the next time your little helpers hear anything about me, you could let me know."

He rose from his chair and paced in front of the window before looking back at me. "What do you do?"

"What?"

"How deep are you in with the crew? If your car is anything to go by, you have the same taste as them. Do you race? What do you do for work?"

Every question he asked had me inching off the desk, ready to bolt out of the room. "I'm not part of their crew or with any gang."

"Then why are they so interested in you?"

"I procure expensive items for people," I said carefully. "And I'm very good at my job. There's an item I'm looking for that Kade and Gray are helping me with. They don't trust me, and I don't trust them. But the payout is worth it."

That was about as honest as I'd ever been with anyone other than Caleb, but it was still vague enough that Rylan would never know what I really do for work. I doubted he'd ever heard of Sapphire before, but I wasn't going to take the chance.

"They like you," he muttered, staring at me. "Gossip is spreading that they have a girl. One girl between the both of them."

"I don't care about rumors." I shrugged. "And I don't care what people think of me. I do what I want over anything."

"And you want to sleep with them?" he asked.

I tilted my head. "In all truth, I only slept with Kade. And I only did it to get something I wanted."

"What did you want?"

"To show them that they have no say in what I do. I can promise you that I am not their favorite person right now." I laughed, Kade's naked image filling my head. "Are you jealous, Rylan?"

"No," he said quickly before running a hand down his face. "Actually, maybe I am. I don't know. You make my thoughts jumbled."

"I will never be a woman that settles down," I told him quietly, once again thinking this was a mistake to involve him.

"I still want to see you again." He walked back to me, placing his hands on the desk on either side of me. "I'll give you what you want. Every time I hear them talking about you, I'll tell you. On one condition."

"What?"

"Go on a date with me."

"A date?" I choked out.

He nodded. "That's it."

I took a deep breath. To him, a date was another normal thing. But not for me. I could deal with Kade and Gray with ease. We were cut from the same cloth of crime, darkness, and danger. Using sex to mess with them was simple. I was more comfortable fighting with them on their turf than sitting here in this office. Rylan was nothing like the men I'd spent time with in the twelve years since I'd been part of the criminal world.

I was out of my element when I talked to him, and I didn't fucking like it. I'd perfected being at ease in almost any situation. And on a surface level, I was an expert at it. But with Rylan, it was more. Because he wanted to get to know me.

"One date," I finally said. "But it will have to wait. I'm going out of town for a while."

He frowned. "Again?"

"It's only for a few days, and it's for business."

"Then I'll see you when you get back," he said with a smile.

I blinked. "That's it? I had plans to be naked and sprawled on your desk tonight."

He ran a hand down my cheek. "We'll save it for after the date."

"Why?"

"Because I want you to go on your business trip thinking about how good it's going to feel when I finally drop to my knees and taste you," he murmured. "I want it to consume your mind."

I swallowed thickly, heat rushing between my legs. "Why wait?"

"Because I plan to see you for more than just one date."

I chuckled. "You can't turn me into a respectable woman. I'm not built like that."

"I'm not trying to change you. I want to know you just how you are."

His words jolted me back to reality. If he knew who I was and what I'd done, then he would never want me. If he knew of the horrors I'd committed and been a part of, he would be looking at me in disgust. I jumped off his desk, striding toward the door.

"I'll see you when you get back, Mili," he called after me as I left his office.

21

Gray

"Is it my turn to choose the music?" Mili grumbled from the back seat.

I reached forward to the radio and turned my music up a little more. "Shotgun chooses music."

"You stole my seat when we stopped at the gas station," she snapped, her head popping up between the passenger seat and the driver's seat. "Why the hell did I agree to drive with you?"

"We only have twenty minutes before we get there," Kade muttered, keeping his eyes on the road as he drove through the mountains.

We were driving with her because we wanted to make sure she didn't try to pull any shit behind our backs. Kade was convinced she was going to screw us over again. Even though I had my doubts, I thought she really wanted to work jobs with us before the Panther job.

But still, I'd been wary for the entire four-hour drive. We were driving in a white SUV since Mili told us we didn't want any cars that stood out.

"You should put your seat belt on," I said, turning my head to glance at her. "It would be a shame if you got hurt if we got in an accident."

She scoffed. "We'd be screwed either way if Kade crashed now."

Looking out my window, I stared at the steep cliff. The guardrail did little to protect cars from going off the edge. We were high up in the mountains, going to a tiny vacation town named Roseville. I'd never been there, but we'd heard about it. Roseville was a place where the rich came to unplug from life. From what I'd looked up, everything in the town was expensive and catered to every need of their guests, even though it was in the middle of nowhere.

"You two remember the plan?" she asked. "Because after we check into the hotel, you'll have to go right away to make it on time."

"We know what we have to do," Kade clipped out.

I smothered my laugh at how short he was being with her. He was still pissed about her locking him in the bathroom, and I had a feeling he wasn't going to forget anytime soon. Keeping one hand on the wheel, he pulled out a pack of cigarettes and took one out. Mili reached over him and snagged one before rolling her window down.

"Do you ever do jobs solo?" she asked casually. "Or do you two work together all the time?"

"We work better together," I answered, seeing the welcome sign for Roseville.

"Who pulls rank when you disagree? Or do Juan and Vic handle all the decisions?"

"Why so curious?" Kade asked tightly.

"I'm trying to understand. There's two of you. So what happens if you two don't agree?"

"We work it out," I told her, having no intention of explaining how we ran things.

Kade moved to flick his cigarette out the window, but before he could, Mili lunged forward and snatched it from his hand. I whipped around, watching her drop the cigarette into a water bottle, along with her own.

"Are you an amateur?" she snapped, glaring at the back of Kade's head. "You don't leave any fucking evidence of being here."

"Are you kidding?" Kade grated out. "We're nowhere near where we're staying. Or the guy's house."

"It doesn't matter. There is no logical reason for you to even be in this town. Once the car gets reported stolen, they're going to investigate. You don't fucking leave anything that could come back to you."

I raised an eyebrow, studying her. Her entire demeanor was different. Her usual sarcastic, playful manner was gone, and in its place was a calm and calculating stare. Her body was tense as she looked out the window as we drove down the main street in town. Roseville only had a few streets, but it was bustling with tourists. Restaurants and shops lined the road, and I glanced at the GPS, seeing our hotel was on the next street.

Kade pulled to the curb and parked in front of where we were staying. It was more of a bed-and-breakfast than a hotel; a place where newlyweds stayed. Why she picked this place instead of the popular hotel was a mystery to me. We climbed out of the car and grabbed our bags out of the back before going up the steps to the wraparound porch.

"Good afternoon," the receptionist greeted us with a smile. "Checking in?"

"Yes, we have two rooms booked under Chelsea Green," Mili answered, her voice a few notches higher than usual.

The smile faded as she looked up the reservation, and she gave us an apologetic frown. "I'm sorry. Our system crashed last night and messed up the reservations. We tried contacting everyone—"

"I didn't receive an email," Mili cut her off.

"Yes, some contact information was lost. I am so sorry." She clicked a few more times before looking at us again. "But we do have one room available if you'd all like to share it."

"Share?" Kade sputtered. "No, we can look at the other hotels."

Mili looked as put out as Kade as the receptionist glanced between us. "There is a convention in town this week. I'm not sure there will be availabilities anywhere else."

Kade had already pulled out his phone, clearly calling the other hotel, while Mili pulled out a credit card and placed it on the desk. "I'll take the one room, thank you."

Kade stepped to the side, muttering under his breath before hanging up. "The other place is booked. And apparently this place and the other hotel are the only two in town."

"Yes, most of our guests own their homes here," the receptionist answered, trying to be helpful. "We usually don't get this many people only staying two nights."

"We have a house to stay at, but isn't ready," Mili lied smoothly. "We'll be here all week for the convention."

"Wonderful. I'm glad it will work out." The lady handed us key cards and pointed in the direction of our room before moving to help another customer.

"Why did you tell her we're staying the week?" Kade asked in a low voice as we walked down the hall.

"Because she said they don't get many people coming for only a couple nights," Mili spoke slowly, as if we should already know. "We don't want to seem out of place. We want to blend in like we belong. We want to be invisible and leave without anyone remembering our faces."

"You're going above and beyond for us to take one car," I muttered, wondering if she was this careful on all her jobs.

We stopped at our door, and Mili turned toward us. "This town is crawling with wealthy people. People who I may or may not have already done business with. Who you might have stolen from before. There's a fucking reason I've planned this so carefully."

Kade rolled his eyes as he unlocked the door and pushed it open. We all stepped inside, freezing while we looked at the room. Thick white carpet covered the floor. There was a large fireplace, and in front of it was a small coffee table with two chairs. There were vases of flowers on every available surface, and floral portraits were on the walls. But it was the bed we were all staring at.

Because there was just one.

Mili bolted forward, throwing herself on the four-poster king bed. She sprawled out, lying on her stomach and resting her face in her hands while grinning at us.

"Looks like you two are sleeping on the floor," she said sweetly.

"Hell no, we're not," I ground out.

She pulled out her phone, glancing at the screen. "We can argue about it later. You need to be at the party in a half hour."

Kade grabbed the garment bag. "Let's go."

"Is she sure he's going to show up?" Kade muttered. "We've been playing this valet act for over forty minutes."

I flicked my tongue over my lip, forgetting for a moment that I didn't have my lip ring in. "She planned this down to every detail. He'll be here."

"She should have come with us instead of staying back in the hotel room," he grumbled, messing with his white dress shirt. "I feel like she's plotting something that we don't fucking know about."

"This is the whole reason we're doing this job with her," I reminded him. "He knows what she looks like."

"And you believe her? I feel like everything she gives us is a half-truth."

"It probably is," I mused. "But she seems pretty serious when it comes to her jobs."

"Too serious." He straightened up when headlights turned into the circular drive.

The red Mustang got closer, and I began backing up toward the entrance. "Looks like our guy. I'll see you in a few."

Kade nodded, stepping up to the car as it stopped in front of him. I spun around, heading into the foyer of the ballroom. Straightening my black tie, I went behind the coat counter, and the girl who was working shot up from her seat.

"I'm sorry, only employees are allowed back here—"

"Why do you think I'm here?" I gave her a charming grin before glancing at my suit. "I wouldn't be wearing this if I didn't work here, would I?"

She pushed back her blond bangs as her eyes trailed over me. "I guess not. I'm supposed to work this whole shift tonight."

I frowned, pretending her words were new to me. "I just started this job, and I could have sworn tonight was my first shift."

The front door opened, and my stomach rolled with anticipation as I locked eyes with the guy I'd been waiting for. He looked exactly like the picture Mili had shown us. Black hair that was styled to the side with gel, brown eyes, and a small scar above his left eyebrow. I was guessing he was in his late thirties, while the petite redhead on his arm looked like she still belonged in college. He helped her take off her shawl before shrugging out of his jacket.

I stepped forward. "Good evening. Please let me take those for you."

The guy all but tossed his jacket at me, his eyes wandering over the girl next to me. The redhead obviously noticed him checking out the employee, but she didn't say a word. I handed him the small paper stub so he could collect his jacket later, and he snatched it up, striding into the ballroom.

"Let me hang these up," I told the girl, who was still staring at me in confusion. "And then I'll go to the office and try to figure out why they put me on the schedule."

"Okay," she said uncertainly, turning to help the next couple that came in.

Slipping behind the thick curtain, I looked over my shoulder, making sure I was alone before opening the guy's jacket. I ran my fingers down the smooth interior until I felt a lump. Just like Mili explained, he had a small hidden pocket with a key inside. The zipper was small, making it hard to unzip. I finally got it open, and I grabbed the tiny key, slipping it into my pocket. After hanging up the jacket and shawl, I walked back out, nodding to the girl and heading toward the offices. Once I was out of sight, I turned down the other hall and pushed open the side exit door.

I made my way to the valet parking lot, scanning the aisles until I spotted the red Mustang. Kade was standing beside it, and the car lights flashed as he unlocked it when he spotted me. He already had gloves on, and I slipped mine on as I got closer.

"You get it?" he asked.

"Yeah." I held up the small key before opening the passenger door.

I slid into the passenger seat as Kade stood outside, scanning the parking lot to make sure we weren't disturbed. I stuck the key I'd taken from the jacket into the glove box lock and twisted. It clicked when it unlocked, and I pulled it open.

"I still don't believe someone would leave a spare house key in their damn glove box," Kade muttered, watching me dig through paperwork.

"Well, this guy does." I finally found the key at the bottom of the glove box and pulled it out.

"Make sure it's exactly how it was," Kade said, watching me rearrange the papers I'd just gone through.

"I know," I muttered, closing the glove box and locking it. "Let's go."

"Now we get to stay holed up in that bed-and-breakfast until tomorrow night," Kade grumbled as we walked toward the building. "We should just do it tonight."

"And that's probably why she didn't give us the code to his house. So we didn't go behind her back."

Kade scoffed. "I still don't trust her."

"I don't think we'll ever trust her," I muttered. "But we agreed to do the job with her, and I'm positive if we fuck it up, she will try to kill us."

"And what's stopping her from trying to do that anyway?"

I arched an eyebrow before pulling the side door back open. "I don't know. But messing with her job wouldn't help."

He rolled his eyes and went to get the car while I went back inside. The girl at the coatroom frowned when she saw me again.

"You were right. I'm not scheduled to work." I grinned sheepishly. "I left my phone in the back. I just need to grab it."

She nodded, turning her attention back to the customer she was helping. I pushed the curtain back, going to where I'd hung up the guy's jacket. Pulling the key out, I slid it back into the small pocket, making sure it was zipped back up. Once I got back to the front, I nodded to the girl and strode out the front door. Kade was parked around the corner, and he took off as soon as I got in the passenger seat.

"Let's go find some food. I'm starving," I said, pulling out my phone to search what fast-food places are in the area.

"And stop at that other hotel to see if they have any open rooms," Kade grumbled.

I chuckled, leaning back in the seat. It would be a miracle if blood wasn't spilled tonight. Sharing a room for a night with her was going to be interesting.

22

Milina

I paced the room for the thousandth time, looking through the curtain to see if the car was back. I'd learned in the past two hours that I was terrible at delegating work. All I was imagining was them messing up the one chance at getting the key. Maybe Caleb was right; I should have done this job alone. This wasn't a regular car heist. It was personal for me, and I should have fucking come here without them. But no—I wanted to prove to Kade and Gray that I'd work with them before the Panther job.

My phone went off, and I nearly sprinted across the room, snatching it off the bed. I arched an eyebrow in surprise when I saw it wasn't Kade or Gray.

Rylan: How's your business trip going?

I grinned as I texted him back.

Mili: Boring so far. Working late again?

Rylan: Always. But the image of you on my desk is making it hard to concentrate.

Mili: We can always skip that date and make that image a reality.

Rylan: And what would you wear if we skipped the date?

Mili: I'd wear exactly what I have on now.

I flopped onto the bed, lying on my stomach while I waited for his response. This was much better than just waiting around for the guys to come back.

Rylan: What are you wearing?

Mili: How about I show you the night I come back?

Rylan: Show me now.

I bit my lip, standing up and looking out the window again. The car was still gone, and I decided I'd have more than enough time to snap a quick picture. Stripping off my clothes, I stood in front of the full-length mirror. The black lace bralette I was wearing covered some of my tattoo, and I slid the straps off my shoulders, lowering it until only a couple of the blue flames were showing. My thong matched the bralette, and I turned, making sure he could see the curve of my ass. I kept the phone high, hiding my face as I took the picture. I didn't mind him seeing my body, but putting my face or tattoo through a message wasn't happening.

Rylan: Fuck me.

I giggled, falling back onto the bed. I scooted back until I was resting against the pillows and started texting back until he sent another message.

Rylan: I'm fully regretting letting you leave my office the other night.

Mili: It's too bad you're not here.

Rylan: Touch yourself as if I were there.

Mili: I'm shocked. The straitlaced mayor wants to sext?

Rylan: Only with you.

Hot excitement flooded through me, but I paused at the slight hesitation creeping through my chest. Rylan was in a whole different world than me. And Gray and Kade. I could play with them all I wanted because we were in the same life. Getting Rylan involved was a mistake, especially since there was clearly bad blood between him and the crew. If I dragged him into this life, he might end up dead.

My hold on the phone tightened as I stared at his message. I barely knew this man, yet there was a part of me that cared what happened to him. Fuck, I didn't like it. Worrying about people made things messy. It made me vulnerable. Something my enemies could use against me if they found out. With a sigh, I texted a quick reply.

Mili: Thanks to this hotel messing up, I don't have my own room. But I'll be back in town in a few days.

Blowing out a breath, I tilted my head back and stared at the ceiling. My text was short and ruined the playful mood. I doubted he was going to respond, and it was better this way anyway. He didn't need me in his life. I'd only ruin it. My phone dinged again, and a smile played on my lips.

Rylan: Are you alone now?

Mili: Yes. But not for much longer.

Rylan: I bet you could get yourself off before then.

Mili: Is that a challenge?

Rylan: If I say yes, do I get a picture with your fingers buried in your pussy?

This man was taking me by surprise every time I talked to him. Which didn't happen often. I was usually good at reading people. I had pegged him for another boring politician in the beginning. I could admit I had been wrong. He had a dirty mind under those pristine suits he wore. And I had a feeling he would be fun in bed.

Rylan: Don't keep me waiting.

My defiance flared even as my lower stomach pulsed. I should have realized he liked control in the bedroom. Kade and Gray were the same. I fucking hated giving up my control. It was something I hadn't done in five years. But apparently, when it came to men, it was clear I had a type. I should listen to reason and leave them all the hell alone.

Instead, I shimmied down the bed, keeping the phone in one hand while pushing my thong to the side and sliding my fingers over my already-drenched pussy. I worked myself up a bit before angling my phone to take a picture. Again, I made sure my face and tattoo couldn't be seen before sending it to him. I continued touching myself as I stared at the three tiny bubbles that showed me he was replying. I glanced at the door as the AC kicked on. Even with the low fan, it would be easy to hear when the door opened. I doubted they'd be quiet when they came back.

Rylan: Fuck. You're stunning. And so wet. I want you to finger yourself until you come. While thinking about what I'm going to do the next time you're on my desk.

Texting back one-handed proved more difficult as I kept my fingers on my clit.

Mili: What are you going to do?

Rylan: I'm going to strip you naked before my hands explore every inch of your skin. Until my tongue takes over and I start all over again.

I circled my clit faster, imagining it. I'd make sure that his desk would be the first place we fucked. Even though I knew it was a bad idea, I also knew I was going to end up sleeping with him. He wanted it—and so did I. I'd just be careful.

Rylan: I can't wait to fucking taste you.

A small moan escaped me, but as close as I was, my movements faltered as I kept my eyes closed. There hadn't been another noise other than the AC fan, but I wasn't alone anymore. I could feel their presence without having to look. I got a small whiff of cigarette smoke for a moment before it disappeared. Apprehension settled in my stomach as my face got hot. I didn't care that they saw my body. But seeing me get myself off was a whole other thing.

"I warned you earlier you shouldn't smoke on a job," I murmured, forcing my eyes open. "They leave evidence—like the smell. It gives you away."

I hid how startled I was when I met their gazes. I figured they'd be near the door. But Kade was only a couple of feet away, while Gray stood at the edge of the bed. How the hell did I not hear them come in?

"I didn't smoke on the job," Kade said through clenched teeth, his gaze dropping to my pussy before moving to my face again. "What are you doing?"

I smirked, refusing to show that they'd surprised me. "I got bored waiting for you two."

I still had my phone in one hand, and my other was still covering my clit. The tension was thick, and I had a feeling the second I moved, they would too. Gray beat me to it and jumped on the bed next to me, his grin wide.

"Let me help you finish," he offered, a wicked gleam in his eyes.

"No."

I moved my hand away from my pussy, and Gray snatched my wrist, pulling it to his lips. He sucked on my wet fingers and groaned. I broke his stare when my phone went off and it was still unlocked, but before I could look at it, Kade ripped it from my grip.

"Hey," I hissed angrily, moving to get it, until Gray tightened his hold, yanking me back to him.

"Holy fuck," Kade muttered, his eyes glued to the screen.

Twisting out of Gray's grip, I jumped to my knees, reaching for my phone. "Give it back. Now."

"What is it?" Gray asked from behind me.

"Our great mayor seems to have a thing for little hellions." Kade lifted the phone above his head when I lunged for it again.

Gray chuckled. "He has good taste."

A surprised cry left me when Gray's arm banded around my waist, tossing me back on the bed.

"Gray." His name came out as a warning—one he didn't heed as he pried my thighs apart and settled himself between my spread legs. I leaned up on my elbows, not making a move to push him off. I remembered how good he got me off before, and even with their interruption, my body was begging to finish.

"You were getting off while imagining another guy," Gray murmured, and I couldn't tell what he thought about that. "I'll touch you so you don't need to fucking imagine it."

I didn't move a muscle, even when his fingers trailed up the inside of my thigh. His eyes were locked on mine, as if waiting for me to shove him off. When I didn't, he bit his lip, playing with his piercing as he pushed two fingers inside me.

"What are you thinking?" Kade snapped, making my attention go to him. He was standing at the foot of the bed, his arms crossed tightly as he glared at his best friend.

"I'm thinking we never stopped for food," Gray answered gruffly, "and I'm starving."

"She's probably doing this to fuck you over," Kade argued.

"Aw. Are you still upset about being locked in the bathroom?" I had meant for the words to come out sarcastic, but Gray's moves were making it hard to talk, and I barely choked them out.

Kade ignored me. "The second you're distracted, she's going to do something."

"If all you're going to do is talk, then you can leave," I said between quick breaths. Gray was plunging his fingers in and out of my pussy as his thumb circled my clit. The pressure building in my lower stomach was promising my release was going to be fucking amazing.

"I'm not leaving him alone with you," Kade said gruffly.

"Then stand watch for me, *brother*," Gray grinned. "Watch her to make sure she doesn't try anything. It looks like you're enjoying the show anyway."

It seemed Kade wasn't going anywhere. He stayed where he was, his eyes darting between Gray and me. I turned my focus back on Gray, stifling a cry when he pinched my clit. Knowing Kade was watching only turned me on more. He might act like he didn't want me, but that wasn't the truth. We both knew it, even if he wouldn't admit it.

"What are you doing—" my words were cut off when Gray lifted me and spun me around on the mattress. Now my head was at the foot of the bed, and I only needed to bend my neck slightly to look upside down at Kade.

"Why'd you invite us to this job?" Gray asked, his fingers going back to my pussy.

I frowned. "I told you. So we could build up trust to work together."

"I think Kade needs more to trust you," he replied, his tone promising dangerous fun. "Don't you, Kade?"

They seemed to have a silent conversation as they exchanged a look. Even upside down, I could tell Kade was fighting against whatever Gray wanted him to do.

"Do you trust us, Rebel?" Gray asked in a low voice.

"I don't trust anyone."

He raised an eyebrow. "Do you trust us enough to know we wouldn't hurt you tonight?"

Hurt me? My stomach dipped when I realized I hadn't worried about them hurting me since the night they tried to arrest me. Even when they chained me in their office, I didn't fear them. I didn't exactly trust them, but I was getting comfortable around them. And that was just as fucking bad. Refusing to give that any more thought, I licked my lips before grinning.

"Am I going to get an orgasm?" I asked, and Gray nodded. "Then even if you do hurt me, I'll probably enjoy it. Do your worst, Gray."

His eyes darkened, and he withdrew his fingers, wrapping his arms around my thighs. "Get the bag, Kade."

"Wait. What bag?" The rest of my questions were lost when Gray's tongue attacked my clit without any warning. My pussy throbbed, and I fisted the comforter when his teeth nipped at me. I was barely aware of Kade moving around the room before stopping near me. Gray's hold on my thighs went tight when Kade grabbed one of my arms. I stiffened, attempting to regain control. But Gray held my body in place as Kade pulled my arm above me.

My eyes widened when he began wrapping some type of rope

around my wrist and tying a knot before tying off the other end to the bed post after he pulled it taut.

"What the hell are you doing?" I tried sitting up, but Gray only tugged me until I slipped back down.

"Trust, Mili," Kade taunted, catching my other arm in his grasp. My half-assed struggling did nothing to stop him from tying my other wrist to the bedpost.

"Why the fuck do you carry rope around?" I snapped.

"We come prepared for jobs," Kade answered, staring down at me. "You never know when you need it."

My heart was racing, and as I tugged against the thick rope, my chest went tight. Giving my freedom over to someone wasn't something I ever wanted to do again. But as Gray continued to feast on my pussy, I realized this was different. They weren't trying to trap me. They weren't Joel. Even if Kade hadn't touched me, I could see the lust in his gaze. They both wanted me. He'd tied me down because he didn't trust me after what I did to him. And I couldn't exactly blame him for that.

I squirmed in Gray's hold when he got me close to the edge, but then he slowed down. Lifting my head, I glared at him as he slowly licked up my slit.

"Why don't you show Kade he can trust you?" Gray's words were barely coherent since he hadn't lifted his mouth from my pussy.

"And how am I supposed to do that when he tied my hands?" I snarked.

"Prove to him that those pretty lips can do more than cause trouble."

"You're not serious," Kade nearly choked out. "I put my dick anywhere near her, and she'll bite it off."

"Not if she wants to come."

"Excuse me?" I hissed out.

He didn't answer, sucking on my clit until I was grinding on his face. Fuck me, it felt so good. He slowed again, and I snarled in frustration. He edged me again, his eyes staying on mine as he kept his face buried between my thighs.

"This is bullshit," I huffed out. "Untie me, and I'll get myself off."

"Not an option," Gray mumbled, clearly intent on bringing me to the brink of insanity. "You want me to stop, I will. But you'll stay tied to this bed for the rest of the night."

"Careful, Gray," I threatened, rocking my hips against his mouth.

"I could do this all night." He released one of my legs to finger me. "When I have you on the edge, it's the most open I ever see you. Your defenses are down. I can see your pleasure. Your need. And I fucking love it."

There was no bluff in his voice. He would really do this all damn night. Craning my neck, I glared at Kade, biting my lip when Gray's fingers hit my sweet spot.

"Pants off," I ordered, daring Kade to argue with me.

"Last time you said that, you cuffed me to the sink."

"Trust, Kade." I mocked his words from earlier. "I promise I'll play nice. No teeth."

He grumbled something under his breath, but I could see his control snapping as he watched my chest rise and fall. Tugging his gun out of his waistband, he tossed it on the small table. He unbuttoned his jeans, slipping out of them and his boxers. With one hand, he grabbed the back collar of his shirt, pulling that off too. He didn't seem to care at all that he was naked in front of his best friend.

My eyes roamed over his hard chest and to his sculpted abs. Black ink covered almost every inch of him, and I couldn't tear my gaze away. He might be an asshole most days, but fuck, he was beautiful to look at. Even when I was looking at him upside down. He fisted his huge cock as he stared down at me. He was still hesitating, and I grew impatient as Gray alternated between licking and fingering me. I needed more.

"Fuck my mouth, Kade," I demanded.

He stepped closer, and Gray pushed my body forward until my head hung off the bed. The blood rushed to my skull, but that was a second thought as Gray brought me back to the edge again. I opened my mouth as wide as I could, and Kade slowly pushed the head of his cock between my lips. I almost wanted to fuck with him and drag my teeth along his shaft, but I didn't want to give Gray a reason to keep teasing me.

I relaxed my throat as I attempted to get used to his size. He hit the back of my throat, and I sucked in breaths through my nose. He couldn't even fit all the way, and he was already blocking my airway. I choked out breaths as he started moving. Slowly at first, but then faster as I flattened my tongue and sucked.

"Fuck," he groaned.

"Just like that, Rebel. Good girl," Gray praised me before returning his attention to my clit.

I whimpered around Kade's cock as my body locked up. This time Gray didn't stop. Even when the shattering orgasm consumed every inch of me, he kept going, drawing out wave after wave of pleasure. I jerked against my bonds, trying to escape when the pleasure became overwhelming. Kade was controlling how fast he fucked my mouth as he chased his release. I could feel him tense up, but he only slowed down for a few moments, apparently not ready to be done. Gray was still devouring me, quickly building me back up again.

"Fuck," Kade grated out as he came, his release shooting down my throat. His cock jerked, and he pulled out, his gaze landing on mine. I licked my lips, swallowing the few drops that spilled out of my mouth. He watched, looking both unsure and still turned the fuck on.

"One isn't enough," Gray growled, pulling away from me. "This time, I want to hear you scream."

I lifted my head, watching as he pulled his wallet out and cursed. I realized he was looking for a condom, and I was as disappointed as him. If his tongue and fingers were anything to go by, he probably fucked like a God. A silver foil wrapper hit him square in the chest, and Gray stared over me at Kade.

"I still think she's going to fuck us over," Kade grumbled. "But if you're going to do it, at least don't make a spawn of her."

Gray grinned, ripping open the condom wrapper that Kade had thrown at him. "If she screws us over, I think feeling her pussy around my cock will make it worth it."

"*She* is right here," I said, my usual attitude absent as I caught sight of something silver on the tip of Gray's cock.

He followed my gaze, his smirk growing cocky. "You didn't think I just had my lip pierced, did you?"

At the base of the head, a barbell piercing ran vertical with a bulb at each end. I knew just by looking at it that I'd feel it even with the condom.

"It's a King's Crown," he told me, sliding the condom on. "I'm thinking of getting another."

Kade was shuffling again, and after he'd tied my hands, I wanted to know what he was up to now. Letting my head fall back, I watched as he slid his boxers back on. My breath hitched when Gray nudged my entrance before slamming into me. My pussy clenched around him, the piercing hitting my inner walls with each thrust.

"Yes," Gray moaned, slowly sliding out and plunging into me again. "Fuck, you feel amazing."

My words were lost as he fucked me. When his fingers played with my clit, I lurched up, only staying on the bed because of the restraints. These men were going to be the death of me. Both he and Kade seemed to know exactly what I needed. I'd never had a man give me such powerful orgasms before. Fuck, I was going to miss them when I left town. My heart thrashed. This. I was going to miss the sex. That was it.

The vibrating of my phone caught my attention through the sex haze, and I protested when Kade grabbed my phone from the bed. Gray didn't slow down, his grip bruising my hips in the best way.

"Who's C?" Kade asked, glancing up from the screen. "He's calling."

Gray distracted me when he lifted my legs over his shoulders, hitting me at an entirely new angle. My nails dug into my palms as he hit my G-spot over and over.

"Want me to answer it?" Kade asked.

"No," I snapped. "I need to take it."

As much as I wanted Gray to keep fucking me, Caleb knew I was with them. He wouldn't call unless he absolutely needed to talk to me. Gray and Kade looked at each other before Kade hit the screen. Anger intertwined with the pleasure Gray was giving me, but it bled into shock when Kade pressed the phone against my ear.

"Yeah?" I clipped out, glowering at Kade and looking pointedly at the ropes. He didn't move a muscle, a smug gleam in his eye. Gray slowed down, but didn't pull out, and I blinked a few times, trying to concentrate. They were really going to have me take my call while Gray was buried inside me.

"Mili?" Caleb asked hesitantly. "You're not alone."

It wasn't a question. Every time I answered the phone like that, it was a hint that I was around people, and we couldn't speak openly.

"No, I'm not."

"You with them?" Caleb kept his voice soft and quiet to keep anyone on my end from overhearing.

"Yes." My voice was hoarse, and it was taking everything in me not to cry out in pleasure every time Gray circled my clit as he kept up with his slow strokes.

"Something came up that you need to know about, but I can call back later—"

"Tell me, Caleb," I forced out, instantly regretting my words.

Kade's face lit up with interest, and I mentally kicked myself for saying Caleb's name. They didn't need to know anything about that part of my life.

"One of your old coworkers reached out to your new partners' bosses," Caleb breathed out.

Ice chilled my veins, his words slicing through the immense bliss Gray was giving me. Old coworkers. Joel's men. Fuck. They reached out to either Vic or Juan.

"They want to work with me?" I asked carefully, ignoring Kade's penetrating gaze.

"I don't think it's about you." He sighed. "They want to run a job. I think it's a bad coincidence. But we can't chance it."

"Send me the details. I'll take care of it."

Gray was moving faster, not liking that I wasn't reacting to him anymore. That changed the next second when he reached over me, slid his hand under my bralette and began pulling at my nipple. I choked out a breath as he plunged back into me, fucking me like his life depended on it. Even with the news Caleb had dropped, my orgasm was about to explode.

"Are you okay?" Caleb asked, worry coating his voice. "You don't sound like yourself."

"I'm fine," I forced out.

"Did they do something to you? If they did, fuck the plan." Caleb's voice got louder as he grew angry.

"No, they haven't."

"Mili. Tell me if you need help."

I could tell by Kade's furrowed brow that he could hear Caleb. Yet I couldn't focus on anything other than Gray's cock. I was on the brink of coming, and my thoughts were no longer coherent.

"I don't."

"Are you worried about the job tomorrow night? I know it's going to be hard—"

"Fuck," I cut him off before he gave Kade my whole life story. "I'm drunk. I'll call you back later."

I could hear Caleb arguing, but I nodded to Kade, and after a moment's pause, he took the phone from my ear and hung up the call. I'd call Caleb when I wasn't being fucked within an inch of my life.

Gray let out a yell as he came, and I got my release at the same time. Every muscle locked up, and I grew lightheaded as euphoria washed over me. It seemed to last forever until I came back to reality when Gray fell on top of me. His heart raced against my chest as Kade untied my arms. I'd have rope burns, but I couldn't get myself to care. It was well fucking worth it.

"Who is he?" Kade growled.

"Who?"

"Don't play dumb." He raised my phone and shook it. "The guy you were talking to."

"Someone who works for me," I answered before yawning.

"He sounded awfully worried about you to be just an employee," Kade said, suspicion flashing across his face. "Are you his girl?"

"Jesus," I muttered, pushing Gray off me and jumping off the bed. "No. I told both of you that I'm not anyone's."

"How about you two fuck again?" Gray grumbled. "Seeing as it's the only time you don't argue."

"Did you get the key?" I asked, the seriousness of the job settling over me now that I could think clearly.

"We got it," Gray answered.

"Good." I snatched my phone from Kade, racing to the bathroom before either of them could steal the shower. I opened my texts, freezing in my spot when I opened Rylan's chat.

Mili: She tastes like ours. Fuck off, Mayor.

I bit my tongue so hard that I tasted blood. If that text wasn't bad enough, below it was an attached picture. Gray's head was between my legs, and my hands were balled up in the sheet. Most of my tattoo was still covered, and at least he made sure not to show my face. But my rage soared as I spun to face them.

"You asshole," I spat out, stalking toward Kade. "You had no right."

Kade shrugged. "We don't want you around him."

My jaw dropped at his audacity. "I don't give a flying fuck what you want. I am not yours. Or Gray's. I can see whoever I want."

"Don't forget that you're staying in our city," Kade warned. "We don't need a connection between us and the mayor."

"Don't forget who the fuck I am," I retorted, texting Rylan back. Not that anything I said would help.

Mili: They took my phone. Sorry, Rylan.

I laughed at myself, staring at my phone. What was I doing? Why did I feel bad that I'd likely hurt his feelings? I shouldn't. But I fucking did.

"I'm going to take a shower." Gray shuffled to the bathroom until I pushed him back, making it to the bathroom first and slamming the door behind me. Making sure it was locked, I turned on the shower and then sagged against the wall. I planned to take my time. They could fucking wait all night for all I cared. My phone went off, and I almost didn't want to read his text.

Rylan: I'll see you for our date, Mili.

23

Kade

As Gray drove up the long driveway, I couldn't tear my eyes off Mili. She sat perched in the passenger seat, her back straight as a rod. I'd never seen her so focused. Maybe she was like this for all her jobs. But after overhearing what that guy Caleb had said about being worried for this job, I had a feeling this one was different somehow.

"My neck is fucking killing me," Gray grumbled as he turned off his headlights.

"Your neck? I'm the one who slept in the middle. How did the smallest person take up half the damn bed?" I said, surprised my words didn't get a reaction out of her.

Last night, I was the last to take a shower, and when I came out, Mili was already passed out. She was sprawled on one side, and Gray was on the other. We had flipped a coin, and I lost. Which meant I was stuck in the middle all night. And I didn't get an hour of sleep. Mili moved in her sleep, and half the night she was practically rubbing on me, causing me to replay what we had done as I sported a semi hard-on all night. Her mouth was the best I'd ever felt besides when we'd had sex at the club. And it was driving me insane.

I didn't trust her. I shouldn't want her. But I craved her more than anything else that had ever touched my tongue.

After she got ready in the morning, she left the room and didn't come back all day. We had no idea where she went, but she was back at eight tonight to get ready for the job. It was only ten now and already dark outside.

"His cameras should go down right about…now." She was staring at her watch, her eyes narrowed with determination.

"You know how to hack camera systems?" Gray asked in surprise.

"Or someone who works for her does," I muttered. "Maybe Caleb."

Mili whipped her head around, her death glare focused on me. "Don't talk about things you know nothing about."

My chest rippled with a foreign emotion as I tried picturing who the fuck this Caleb guy was. It bothered me that she was defensive about him. Picturing her with anyone other than Gray or me made me see red. My breath hitched, and I looked away from her to stare out the window into the darkness.

I was jealous. I didn't get fucking jealous.

"Park in front of the garage. It's a blind spot from the house," Mili ordered, pulling me from my thoughts.

"I thought you said he wasn't home," I said, my heart rate accelerating as Gray shut off the car. I loved the thrill of working jobs, but we were out of our element with Mili here, and it had me on edge.

"He is. Or he's supposed to be. So just in case." She took the key that Gray and I had stolen out of her purse before pulling on her ski mask. Gray and I followed suit, covering our faces. Only our eyes and mouths showed as Mili carefully tucked her hair under the thick wool.

"I'll go into the house to get the car key," she said, even though we already knew the plan. "You two stand watch."

"Maybe one of us should go in with you," Gray started to say.

"No," she said sharply.

"Why not?" I asked.

"Because I know the security code to get into the house. This place is a fortress. You can't get in without it unless you want to trip the alarm."

"I looked this guy up," I said, watching her tense. "Everything he owns is locked down. He runs in big circles. Illegal circles. How the hell did you find out the code to his house?"

"I do my research," she snipped. "That's why I'm so good at my job."

We got out of the car, silently closing the doors before following Mili to the side of the house. Taking out the key, she stuck it in the lock while glancing at us.

"I'll open the small garage door once I disarm the alarm."

With those words, she slipped inside, closing the door soundlessly behind her. My gut twisted, wondering if we'd made a mistake doing this with her.

"We'll be fine," Gray murmured, knowing what I was thinking. "She takes her jobs seriously."

The five minutes we stood there felt like an eternity until we heard the small click we were waiting for. The garage door opened, and Mili's brown eyes peered at us through the ski mask. She motioned for us to follow her, and we flipped on our flashlights as we went into the pitch-black garage. I smiled in appreciation once we stopped in front of the car we were taking.

An Alfa Romeo 33 Stradale. Worth at least three million dollars with only eighteen of them in existence. This man must bleed money because this wasn't the only rare car in this huge garage.

"You know there's three of us," Gray muttered, looking wistfully at the car next to us. "We could take another—"

"No. We don't deviate from the plan," Mili interrupted him.

She hit a button on the wall, and the large garage door rolled up. As it moved slowly, she unlocked the car and opened the passenger door.

By the time I got close enough and shined the light on her, she was already straightening back up after messing with the cupholder.

"What are you doing?" I asked tightly.

"Nothing." She tossed me the key. "You and Gray take it. You know where the drop is."

My lips parted in surprise that she was trusting us to do this without her. "We'll wait for you."

She waved her hand. "No need. I'll drive the other car and pick you both up after I reset the alarm."

Her usual sarcastic banter was absent as she waited for us to move. Gray trusted her more than I did, and even he was hesitating. Her eyes clouded with anger as she clenched her hands.

"You agreed to do this my way. It's my job," she hissed. "Let's not sit here and argue until he comes home. Get in the damn car."

I bristled at her demand but moved toward the driver's door. We didn't need to get caught doing this. Gray stepped in front of me, raising an eyebrow. I sighed, raising my hand.

"Come on," Mili said, her voice hard and cold.

"Give us a minute," Gray told her. "This might be the only time we get this close to a car like this."

"So?" she asked, clearly not understanding.

Without explaining, Gray and I closed our hands into fists and played a game of rock, paper, scissors. I gritted my teeth when he won. We did it again, and my heart skipped when my paper covered his rock. I wanted to drive this car.

"Are you serious?" Her voice was smothered in annoyance, but I detected a small note of amusement as Gray and I played the last round.

"Shit," I cursed when I lost again. "Son of a bitch."

"If you're nice, we'll stop halfway and you can drive." He smirked, holding his hand out for the key.

After dropping it into his palm, I stalked to the passenger side and jumped in, not even opening the door. It was a convertible, and luckily, there was no rain forecasted tonight. Gray started the car, and the engine purred to life.

"Go," she urged, her finger on the garage button. The second the car cleared the door, she was closing it. Instead of racing down the driveway like I expected, he put the car in park.

"Let's wait a few minutes," he said, not looking at me.

"I'm not the only one who thinks something's up," I mumbled.

We waited in silence for over three minutes before I got impatient. She should be out by now. Nerves created a pit in my stomach as I climbed out of the car and headed to the door she had used to get into the house.

"It's fucking locked," I said incredulously. "She shouldn't have locked it until she came out."

"We would have seen her if she left the house," Gray said, his gaze moving over the windows. There wasn't a light on, and for a moment, it was silent until we heard a muffled crash. We stayed still for a second before a second crash came from inside the house. I twisted the door handle again, knowing it was useless.

"These doors are all reinforced," I muttered, remembering what Mili had told us. "We need to find another way in."

My ears pricked up, hearing yelling in the house. Whoever it was had a deep voice, which meant it wasn't Mili. What the hell was she doing? Even though I knew she could handle herself, I couldn't stop the slice of panic that was spreading through me. We ran to the back of the house, picking up our speed when a light suddenly turned on. Skidding to a halt, we peered through the glass doors at some sort of study. One lamp was on, and it kept the room bright enough for us to see.

I didn't try to hide, knowing they couldn't see through the dark window with the light illuminating the room. Mili was standing in front of the doorway of the study, her mask still in place. The guy had his back to us, his arms raised in surrender as Mili swung a bat in her hand. A weapon she didn't have before entering the house. The guy was yelling, but we couldn't hear anything through the glass.

Mili raised the bat and swiped the shelf on the wall beside her, knocking down pictures and other expensive-looking shit. Making a decision when she went for another shelf, I planted my feet. When she smashed the third shelf, I shoved my elbow into a pane of glass in the door. Brushing the specks of glass off my hoodie, I kept my eyes on Mili, but she hadn't even noticed. She was completely focused on the guy in front of her.

"What do you want?" the guy asked. "Money? Take it."

"I don't want your money."

The guy paused. "A woman? A fucking woman broke into my house?"

I sucked in a breath when Mili pulled off her mask. Gray went rigid next to me, neither of us moving. Her face revealed no emotion. Nothing. It was a look I hadn't seen on her before, and it made me uneasy. I shifted, waiting for her eyes to spark with some type of life.

"Milina?" the guy choked out, sounding like he'd seen a ghost. "Holy shit. The rumors are true. You are alive."

My eyes widened as I stared at Mili. No wonder she wanted us to leave. Whatever this job was, it was personal. Something she didn't want us to be a part of. Excitement churned in my stomach. Maybe we'd actually figure out some of her secrets tonight. Gray looked uncomfortable, like we shouldn't be eavesdropping. But he didn't move away from the door either.

"It's been a long time, Rhett." Her voice still lacked its usual vigor, but her eyes were suddenly burning with red hot anger.

"Why'd you come here, darling?" Rhett asked, his attitude flipping now that he knew who she was. "Did you miss me?"

I gritted my teeth, forcing myself not to move. I'd rather this fucker go back to being scared like he was when she had the mask on. He was acting like she was nothing to him. Powerless. Like he was in control of her. I didn't fucking like it.

"You could say that," she mused, her posture relaxed even when he took a large step toward her. "It took me years to track you down. You hid this house well."

She shuffled to the side, and he did the same, still keeping a wide distance between them. Where they were standing now, I could see both of their faces, and bile crept up my throat at the sight of Rhett's. The hungry look in his eyes was one of a predator. He wanted her. Shit, maybe she used to be with him. It was obvious we knew nothing about her.

"How did you find me?" he asked, studying her.

"Everything can be bought. Especially when your security alarm system is online. Makes it easier to track."

He was silent for over a minute. "Caleb. He's alive too, isn't he? You couldn't have hacked your way through that yourself."

"You haven't seen me in six years," she snapped. "You know nothing about me anymore."

"You couldn't have changed that much," he said, creeping closer to her. "I remember everything about you, little Lina—"

"Call me that again and see what happens," she hissed, the rage making her voice tremble. Her grip on the bat tightened until her knuckles turned white as she watched him inch closer. I internally screamed at her to swing, but she stayed completely still.

"Everyone wanted you," he said, his voice thick, as if he were reliving memories. "But Joel never was one to share."

A flash of fear crossed her face for a split second before she schooled her features. Joel. That name was important to her. And from her reaction, she wasn't fond of him.

"That didn't stop you from trying, did it?" she spat out, making him freeze.

"I offered you an out—"

She laughed coldly. "An out? You wanted me to become your doll. To be your special little fuck toy."

"It was still better than the life you were living," he tossed back, losing control of his emotions. "When I found you, I risked my fucking life to not bring you back to him."

"Found me? You tracked me down. On his orders," she screamed, her voice hollow. "Then you threatened me with the options to let you fuck me or bring me back to Joel. You really think I would have traded one devil for another?"

"I'm not going to pretend I'm a good guy," he murmured, getting within hitting range of her. "But I was still a better choice than him."

"Really?" she tilted her head. "Because I got free of him. I'd say I made the right fucking choice."

Without warning, he lunged at her, and my heart leaped in my throat. But she was ready. She swung the bat right into his kneecap, and he crumpled to the floor, roaring in pain.

"You stupid bitch," he bellowed, trying to scramble away from her. "You think you can get away with this? I'll make your years with Joel seem like heaven compared to what I'll do to you now."

A grin spread across her face, and this one was a far cry from the one she gave us. This was her Sapphire smile. Or maybe her real one. In this moment, I could easily see why she was so good at what she did. She was fucking ruthless. That smirk she was casting at Rhett promised to drag him to the depths of Hell.

"I'm simply repaying a favor," she told him calmly. "When you shoved me in the trunk to cart me back to Joel, you broke my leg when you slammed the trunk lid on me."

My chest tightened painfully, the image of a younger Mili enduring that kind of life.

"I didn't break your leg. I-I broke your arm," he finished lamely, realizing the truth didn't sound any better.

"Oh shit," she said brightly. "You're right. Bad memory. Let me fix that."

She stepped forward, this time swinging the bat into his right arm. The crack of his bone was barely heard over his howls of pain as he rolled on the floor.

"I was going to make this look like an accident," she informed him over his screaming. "But after seeing you sleeping so peacefully, I couldn't do it. You needed to pay for it all."

I wasn't sure Rhett was even comprehending her words at this point. His eyes were wild from the pain, and fear was finally breaking through as he looked at her.

"What the hell happened to you?" he sputtered out. "When did you become this person?"

"I got free," she stated, as if he should understand. "You think I'd ever allow someone else to steal my life like he did?"

His breaths were shallow, and his face was pale as he cradled his smashed arm. "You'll never be free. Even if he's gone, others aren't."

"Actually, I'd say there are only about three of you left. You aren't the first one I've found."

Confusion swamped me, and I hoped they kept talking about who the hell the others were. It made sense why she was so protective of her name. It wasn't just because she was Sapphire—it was because she was hiding.

"Even if you kill me, you won't get what you need—"

"You mean this?" She held up a small, narrow piece of paper. "How arrogant of you to keep it in your most prized car. You really thought no one would be able to find that secret compartment under the cup holder? If you were smarter, you would have kept it in a fucking safe."

She was patronizing him, and even with his body broken, he wasn't taking it well. Baring his teeth, he grabbed the edge of the small sofa and pulled himself up on his one good leg.

"You won't find them all. You can't shut us down for good," he hissed. "We're too large for that."

"Not anymore. Not since Joel died," she replied with a feral grin. "It's too bad you won't be here to see when I bring it all down."

"Did he die?" Rhett shot back. "Because we thought you died with him, yet here you are."

"You think I'd be here if he was still breathing?" The blank look crossed her face again. "If you have any last words, better spit them out. Because you're about to meet your friends in hell."

"Wait—wait," he cried out. "What do you want? We can work out a deal."

"Beg," she taunted him cruelly. "It's music to my fucking ears."

"Milina, I can help you—"

"Caleb wanted me to give you a message. He's sorry he couldn't deliver it himself."

Rhett brought his one good arm up, as if he could shield himself, as she advanced toward him. "I'm sorry for what I did to him. He didn't deserve it—"

He screamed bloody murder when she swung the bat into his side, no doubt breaking at least a couple of ribs. He crashed back to the floor, his breaths coming out in short wheezes. He tried crawling away, getting closer to the door we were hiding behind.

"If I had time, I'd shatter every bone in your body for what you did to us," she said, her voice shaking as she glared at him with hatred. "Lucky for you, I need to go."

He didn't have a chance to respond before she raised the bat again before smashing it against his skull. He fell to the side, his lifeless body leaning against the side of the couch. Dropping the bat, Mili pulled out a handgun, aiming it at Rhett's head.

"Fuck," I muttered under my breath.

She was a good shot, but if she missed, or if the bullet went through him, it would go right out the window at us. Gray carefully stepped to the side, realizing the same thing I had. I took one step back and flinched when my shoe crunched on a piece of glass. I didn't even have a chance to glance up to see if she'd heard because a second later, a bullet went through the glass. I dove to the side, out of the way, while Gray crouched and ran in front of the doors until he was beside me.

"Who's out there?" she called out.

Neither of us answered, and my heart thudded as I debated whether we should tell her it was us. We'd built up enough trust with her in the last couple of months that even with her pranks, we hadn't been worried about her killing us. But now I wasn't so sure. Whatever her past was, she didn't want us knowing anything about it. That conversation revealed a lot. Too much.

"If we can get to the car before her, we can get out of here before she knows it was us," Gray whispered.

I forced a grin. "You mean you don't want to come clean that we were listening?"

"Fuck no. She'd use that bat on us."

Another bullet rang out, and we leaped to our feet, racing across the back patio. We tried stepping lightly, but our steps weren't completely silent. We rounded the garage, skidding to a halt when we saw her coming out of the house. The front door was still wide open, and dim light spilled over the lawn. An outside light popped on when she hopped off the porch.

"Shit," Gray muttered.

"Is it hard for you two to follow directions?" Her voice was dangerously soft. "All you had to do was drive the fucking car ten minutes away."

"In our defense, we wanted to make sure you were okay after we heard the screaming," Gray told her nervously, his eyes staying on the gun in her hand.

She observed us silently as she leaned against the expensive car. "How much did you hear?"

My fingers twitched, instinct telling me to go for my gun. I could see it in her eyes—the struggle to put a bullet in us to keep her secrets safe. I resisted the urge to reach for my weapon, staying still. Even if I did, she'd get a shot off before I could even grab it.

"We took the car like you wanted, and waited for you to pick us up," Gray said carefully. "The poor asshole died during a break in."

Her mask was impenetrable, her gaze not giving anything away. "Take the car to the truck. I need to make sure I didn't leave anything behind, and then I'll meet you there."

She spun around, tucking her handgun in her waistband before striding back into the house. I blew out a breath, relaxing my muscles. There wasn't a doubt in my mind that she had considered shooting us. But she'd chosen not to. That had to count for something.

"I'll wait and drive with her," I muttered, glancing at Gray. "You good to drive it yourself?"

"Don't push her, Kade," he warned me. "No questions. No prodding into what we heard. Or she will fucking kill you."

"I know."

He nodded and then hopped into the car. I watched him drive away before walking back to the car we had driven here. I wasn't about to walk back into the house. But I wanted to make sure she was okay. She hid it well, but I'd seen the pain flash in her eyes when Rhett spoke about her past. Whatever hell she'd endured had scarred her. Anger licked down my spine as Rhett's words replayed in my mind. I wanted to help put the rest of the monsters who'd hurt her in the fucking ground. Not that she'd ever accept our help. Or want it.

But the door was cracked open tonight. We'd learned about her, and now I wanted to dig until we found out everything.

24

Gray

I walked stiffly through the entrance of the small restaurant area of the bed-and-breakfast. I swiped my tongue across my lip to mess with my piercing until I remembered I'd taken it out. The black slacks and business button-down shirt I wore were making me itch. Kade walked next to me, looking just as uncomfortable. We'd gotten back from the job less than an hour ago, and Mili had stayed in the room just long enough to change. She warned us to blend in if we came down to the bar, so here we were, wearing clothes we hated.

The bar area was packed. Wealth saturated the room, and I knew Mili had been right. If we were to walk down here in our regular clothes, we would have been the center of attention. Although, even with my outfit, I was sure I didn't fit in completely. I was the only guy in here whose hair wasn't cut short. Scanning the tables, I saw Mili sitting by herself. With the navy-blue cocktail dress she had on, she blended in perfectly. Or as well as she could. She was easily the most stunning woman in the room, and half the men in here were stealing glances at her.

She sipped on a martini as she scrolled through her phone, a pinched expression on her face. If I were to guess, she was probably still thinking about Rhett. She hadn't said a word about it to us, and I guessed she didn't plan to.

"Sit at the bar?" Kade asked, purposely not looking at Mili.

I was about to agree with him because I had a feeling she didn't want our company right now. But I halted in my tracks, watching a guy saunter to her table. He was staring at Mili as if undressing her in his head, and heat raced through my veins. Before I could say a word, Kade cut in front of me, moving straight for her table. I followed, and we sat down on either side of her right as the guy got to her.

"Can we help you?" Kade asked, a clear warning in his question.

"Oh, uh, no," the guy stammered out. "I thought she was alone."

"Nope," I said, giving him a grin while my gaze dared him to try and talk to her.

He mumbled something under his breath as he turned and shuffled away. Mili stirred the olive in her drink, her eyes trailing over us.

"Don't tell me you came down here just to chase off men for me," she murmured. "After the night I had, sex is the perfect way to end it."

"Good thing there are two guys right here who would love to take you up on that offer." I cleared my throat after seeing Kade's scowl. "Well, maybe just one."

She laughed lightly as her eyes flashed with danger. "I'm pissed at you two. You don't want to be alone with me right now."

"I'm going to get a drink," Kade muttered, standing up and heading toward the bar.

I watched him leave before focusing on Mili. She was acting like herself, as if she didn't beat a man to death less than two hours ago. Dredging up her past had to have shaken her, but she was hiding it well.

"I bet the payout for that car is going to be big," I said, carefully starting the conversation.

"I wouldn't know," she replied. "I didn't look."

"The job was never about the car," I said softly, wondering how far she'd let me push until shutting me down.

Her eyes cut to mine. "No, it wasn't."

"Is a broken arm the worst he did to you?" The question was out of my mouth before I could stop it.

She straightened up, anger flashing across her face. "I don't want or need your fucking pity. So drop it. And don't ever talk about it again."

Bouncing my leg, I stared at her for a moment before unclasping my cuff link and rolling up the sleeve. She watched me curiously as I turned my arm, letting her see the inside of my wrist. My full sleeve tattoo covered the skin, but I knew she saw the scars when her eyes widened slightly.

"One surgery and two steel pins," I said in a low voice. "All because I accidentally dropped my dad's beer when I was seven."

Her fingers lightly traced my scar as she stayed quiet. My heart hammered against my ribs while I wondered why the fuck I was sharing this with her. No one other than Kade knew how badly my dad used to beat on me. But I wanted her to see that I wasn't pitying her. I understood—at least partly.

Unbuttoning the top of my shirt, I tugged it to the side, showing her my collarbone. Her gaze zeroed in on what I was showing her, and she pressed her lips together as she stared.

"This was the only time he put out his cigarette on my chest." Rage made my voice thick as images of my dad popped into my mind. "Most are on my back. Can't see them now though, thanks to my ink. I've had my nose broken—twice. A few concussions. A shattered knee that kept me in a wheelchair for months."

I stopped talking, shaking my head. Fuck, I hadn't dug this deep into my past in years. I looked away from her to see Kade watching us. He had our drinks but was staying at the bar. He couldn't hear us, but he could probably guess what I was telling her since he knew me better than anyone.

"Why is he still alive?" she asked, anger for me present in her voice.

I ignored her question. "I got out when I was thirteen. How long were you trapped?"

She bristled, her fingers going tight around her glass. "It doesn't matter."

"It matters," I said firmly. "Because you survived."

She stared at me, her anger evaporating. Since she wasn't leaving or threatening me, I attempted to push a little more.

"What was your escape?" I asked gently. "Mine was music."

I could tell she understood what I was asking. Her outlet to escape her mind when the pain came. If it wasn't for classic rock, I would have lost myself decades ago.

"Books," she breathed out. "I lived in fictional worlds."

"For how long?"

I needed to know if her childhood was a replica of mine. Were we suffering at the same time? Or did her nightmare come later in life?

She hesitated, her walls coming back up. "I didn't grow up like you. I made my own hell when I was sixteen by walking into a world I knew nothing about."

My fists clenched as I took in her words. That most likely meant the guy she was talking to Rhett about, Joel, wasn't her father, or family at all. My gut knotted, wondering what else he did to her.

"And no," she whispered, "a broken wrist wasn't the worst they did to me."

My heart cracked at the pain in her voice. I opened my mouth to ask something else but closed it when a lady walked up to our table. Frowning, I shot the blonde a glare for interrupting us when I was finally getting somewhere with her. She didn't pay me any attention as she smiled at Mili.

"I remember you," she said, her eyes brightening. "You were at the conference today."

Mili was already back in character, and she smiled warmly at the woman. "I was. It was an interesting topic, wasn't it?"

My confusion grew as they chatted. Was that where Mili had spent the entire day before we went on the job? A shadow fell over the table before Kade took the empty seat next to Mili. The woman glanced at us as if remembering I was there.

"Were you two there as well? I don't remember seeing you," she said, her gaze falling to Kade.

"They were." Mili giggled. "But they like hiding out in the back of the room."

"What did you think about the business model they were discussing?" the woman asked me. "It could be great for small businesses, don't you think?"

I was caught off guard, so I reached for the beer Kade had brought me and sipped it as I thought about what to say. Mili's eyes danced with amusement for a few seconds before she bailed me out by answering the question with ease. Shock was plastered on Kade's face as he listened to Mili talk about start-up businesses as if she were an expert.

"I need another drink." The woman glanced at Mili's empty drink. "Join me?"

"Sure," she replied as she stood from the table. Before leaving, she leaned into me, her lips brushing my cheek. "Don't look so surprised. I told you we needed to act like we belong."

Giving me one last look, she turned on her heel and followed the woman to the bar. I finished my beer, not taking my eyes off her.

"What did you two talk about?" Kade asked the second we were alone.

"Whatever happened to her, it didn't start until she was sixteen," I answered quietly. "I don't think it was family who hurt her."

Kade's jaw dropped. "She actually told you that?"

"That was pretty much the only thing she told me." I sighed. "I doubt she'll tell us anything else."

"We need to look into Rhett's life more," he said gruffly. "It might lead to who Joel is."

"If she finds out we're digging, she'll lose it," I warned him, even though I knew it was useless. We were both too invested to drop it now.

I glanced back over at the bar, my gaze wandering when I didn't see Mili. I found her on the makeshift dance floor, her offbeat dance moves nothing like how she'd danced at our club. But her moves fit in perfectly with everyone else around her. The woman was dancing with her, and they were both smiling. I doubted Mili was enjoying herself, but we'd never know it from looking at her.

"That fucker is going to try it again," Kade grumbled, his eyes focused on the bar.

Following his gaze, I saw the guy who had gone up to Mili before we joined her at the table. His obsessive stare was on her as she danced. He ran a hand through his curly brown hair, a vile smirk forming on his face as he jumped off the barstool. The back of my neck flushed with heat as he began dancing with Mili. She expertly inserted the blond woman between her and the guy, but that didn't deter him.

He pretty much shoved the poor woman out of the way, roughly grabbing Mili around the waist and pulling her into his chest. His hands roamed over her ass until she grabbed his wrist and shook her head, laughingly telling him no. Kade rose from his seat, and she glanced over her shoulder, as if sensing that we were about to intervene. Her look said more than any of her words could have. She didn't want us to come anywhere near her.

I swallowed thickly, trying to rein in my anger at seeing another guy touching her. That in itself was a problem. She'd been very clear from the beginning that she had no interest in being with me. I knew from the start she'd disappear as soon as the Panther job was done. But the more time I spent with her, the more I wanted her.

"If he touches her again, he's dead," I muttered, deciding I didn't give a shit that Mili wanted us to stay out of it. I wasn't about to sit and watch while this asshole groped her.

I shot up from my seat when the guy grabbed Mili above her elbow and all but dragged her off the dance floor. Her body tensed, but she didn't fight against him besides pretending to feebly tug out of his grip. She could fucking drop him, but no—apparently not causing a scene was more important to her.

Fuck that.

Kade and I followed to where he was pulling her into the hall. We rounded the corner, catching sight of her pressed against the wall with him grasping her chin as he tried kissing her. She twisted his wrist, tearing his grip from her face before ducking under his arm. Teetering on his feet, he spun around, as if not understanding how she'd moved that quickly. I realized he was drunk, and from the way he could barely stand straight, he was a drink away from passing out.

"You should know we can't have any fun without protection," Mili teased, running a hand down his face. "I'm going to run up to my room real quick. Why don't you go get us a drink and meet me back here?"

His gaze dropped to her breasts, and she rolled her eyes in disgust, masking it before he met her stare again.

"My cock is going to look so good in your mouth," the guy slurred.

Jesus fuck, I wanted to strangle him right there. Mili hadn't even realized we were watching, and Kade's jaw clenched as he forced himself to stay still.

"Go get another drink," she urged with a seductive smile. "I'll be right back."

He nodded eagerly as she walked away. With each step she took, she relaxed, taking her time going down the hall. She wasn't coming back; she fully expected him to be so wasted that he'd forget about her. Once again, the way she controlled the situation surprised me. I wondered if she ever lost it.

Kade strolled up to the guy, getting in his way so he couldn't go back to the bar. I moved beside him, and the guy barely gave us a glance until Kade slid his pack of cigarettes from his pocket.

"Want one, man?" Kade asked, holding a cigarette out.

"Hell yes." The guy took the cigarette, stumbling as he looked for the exit.

"Shit," I mumbled, patting my pockets. "Left the lighter in the car. You good to go to the parking lot?"

"Sure, it's not like we can smoke in here anyway." The guy laughed, his eyes losing focus as he looked at us.

We let him walk in front of us, and I scanned the hall, making sure no one saw us leaving with him.

"Here," Kade said under his breath, holding out the car key. "You follow."

I frowned. "Who the fuck says you get all the fun?"

He scowled. "Fine."

As we got outside, we played rock, paper, scissors for the second time tonight. We used to do this all the time as kids when we couldn't agree, but as adults, we barely ever had to do it because we usually agreed on everything. Until Mili came into our lives.

I chuckled when I won again, making Kade curse under his breath. He unlocked the car before pretending to search for a lighter. I kept my eyes on the guy as he went to his car and pulled out a bottle of whiskey.

"Nice car," I lied, pretending to be in awe of his beat-up Porsche. "I bet the women love that."

"They do. I'm hoping to impress the bitch I met tonight with it." He lit his cigarette after Kade tossed him the lighter. "I'm Pete."

"Gray," I said, not caring if he knew my name. He wasn't going to survive long enough to tell anyone.

Pete gave Kade the lighter back, not noticing that neither of us were smoking with him. I gave Kade a side eye, shocked he hadn't lit one up. Apparently, Mili's words about leaving evidence had stuck with him.

"You got a wife?" Kade asked him.

"Nah," Pete answered after blowing out a long drag of smoke. "You?"

I shook my head. "Too many ladies to be tied down by one."

Pete bellowed a laugh. "You got that right, man."

"Kids?" Kade asked, trying to sound interested instead of pissed off, but he wasn't doing half as good a job as Mili had. He was staring at Pete like he wanted to stab him in the neck. But at least we knew this asshole would have no one missing him.

"Nope," Pete said unevenly. "Thanks for the smoke, but I have someone waiting for me."

"Can I take this baby for a drive?" I asked, hoping my voice was hitting the excitement I needed for him to stay interested. I knew his type. He was cocky and loved to brag—whether it be to men or women. He wanted people to think he was important.

"I would, but like I said, I have a woman waiting."

"Come on," I coaxed. "I saw you with her, and she was smitten. She'll wait for ten minutes. I just want to tell my friends that I was behind the wheel of a car like this."

He hesitated, and I was surprised he was suspicious with how drunk he was. After a few moments, he finally nodded slowly. Digging his keys out of his pockets, he handed them to me before getting in the passenger seat. Biting back my grin, I glanced at Kade before getting in the Porsche.

"You live around here?" I asked as I started the engine, immediately noticing it wasn't as smooth as it should be. This guy treated his car like shit.

"No, here for the conference."

Pulling out of the parking lot, I turned toward the mountain road, opposite of town. I revved the engine, and my head hit the seat when I accelerated.

"Whoa." Pete laughed nervously, grabbing the dashboard. "Careful."

"I need some advice. How do you get the ladies?" I asked, acting curious. "I saw you dancing with the black-haired woman, and she looked like she didn't want you. Then, in the hall, she was all but panting after you. What's your secret?"

Pete relaxed, shooting me a smirk. "They all want it. Even if they play hard to get."

They. This fucking prick had probably forced himself on women in the past. I was doing this because he did it to Mili, but at least I was ridding the world of one more dirtbag at the same time. Headlights appeared in my mirror, and when they blinked three times, alerting me that it was Kade, I shifted gears. Pete sucked in a breath when I turned a corner without slowing down.

"I think we should go back," he said, shaking his head as if trying to think straight.

"You know, driving drunk is dangerous," I murmured, letting my voice grow cold. "Especially on roads like this."

"You're drunk?" Pete screeched. "And you asked to drive my car? Not fucking cool."

I threw my head back and laughed. "No, you are. I wonder how many other drunk drivers have lost control and gone over the cliff. I should probably look that up later."

Pete was full-on sweating now. We were coming up on another curve, and he blew out a breath when I slowed down. But instead of turning with the road, I kept the wheel straight.

"What the hell are you doing?" he screamed.

He leaned over the center console to try and grab the wheel, and I threw my elbow into his face. His nose started gushing blood, and he choked as he held his face. I could have hit him harder to knock him out, but I wanted him alert for this.

"Please," he cried. "I didn't do anything to you."

"You touched what isn't yours."

With that, I let go of the wheel and punched him in the face to make sure he didn't have a chance to recover before it was too late. Straightening the car out again, I pushed open my door before using my other hand to unbuckle his seat belt. His yelling was garbled as he attempted to shake off my hit. Taking a deep breath, I jumped out of the Porsche and hit the ground, with my shoulder and hip taking most of the fall before I rolled over the pavement.

The car hadn't been going that fast, but I jumped out close enough to the guardrail that it hit before it could stop on its own. I watched, not getting off the ground, worried for a second that the speed wasn't enough. Until Kade drove up behind and clipped the back bumper. The metal of the old guardrail bent as the wooden posts slipped from the dirt. Since the windows were down, I heard Pete screaming as it teetered on the edge. Kade reversed and then drove forward, this last bump enough to send the Porsche over the cliff.

By the time I jumped to my feet and ran to the edge, the car had already hit. The headlights were still on, showing exactly when it landed. The drop was three hundred feet. No way he survived that. Especially since he wasn't buckled. He probably flew from the car, and no one would ever know I was there. We'd keep up with his death investigation once he was found, but I wasn't worried in the slightest about getting caught.

"Let's go," Kade called out from the car.

With one last glance down the steep cliff, I studied the front of our SUV, seeing a scratch or two but nothing super noticeable. I hopped into the passenger seat, and Kade sped off. My heart was still racing from adrenaline, and I shot Kade a grin.

"The guy died terrified out of his mind," I informed him.

"Good." Kade jerked a nod to the back seat. "You should change before we go back to the room or she's going to figure out what we did."

My clothes were full of dirt and specks of blood from hitting Pete. Peeling off my shirt, I reached over the seat and dug into the bag until I found a new one.

"We just killed for her," I muttered, voicing my thoughts out loud.

"I know."

"We don't do that for anyone outside the crew."

Kade gritted his teeth. "I know."

"Because it's more than just sex with her. At least for me."

I glanced at him, knowing even though he didn't answer, he agreed. And I wasn't sure what the hell that meant for us. We'd shared girls in the past, but only in the bedroom. It was for sex, and that was all.

But Mili, she was different.

25

Milina

Confusion swept through me as I sat in the dark corner of the bar. Something wasn't right, and I had a feeling Kade and Gray had something to do with it. I hadn't spoken to them in a couple of days, ever since coming back from Roseville. I was still shaken from knowing they'd heard my entire conversation with Rhett. They knew Joel's name. I wasn't worried about them trying to look into him like I knew they would. They wouldn't find anything helpful. I didn't even care too much that they knew about Caleb. Again, they'd never be able to find him.

The thing that had put a weight on my chest was that they'd seen my weakness. They'd gotten a peek into the hellhole of abuse I'd lived through, and I could see the pain they felt for me every time I looked at them. I detested it. And opening up to Gray had only made it worse. I didn't want to share my life with any of them. I should have just shot

Rhett in the head, but no. I wanted to make sure he knew it was me who killed him.

My phone rang, bringing me back to the present. My stomach flipped when I saw Rylan's name on the screen. I'd been avoiding him too. Although I doubted he wanted to see me after the picture Kade had sent him. Rushing out of my chair, I jogged to the entrance, answering the phone as I ducked out of the bar.

"Hi, Rylan."

"Why didn't you tell me you were back in town?"

I chuckled. "I honestly thought you'd reconsidered after what happened."

"I told you I'd see you for our date."

"How did you know I was already back?"

"The crew aren't the only ones with ears in the city."

I leaned against the old bricks. "Are those ears hearing anything about me?"

"Nice try. You'll have to go on that date to find out."

I grinned, not remembering the last time someone had tried so hard to do something with me that didn't involve sex. I stepped to the side when a group of guys strutted down the sidewalk to go into the bar. One of them shot me a flirty grin before they disappeared through the door.

"Why doesn't it bother you?" I asked, turning my attention back to my phone call.

"What? That you're seeing other guys? Especially two guys who hate me?" He sounded amused, which only enhanced my confusion about him. "Are you seeing anyone other than Kade and Gray?"

"I'm not seeing them," I snapped. "I've just fallen into bed with them a couple of times. And there's been no one else since coming to town. I've been too busy to find guys to sleep with."

That wasn't exactly true. I didn't want any other guys—except these three. I ran a hand down my face, seriously considering just leaving Ridgewood now. They were getting too close. I was thinking about them more than I should be. They were figuring out my secrets, and I couldn't let that happen.

"How was the rest of your business trip?" he asked, sounding genuinely curious.

"If it makes you feel better, I almost killed Gray and Kade."

He let out a laugh, thinking I was joking even though I was actually dead-ass serious. When I found out they'd heard my conversation with Rhett, that had been my first thought. I never left witnesses. If it had been anyone else, I would have shot them without hesitation. But I couldn't. I couldn't pull the trigger because I didn't want them dead. And that was a problem. I'd come here to use them for a job, but somehow they were forcing me to feel things I'd long ago given up on.

"What are you doing tonight?" he asked.

"Why? Going to ask me on that date?"

"Depends on where you are."

I sighed. "I can't tonight. I'm working."

He paused. "With the crew?"

"Nope. By myself this time."

Someone pushed open the bar door, and the music got loud until the door shut.

"Sounds like a good time," Rylan said, sounding a bit upset.

"I'm not partying. My work takes me to interesting places."

"Like where?"

"I'm at some dive bar on the north side." I craned my neck to look at the sign. "The Bar Room. Real original name."

He chuckled. "That place has been around since before I was born."

"You never answered me." I tapped my fingers against my tight jeans. "Why don't you care that I slept with Kade and Gray?"

"Because I think I'm a better man than them, and I plan to win you over."

His words shocked me into silence as a warm flush traveled down my neck. "Do you talk to all the women like this?"

"No, Mili. I'm only talking to you."

I cleared my throat. "I'm available tomorrow night. For the date."

"I can't. I have a meeting. How about Friday night?"

That was two days from now, and I had no plans at all this weekend. "Sure."

"Can't wait to see you, Mili. Stay safe tonight."

"Goodnight, Mayor."

I slipped my phone back into the clutch I had looped around my wrist. My stomach was still fluttering from the phone call with Rylan as I went back inside the bar. It was busy but not packed, which was perfect. If only one of the men in here would dance with me. At first, I thought it was an off night, but as I walked back to my table, I knew I wasn't imagining it. The second any man in here met my eyes, they averted their gazes just as fast.

My plan was not going to work if I couldn't make people remember me tonight. I was dressed to perfection. Blue jeans that stuck to me like a second skin. My black crop top dipped down, revealing more than an eyeful of my breasts. My eyes were surrounded by thick black and gray makeup. I looked like a girl who loved to party at these kinds of bars. But not one guy had asked me to dance or bought me a drink, and I'd been here for an hour.

I panicked for a moment, wondering if somehow people were finding out I was Sapphire. But no, it wasn't that. There were a few women in here that I knew were close to the crew, and they weren't ignoring me like the men were. Although I noticed a couple of them giving me scathing glares.

I needed an alibi tonight, and this place was perfect. The crew owned it, and it was one establishment where there weren't cameras. There was enough of a crowd for people not to notice when I slipped out, but it small was enough that I'd get noticed and could prove I was there if asked. But no one was fucking paying attention to me. I checked the time, clicking my tongue. I had a backup bar to go to, but I didn't like it as much as this one.

Cursing under my breath, I stalked to the bar. "Can I pay my tab, please?"

The bartender glanced at me as he wiped a glass. "You're all set."

I frowned. "I had three drinks."

"They're on the house."

Like all the other men in here, he quickly looked away from me and hurried to the other end of the bar, even though there were no customers waiting. Narrowing my eyes, I bit the inside of my cheek before hopping over the counter and striding to the bartender.

"Hey, you can't be back here," the guy said, panic swirling in his eyes.

"Who paid for my drinks?" I asked.

"You're covered," he stammered out, taking a large step away from me.

I inched closer to him, growing more curious with each step. It was like he was terrified to be within five feet of me.

"Do you know me?" I asked, tilting my head.

"What? No—"

"Then why won't you or any other guy in here look me in the eye?"

"You're their girl," he said quietly.

My heart stuttered. "Excuse me?"

"The crew," he muttered. "Kade and Gray. Everyone knows that you're theirs."

"Everyone?" I choked out. "Who the fuck said that?"

He frowned. "They did."

"They?" I growled, a fire lighting through me. "Kade and Gray said I'm their girl?"

He nodded. "At their club last night. People were asking about you, and they told the entire club you were theirs and off-fucking-limits. Those were their exact words."

"People don't even know me here," I mumbled, thinking out loud.

"Uh, everyone knows you. You've been hanging out with them for a couple of months now." The bartender was a bit calmer and more open since I was keeping my distance from him. "Talk on the north side flies."

"Those fucking assholes," I seethed.

He threw up his hands. "I'm sorry, but I don't want to get involved."

I grinned. "Of course. Thanks for letting me know."

With rage coursing through me, I hopped back over the bar counter, scouting the crowd until I found someone I could use. One guy was blatantly staring at me from one of the tables, even as his friends were trying to discourage him. Fluffing my hair, I walked over to him and straddled his lap. His hands went to my hips, his fingers already digging into my skin.

His leather cut told me he was in a biker club, and although I vaguely recognized his patch, I didn't know which club it was. He was at least ten years older than me, with long black hair that had a few gray streaks. He smiled, and he was handsome enough. His brown eyes screamed trouble, but that didn't make me shy away. He could be a monster, and I'd still eat him for breakfast. Because I was the largest threat in this place. They just didn't know it.

"Do you know who I am?" I asked, slowly biting my lip.

"My boys tell me that you're spoken for." His eyes stayed on my mouth. "But if that were true, why are you on my lap?"

I avoided his question. "Dance with me?"

"Sure, sweetheart."

I nearly lost it when he slapped my ass while walking to the dance floor. Reining it in, I let him wrap his hands around me while we began dancing. I didn't have time to seduce anyone else in here. I needed to leave in twenty minutes. If I danced through a few songs with the biker, I'd be seen enough for people to remember I was here.

I just had to get through it without killing him.

I dodged out of the way when he tried kissing me, grinding on him to the beat of the song. I could feel the heat of eyes on me, and nerves skated up my spine. My idea might be working too well. They'd all remember I was here. Hopefully, it wouldn't be a big scene when I left so I could slip away quietly.

"Playing hard to get?" he asked gruffly.

"Why are you in a hurry?" I asked, trying to keep it flirty.

I yelped in surprise when he grabbed my chin hard enough to bruise. His eyes locked on to mine, hunger burning in them.

"I can see why the crew wants you," he rasped. "You look downright fuckable."

"Let me go," I snarled, giving him one chance to remove his hand before I did it myself. Fuck my alibi; it wasn't worth dealing with him.

"You're mine for the night."

He leaned down to kiss me but was ripped away before my knee connected with his balls. Shock filtered through me when I found Kade standing next to me, his gun pressed against the biker's forehead. I didn't need to look over my shoulder to know who was holding on to me. How the hell had Kade and Gray gotten here so fast? I figured they'd hear about it, but I had planned to be long gone. So much for my fucking alibi now.

"Making trouble, Rebel?" Gray murmured as he rested his chin on my shoulder.

"Me?" I forced out a laugh. "I'm not the one storming into a bar with guns raised."

"What the hell are you doing?" the biker spat at Kade.

"One question," Kade said, his voice dangerously quiet. "Did you know who she was when you started dancing with her?"

I wanted to scream that I was nobody. I wasn't theirs. Kade had no right to try and come to my rescue. I didn't want it, and I sure as fuck didn't need it. But I kept control, biting my tongue as the biker's friends edged closer, their weapons tight in their hands. One wrong thing, and this whole bar was going to end up in a damn shootout.

"She's a bitch who wanted me." The biker laughed gruffly, apparently not giving a shit that a gun was pressed to his skull.

Kade gritted his teeth, his finger resting on the trigger. I didn't try to move from Gray's grip, even when it loosened as he shifted to lean closer to Kade.

"We're friendly with his motorcycle club," he muttered to Kade, keeping his words quiet.

"Keep the peace and just go," I said, glaring at the side of Kade's head. "This is none of your business."

Gray chuckled. "You're our business."

"Why?" I hissed. "Because you told the city I'm yours? Spreading lies isn't smart, Gray."

"Look at that," the biker said, staring at me with a smirk on his lips. "Doesn't sound like she wants to be yours. So you two can fuck off and let me finish what I started."

"We don't care that you party in our city," Kade grated out. "But you know the rules. Disrespecting us doesn't happen."

The biker scoffed. "She came up to me."

"Get the fuck out of here," Gray demanded, letting me go and stepping beside me. He tried pulling me behind him, but I planted my feet, staying between them.

"Sure. But I'm taking her with me."

I raised an eyebrow. "No, thanks. A dance was enough."

His jaw clenched at my words, but he stayed still as Kade finally took the gun off the biker's head. The bikers surrounding us were tense but still not intervening. My gut twisted, and I realized doing this had been a mistake. I thought I could have a night out in this town without Kade or Gray finding me. I underestimated them, and now I needed to get the hell out of here so I could do what I planned.

"I'm just going to go..." I trailed off, taking a step back.

"No," the biker snarled. "You started all this by throwing yourself at me. Fucking slut."

I froze when he whipped his gun out, aiming it straight at me. There was no time to pull my own weapon out. My heart was in my throat as I stared at the biker. If I had observed him for a minute before going up to him, I would have known he was a bad choice. But my anger at learning what Kade and Gray had done distracted me. Along with being on a time crunch. This was why I needed to keep my relationship with them just business. I was getting sloppy because they were in my fucking head.

"Put it down," Kade ordered.

"Make your choice, sweetheart," the biker drawled. "A bullet or my dick. Which one are you going to choose?"

"Shoot me," I taunted. "Because the only way your small dick will go anywhere near me is if I'm dead."

Rage flared in his eyes, and his finger went to the trigger. I went rigid when a shot rang out through the small bar. It took me a moment to realize it wasn't the biker who'd shot—it was Kade. The biker fell to his knees, and blood seeped through his shirt from where Kade's bullet had pierced his stomach. The room erupted in yelling, and I turned to see more than a few crew members coming to back up Kade and Gray.

"Fuck," I muttered, glancing at my watch. I needed to leave now to make it in time. Gray's eyes locked on to mine and he frowned, watching me inch back. But he wouldn't leave Kade's side. Not when there were so many weapons raised at them.

"I didn't ask you to do this," I told him coldly. "This isn't my fault."

"I never said it was," Gray replied. "Where're you going?"

"Away from here," I muttered.

"Mili, wait."

I ignored Gray's call and pushed through the wall of men, making it to the exit. I couldn't stop the relief that seeped in when it stayed silent. No more gunshots rang out, meaning Kade and Gray were going to be fine. I shouldn't care either way, but I did. Shaking off the nerves, I glanced at Kade's black Jaguar parked on the street. I was tempted to boost it but didn't need them chasing after me tonight. Instead, I found a gray sedan, and it was my lucky night because it was unlocked. I took my small tool out of my clutch after shutting the door. Hotwiring it only took me a minute, and then I was racing down the street.

As I drove, I pulled out my phone and called Caleb.

"No changes?" I asked him once he answered.

"No. Ryan is still scheduled to meet with Juan and Vic in fifteen minutes," Caleb answered.

"Good. I'll be there in two."

"Let me know when it's done, and I'll send the message from his email, telling the crew he changed his mind about the job."

I wasn't sure if it was just bad luck that someone who worked with Joel wanted to run a job with the crew or if they were on to me. But either way, it wasn't fucking happening. It was a good thing Caleb had been keeping an eye on the men we used to work with. Hacking into Vic and Juan's email was difficult. But it was easy to snoop into Ryan's email. He hadn't been in Joel's inner circle, but he knew me. And everything would be ruined if anyone from the crew even mentioned my name in front of him. I couldn't take that chance. Which was why the meeting wasn't happening.

"I'll text you when it's done," I said before hanging up. I was running late already and needed to get set up before Ryan showed up. I knew he'd enter the building from the back alley that I had just parked in. I'd scoped the place out this morning and made sure there were no cameras. No need for a mask, which would make luring him much easier.

Turning off the car, I pulled my small gun out of my clutch and stuck it in my waistband, then I hopped out after popping the trunk. Adrenaline rushed through me when I heard footsteps. Poking my head to the side, I saw Ryan walking slowly toward me. He was suspicious, seeing a car in the middle of the alley. And I was surprised he was alone. I figured I'd have to deal with at least two people.

"Excuse me," I called out in a whiny voice. "Can you help me? My tire is flat, and I can't lift my spare out of the trunk."

Ryan stopped, indecision crossing his face. Seeing him had panic flaring in my chest. He was a reminder of Joel. Of everything. My past had been coming up way too much lately. I wanted it all buried again like it had been the past five years.

"Please," I said, pretending to sniffle. "I've been stuck here for twenty minutes."

The shadows were hiding my face, and he finally moved closer. I dropped my head, letting my hair cover my face until he was next to me.

"All your tires look fine," he said uneasily.

"My mistake." I lifted my face, and recognition flared in his eyes when he met my gaze. "You shouldn't be here, Ryan."

His eyes hardened. "You're supposed to be dead."

"Hmm, I guess neither of us should be here then."

Before he could make a move, I gripped the tire iron and swung it at his head. I didn't hit him hard because I didn't want to leave a trail of blood on the ground. But it was enough for him to stagger, giving me a chance to kick him between the legs. When he doubled over, I grabbed his arm and yanked him closer before pushing him into the trunk. He began struggling, kicking me in the gut before I could get his feet off the ground.

"Bitch," he choked out as I shoved his face into the carpet in the trunk. "When they find out you're here—"

"And that's why you won't have a chance to tell them."

I pulled my handgun out of my jeans, pressing it to the back of his head. He froze, but I didn't hesitate, squeezing the trigger. Nerves swarmed me when the shot echoed in the alley. I needed to get out of here before someone came looking. I grunted, lifting his body into the trunk. I slammed it shut and glanced around. I was still alone, but I knew it wouldn't last long.

Getting back into the car, I drove off, making sure to stay within the speed limit as I left Ridgewood. I already had gasoline and matches two hours from here where I was going to burn the car. It was in the middle of nowhere, and by the time someone stumbled onto it, his body would be burned enough that it would be impossible to identify, except with maybe dental records. But that didn't worry me. Joel's men had always been trained not to be in any system. Even if they had dental records, they'd never match them.

As long as the crew didn't catch me leaving the city with the body, I'd be fine. I'd wanted an alibi just in case, but that had obviously blown up in my face. I calmed down once I reached the edge of town, knowing I was home free.

For now, at least.

26

Kade

"She's not going to come," Gray muttered, leaning back on the couch. "Not after last night."

I continued pacing in front of the window, my anger making it impossible for me to keep still. "She'll come. She's not scared of us. And I can guarantee she's pissed that we told the city she's ours."

We were in our private room above the club, and I peered through the one-way glass, waiting to see her come through the front doors. Last night had been a shit show, and she'd just disappeared from it all. Vic and Juan were angrier with me than ever because the biker I shot ended up dying. And now other motorcycle clubs were not happy. But I'd deal with that after we talked to Mili.

"I'm just gonna say, she probably never would have egged on the biker if you didn't try making her feel trapped," Gray said quietly. "You knew she would flip out."

I ground my teeth. "The bartender told us she'd been there an hour before he blurted out what I said at the club."

"Yeah, but she didn't get the biker's attention until she found out."

"I don't know why the fuck we're arguing about this. That's not even the reason we need to talk to her."

The other night played back in my head again. Gray and I were having some drinks at the club until we overheard a group of guys talking about Mili. Not many in town knew her name, but it was obvious who he was talking about when he described her. And when they started discussing what they wanted to do to her, I lost it. Fucking saw red and told the entire club she was off-limits.

Looking through the glass, I spotted her pushing her way through the thick crowd, and my heart skipped. This wasn't going to be a fun conversation, but we needed fucking answers. She was messing with business now, and it had to end. Either she fell in line, or we needed to get her to leave Ridgewood.

A few seconds later, the door swung open, and she strode inside. If she was nervous about what happened yesterday, she wasn't showing it. Not that I expected her to. She was dressed casually in leggings and a T-shirt. Her hair was pulled back, revealing the small bruises that asshole biker left on her jaw last night. Her eyes trailed over each of us, most likely taking note that we'd come unarmed. Something I doubted she did.

"You needed to talk?" she asked, not coming any closer to us.

"You left us last night," Gray said, staying on the couch.

"After you started it. I didn't tell you to shoot that prick. Or help me at all." Her gaze fell to me. "Or tell your fucking city that I was your girl."

And that was why she was here. Not because we asked her to come, but because she wanted to make it clear that what we did wasn't going to stand.

"How the hell did you even find me last night?" she asked, suspicion flitting into her gaze.

I just smirked, knowing it would aggravate her.

"Are you tracking me?" Her voice got higher as she thought of that. I was sure once she left, she'd be checking everything we came into contact with to see if we'd bugged it.

"We have eyes everywhere," Gray murmured. "We know where you are in this city the second you're in public. Especially on the north side."

"Where'd you go after you left the bar?" I asked, trying to keep my voice casual while getting to the reason we were here.

"Home. After everything, I needed a nice bath to calm down."

Her lie fell from her lips, and if I hadn't already known what she was really up to, it would have been easy to believe. My stomach knotted, wondering what else she'd lied to us about.

"Interesting." Gray jumped up, and she tensed for a moment until he turned away from her, heading to the bar. "Care to explain this, then?"

Her curiosity got the better of her, and she finally inched forward, leaving the doorway. I stayed where I was while Gray grabbed the remote, flicking on the screen that was mounted behind the counter. Camera angles from outside the club appeared on the screen until he pushed a button, playing the tape.

The screen wasn't large, and she moved closer, her eyes glued to the TV. I watched her, studying her reaction as she stared at the video of herself. The one recorded last night of her shoving a guy in a trunk before shooting him and driving off. Her entire body locked up, the blood draining from her face. For the first time since we'd met her, we'd completely blindsided her. From the genuine shock on her face, she had no idea she'd been on camera. Probably because at some point she had checked for them. Gray and I put up temporary cameras before the meeting Vic was supposed to have so we didn't need to worry about an ambush. When the guy didn't show up, we played the tape. Mili killing him was the last thing I expected to see.

I silently stepped to the side, putting myself in the way of the door. A second later, she whirled around with the clear intent to bolt. She caught my stare, and her eyes narrowed.

"Get out of my way," she hissed.

"How the hell did you know about that meeting?" I asked, my voice hard. "You spying on us?"

Gray crept toward her as she faced me. "Or did you know that Ryan guy?"

She turned, making sure neither of us were out of her sight as she backed up until she hit the window. Her eyes were darting between us, as if figuring out what to tell us.

"No lies," I snapped. "You're fucking with our business. Vic and Juan want answers."

"They know too?" she asked, swallowing hard.

"They were there when we watched the tape." Gray crossed his arms. "Why'd you do it?"

After a deep breath, her unfazed demeanor was back, and she waved her hand dismissively. "He wouldn't have been good for your business."

"And how do you know that?" I stopped stalking toward her when her fingers twitched, most likely getting ready to pull whatever weapon she'd brought.

"Because I worked with him in the past," she replied stiffly. "And he screwed me over."

"So he deserved to die?" Gray asked with a frown.

"Why'd you do it?" I asked at the same time.

"Because he was going to interfere with my business," she stated coldly.

I raised an eyebrow. "How?"

"That's not your concern."

"Jesus fuck," I snarled. "Do you realize what you did? Vic and Juan think you're going behind our back to screw us over. Just fucking tell us how you knew and why you did it."

She sighed. "All you need to know is that he would have fucked you over if you worked with him."

"We're going to pull out of the Panther job," Gray murmured. "The crew won't have any part of it if we think you're going to hurt us."

Her lips parted in surprise. "The payout for that job is more than you make in a fucking year. You're really going to turn that down?"

"Don't care," I said bluntly.

"He's early," Gray interrupted the conversation as he looked at the screen, which now showed the security cameras at the club. I saw the guy walk in through the front entrance, and blew out a breath, looking back at Mili.

"We need to talk about this later," I said gruffly. "But if you want us to work with you, then we need answers."

"You scheduled a meeting for the same time you wanted to talk to me?"

"Go," I demanded. "You being here for this will only make it worse."

She tilted her head. "Why?"

"Because we're meeting with the MCs to try and fix what happened last night," Gray answered. "And Juan and Vic are coming too."

I could see her calculating the odds of getting out of here if things turned bad. Apparently, she figured she could handle herself against us, but she was smart enough to know five to one wouldn't work out in her favor.

"Hmm," she hummed out, suddenly rushing toward me. "Speaking of last night, you need to fix it."

My grin was smug. "Fix what?"

"Tell everyone you made a mistake. That I'm not yours. Or Gray's."

Her chest brushed mine, and I looked down at her, making sure she didn't miss my answer. "No."

My breath hitched when something sharp pressed against my jeans, right where my dick was. She smirked at my reaction, pressing whatever she had in her hand harder against my crotch.

"I fucking *dare* you to try to keep your claim on me," she whispered, her eyes lighting up in challenge.

There was a knock before a new voice filled the room. "Am I interrupting?"

I glanced at the doorway, just now realizing that Mili had left it open when she came in. Most likely for an easy way out if the conversation went south. The biker we were meeting with filled the doorway, his wary stare on me and Mili.

"No. She's just leaving," I said, nearly sagging with relief when she backed away. I caught a peek of her blade before it disappeared in her pocket. "This isn't finished, Little Hellion. We still want answers."

I purposely didn't use her name in front of the biker, knowing it would only piss her off all over again. She studied me for a moment before turning on her heel and walking toward the biker. She slowed her steps, studying him and his leather cut.

"You're not wearing the same patch as the bikers I saw last night," she stated, making Gray groan.

"No. I'm here as the middleman," he answered, sizing her up. "Who are you?"

I opened my mouth, but Mili spoke first. "I'm the reason your biker friend is dead. If you have an issue with that, then you can talk to me."

Shock coursed through me, wondering what the hell she was doing. Was she trying to put the blame on herself? Why? It sure as fuck wasn't to protect me. The guy raised his green eyes to me, arching an eyebrow.

"I thought you shot him?" he asked me.

"He did," Mili piped up. "But only because I started it. The asshole touched me. If I'd gotten to my gun first, I would have done it."

His gaze fell back on her. "You with their crew?"

"No." I could hear the smile in her voice. "But if you ever get tired of your motorcycle and need a good car, I'm the one you can call."

He stared at her for a moment before chuckling. "You remind me of someone I know."

"Why?"

"Because you both scream trouble."

Her body relaxed slightly, not seeing him as a threat. "Only when it finds me."

He extended his hand. "I'm Don. President of the Dusty Devils."

She shook his hand, not introducing herself. "Nice to meet you. I'll leave so you big men can get down to business."

Without another glance at me or Gray, she bounded down the stairs. Don glanced over his shoulder, watching her leave before turning his attention back to us. Gray moved behind the bar and pulled some beers out of the fridge, offering one to Don.

"You heard her," I said, leaning against the counter. "The guy was feeling her up. In our city. We gave him a chance to walk away, and he chose violence."

Don seemed to ponder that as he took a swig of beer. "She yours?"

I glanced at Gray. "Yes."

That one word would change it all now, and Mili was going to rage when she found out. It wouldn't just be the people in our city who saw her as ours now. It would be the entire criminal circle we ran in. Don would tell his MC, and it would spread from there.

"If that's true, why did she have a pocketknife to your junk when I walked in?" he asked, a twinkle of amusement in his gaze.

"She doesn't like being told what to do," Gray grumbled.

The back door opened, and I straightened up when Vic and Juan joined us. They nodded to Don before turning their scowls on me. We made polite conversation with Don, making sure he knew what happened last night. The other biker club had no reason to retaliate since I technically did nothing wrong. I was protecting my girl—in my city. Or that was what they'd believe. They didn't have to find out Mili would rather slice off my dick than be called mine.

"I'll talk to the MC president, but I don't think there will be an issue," Don assured us. "This isn't the first time they've had trouble with that guy."

I really didn't care either way. We could have handled the MC, and I was itching for a fight to take out my anger. Or a race. I needed to do something or I would go insane. Don finished his beer and stood from the stool.

"The Aces need an extra vehicle," Don said, mentioning another MC that we did business with. "It's a busy month."

"No problem," I muttered. We supplied their cars to ship the guns they sold, and it was an easy job. We never had issues with the Aces, and they always paid their bills.

Don left, shutting the door behind him. Vic and Juan focused on me, and I bit my tongue to keep quiet.

"Did you talk to her?" Juan asked.

"Yes," Gray answered before I could. "She told us she used to work with the guy, and that he was a piece of shit."

"How did she know about the meeting?" Vic snapped. "We're careful to make sure our business dealings stay quiet. She clearly knew every detail about it."

"She won't tell us," I admitted gruffly, moving to grab another beer.

"Unacceptable." Juan stared at the security camera screen. "She's in your city, and she agreed to respect it. We have a fucking reputation to uphold. Between her killing a potential business partner and getting you to kill for her, she's done too much."

Vic nodded in agreement. "Get her under control. Or we will."

I bristled, anger rushing through me. "What will you do?"

Vic stared at me. "What changed?"

"What?" I asked, falling onto the couch.

"Neither of you wanted her here, and suddenly you're puffing your fucking chest out—at me—when I threaten her." Vic kept his glare on me, waiting for an answer.

"She's *Sapphire*," Gray said, as if they should know. "She isn't someone we can bend to our will. Or get rid of. Not without consequences. She has people with special skills working for her. She's not a one-person operation."

"She's more trouble than she's worth," Juan said quietly. "Did you two forget how large we are? We aren't some small-time gang. We can handle her."

Vic clicked his tongue, looking at me. "And we will if you two can't. I want her connections. I want her to work for us. If that's not possible, we get rid of her."

I kept a blank expression on my face, nodding as if I agreed with them. They didn't know her like we did. If we killed her, she'd bring us down with her. But that wasn't what was plaguing my soul. It was the fact that I didn't want her dead. Or gone. I wanted her to stay here. No matter how infuriatingly angry she got me every time she opened her mouth. But that wouldn't happen. Not if Vic and Juan didn't trust her. The other option was to force her out of Ridgewood.

"We have to go run a job," Gray lied, shooting to his feet.

"What job?" Juan asked.

"Off the books," I replied, following Gray to the door. "A favor for someone."

"Figure it out with her," Vic called after us. "Or we'll intervene."

I gritted my teeth as I went down the stairs. Ridgewood was mine and Gray's. But the crew was still theirs. And they would do anything to make sure nothing happened to their legacy. They were the bosses, and our men followed their orders over ours. We answered to them. But when it came to Mili, I wanted them to stay the fuck out of it.

"She's not going to suddenly start listening," Gray mumbled as we pushed through the crowd until we got outside. "And she won't tell us anything she doesn't want to share, no matter what we threaten her with."

"I know." I leaned against my Jaguar, a heaviness filling my limbs. "We need to get her to leave. For good."

"Force her out?"

I nodded. "Yeah. Either she stays and Vic and Juan get involved, or we make her leave."

"She doesn't want to go. She won't make it easy."

"We're not going to give her a choice." I could feel Gray's stare, but just kept looking ahead. "We're going to push her past her limits and hope to fuck she doesn't kill us. Which will still be a huge possibility."

"We only got a peek of her past, but it was enough to know that if we do something that horrible to her, she won't forgive us," Gray said carefully. "You can admit she's gotten to you since she came to town. I know she got me."

"She either hates us and leaves—or stays and possibly dies or gets blackmailed into work for the crew." I finally turned my head, meeting his stare. "Which would you want for her?"

Gray didn't answer, but he didn't have to. Because I felt the same way. I fucking wished the lies I'd told the biker president were true. That she was our girl. Last night, when I shot the asshole, I didn't give it a second thought. I saw his hands on her and went into a blind rage. I wanted her. But if the tattoo on her spine was anything to go by, she wanted to live her life free. She didn't want to answer to anyone or be tied down. And if we showed her that was exactly what we wanted, she'd bolt in a heartbeat.

Which was why I planned to use that to get her to leave town.

27

Milina

"This is where we're going?" I asked as Rylan helped me out of the car.

He raised an eyebrow. "Is this not a good enough place for a date?"

"It's great," I said quickly, not enjoying how awkward I was feeling. "I'm just surprised."

"Why?"

"I was expecting a classy, five-star restaurant."

He chuckled, holding the door open for me. "Because I'm the mayor?"

"Yes."

"I didn't grow up with money," he said quietly. "I grew up here. It's still my community. That's why I stayed on the north side even when I went into city politics."

The building we stepped into had dim lighting, and a lady walked up to us with a wide smile. I glanced down the short hall, hearing music from behind the closed doors. I'd never been here, but it was one of the places I'd researched before coming to Ridgewood.

"Welcome, Mayor," the lady greeted him. "Your table is ready."

Rylan placed his hand on my lower back, leading me down the hall as I fought to relax. My body was stiff, and I took a deep breath. This was fucking ridiculous. I'd been in situations where I had to fight my way out, yet I was more nervous to be on this damn date.

Although, the conversation with Kade and Gray last night had me on edge too. They were never supposed to find out about Ryan. I needed them for the Panther job. But I refused to tell them what they wanted to know about my past.

The lady pushed open the door, and music filled the air. A smile played on my lips as I gazed around the large room. It was a jazz club and was decorated like the Prohibition period. A live band was on the stage, and the giant dance floor was packed. Women were being spun, and the atmosphere was light. We followed the lady to a table that was a little higher than the dance floor. It was a small round table, and our chairs were close.

I smoothed out my white, shimmery dress before sitting down. Rylan unbuttoned his suit jacket and shrugged out of it, putting it on the back of his chair. After ordering drinks, he scooted his chair closer, and I tore my eyes from the dancers, meeting his gaze.

"Do you not like the club?" he asked with a slight frown.

"Of course I do," I answered, giving him a smile.

"You seem more uncomfortable than when I found you outside the police station with guns aimed at you."

I straightened up, taking a deep breath. I'd learned to act natural in any setting. It wasn't the place we were in that was keeping me on edge.

"I don't date," I muttered, making him lean closer so he could hear me.

His eyes widened. "You're nervous about being on a date with me?"

"Not with you. Just being on a date in general."

I bit my tongue when he was close enough that his shoulder brushed mine. I shouldn't have blurted that out. I never shared things about myself, and even if he wasn't part of my world, it didn't mean I should trust him.

"When's the last time you were on a date?" he asked.

I didn't answer, keeping my gaze on the band. Rylan's hand gently grasped my chin, turning my head until I was staring at him.

"Part of being on a date is learning things about each other," he murmured. "I'll go first. You're the first woman I wanted to take on a date in over a year."

He was so open about his life, which was the complete opposite of the way I lived. I kept my eyes on him, debating whether to lie or tell the truth. It wasn't like this truth would reveal anything important. Pulling my face from his grip, I rolled my eyes and took a large sip of my drink.

"I haven't been on a date since I was fifteen when I went to the homecoming dance at my high school."

I giggled in amusement at the absolute shock that covered his face. He opened his mouth to respond and then closed it again before studying me as if he were trying to see if I was telling the truth.

"Why?" he finally asked. "You're my age, aren't you?"

I grinned playfully. "I don't know. How old are you?"

"I'll be thirty this year."

"Then yes, I'm around your age."

He broke our stare, taking a long sip of his whiskey. "You're telling me you haven't been on a date in, like, fifteen years?"

I shrugged. "I guess not."

"You were in a long-term relationship," he stated, watching me carefully. "Am I right?"

I bristled, not enjoying this conversation anymore. I didn't want to think about Joel tonight—or ever. The only person I'd talk to openly about him was Caleb.

"Why did you choose this club?" I asked, purposely changing the subject.

"Because I have no idea what you like," he answered. "You're a mystery, Mili. But after seeing you dance at the crew's club, I got the feeling that you enjoy dancing."

"I do," I muttered. "It feels freeing. But why this place?"

He grinned. "You think I don't know who owns this place?"

Like many other businesses in this city, the crew owned this jazz club. Although from what I could find out about it, it was one of their legitimate businesses, and it was in the middle of the city. Not completely on the north side like their other club was. But as I glanced around, I noticed more than a couple of people were stealing looks at me. Gray and Kade hadn't been kidding about rumors circulating after I'd been seen with them.

Not that I gave a fuck. I didn't care what people thought. But for some reason, I didn't want Rylan caught up in it all. And after finishing business here, I'd never be able to come back since people knew my face.

"If I avoided all the places they owned, I wouldn't have anywhere to go in my city." He chuckled, leaning back in his chair. "And I think it helps that I show my face. It makes them stay more on the legal side if they have to worry about people like me coming into their establishments."

"There's a history between the three of you." My words had him tensing, and I grew more interested.

"I knew them when we were kids," he said gruffly. "But obviously we went our separate ways."

He didn't elaborate, and I tilted my head, watching as he relaxed again. Maybe I'd been wrong about him being an open book, because he was being very tight-lipped about how he knew Kade and Gray.

"And what about you?" he asked, looking like he almost didn't want to know the answer. "You went out of town with them. You're seeing them."

"I don't see anyone," I told him bluntly, repeating what I told him on the phone last night.

"But you've slept with them. You like them."

"I tried sleeping with you too, but you refused," I teased before growing serious. "If you're looking for a wife, I'm not the right woman for you. And I never will be, Rylan. If that's what you want, then this date was a mistake."

He grabbed my wrist when I tried moving away from him. "This is not a mistake. I don't want another woman. You're the one I can't get out of my head."

"That's not exactly a good thing," I mumbled.

"I'm not stupid. I know that whatever you do isn't exactly legal." He looked around, making sure we weren't being overheard. "But I can't stay away from you. And I don't want to."

"Then let's move this somewhere more private," I purred, dragging my fingers down his shirt sleeve.

He laughed, standing up and pulling me with him. "Let's dance first."

I let him bring me to the dance floor, and my stomach fluttered with nerves as he spun me around. I had no idea how to dance like everyone else here was, but it would be fun trying. Rylan took the lead, and he knew what he was doing more than me. I grinned when he pulled me into his arms, letting all my troubles disappear as I lost myself to the upbeat music. I was light-years away from my hellish reality, and I was enjoying pretending to be just a girl who was on an innocent date.

We danced through two songs, and the floor got more crowded as the night went on. A slower song came on, and he tugged me closer, his arm wrapping around my waist. I tilted my face up, and his lips crashed onto mine. Pressing myself against him, I opened my mouth, letting him deepen the kiss. We made out like horny teenagers until another faster song began playing. His hazel eyes seemed to brighten with amusement as he spun me around again.

Until someone got a hold of my wrist and I was yanked away from him. My chest collided with someone else's, and I glared when I looked up to meet Gray's stormy gaze. Surprise jolted through me. I'd thought I'd have a longer reprieve after talking to them last night. His arm locked around my back when I attempted to pull away, and I mentally cursed myself for leaving my knife in my purse at the table.

"What the fuck are you doing here?" I hissed.

"I don't think so," he tsked, tightening his hold. "What are you doing? I think Kade and I were pretty clear when we told you that people think you're our girl. And how bad it fucking looks when people see you with someone else."

"Are you kidding?" I spat out. "I don't give a shit what other people think. You should have kept your hands to yourself if you didn't want rumors flying around. Because I sure as hell don't belong to you. Or Kade. I will do whatever I want, anywhere I want. And if you don't get your hands off me in the next few seconds, we're going to have a fucking problem."

I craned my neck, seeing Rylan arguing with Kade on the side of the dance floor. Gray slid his hand up the back of my neck, fisting my hair and forcing me to look back at him.

"You might be the great Sapphire," he murmured. "But right now—in this city—you're a girl who has the attention of everyone because you're bouncing between the men who own this town. Mixing the mayor into it was a mistake. It only adds to the talk going on about you."

"You think I care what people say about me? Or what they say about you?" I snapped. "I told you before—I am not yours. You and Kade gave me attention, so what people are saying is all on you."

"You want to spend the next few months here?" he asked, his eyes narrowing. "Then you play by our rules—"

I lifted my knee, hitting him in the balls while twisting out of his grip. He grunted, attempting to get a hold of me again, but I was already out of reach as I raced back to the table. I snatched my purse before heading straight to Rylan and Kade. Rylan saw me first, and he shook his head, not wanting me to intervene. I ignored him, slipping between him and Kade.

"It's rude to crash a date," I murmured, my voice dangerously low as I stared at Kade.

"You shouldn't be here," he replied coldly. "Especially not with him."

"I'm going home with him," I stated loudly, causing others to stare.

"No," Kade growled, wrapping his fingers around my arm. "You're coming back with me."

"You are out of your fucking mind." I opened my free hand and smashed it against his nose, ripping away when his hold went lax. "Come on, Rylan."

Grabbing Rylan's hand, I pushed through the growing crowd, hearing Kade curse behind us. I didn't hit him hard enough to break his nose, but I was sure he wouldn't be moving very fast for the next few minutes. We made it to the front entrance, and the outside silence had my ears ringing from the absence of the loud music.

"Let's go before they catch up..." I trailed off when I saw three guys surrounding Rylan's Mercedes Benz. It was clear they were part of the crew, and they all stiffened as I got closer.

"You boys better get the hell away from my car," Rylan threatened, stepping in front of me.

One of the guys scoffed. "You think we're scared of you calling the cops on us?"

Rylan unbuttoned his shirt cuffs and rolled up his sleeves. "I don't need to call anyone to deal with you."

My jaw dropped at how menacing Rylan sounded. He was nothing like the respectable mayor I'd come to know. Guilt slithered through my chest, and I darted forward, grabbing his forearm. From everything he'd told me and the things I'd learned online about him, this wasn't how he usually acted. He was careful, and he never got caught up in scandals. And now he was about to brawl gang members to protect me.

"Stop," I muttered, keeping my words quiet. "I can take care of myself. You should just go home before people hear about this."

"I'm not leaving you here—"

Anger bubbled in my veins when, once again, I was jerked away from Rylan. I caught sight of Gray's leather jacket as I opened my purse, and my heart stuttered when I realized both my knife and gun were missing. Gray tugged me farther down the sidewalk, purposefully dragging me backward, making it harder for me to get my footing.

"You really shouldn't leave your bag unattended," he taunted in my ear, stopping when we were feet away from Rylan.

I forced out a laugh. "This is way over the line of your usual pranks to get me to leave town."

"This isn't a joke." He brought my arm behind my back, bending my elbow and pulling my wrist high enough to make it hard for me to move. "You're messing with our city. People are talking about us—and not in a good way. You're making it look like we can't control a girl we're sleeping with. We don't need our enemies thinking we can't deal with things in our city."

"You can't control me," I spat out, watching as Kade got in Rylan's face in front of the car. "You're going to fucking regret this."

"You fucked up, Mili," he murmured, pushing my chest against the side of Kade's Camaro. "You took it too far. We warned you not to get with guys in Ridgewood. Especially on the north side. You asked us not to blurt out your name, and we asked you this. Yet here you are, practically fucking the mayor in the middle of one of our clubs. And let me tell you, we don't need rumors circulating where he's involved. People are going to think we're under investigation or cooperating with the fucking cops."

"That's not my problem," I snarled, pushing off the car, only for him to shove me back, pulling my arm higher.

"Let her go," Rylan demanded, moving closer to me before Kade stepped between us.

"We need to talk to her," Gray said as he opened the car door next to us. "Run along home, Mayor."

"Not happening." Rylan's eyes darted to the growing crowd around us. "This time there are witnesses. You can't kidnap a girl in front of everyone."

Kade tilted his head. "Kidnap? She's coming with us willingly."

"No the fuck I am not." I fought against Gray when he tried pushing me into the car. I wasn't worried they were going to kill me, but they were more heated than I'd ever seen, and it was smart to let them cool off before they got me alone.

Rylan went still when Kade slammed his palm against his chest, keeping him away from me. Gray was putting all his weight against me, pressing me on the car, not moving even when I crushed my heel onto his foot.

"Look at you two." Rylan huffed out a harsh laugh. "Need to show her how big you are, don't you?"

Kade smirked. "Oh, she knows."

Fury slammed into me, and I struggled harder to get free. I didn't give a fuck that this was their town. No one treated me this way.

"But don't worry," Kade continued in a low voice. "I'm sure she was thinking of you when she was worshipping my cock."

"You son of a bitch," Rylan growled.

Gray tightened his hold on me. "We'd love to keep chatting, but we have things to do. Bye, Mayor."

28

Milina

Gray kicked the back of my knees, making me fall, and he shoved me into the back seat of the Camaro. I heard the door shut while I wrestled to get out from under him.

"You two really have a death wish, don't you?" I grated out.

He captured my wrists, pressing them against my spine as he sat on top of me. "All we want to do is make sure you understand that you can't undermine us in front of the public."

"You think this was undermining you? No, this was me being nice."

Kade must have gotten into the car because we suddenly lurched forward before sharply taking a turn. Gray stayed on top of me as we drove, and my rage was quickly building. It was time to rethink my Panther plan because there was no fucking way I was working with them anymore.

"I thought you wanted to talk," I snarked when they both stayed silent.

"Once we're out of the car," Gray answered stiffly.

We didn't drive very long before the car stopped. Gray finally climbed off me, pulling me out of the car with him as Kade held open the door. My eyes darted around, quickly realizing we were in front of their usual club.

"Now, we're going to go sit at the bar and talk," Kade told me as we walked toward the door. "And if you don't, then we'll go somewhere more private."

I chuckled. "Don't trust yourselves alone with me? Probably a good idea. Even without my weapons, I could kill both of you in five different ways."

I held my breath when Gray's lips brushed my ear. "I think we've all learned by now that the best way to talk to you is when you're tied up. So if you don't want a repeat of the hotel room, then be a good girl and sit at the bar."

I was seeing red by the time Kade pulled open the door to the club. They had no idea what those words were doing to me. I'd spent years being a good fucking girl. Those days were long gone, and hell if they thought they could bend me to their will. I couldn't kill them because I wasn't stupid. Their crew members were everywhere, and I doubted I'd make it out of the club alive. But I had no plans to talk to them either.

The second we were through the doors, I dug my elbow into Gray's ribs. I planted my foot in front of his before shoving him with my free hand. He went down, and I spun around, catching Kade's wrist. He tried reaching for me with his free hand, but I was already twisting his wrist while kneeing him in the stomach. He choked out a breath as I swung him into Gray, making them both stagger to stay on their feet.

I weaved through the crowd, heading for the busy dance floor. They thought they could dictate who I spent time with? I was going to find the first semi-decent guy and walk out the back door with him. I spotted a guy standing by himself, and I sauntered up to him, wrapping my arm around his waist.

"Hey, you," I said, shooting him a wicked smile. "Want to get out of here with me?"

His surprised grin melted when he met my gaze. "I know you. You're the crew's girl."

My jaw clenched. "I think you have me confused with someone else."

His eyes trailed down me as he gently pulled my arm away from him. "No. You're definitely the girl everyone's been talking about."

The music suddenly died before Kade's voice boomed over the mic. "Everyone out. We're closing early."

People scrambled toward the door, and the guy shot me a sheepish grin. "Sorry, but I really don't want to be seen talking to Kade and Gray's girl."

"Oh my fuck. I'm not theirs," I hissed, moving forward to get lost in the bodies that were cramming toward the entrance.

"I don't think so, Rebel." Gray's arms banded around me, trapping my arms next to my sides. I whipped my head back, barely clipping his chin. He dragged me back toward the bar, and Kade popped up in front of me, reaching down and lifting my legs. I could handle myself against one of them, but without my weapons, they had me at a huge disadvantage when it was the both of them. Their hold on me was iron tight, and Kade released my legs before helping Gray smash my chest against the bar. I snarled with rage when a hand wrapped around the back of my neck, keeping me in place. My cheek was pressed against the bar top, and I saw Kade racing up the stairs to their personal room above the club.

"This is fucking done," I screeched, my palms pressing against the wood. "The deal—the Panther job. It's all gone. So have fun telling your bosses how badly you fucked up."

"We're nowhere near done," Gray murmured, his fingers staying tightly around my neck. "You've knocked us on our asses again and again ever since you came here. I think you've forgotten who we are.

We are not some low-life criminals. This is our city, and you're making us look like fucking jokes."

"I'll fucking burn your city to the ground," I threatened. "You have no idea what I can do."

"If you would have listened to us the first time, then we wouldn't be here right now," Kade said as he came back down the stairs. "We only asked one thing."

"I let you fuck me with the very clear understanding that it didn't mean anything." I kept my voice calm as every cell in my body raged. "No one fucking claims me."

"People in this city recognize you now." Kade leaned on the counter next to me. "They all think you're ours. And being seen with any other guy makes us look like fools. And out of all fucking men, we hear that you're with the mayor at one of our clubs?"

I grinned, licking my lips. "He really is a gentleman. More than I can say about the two of you. And his kisses put your mouths to shame."

"Mili, work with us," Gray said softly. "We know you need us for the Panther job. Stay here and let's plan. All we want is for you to keep up appearances."

I laughed coldly. "What is this? Good cop, bad cop?"

"In the eyes of this city, you're ours," Kade growled.

"You know what I think? I think you're possessive as fuck." I stared at Kade, not fighting against Gray's hold. "I should have known after the first night you fucked me and gave me that hickey. You can't handle seeing me with anyone else—unless it's your best friend."

Even though I was looking at him sideways, I could see his jaw muscle tick. "That's not true."

"It's not?" I questioned. "Then why do you want to make sure everyone thinks I'm yours?"

"We told you," he ground out, "it looks bad for us—"

"I'm calling bullshit," I cut him off. "Is my pussy so good that you want it all for yourself?"

I bit back a cry when Kade fisted my hair. Gray let go of my neck but moved his hand to my back to keep me pressed against the counter.

"You drive me fucking crazy," Kade murmured. "But maybe you're right. Because when I see another guy's hands on you, I want to fucking kill him."

"Like you did the other night?" I snapped. "Can't control your temper, Kade? Killing one man because he touched me?"

"Two," Gray said.

"What?"

"We've killed two men. We probably should have kept that guy alive in Roseville," Gray replied, making my stomach flip. "No one even knows we did it. Not really good to send a message. But killing that biker? That was a clear message. That you're ours."

"Why do you want to get with the mayor so bad?" Kade asked, studying me. "You plan to use him for something?"

"No, I'm using you two." I grinned. "You were nothing more than a way to get a job done. But your dick energy screwed that up. Our business is fucking done."

"So, you're leaving town?" Gray asked stiffly.

My laugh was cold. "Nope. I plan to stay and show Rylan exactly how much I like him."

"That's not going to work for us," Kade said in a low voice. "If you stay in Ridgewood, then we'll make sure everyone knows you're ours."

Gray gripped my wrists, keeping my arms on the counter as Kade leaned over me. Something cold touched my throat, and I thrashed when it got tighter. A small click had chills running down my spine, and they both released me. My hand went to my neck, and I tugged at whatever the fuck Kade had put on me. Bolting up, I spun around to see them both staring at me, their faces blank. Whipping back around, I jumped over the counter, shoving bottles to the floor so I could look in the mirror that lined the wall behind the bar.

Pressing against my throat was a thick silver chain. My fingers were shaking as I touched it, gripping the small padlock that rested on my chest. It had the crew's symbol on it, and fire scorched my veins as I turned to face them again.

"I will fucking kill you," I hissed, my glare darting between the two of them. "You think you can show the world I'm yours?"

Kade was tense as he answered. "Not the world. Just our city. We're done playing by your rules. If you stay here, then you will do the one thing we ask."

The weight of the chain felt suffocating, but I ignored it, advancing toward them. "The game we were playing was fun, but you just fucked it up. I'm done."

"You won't kill us," Gray told me, his muscles flexing as I got closer.

I cocked my head. "Why do you think that? Because we did a job together? Or because we fucked? Let me tell you something—that doesn't mean shit."

"You won't kill us because we'll make sure everyone knows it was Sapphire who did it," Kade answered. "We have videos of you from our club cameras. We know your tattoos. It's not much, but it seems you try really hard to keep your identity a secret."

My heart thudded as I stared at them. "You think I care if people find out who I am?"

"We do." Gray crossed his arms. "And we'd let everyone in our world know who you are and what you look like."

I clenched my teeth, attempting not to give them the reaction they were looking for. If any of Joel's people got word that I was alive and in California, I was fucked. I'd have to hide, and doing the Panther job would be fucking impossible.

My eyes darted between them as I inhaled a deep breath, calming my shaking muscles. I'd never lost control before, but what they'd just done nearly had me at my breaking point. Not one man had tried owning me since I escaped Joel. This piece of metal around my neck was nothing compared to what Joel had done to me, but it was a reminder of why the fuck I never got close to anyone.

Without even realizing it, I'd begun letting my guard down around these two. That had been a fucking mistake. One they were going to come to regret. My gaze snapped to the bar, and I stared at a beer glass.

Kade lunged forward, as if reading my mind. Losing my last thread of common sense, I lashed my arm out, snagging the glass the exact second Kade's fingers latched around my wrist. Gray came up, grabbing my other arm before my fist could meet Kade's cheek. My spine dug into the edge of the counter as I fought to get my wrist out of Kade's grip while still gripping the glass. His jaw ticked, and he pressed his body into mine to keep me pinned against the counter.

"You think you can threaten me?" I murmured, my voice steeped in danger. "I could kill both of you here and leave town without giving either of you a chance to expose me."

Kade's other hand went to the glass, forcing my arm down. My anger boiled over from not being able to fight my way out of this. My strength wasn't even close to theirs when combined. Gray pressed my arm against the wood while Kade finally got the leverage he needed, forcing the glass from my hold. It rolled to the floor, the shattering glass only making the tension in the room worse.

"You won't kill us," Gray said stiffly, tugging me away from the counter. He moved behind me, pulling my arms together and holding them against my ass. Before I could even think of breaking his hold, Kade was in front of me, his hand wrapping around my throat, right above the fucking collar they'd locked on me. My pulse thrashed under his hold as his grip tightened, stopping right before I lost the ability to breathe.

"So many secrets. Mili. Milina. Sapphire." Kade's voice was as cold and ruthless as his stare. I'd gotten to know them so well; it was easy to forget who they were. What they were. They were just like me. Monsters in the dark who would do anything to hold on to their power. And right now, I was a threat to their livelihood.

"You have no idea who I am," I spat out, my voice trembling with rage.

"You've given us some clues, even without meaning to," Gray whispered against my cheek. "Going on that job with you revealed a piece of your past."

Chills ran down my spine, even though I had been expecting this conversation. I never should have fucking brought them. I never wanted them to hear Joel's name. To know I used to be a weak girl who couldn't fend for herself. They saw me as someone other than Sapphire. And I fucking hated it. Sharing pieces of myself with them was never supposed to happen.

"Joel," Kade spat out the name as if it burned his tongue. "Was that the ex-boyfriend Andy was talking about?"

I pressed my lips together, having no intention of giving them anything. Kade's eyes bored into mine, as if staring hard enough would draw out my secrets.

"Caleb," he murmured in a softer voice.

Panic clawed at my chest, making me struggle against them. My reaction gave them the answer they were looking for, and I cursed at myself for not being able to rein in my emotions. Kade's eyes widened a fraction at my response before confusion saturated his features. While Gray kept my wrists captive, Kade released my throat, only to tug on the chain around my neck.

"He's your weakness," Kade grated out, resentment in his tone. "Whoever he is, you care about him. You have someone to protect."

"And what does any of that have to do with me not killing you?" I hissed, my stomach roiling at this conversation.

"You seem to forget that it's not just Gray and me. We're part of a much larger organization." Kade grasped my chin. "We have silent partners. People you have no fucking idea about—even with all the digging you've done on us. We're not easy targets like you seem to think."

His words sounded like they held truth. Maybe with all the research Caleb and I had done, we'd still missed something. I doubted they'd ever get to Caleb, but I wasn't going to chance it. At least not until I was sure their crew couldn't touch us.

"Here are your two choices. Leave town for good. Or stay here."

Kade finally stepped back. "But if you take the second option, then you better remember that as long as you're in Ridgewood city limits, you're ours. You don't interfere with our jobs. Or fuck around with anyone. Especially the goddamn mayor."

I choked out a sarcastic laugh. "Holy shit. That's it, isn't it?"

Gray's rapid breathing fanned over my hair as I held Kade's gaze.

"You didn't do all this after I got in the way of your job. You did this after seeing me with another man." I tilted my head, knowing I was right when Kade's eyes darkened. "It's cute. Trying to claim me out of jealousy. I was right earlier. You can't stand seeing me with anyone else after fucking me."

"Leave town," Kade ground out. "It's best for all of us."

Gray reluctantly let go of my arms, and I casually stepped away from him, a half-smile plastered on my face. I was back in control now. They wouldn't see the storm they created until I was ready to show them.

With a sinister grin, I snatched my purse from where it had fallen on the floor. "I'll see you boys later."

I didn't miss when Gray swallowed hard as I sauntered past them. At least he was smart enough to be worried. Kade didn't say another word as I turned my back on them and strode toward the exit. I resisted the urge to try and rip the chain from my neck, pretending it didn't bother me at all.

I rushed outside, scanning the street for a car I could take. My mind was racing with my plans. I was leaving Ridgewood. There was no doubt about that. But I had a few things to do first. And I couldn't wait to show them exactly why fucking with me was a mistake.

29

Rylan

I stared at the numbers on the elevator, mentally willing it to move faster. It was four in the morning, and when Mili texted me to meet her at my office, I was already in my car. Because I'd been driving around the city looking for her. Kade and Gray had grown up pulling power moves like this because they could get away with it, but bringing her into it changed things. Because I didn't want to see her hurt.

The elevator dinged, and I flew out the doors as soon as they were open. The entire building was empty, and it would be for a couple more hours until people started coming in for work. I nearly jogged down the hall, stopping in front of my door and hesitating for a moment. Kade and Gray seemed as obsessed with her as I was, and I honestly didn't think they'd hurt her. Seeing them shove her into the car earlier had me doubting that now.

I slowly pushed open the door, freezing when I saw her perched against the front of my desk. She had a trench coat on, buttoned up high to cover her neck. Her red heels added at least five inches to her height. My gaze traveled back up her bare legs, and I studied her face, taken aback by the heat in her gaze.

I cleared my throat, closing the door behind me. "Are you okay? I'm sorry I couldn't stop them—"

"I'm fine," she interrupted me, her voice softer than usual. "I wanted to see you before I left."

"Left?" I repeated, my stomach dropping. "You're leaving town?"

"My business with Kade and Gray is done. It's time to go."

"When are you leaving?"

"In a few days…there are some loose ends I need to tie up," she murmured, and my heart thudded, hearing the promise of vengeance in her voice.

"You're just going to disappear in the dead of the night, like how you showed up here?" I asked as I took a couple of steps closer to her.

She chuckled. "No. Night is when they'll be looking for me. I'll slip away unnoticed during morning rush hour where they won't expect me to be."

"Looking for you," I muttered, stopping in front of her. "Did you hurt them tonight? If you did, they fucking deserved it."

She grinned. "I think you're better off not knowing what I'm going to do to them, Rylan. You can stay on the right side of the law like you strive so hard to do."

"I'd cross that line for you," I muttered.

"I know you would. Seeing you try to fight the crew tonight showed me that." She began unbuttoning her jacket. "But I don't want that for you. I'm not bringing you into a life that could get you killed."

"Did you forget where I grew up?" I asked, my eyes glued to her hands as she undid another button. "I was surrounded by crime and death as a kid. I know how that world works."

"And you got out," she said softly. "Stay out, Rylan. But I want one night with you first."

I swallowed thickly when she slid the jacket off her shoulders, revealing that she was wearing absolutely fucking nothing. The coat fell to the floor, and every one of my logical thoughts disappeared. She was all I fucking wanted.

My gaze trailed over her bare skin, taking in every inch of her. In all the times I'd imagined her naked, it was nothing compared to her standing in front of me. She was fucking gorgeous. The tattoo sprawled under her breasts made my breath hitch, and my eyes cut to hers. She was watching me curiously, as if waiting to see if I'd recognize it. I did. It was the Sapphire calling card. I'd grown up around cars and racing, just like Kade and Gray had. If I was being honest with myself, I missed those parts of my life. Some of my best memories revolved around going to races.

My questions died when my eyes landed on her throat. A thick chain was tight against her neck with a small padlock resting on her chest. It was easy to see the crew's crest on it, and I lunged forward until I was inches from her. My fingers ran along the cold metal, and she stayed still as rage boiled in my veins. Who the fuck were they to try and claim her?

"They did this?" I asked in a low voice, already knowing the answer.

"They were desperate to try and get me under control," she answered, her rage making her voice tremble before she cleared her throat. "As if a piece of fucking metal would make me bow to them."

"Let me help you cut it off—"

"I can do that myself." She reached forward, unbuttoning the top of my dress shirt. "Tonight, I'm yours."

My eyes widened. "What?"

"Own me, Rylan," she whispered. "You wanted me on your desk—here I am. I'm yours until I walk out of this office."

My hands went to her hips, and I pulled her into me. "Is that what you want?"

"As long as you're okay with being on camera."

I blinked, processing her words. "You want a picture of me?"

She giggled, glancing over her shoulder to my desk. "No. I want a video."

My gaze followed hers, and I saw her phone propped up on my little phone stand on the corner of my desk. My stomach rolled with apprehension, even though I knew I wouldn't deny her.

"You're using me," I muttered, not sure how I felt about that.

"No. I want you," she said firmly. "I could have found a random guy to make a video with. But I came here because I don't want anyone else."

I hesitated, looking back at her phone. She sighed, pulling away from me, and I scowled, wrapping an arm around her waist and tugging her back.

"You don't want to do this. That's fine," she said, looking at me with understanding. "I'm yours tonight either way."

"And tomorrow?" I questioned.

She kept my stare. "Tomorrow I'll find someone to make the video with. I want to show them how much their little necklace worked to keep me in line."

"No," I growled, a possessiveness that I'd never felt before holding me hostage. "I'll do it."

"Rylan—"

She cried out in surprise when I gripped her ass and picked her up. Rounding my desk, I set her on the smooth wood in front of my leather chair. She leaned back on her palms, her eyebrows raised in surprise.

"Turn on the camera, Mili," I told her, unbuttoning my shirt the rest of the way.

"Are you sure?"

I tsked, running my fingertips down her chest, stopping just below her belly button. "You want to be mine tonight, which means you'll listen to me. Understand?"

That got her attention, her eyes glittering with rebellion. But the desire was there too, and as my fingers inched closer to her pussy, she spread her legs wider.

"Turn on the camera," I repeated gruffly, my dick twitching when I felt how wet she was.

She broke our stare, turning and messing with her phone for a few moments. She had it angled to keep her head out of the frame. If I stayed where I was between her legs, my face wouldn't be seen either.

"Don't use my name," she said quietly. "I can't leave them with evidence to use against me."

I nodded, understanding. I figured she didn't want her face on camera when she'd sent me those pictures last week. Before she started the video, she glanced at my bare chest, her gaze zeroing in on the one tattoo I had over my heart. It was the only ink I had, and no one ever saw it since I didn't make it a habit to be in public with my shirt off. Her fingers grazed the colorful tattoo as she studied it.

"A chameleon?" she asked curiously. "What does it mean?"

I stiffened, never having had to explain its significance before. "Growing up, I always thought I'd go down the same road as Kade and Gray. Even after all these years, sometimes it still feels like I'm wearing a costume. Changing how I look and act to succeed in politics."

"Adapting to change so you can blend into the world around you," she murmured.

She understood better than I thought she would, and it made me hesitate. She noticed my change, her curiosity heightening.

"Is there another meaning behind it?" she asked.

I traced her tattoo. "Why don't you tell me about yours first?"

We stared at each other in silence, and her jaw clenched as she shut down. I didn't expect her to tell me anything. She had secrets, just like everyone else in this world. And I was no fucking exception. She saw me as an honest, straightforward guy. On paper, I was. But I wondered what she'd think if she knew my truths.

Instead of continuing the conversation, she turned away from me and hit the record button on her phone, signaling that she was done talking. I grinned, shaking away the seriousness of the mood and bringing my hand back between her legs. She lay down, ignoring the paperwork under her as I brushed my fingers over her clit. I bit back a groan, watching her eyes flutter from my touch. I'd been waiting months to do this, and I wanted to savor every fucking moment.

"Is this what you were imagining when we were texting?" I murmured, pushing a finger inside her.

Her eyes widened, and she glanced back at the camera. She was worried they'd recognize my voice. I was positive they would.

"I want you screaming my name by the end of the night," I rasped, adding a second finger inside her and curling them.

Her back arched off the desk, her hands pressing into the wood as she cried out. Scattered papers fell to the floor as she writhed. Her chest heaved, and I pumped my fingers in and out of her while rubbing my palm against her clit. My need to claim her surged through me as I fingered her, not stopping when her muscles locked up. Her pussy clenched around my hand as she came, a hoarse cry falling from her lips.

I let her ride out the waves of pleasure until she sagged on the desk. Withdrawing my fingers, I brought them to my mouth, tasting her. My cock pressed against my slacks, and I leaned down, planting kisses on her soft skin. I moved from her stomach up to her chest, taking one of her nipples in my mouth and teasing it before going to the other. She squirmed under me, her breathless moans better than anything I'd ever heard.

With my body on top of hers, I kept kissing her until my lips reached her throat. Ignoring the chain around her neck, I nipped at her earlobe, knowing full well my face was in the video at this point.

"Whose mouth do you want on your pussy?" I asked gruffly, making sure I was loud enough for the camera to pick up.

"Yours," she breathed out.

I lifted myself off her, wrapping my fingers around her neck. "Whose hand do you want around your throat while you're getting fucked?"

"Yours," she said again, making me want to take her right there.

"Who do you belong to tonight?"

She bit her lip, her stubbornness making her pause. I tightened my hold on her throat, bringing my other hand back to her pussy and pinching her clit.

"Who?" I asked again.

"You," she choked out, her eyes rolling from pleasure. "I belong to you."

"Every scream. Every moan. Every orgasm is *mine*."

I glanced at the camera, showing my entire face before planting kisses back down her body. I wanted Kade and Gray to know exactly how much she wanted me. And I her. There was no doubt that they'd keep this video to themselves. The city saw her as theirs, and they wouldn't ruin that to blackmail me.

I lifted her legs, putting them on my shoulders after dropping to my knees. Her pussy was glistening from the orgasm I'd already given her, and I licked my lips before diving between her thighs. Flicking my tongue over her clit, I groaned, knowing I could eat her for the rest of my life and die happy.

"You taste fucking delicious," I muttered, not lifting my lips from her.

Her fingers tangled in my hair, pulling my roots as she ground her pussy against my face. I slowed, and she protested, her thighs squeezing my head.

"Hands on the desk, Lynx." The nickname fell from my mouth, and I pulled away when her hand stayed in my hair.

"Lynx?" she mumbled when I raised my head high enough to meet her gaze.

"You're stealthy. Quiet. Unseen until you're ready to reveal yourself." I grabbed her wrist, pulling her hand from my hair. "I know enough to know you're a predator. A deadly, beautiful one." She didn't say anything as I pushed her arm onto the desk. "Hands stay on the desk or I stop."

Lowering my head, I swirled my tongue around her clit, hearing her sharp intake of breath. I teased and sucked, enjoying every moment. Her hands stayed pressed against the desk, her nails clawing into the wood as she came undone again with a loud scream. Unable to wait another second, I unbuckled my belt and unzipped my pants. She was still writhing with pleasure as I pulled my cock out and pressed the tip against her entrance.

"Don't make me wait," she panted, lifting her hips. "Fuck me, Rylan. Please."

Hearing her plead my name shattered any self-control I had left as I plunged into her. Her legs were still on my shoulders, and I grasped her hips, burying my cock until I filled her completely. There was a nagging of unease that filtered through my mind before I shoved it away as I thrust into her again.

"You take me so well," I said gruffly, reaching one hand between us and giving her clit attention. "Do you feel it? You're meant to be mine."

"Rylan, I can't," she choked out, clearly only focused on the euphoria I was giving her. "I can't handle another one."

"You can. You will." I slammed into her again. "I need to know how it feels when you come around my cock."

She reached up, grabbing the back of my neck and pulling me on top of her. My lips crashed onto hers, our kiss primal and needy. Her tongue clashed with mine as I kept plunging into her. Her legs quivered, and she turned her head, taking a moment to catch her breath. A moment was all I gave her before I fisted her hair and claimed her lips again. The desk shook and my picture frames were in pieces on the floor, but I didn't stop, feeling my release build. She tensed, her nails digging into the skin on my back.

"Not yet," I ordered, making her eyes flash dangerously. "Do not come yet."

She bit her lip, squeezing her eyes shut as I moved faster, my body rippling with pleasure.

"Now," I rasped. "Come for me."

If my demands bothered her, I didn't see a hint of it as she arched her back to meet every one of my thrusts.

"Fuck," she screamed. "Yes."

We came at the same time, her body shuddering as if unable to handle another orgasm. Her heart was racing at the same pace as mine as we lay tangled in a heap. She didn't attempt to move, and I stayed on top of her, knowing the second I moved, this would be over and she'd leave.

"Fuck, that felt so good," I muttered in her hair.

I froze, my mind clearing enough to realize what had bothered me earlier. I pulled out of her, shooting up and looking at her in a panic. She sat up, frowning as she stared at me.

"I didn't use a condom." I ran a hand through my hair. "Shit. Mili, I'm sorry."

She rolled over and grabbed the phone before standing up. "It's fine. I get tested—"

"So do I," I cut her off. "That's not the point. What if I got you pregnant?"

She was rigid as she bent down and grabbed her jacket. "You didn't."

"You're on birth control?"

"Yes." Her answer was instant, but it didn't sit right. I rounded the desk, stopping her as she put the coat on.

"I'm not going to let you walk out of here and disappear, not knowing if you're going to end up raising my baby—"

She yanked out of my grasp, the calculating blank look returning to her face. The openness she'd had while she was on my desk was already long gone.

"You didn't get me pregnant," she said curtly. "I need to go."

"Call me. When you know for sure."

She sighed. "You're not going to hear from me again, Rylan. Maybe this was a mistake—"

"Don't," I warned. "Don't act like this was nothing to you."

Her eyes softened. "It wasn't nothing. It was amazing. But the night is over."

"I'll come looking for you."

She laughed. "You couldn't find me if you tried. But I'll ease your worry. I can't have kids."

My stomach plummeted, and I grabbed her arm, pulling her into my chest. "I'm sorry. That must be hard to talk about—"

"Don't pity me," she snapped. "I made that choice. I can't have babies because I chose it."

I frowned. "Why?"

She shook her head, tugging me down and kissing me instead of answering. She pulled away much too quickly and ducked before I could grab her again. She buttoned her jacket as she backed away.

"Bye, Rylan," she said quietly before disappearing out the door.

30

Gray

Thanks for the jewelry. It really complements his hand, doesn't it?

I stared at Mili's text for what felt like the thousandth time in the last three days. But it wasn't her words that kept me coming back to the message. It was the video under it. The one where she was sprawled on Rylan's desk, wearing nothing except the chain Kade had locked around her throat.

I had no idea I could be so fucking turned on and pissed off at the same time until I watched that video. She had been careful not to show her face and to shield her tattoo. But I didn't need to see her eyes to know what she'd been thinking in that moment. Her body said it all. She'd submitted to him. Even if it was for the time she'd been on his desk, she'd given the fucking mayor what she refused to give me. Or Kade.

There was no tension. No hesitation. Her feistiness was still present, but she let Rylan control it. She gave him what she would never give us. And she made sure we knew it.

"Ready?" Kade asked as I hurriedly slipped my phone back into my pocket.

I glanced at the warehouse and nodded before we climbed out of the car. The knots in my stomach had been growing since we'd tried running Mili out of town. With every little thing that happened, my first thought was that she was coming to pay us back. None of our men had seen her, and everybody had been on the lookout. But with her ability to blend in and her fondness for wigs, I had a feeling she could be right under our noses and we wouldn't know it.

But we knew she hadn't left town. At least not yet.

For the most part, it had been quiet. But odd things were happening, and although neither Kade nor I voiced it, we were guessing she was behind it. Last night, the employee entrance to our club was found unlocked, even though everyone on shift swore it was locked. Nothing had gone missing, and the cameras didn't show anything suspicious. Kade hadn't pulled his Jaguar out of the garage because we worried she'd try to blow up a car again.

I wasn't used to walking on eggshells in my own city, and it made my annoyance flare. What we'd done to her was to make her run. And I felt guilty every time it replayed in my head. I felt like a complete piece of shit, knowing what we did hurt her. But it was supposed to fucking work.

"Front door?" Kade asked as we got closer to the warehouse.

"Yeah," I muttered, knowing we wouldn't find anything if it was Mili. Unless she was already long gone. I half expected to see our cars gone when we opened the door.

Kade pushed open the door, and the alarm echoed through the large building until Kade punched in the code, shutting it off. My gun was out, and I scanned the area once we flipped the lights on. Everything was exactly how it had been the last time we were here. The cars sat in perfect rows, not one out of place. We moved slowly, peering into each car until we covered the whole building.

"This doesn't mean it was her," Kade mumbled as we got to the back of the warehouse. "It's not like this is the first time this has happened."

He was right. Sometimes, kids would come and try to fuck around, not knowing that this was our warehouse. Or homeless people would try to get in to find a place to sleep. The alarm had been tripped more than once in the past.

Pulling out my phone, I hit Vic's number.

"False alarm," I told him gruffly when he answered, still scanning the room as if she was going to pop out. "Nothing on the cameras either."

"Was it her?" Vic asked tightly. They were pissed when we told them Mili skipped town, but they had no idea why she did it.

"Doubtful. If it was her, she wouldn't have left the cars untouched."

Beeping in my ear alerted me to another call, and I glanced at the screen, my heart jumping.

"I gotta go," I told Vic before nudging Kade and showing him the screen. A muscle in his jaw flexed as he stared at the unknown number. Hitting the button to connect the call, I put it on speaker so Kade could hear too.

"The midnight blue Mustang is my favorite." Mili's bright voice came through the speaker. Apprehension flitted through me as I lifted my head, my gaze trailing down the aisle of cars until I saw the one she was talking about.

"You couldn't have loved it that much," I replied as we looked around, wondering if she was somehow watching us. "You left it behind."

"I like my Corvette more."

"Where are you, Rebel?" I asked. "What's so important in here that you'd risk us finding you?"

She laughed. "Risk? I've had eyes on you since I walked out of your club. The men you ordered to keep a lookout for me? One of them flirted, not even realizing who I was."

A horn of some kind blared through the speaker, and my gaze went to Kade. A train horn. There were tracks behind the warehouse. Was she really so confident that she stayed on the property while calling us?

Kade jerked his head, silently telling me which way he was going. I nodded, following him back through the warehouse. He turned left to go out the side door, while I kept going straight to cut her off in case she bolted when she saw him.

"You should have left town," I said, trying to get her to keep talking. "We told you what would happen if you stayed."

"And you should have stayed with Kade," she murmured, her voice dripping with threat. "See you soon, Gray."

Ice dripped down my spine as she cut the call, and I whirled around toward the door Kade had disappeared through. Fuck.

"Kade," I bellowed, hesitating about which way to go. She was expecting me to chase after him. Silence smothered the warehouse, and I gritted my teeth, deciding to go through the back like I planned. Quietly pushing the back door open, I kept my gun raised as I scanned the parking lot.

A lone old van was parked in the center, but what got my attention was the body slumped on the ground in front of it. I stared at Kade, my breath returning when his chest moved up and down, proving he was still alive.

"Ready to play?" Mili's voice came from behind me, and the metal of a gun barrel was jammed into my spine before I could move an inch.

I stayed still, keeping my eyes on Kade. "We've been playing with you ever since you came to town. If you wanted to kill us, you would have done it already."

Her small laugh promised hell as she kept the gun on me. "No. You've seen me play as Mili. Child's play. I was having fun. But now? You get to see Sapphire."

I hissed out a breath, feeling a prick in my neck. My hand shot to my throat, but whatever she'd given me was already working. My movements were sluggish, and keeping my eyes open became impossible. I fell to my knees, my head swimming in darkness before everything went black.

31

Kade

I groaned, lifting my head and flinching at the stiff ache in my neck. I licked my lips, my tongue feeling like sandpaper. There was a tiny pulse of a headache, but it wasn't nearly as bad as I was expecting after being drugged with a fucking sedative. Had I been passed out long enough for most of it to leave my system? Forcing my eyes open, I was met with darkness. Pitch-black, making it impossible to know where I was.

"Gray?" I choked out, going rigid when I realized I couldn't move my arms. I was sitting in a chair with my hands cuffed behind me. I pulled against the restraints, feeling the metal bite into my wrists with every move. Attempting to shift my feet, I learned my ankles were tied to the legs of the chair.

"About time you woke up," Gray grumbled hoarsely from somewhere in front of me. "I thought she accidentally killed you."

"If either of you die, it won't be by accident." My heart thundered against my ribs at the echo of Mili's voice. Wherever we were, it was a large room.

Overhead lights flickered on, and I blinked until my eyes adjusted to the brightness. After a few moments, I was able to focus, seeing Gray cuffed to a chair about five feet in front of me. His ankles were zip tied to the chair legs, just like mine. After a quick look at his chair, I realized there was no point in trying to rock the chair. If it was wood, I'd attempt to fall and let it break. But the chairs were fucking metal. I shifted again, my muscles burning as I tried to pull my hands out of the cuffs. All I managed to do was cut up my skin.

The clicking of heels turned my attention to the left, where Mili was walking toward us. The first thing I noticed was that the chain around her throat was gone. Not that I expected to see it. I still wondered how hard it was for her to figure out how to cut it off. She was wearing tall black heels that matched her tiny dress. The thing was sheer, revealing every detail of her body. Her nipples were hard and pressing against the fabric, and her lace panties were bright red.

My eyes traveled to her face, and unease skated down my spine when we locked gazes. She had the same ruthless stare she'd worn when she confronted Rhett. But this time, a smug grin was playing on her lips. She moved her stare to Gray, and I took a second to look around the room behind her. The floor was an old white tile, and the walls were painted cement. If I were to guess, it looked like an old factory of some kind. There were a few abandoned buildings like this on the north side of town. Or she could have taken us out of Ridgewood. There were no windows, making it impossible to know what time it was or even guess at how long we'd been here.

"Better make sure you bury our bodies if you don't want the crew going after you," I grated out, refusing to fall into whatever game she was playing.

She arched an eyebrow. "Kill you? No, Kade. You'll survive this. I'm just saying goodbye."

"Goodbye?" Gray questioned, not hiding the fact that he was trying to wiggle out of his cuffs.

Her gaze moved past us, and I turned my head, confusion shooting through me. About fifty feet away were two cars. I had to study them for a second before I recognized them. The lights directly above us were bright, but the rest of the building was dark. My Jaguar and the Mazda Gray had raced. Rage boiled my blood as I stared at my prized car. I'd rebuilt every inch of it. She slowly walked between us, heading for the Jaguar. I struggled against the cuffs uselessly as she opened the driver's door. But all she did was turn on the radio. Club music drifted through the air, and she left the door open as she crossed the room, coming closer to us.

"I know when I'm not welcome anymore." She sauntered up to Gray and lowered herself onto his lap, straddling his legs. He tensed when she trailed her fingers down his cheek. "Killing you would be boring. Not when I can do something else."

"Do what?" I forced out, my eyes darting between her and my car. I highly doubted she'd driven it here just to play music.

"I'm going to leave, just like you two want," she purred, beginning to grind on Gray's lap along with the beat of the music. His jaw dropped in surprise, and he glanced at me before focusing back on Mili. "And you'll never see me again. Or maybe you will."

I frowned, trying to pay attention to her riddles while my dick was stirring from watching her dance. She had me cuffed to a chair, but my body didn't seem to give a flying fuck. If I was getting hard from just watching, I was sure Gray was worse off than me. His jaw was clenched, and he wasn't moving a muscle as Mili continued to dance.

"You get to live wondering if I'll ever come back to finish this," she murmured, draping her arms over Gray's shoulders. "Instead of comfortably ruling your city, you'll be spending your days looking over your shoulder, waiting for me to make my move."

"You do that, and we'll release the footage we have on you," I growled. "Then you'll be too busy hiding from whoever you're running from."

Glancing over her shoulder at me, she grinned. "Oh right. The cameras from the club. You don't have those anymore. It was smart to keep everything on the hard drive so it couldn't be hacked. But you really should have locked it in a place I couldn't steal it from. Leaving it at the club? Not smart."

I didn't answer, realizing that was why we'd found the club door unlocked the other day. She'd broken in. A small flash of panic sliced through my anger. If she had the tapes, we had nothing on her to stop her from killing us.

"I went to every establishment I visited while living here, making sure my face was nowhere to be found," she continued. "When I leave, the only way you'll remember me is by memory. And that video I sent you of Rylan and me. But my face wasn't the star of that show, was it?"

I pressed my lips together, attempting not to react the way she wanted me to. Seeing her with Rylan—watching her come apart while screaming his name—made me fucking lose it. Yet I still watched the video more times than I'd ever admit.

"I need to take an extra car with me when I leave," she said, a wicked gleam flashing in her eyes before she turned back toward Gray. "I decided to see why you two love these cars so much."

"Take mine," Gray rasped, his voice revealing how much her grinding on his lap was affecting him. "It's faster."

She giggled. "It's cute how you're trying to protect Kade."

Gray knew how much I loved the Jaguar. He liked his Mazda too, but it was replaceable.

"But I am a bit confused," she pouted, tugging on Gray's hair. "If you want me gone so badly, why are you enjoying me on your lap so much?"

Gray didn't respond, grunting when she yanked on his hair again. She leaned forward, pressing her lips to his. I gave him credit for holding out for a long few moments before he opened his mouth, kissing her back. The handcuffs clanged on the back of his chair as he strained to touch her. She finally pulled away, her chest heaving as she caught her breath. Gray bit his tongue, as if swallowing his protest when she slid off his lap. Her red lipstick was smeared across his lips, and even tied here at her mercy, I was jealous that it wasn't me kissing her.

"Like I said, I only want one car." She tapped her chin. "But how will I choose which one?"

Dread pooled in my stomach as she glanced at me, raising her arm and pointing her finger at me before moving it toward Gray.

"Eenie meenie miney mo. Who's going to be the lucky *asshole*?"

Her finger landed on me as she said the last word, and I swallowed thickly, not knowing what that meant. Her devilish expression gave nothing away, but my gaze dropped to her body when she slipped her panties off. She balled them up in her fist before grabbing a bag from the floor and pulling out duct tape. We both stiffened when she ripped off a length of tape and stuck an edge of it to Gray's jeans.

"Open up," she told him, gripping his jaw with one hand while holding her panties in the other.

He frowned, keeping his mouth shut. She tsked, shaking her head before leaning down and whispering something in his ear. His eyes widened slightly, his gaze going to me as she spoke. I couldn't hear her, and it was driving me crazy. When she pulled away, Gray glared at her as he relented and opened his mouth. She pushed her panties in before grabbing the tape and pressing it over his lips.

"Good boy," she praised him tauntingly. "Enjoy the show."

Her gaze went to the cars again before she focused on me. Vengeance brightened her eyes as she stopped in front of me.

"Do you want a goodbye kiss too?" she asked, running her tongue over her bottom lip.

That was a fucking loaded question. I could guarantee she had every detail planned out, no matter what I said. She was just toying with us.

"What did you whisper to Gray?" I tossed back, holding my breath when she climbed onto my lap.

"I told him what I really planned to do with your cars. But promised that if he behaved, I'd reconsider."

She began moving against me like she had on Gray, causing all the blood to rush to my dick. The fact that she wasn't wearing panties didn't help at all as I tried to concentrate on her words. She dipped her hand into my front jeans pocket and pulled out my cigarettes, along with my Zippo lighter.

"You look stressed, Kade. Let me help." She put a cigarette between her lips and lit it, inhaling a long drag before coming closer and kissing me. She blew the smoke into my mouth, and I sucked in on reflex, feeling the toxic addiction filling my lungs. She attempted to pull away, and I closed my teeth on her bottom lip, not ready to commit her taste to only memory.

Her hand went around my throat, and she pushed me back. "You do not get to fucking control this."

Even with her anger, I could see the lust building. Her dancing on us was affecting her too. I smirked, letting my eyes fall on her body as she climbed off me. The inside of her thighs were slick, and I could bet her pussy was throbbing to be touched again.

"Did you know that a lit cigarette can't set things on fire?" She stared at the cigarette in her hand as though inspecting it. "But let's see if that's really true."

After taking another puff, she walked about five feet away, stopping in front of a puddle of water. I frowned, following the trail of water to Gray's Mazda. I spotted a second puddle of liquid a few feet away that went all the way to my car. Fuck me. That wasn't water. It was some kind of gas or accelerant. My heart lurched when she dropped the cigarette into the middle of the liquid, drawing a breath when it died instead of going up in flames.

"All the hard drives are in the Mazda," she murmured, going back to the bag where she'd pulled the duct tape from. "I need to get rid of the evidence."

"Wait," I yelled hoarsely. "You can't light a fucking car on fire in here."

She pulled out a blank piece of paper from the bag. "It's not going to explode. I drained most of the gas. You think I'm stupid enough to do that? And the ceiling is full of vents. The smoke won't even touch us."

I raised my eyes, seeing she was right about the vents. Just like I'd thought—she had this entire thing planned out.

"Give me a reason not to do it," she said, staring at me. "Give me a reason to walk out of here right now and forget about it all. You. Gray. The last three months. Give me a truth, and I'll spare Gray's precious fucking car."

I hesitated for only a second, but it was a second too long for her. Gray let out a muffled yell as she lit the paper and then let it fall to the puddle on the floor. This time, the flame grew instantly, racing over the liquid trail until it went under the Mazda. Flames licked at the side of the car as it grew, and soon the whole car was ablaze.

"One more chance, Kade." She crawled back onto my lap. "I never planned on driving your Jaguar. I have every intention of burning it."

"Don't," I snarled. "What do you want?"

"I want you to feel how I did when you locked that chain around my neck."

My chest constricted with guilt when the tiniest flash of pain slithered through her mask.

"How about I make you feel good instead?" I asked in a low voice. I couldn't tell her what that car was to me. It was personal, and if she knew how much it meant to me, she'd light the match in a heartbeat just to get even with me.

Suspicion lit her gaze. "Excuse me?"

"I can feel how wet you are through my jeans, Mili." My confidence grew when her face flushed. "Use me. Make yourself feel good. I give you an orgasm, you leave my Jaguar alone."

"I don't need you for that," she sneered.

"Can't do it with an audience?" I taunted her, looking over her shoulder at Gray.

She rolled her eyes. "You're being very transparent. You're not going to make me angry enough to agree with you. It only shows how much you really want to save your car."

"Come on, Little Hellion." My gaze dropped to her lips. "What's stopping you? You could do both if you really wanted. Use me and destroy my car. I'm just giving you a little more time to think about it."

It would give me a chance to talk her out of doing it. I wondered if Vic and Juan knew we were missing. Our cars had trackers on them, but for all we knew, she'd already disabled them. She shifted in my lap, sliding my lighter back into my pocket. I straightened up as much as the cuffs allowed me when she went for the zipper on my jeans.

"What are you doing?" I hissed, swallowing a groan when she fisted my cock.

"You told me to use you. You didn't think I'd just grind against you, did you?"

That was exactly what I thought she'd do. I certainly didn't expect her to want to have sex. She held my stare, as if waiting for me to shut it down. She'd be waiting a long fucking time. There wasn't anything in the world that would get me to turn down a chance to bury myself inside her. When I didn't say a word, she grinned, falling off my lap and getting on her knees.

"Holy fuck," I groaned out when she flicked her tongue out and licked me from the tip of my cock all the way to the base. She did it again and again until I had to bite my lip to keep from telling her to stop fucking teasing. If I began making demands, she'd stop.

She finally stopped, and I caught my breath, glancing at Gray to see his eyes burning with desire. We'd done stuff together with women before, but this was something fucking new, seeing as I was the one restrained. I waited for her to look for a condom, but instead, she straddled my legs again. She sank down until the head of my cock nudged her entrance, pausing to see if I'd protest. My heart raced, keeping my gaze locked on hers. I'd never fucked anyone without a condom.

She would be my first.

I witnessed a quick speck of indecision fly through her eyes, and I jutted my hips up. "Sit down and fucking ride me."

She bristled at my command, and I reminded myself not to do it again. She'd only do this if she was in control. She lowered herself, slowly adjusting to my size. Her fingers dug into my shoulders as she began rocking back and forth, and it was frustrating as fuck not to be able to move in rhythm with her. A quiet moan escaped her when her clit rubbed against me as she moved. Her breasts were in my face, but I couldn't lean forward enough to tease her nipples with my mouth.

"Did it work?" she panted as she upped her speed.

"What?"

"Trying to distract me so you'd have time to convince me to save your car."

Shit. That had been the whole point. But the second her mouth touched my cock, all other thoughts flew out the window. My hands curled into fists, and I fought against the cuffs as she danced on me. All I wanted to do was to touch her. And hold on to her so she couldn't fucking leave. As we stared at each, her cheeks pink from all the moving, I decided I didn't want her to go.

"If you're stalling so your crew can save you—they won't," she forced out as her body locked up. "Not until I'm long gone."

"I'd rather stay chained up all night if it means my cock stays in your pussy."

"Oh my God," she screamed hoarsely. Her pussy clenched around my cock as she came hard. My eyes never left her face, loving that the only time all her defenses came down was when she was in the throes of pleasure. She almost leaned forward to rest her head on mine after she came down but caught herself. I figured she'd stop after she got what she wanted, but she started moving again.

Heat pooled in my stomach, and I could feel myself getting close. Until something snapped in her gaze, making me tense. She was going to leave me high and dry—again.

"Shit," she said, her voice smothered with dramatic concern. "I messed up. I didn't put the hard drives in Gray's car. They're in yours."

Even as she spoke, she continued to grind on me. Her words did nothing to stop my release. I was too fucking close.

"Don't do it, Mili," I gritted out.

"Give me a reason."

I wouldn't tell her what that car was to me. She wasn't the only one who didn't want to share parts of their past.

"We were trying to get you to leave town," I said through breaths as my balls tightened. "That's why we did it."

"Not good enough."

Anger boiled my veins, and the words were out of my mouth before I could stop them. "I fucking swear I'll come after you. You'll be lucky if you leave Ridgewood."

I caught Gray shaking his head in warning, but it was too late. I saw it the second she made the decision. She lifted the lighter, and I stared at it, wondering when the hell she'd pulled it from my pocket.

"Do you know what the last person did when he tried to own me?" she murmured, pain lacing her voice.

She was still riding me, and I shook my head, trying to separate her words from how my body was reacting.

"Your little necklace was nothing compared to that. But it reminded me that men are all the same. They take what they want and will do anything to keep it."

"Mili—"

Out of the corner of my eye, I saw her lift the lighter and flick it until a small flame appeared. She sped up, her pussy gripping around my cock like it owned it.

"Fuck," I grunted, feeling my release explode inside of her. I was still coming when she gripped my jaw, making sure I was looking at her.

"Don't ever fucking underestimate me," she hissed, the promise of death in her voice. "Try to make me yours again, and I won't hesitate to kill both of you."

"Drop that lighter, and I won't hesitate to chase after you." I didn't bother to mention we'd try to find her either way.

She grinned, her emotions fading until she was almost looking through me.

"No—"

My yell did nothing as she tossed the Zippo the few feet to the accelerant. It lit up the floor, hitting my car in seconds. She must have tossed more gas on the Jaguar than the Mazda because it was burning faster. The inside would be nothing but ashes by the time I got out of these handcuffs. A weight fell on my chest as I watched the smoke billow to the ceiling.

Mili slid off me, and she pushed my dick inside my boxers before tugging her dress over her ass. My chest heaved as I glared at her while she lifted the bag over her shoulder. Gray's eyes were filled with pity as he looked at me, knowing what I'd lost in that car.

"See you boys never," she called out, her back already turned.

Her heels echoed on the tile until she disappeared through a side door. I threw my head back, staring at the ceiling, not wanting to watch my car burn. Now that my dick wasn't inside her, my mind was crystal clear.

And I decided she wasn't fucking leaving.

32

Milina

"Lina, Lina. You've been a bad girl," Joel murmured as he pulled me out of the trunk.

"I'm sorry. I didn't mean it," I cried, tears streaming down my face.

I was barely aware of his men around us. Liam was there, and Rhett was leaning against his car. The one Joel had just pulled me out of. There were a couple others I knew, but I didn't see Caleb. Hopefully, he was smart enough to stay away.

"You didn't mean to run away from me?" He cocked his head to the side as if trying to understand.

Fear clung to me like a second skin, and my body trembled as Joel stayed quiet, waiting for the answer we both knew I didn't have. I'd just turned eighteen a couple of months ago, but it felt like I'd been trapped with him for a lifetime.

"Who helped you leave?" Joel asked softly, breaking the silence. "I can't have a man I can't trust in my circle."

"No one," I choked out. "I did it myself."

His hand lashed out, and he grabbed the arm that Rhett had slammed in the trunk. Pain swarmed my body, and I screamed bloody murder when he yanked me forward. Black dots filled my vision, and I heaved, my stomach swirling with nausea.

"Who. Helped. You?" This time, he wasn't keeping the calm and collected pretense up.

"No one," I stuttered out. "Joel, please. It hurts. I need an X-ray. I know it's broken."

"Then you have a hint of how bad it hurt when I woke up to see you gone." His hold on my arm stayed tight. "I can't live without you, Lina."

"I won't leave again," I whispered, my stomach sinking.

Liam was watching me with pity, but no matter how bad he felt for me, he'd never stick his neck out for me. He was too loyal to Joel.

"You are mine," he hissed. "No one else's. Were you running off to find a guy you thought could treat you better than me?"

"No," I promised, my voice hitching. "I just—I'm not ready for all of this. I'm only eighteen."

His eyes gleamed cruelly, and I flinched, knowing I'd said the wrong thing. "You want to date other people?"

"No," I nearly screamed, clutching his shirt. "I love you. Just you."

I resisted the urge to move when he brushed hair out of my face. "You are beautiful. I know every man in here would fuck you if they had the chance. If I allowed it."

I swallowed through the lump in my throat, keeping my eyes on the floor. That was all Rhett wanted. He would have locked me away in one of his houses and kept me from Joel in exchange for sex. I'd been horrified when he offered that. But now...maybe I should have taken it.

Joel fisted my hair, and I yelped when he jerked my head up. "Go lay on that table, Lina."

My gaze flicked to the coffee table in the middle of the room. "Why?"

"I'm going to make sure everyone knows who owns you—even if you try and leave again."

"No, I learned my lesson. I promise," I begged, panic clutching my heart. "I won't leave. I'm yours."

"Get on the table."

"Joel, please—"

"Liam." All Joel had to do was jerk a nod for Liam to snap to attention. I didn't make it two steps before Liam's arm wrapped around my waist.

"Don't. Please." I couldn't see through my tears anymore, and I dug my nails into his wrist with my good hand.

"Don't fight it. You know he gets off on it," Liam breathed in my ear, making sure no one else could hear him. "I'm sorry, Mili."

Liam laid me on the table, pressing my chest into the wood and keeping a hand on the back of my neck to keep me in place. One of the other men stepped forward and tied my uninjured arm to the leg of the table. He reached for my broken arm, but before I could do anything, Liam shoved the guy away.

"Don't move that arm," he whispered. "Or he'll make them tie that one down too."

I tried as hard as I could to stay still, not sure I'd be able to handle any more pain done to that arm. I could hear Joel moving closer but didn't dare turn my head to look. I focused on my breathing, closing my eyes to try and block it all out. My heart dipped when someone lifted my shirt to reveal my lower back. But I still didn't question it. It wouldn't do any good anyway. Joel would finish what he was doing, whether I was silent or screaming.

And then it felt like my skin right above my ass was on fire. The pain seemed to go to my bone, and the only thing keeping me from flying off the table was Liam holding me down. As hard as I tried to stop them, tears still leaked through my closed eyelids. Until I couldn't stand the pain anymore.

"Joel," I choked out. "I can't take it anymore."

"I'm almost done, Lina."

My blood ran cold. "Done with what?"

"Making sure if a man gets close enough to see this, they'll know you aren't theirs to touch."

I swallowed a sob. "See what?"

"My name. Carved into your skin."

"Her face is getting white, and she can't focus," Liam said, his grip on me gentler than before. "I think she needs to see a doctor, Joel. Now."

"Five more minutes, and I'll be done."

My ears buzzed, muting the voices around me. I could tell I was about to pass out, and I welcomed it.

Darkness was always the better choice.

I snapped my eyes open, the nightmare still swallowing me whole. My heart was hammering against my ribs, and I sucked in breaths, barely realizing that I was sitting up in bed. The room was still dark, but as I looked around, a large shadow in my corner chair made my breath catch. Someone was in here, and it was too dark to even guess who it was. No one in this city knew where I was staying. Pretending I didn't notice anything, I lay back down, stretching my arms above my head. Inching slowly, I stuck my hand under the pillow next to me, my stomach dropping when I realized my gun wasn't there.

"You won't find the gun. Or the knife you keep under the mattress. Sit up, Rebel. We need to talk."

I froze when Gray's voice filled the room. How the hell did they find me? How did they get out of the cuffs? I figured it would have taken their crew hours to find them. I had planned to be long gone by the time they'd gotten free. I just needed a couple of hours of sleep since I hadn't gotten any in the last couple of days.

My gut twisted as I slowly sat up, turning my body until I was perched on the side of the mattress. I couldn't see him, but there was no doubt he had some type of weapon pointed at me. Leaning forward, I flicked on my small nightstand light, hoping I had something within arm's reach that I could use to protect myself.

"Sit back on the bed," Gray ordered, making my eyes snap to his. He was sitting on my small chair, his elbows resting on his knees. The gun I usually kept under my pillow was in his hand, and he had it pointed to the floor. But his tension was coiled like a snake as he studied me. If I made one move, he'd have that gun to my head in a second.

I scowled. "I am sitting on the bed."

"Scoot to the middle."

Not breaking eye contact, I gritted my teeth, pushing myself back until I was in the middle of the mattress. Smart on his part. My bed was up against the wall, making it impossible for me to escape that way. And now I was far enough away from him that he'd see my moves coming before my ass left the mattress.

"Where's Kade?" I asked, not revealing how shaken I was that they'd found me. "Off crying about his Jaguar?"

Anger flooded his gaze. "You have no idea what that car meant to him."

"Probably about as much as my freedom means to me."

"We were giving you your freedom. By getting you to leave town."

I glared at him. "I don't need you to give me anything."

"Nice place." He pretended to study my room. "How do you think the residents would feel if they knew a killer was living on the prominent south side?"

"How'd you find me?"

He smirked. "We've known for a while."

My heart stuttered. "Bullshit."

"Months," he drawled out, lazily holding the gun. "At first, we didn't want to spook you because we knew you'd move. And then we gave you a chance to leave town. You should have taken it."

My eyes wandered over my things, as if I'd be able to tell where the hell they'd stuck a tracker. That was the only way they'd be able to find me. My purses? No, I always checked those. Maybe they stuck something to my Corvette. But I always parked that a block away and kept a more discreet car in the apartment garage. Gray stayed silent, looking amused at me trying to figure it out.

"Do you always have nightmares like that?" he asked, turning the conversation in a direction I had no intention of talking about. "You didn't have them when we stayed at the hotel."

"What do you want?" I ground out.

"I want you to come back to our house with me."

I laughed coldly. "Not happening."

He frowned, turning serious. "You think we're going to let you walk away and leave us wondering if you're going to come back and kill us?"

"I'll kill you faster if you try to make me stay in town," I told him sweetly, climbing to my knees. A movement he caught immediately as he straightened up.

If I could get to my nightstand drawer, I'd have a chance. Under the pile of magazines was a stun gun. He might have found my gun and knife, but I doubted he'd found my other hidden weapons. I scanned the empty nightstand, realizing the key to the Jeep I'd been driving was gone too. But I could easily hot-wire it if I could get away from Gray.

"Don't," he warned, standing up and aiming my own gun at me.

I tilted my head, a grin spreading across my face. "What did you think I'd do? Fall on my knees and beg you not to hurt me? Or follow you out of this building willingly? If you thought that, then you don't know me at all, *Grayson*."

A stab of guilt hit me in the gut when shock flashed through his eyes. It was a low blow, especially after he shared what his dad had done to him as a child. I shook off my moment of feeling bad and let my glare turn frigid.

"You should have tied me up when I was still sleeping. You would have had a much better chance than you do now." As soon as I spoke the words, I frowned, wondering why they hadn't. Fuck, they could have killed me when I was trapped in the nightmare of my past and I never would have known.

"Better be ready to pull that trigger," I murmured, my muscles tensing as I got ready to move.

"Mili," he grated out, his finger hesitating over the trigger.

I lunged, ripping open my nightstand, ignoring his footsteps behind me. Shoving the magazines to the side, my fingers closed around the small stun gun just as Gray got an arm around my waist. He jerked me back, but he moved too slowly. Twisting in his hold, I jammed the stun gun into his ribs, making him flinch.

His gaze dropped, and his mouth fell open. "Son of a bitch."

"Sorry, Gray. But I'm not going with you."

I pressed my thumb into the button, and Gray grunted, going rigid when the shock hit him. Keeping the stun gun on him, I pushed his arm off me with my free hand, shoving him to the bed before fleeing the room. I skidded to a halt in the kitchen, dropping to my knees and opening the cabinet. I grabbed my emergency backpack, taking a gun out before putting it on my shoulders and running to my front door. I stopped, taking just enough time to slip on my shoes before leaving the apartment.

My head was on a swivel, looking for Kade as I raced into the parking garage. He had to be around here somewhere because there was no way Gray had come by himself. My Jeep was where I'd parked it, and I flipped the safety off my gun as I got closer. I needed to break the window somehow so I could hot-wire it. The noise was going to attract attention, but I'd be gone before anyone showed up. Before I could raise my weapon, someone slammed into me from behind. My breath got locked in my chest when I hit the passenger door.

"I was wondering where you were," I choked out once air returned to my lungs.

Kade pried the gun from my fingers while keeping his body against mine. "You think we didn't see the keys in your room? It didn't take long to figure out what car they belonged to."

I laughed hoarsely, covering up my nerves. "How long did you two watch me sleep? A little creepy, don't you think?"

Footsteps alerted me that soon it would be two against one, and my odds of getting away would grow slimmer. Throwing my elbow into Kade's side, I faked twisting left, and when he moved his arm to block me, I ducked to the right while stomping on his foot. It gave me just enough leeway to slip away from him, but I was stuck between him and the car. Holding my breath, I gripped the handle on the door of the Jeep, hoping it was unlocked.

Relief shot through me when the door swung open, and I dove onto the back seat, going straight for the gun I had under the driver's seat. Kade got a hold of my ankle, yanking me back toward him. Lifting my other leg, I threw a kick into his gut, clawing farther away from him. I fell halfway onto the floor, reaching for the gun as Kade climbed on top of me. I gripped the handle of the pistol as he put his arm around my waist, pulling me back onto the seat. He was on top of me and froze when I pressed the barrel to his forehead.

"Wow, life really comes full circle, doesn't it?" I murmured, not looking away from his glare when Gray opened the driver's side door and jumped inside the Jeep.

"Mili, put it down," Gray demanded from the front seat.

I ignored him, keeping my attention on Kade. "You're going to get the fuck off me and scoot your ass out of this car."

He narrowed his eyes, clearly remembering those were the same words I'd told him two years ago when we were fighting in the Rolls-Royce. Back then, I hadn't shot him because the crew had a reputation I didn't want to mess with. And now I didn't want to shoot him for a slew of other reasons. Was I still enraged over what he and Gray had done? Yes. But I'd gotten even by burning their cars. I planned to leave and never come back. I didn't want them dead, even now.

"You going to shoot me?" he questioned, my hesitation not lost on him.

"Get out of my car and let me leave," I demanded.

His lips quirked up in a smirk. "No. We gave you a chance to leave."

"She still could," Gray muttered.

I wanted to look toward the front, but Kade would gain the upper hand in a heartbeat if I turned my attention away from him. His eyes darkened at Gray's words, and I tilted my head, curious about what was going on.

"You two aren't agreeing when it comes to me, are you?" I asked, knowing I was right when Kade's jaw muscle ticked. "Gray wants to let me go, and you don't?"

"It doesn't matter. He lost the vote."

Kade's answer was met with strained silence, and it was clear he hadn't meant to say that. My grip on the gun tightened when he shifted slightly. I shook my head in warning, not ready to let him move. I might not want to kill them, but I sure as fuck wasn't letting them keep me from leaving.

"Vote?" I purred. "How does a vote work with only you two? Or did Vic and Juan pull rank? I'm sure they aren't happy with me either."

Neither answered. I was missing something, but getting the truth out of them wasn't happening. My heart pounded as I considered my options to get out of this. With both of them here, I couldn't make a mistake.

"Get off me, Kade," I ordered, my voice cold. "Like I told you two years ago, I'll choose my freedom over anything."

"The only way that's happening is if you shoot me."

My stomach flipped when the Jeep roared to life, and panic flooded through me. Gray began driving slowly through the parking garage, and my finger hovered over the trigger, my indecision eating me up and pissing me off all at the same time.

"Let me go," I said again, despising that I sounded like I was begging.

"Put the gun down." Kade's eyes bored into mine, and I bit the inside of my cheek.

Taking a deep breath, I pulled the gun from his head, moving it down and slamming it into his shoulder. Before I could talk myself out of it, I pulled the trigger, bracing myself for the kickback.

But there was none. All the gun did was click.

Kade's eyes bulged, and my heart lurched as we both stayed frozen. I shifted the gun slightly, cursing inwardly when I realized how light it was. There were no fucking bullets in it. Something I should have known the second I picked it up.

"You fucking shot me," Kade growled, his hand snatching my wrist.

"No," I said slowly. "Not technically. Since the damn thing is empty."

"Because I found it while Gray was in the apartment with you," he hissed, his eyes blazing with fury. "If I hadn't, I'd have a hole in my fucking shoulder."

"It wouldn't have killed you," I snapped, wincing and dropping the gun when he pressed on a pressure point in my wrist. "You and Gray would have had matching scars."

His hand went around my neck, and a snarl burned my throat when he pressed me down, keeping me under him.

"Do you believe in fate or chance?" he murmured as Gray turned out of the garage.

"I think there's a good chance my knee is going to meet your dick if you don't get off me."

"I think us meeting two years ago was chance," he continued, his voice gruff. "But you coming to our city? That's fate. And fuck, even after everything, I can't let that go. Let you go."

I searched his eyes, my heart hammering. Distrust. Anger. Guilt. All those emotions were there. But the one thing missing was the reason I hadn't shot him. Because, after all of this, there wasn't an ounce of hatred in his gaze. But it wasn't enough.

"Life dealt my hand of fate years ago," I whispered hoarsely. "And I'm still fighting to escape that."

The Jeep slowed, and I took advantage of Kade's stunned moment to lift my leg and knee him in the balls. He groaned in pain as I hit the inside of his elbow, breaking his hold on my neck. My hand smashed into the side of his face, and I shoved him off me. He fell between the seats, already scrambling to get back up. I glanced through the windshield, seeing the red light turn green. Lunging across the seat, I opened the door. Gray must have heard because even though a car behind us was honking, the Jeep didn't move.

Gray was yelling at me to stay in the car, but I ignored him and jumped out. My feet hit the pavement, and I started running. I bolted between two buildings where the street was too narrow for the Jeep to follow. Glancing over my shoulder, I didn't see them before I turned the corner, going behind my apartment building. My chest tightened the longer I ran, and I sucked in quick breaths, but I didn't stop until I was two blocks away.

I finally stumbled a few steps as I slowed down, walking down the sidewalk and then bounding down the steps to the underground parking lot under a hotel. Slipping my backpack off, I dug through my bag, finding my Corvette key. Once I was farther away, I'd check to make sure there wasn't a tracker on it, but it would work for now.

I got in the Corvette and pulled out of the parking lot, glancing in the rearview mirror every few seconds. After they'd found my apartment, I was more anxious than usual. I didn't breathe easy until I got on the highway.

"Bye, Ridgewood," I muttered, pressing the gas pedal. I was leaving like planned and had no intention of ever coming back.

33

Milina

"Give me another," I told Caleb over the phone as I tapped on the steering wheel.

He sighed. "Mili, maybe you should take a break—"

"I want to work," I cut him off sharply. "I know there are more jobs. Give me the details, Caleb."

"You should come to Florida and visit me. I miss you."

"I'll come next month."

"I don't think you should be alone."

I frowned. "Why? This is how we've been working for years. I'm always alone."

"I know," he said carefully. "But this time it seems different. Ever since you left Ridgewood."

"It's been three weeks since I left, and I feel fucking phenomenal. They were trying to trap me."

"Even the mayor?"

I scowled. "I never should have told you about him."

"You're hurt. Because you liked them. All three of them. It's okay to admit that."

"No, I'm pissed because now I can't do the Panther job," I argued. "Now we have to wait an entire year for our next chance. And I need to come up with a whole new plan because next time I'm doing it myself. No more relying on anyone."

"You'll always have me," he said softly.

I half-smiled. "I know."

"Come home. I'll grill. You and Tucker can argue over the music as I cook. It'll be fun."

I stared at the sun setting, thinking about his words. "Not yet. I need to keep my mind busy a little longer."

"Fine," he said, defeated. "I'll email you details."

"Thanks. I'll call you tomorrow."

"Stay safe, Mili."

"Always." I hung up and tossed my new phone on the passenger seat. All my phones were easily replaceable, but I'd left my main one in Ridgewood when I fled. I was sure by now Kade and Gray had attempted to hack it. Even if they did, they wouldn't find anything.

"Fuck me," I muttered, lightly banging my head on the wheel. I was exhausted from running jobs nonstop over the last few weeks. But it was better than sitting still and being stuck with my own thoughts. After this next job, I'd have to take a break and sleep, or I'd start making mistakes.

I glanced at the phone, resisting the urge to call Rylan for what felt like the thousandth time. I felt bad about how I'd just left. And if I was being honest, I missed him. Even Kade and Gray—as much as I detested it. Life had been fun when I was in Ridgewood until they had to go and fuck it up. I wondered if they were looking for me. It wouldn't do them any good. I was two states away, and even while working jobs, I'd be impossible to find. I wasn't in their city anymore, where eyes were on me. I could slip under the radar like I always did.

My leg bounced as I glared at the phone before my resolve fucking broke. I wouldn't call Rylan. Because leading him on wasn't fair to him. I had told him he wouldn't hear from me again, and I didn't want him to think I was coming back. Instead, I found Gray's number. Caleb had all my numbers from my old phone, and I stupidly told him to give them to me for my new phone. I shouldn't have asked, then I wouldn't be calling right now.

"Yeah?" Gray's curt tone had a rush shooting down my spine. It was the first time I'd allowed myself to feel anything since leaving.

"Have you been hunting for me?" I asked sweetly. The pause was so long, I thought he'd hung up. Until the volume changed and I realized he put me on speaker. "Mm, let me guess. Kade is there too."

"What do you want?" Kade snapped, his voice colder than ever.

What did I want? I had no fucking idea. Caleb was right about me being lonely. It had never bothered me before. Before I went to Ridgewood. Before I met Kade, Gray, and Rylan. Now I felt restless being by myself. Which was ridiculous because I had been alone half the time I was in Ridgewood too.

"I asked you a question first," I tossed back.

"We wanted you gone," Gray answered stiffly. "Why would we look for you?"

"Liar," I purred. "I haven't been gone long enough to forget that Kade, at least, was trying to force me to stay."

"Planning on coming back?" Kade asked.

I laughed. "Absolutely not."

"I thought you'd go underground after running," Gray grumbled.

I bit my lip, stopping my grin as I heard a loud thump that was most likely Kade hitting Gray. "How do you know I'm not underground?"

They both stayed quiet, and I chuckled, leaning back in my seat. "You two are looking for me."

"There's been talk about Sapphire running jobs," Kade muttered. "Everyone has heard about it. Especially since you barely took any during the last few months."

"There are always rumors surrounding me," I said in a bored voice. "But even with all the talk, no one ever knows where I am. By the time people hear of my jobs, I'm already long gone."

"We know," Gray grated out.

My heart flipped. "You've tried finding me."

"You owe me a car," Kade stated.

"You stole my Jeep. Consider us even."

Gray snorted. "You stole that Jeep."

"Stop looking," I demanded. "You won't find me."

"You think we'd have better luck looking for Caleb?" Kade asked.

My blood ran cold. "You'd have better luck finding me."

"Maybe we'll test that."

I took a deep breath, realizing what he was doing. "Trying to draw me out, Kade? Nice try, but it won't work."

"Why'd you call, Mili?" Gray asked.

I hesitated, and it was Kade's turn to laugh. "You don't have a reason, do you?"

"I wanted to tell you to stop looking for me," I snapped, not enjoying how quickly they'd picked up on that.

"Sure you did, Rebel," Gray piped up.

"Be careful," I warned. "Or I'll come back to finish what I started. You wanted me gone, I'm gone. If I come back, you won't like what I do."

"Is that a threat or a promise?" Kade asked in a low voice. "Because I think Gray and I would love the chance to see what you'd try to do if you came back."

"Not just us. There's a certain heartbroken mayor who would probably lock you in his office if you showed up."

Gray's words were like a slap to the face. What was I doing? I never should have called.

"You better be leaving him alone," I snarled. "He isn't involved in this—"

"He got involved the second he touched you," Kade cut me off.

"You want to make sure he stays safe, then maybe you should come back."

I rolled my eyes. "Even you aren't stupid enough to kill him."

"So you're not doing the Panther job?" Gray asked, changing the conversation.

"That's none of your concern anymore."

I hung up before either of them could answer. Staring at Kade's number for a moment, I deleted it and then did the same with Gray's. They were temptations I didn't need. My finger hovered over Rylan's number, and a notification popped up that Caleb had emailed me. Keeping Rylan's number, I read the details of the new job, forcing my thoughts away from the guys in Ridgewood.

34

Gray

I stared through the glass, watching the partygoers filling our club. My eyes searched for the one person I knew wouldn't be here. Just like every day for nearly the past month, I'd hoped she would just show up like she did the last time she disappeared. But I knew that wouldn't happen. She was gone and wasn't coming back.

Not that I blamed her. What we did to get her to run was about as low as we could have gotten. I never expected her to get the slip on us and hold us hostage while she burned our fucking cars. The one thing we had to track her was left at her apartment when she fled. We'd known where she was living for a while but wanted to save it for when we needed it. Not that it did any good—she still got the drop on us.

"Vic and Juan are on their way," Kade told me, coming to stand next to me. "They're going to want an update about her."

I scoffed. "What update? It's been a month. She's fucking gone."

"You really think she's done with us after calling last week?" Kade raised an eyebrow at me. "She's probably making a plan to come back and murder us in our sleep."

"She had a chance to do that," I muttered before taking a sip of my beer. "She left us alive."

He shook his head. "We'll see her again. Not sure if it will be a good thing."

I shifted my gaze back to the club floor, my lips tipping in a grin when I saw Rylan walking to a table. He'd been showing up more often than usual since Mili had disappeared. He was hoping she'd come back too. The smile faded when I heard the back door open. When I turned around, Vic and Juan were already halfway across the room, getting drinks from the bar.

"Any word from her?" Vic asked.

I shook my head. "Nope."

We hadn't told them about her calling. It didn't mean anything, anyway. They were pissed about what she did to us. They didn't have the entire story, but they knew she'd drugged us and left us cuffed there until members of the crew found us. They saw her as a threat and wanted it under control.

"I don't want to have to worry about her coming back and trying to fuck with the crew," Juan muttered, settling on the couch.

"It's not the crew she'll go after," Kade bit out. "It'll be us."

"You'll be running this crew when we retire," Vic shot back. "Dealing with her falls on you either way."

"She's just one girl—"

"She's not," Kade snapped. "Underestimating her is what got us here. Leave her alone, and she'll do the same with us. We lost the chance for extra money, but who gives a fuck? We make enough on our own."

Juan frowned. "It wasn't just money. It was connections."

"We have enough of those too," Kade ground out. "She's gone. Not coming back. The last time we tried finding her, it didn't happen until she sought us out two years later. I'm not wasting any more of my damn time on her."

His shoulders were tense, and I didn't say anything. He might have been acting like he was glad she was gone, but he thought about her just as much as I did. Our story with her didn't feel over. Or maybe I just didn't want it to be. She fucking hated us, yet I couldn't make myself feel the same about her.

"A group reached out to work with us," Vic said, changing the subject. "They worked with that guy, Ryan."

My ears perked up at that. "The guy Mili knew?"

"The guy she killed," Juan shot back. "But yes. They want help on a job and are willing to pay a lot."

Unease skated up my spine as Kade and I exchanged a glance. Mili had killed the guy for a reason. Was it really because he screwed her over, or was there another reason? I wasn't sure we'd ever find out.

"I'm not sure why you're acting like the choice is only up to you two," Juan said, a frown on his face. "We already accepted. We'll meet with them in a couple of weeks to go over details."

I didn't argue, deciding we'd do our own research on them before the meeting. We usually did that for any new meetings anyway. My attention drifted back down to the club, and I noticed Rylan was staring at the glass. He couldn't see me, but it was clear he was trying to get our attention.

"Is that all?" I clipped out, pulling on my leather jacket.

Vic scowled. "That's it. If you hear anything from the girl, you tell us."

I jerked a nod before bounding down the stairs. Booming music met me, and I pushed through the crowd, stopping in front of Rylan's table. People were already sneaking glances at us, and I cocked my head, grinning.

"Need something?" I drawled, taking the chair across from him. "You know, people are going to start talking if you keep showing up here."

"Has she contacted you?"

I swiped my tongue across my lip ring. "And if she has? What does that have to do with you?"

He hesitated. "I just want to make sure she's okay."

"Believe me, she's fine," I grumbled. "Like I told you last time, she's gone for good. Stop fucking pouting and get over it."

Annoyance flared in his eyes, and he stood up, purposely knocking his drink over on the table. I jumped up, moving before it could hit my jacket.

"Her leaving is your fault," he sneered. "Yours and Kade's."

I bit back a reply, seeing how pissed he was. We didn't need to bring any more attention to us than he already had.

"Go home, Mayor." I glanced over my shoulder as I walked away. "All you're doing is ruining your reputation by being here. You really want to do that, just ask, and I'll do it for you."

If he replied, I didn't hear it as I went to the bar. Kade was already there, his gaze going behind me, most likely looking at Rylan. I sat next to him and ordered a drink. Life was going back to normal. Once Rylan calmed the fuck down, all would be right in Ridgewood again.

Too bad that wasn't what I wanted.

35

Milina

I slowly drove around the block for a third time, making sure I didn't miss anything. I was wearing all black, and I tugged my hood over my hair before pulling up to the gate. Reaching out the window, I scanned the security card I'd stolen a couple of days ago. I pulled around the building and parked before stepping out of the small sedan I'd brought for the job. Dread coiled in my stomach, and it only got worse as I walked away from the car. I was back in California, only hours from Ridgewood. Caleb had practically begged me not to take the job, but I decided it wouldn't hurt. By the time anyone found out I was in California, I'd be in Florida with him, sipping martinis on the beach.

The car I was taking tonight was one I'd never driven before, and excitement slowly pushed out my nerves as I crept closer to the building. Inside was a cherry red 1969 Chevy Camaro ZL1. The job would be one of my easier ones. The owner was on vacation and had brought all his vehicles here to be stored safely. Whoever wanted this car was aware and gave us that information, which meant it was most likely someone the owner knew. A friend or family member was stabbing him in the back. Yet another reason I'd only trust Caleb in the future. People were assholes.

I picked the lock in record time and quickly punched in the security code that Caleb had gotten. The alarm stopped beeping, and I shined my light around, seeing only a couple of cars in this massive building. After making sure I was alone and cutting the camera feed, I grinned, catching sight of the car. She was beautiful. I bet she drove like a fucking dream. I checked my phone, almost wishing I could take it for a drive. But I wouldn't risk getting caught by playing around. Rare cars like this were targets for cops.

Like I expected, the car was unlocked, and I slid into the seat, studying the pristine interior. The keys were in the center console, and I picked them up, pausing for a moment. The hairs on the back of my neck stood up, and my senses tingled. Something was off. Keeping the keys in my hand, I pretended to inspect the car more while I scanned the room again. A flash of movement caught my eye, and my stomach tightened. Moving slowly, I pushed the lock down on the door and moved to reach down to grab the gun strapped to my ankle.

Until I heard shuffling from behind me. Inside the fucking car.

Before I could reach for a weapon, something tight was cutting off my air, pressing me to the seat. My fingers wrapped around the rope that was strangling me but pulling it did nothing. Panic swarmed me, knowing I only had seconds before I passed out. Sliding my other hand under my shirt, I grabbed my knife from its holder and blindly swung behind my head. A grunt alerted me that I hit him somewhere, but it wasn't enough. Angling the blade sideways, I swung again, and this time the rope loosened, and I sucked in a lungful of air. The guy let out a pained yell when I stabbed his arm again.

I ducked away from the rope, but before I could move, the driver's window suddenly shattered. I flinched, shielding my face from the glass shards. Someone grabbed me under the arms, hauling me through the broken window. My spine hit the ledge of the window frame, and pain shot up my back. I overplayed my pain, screaming and sagging like I couldn't move.

"You made this easy," someone said gruffly. He was still pulling me backward, and the second my ass hit the cement, he let go of me. I reached forward, freeing my gun from my ankle, then fell onto my back, aiming at the man who'd dragged me out of the car. His eyes widened, and I pulled the trigger, not giving him a chance to say anything. A bloody hole appeared on his forehead, and he slumped forward, dead before he hit the ground.

I scrambled to my feet while the other man fleeing the car from the passenger side. My heart lurched at the sight of a walkie-talkie in his hand. He wasn't alone. I shot at him, but he ducked behind another car. I cursed, debating whether to go after him or leave. Since I didn't know how many others were here, I spun around, racing back toward the entrance. I slammed open the door, only to be taken to the ground. My head cracked on the pavement, and I groaned, my head swimming in pain. A heavy body was on top of me, and he was going for my arms. Flailing around, I ripped out of his grip and blindly jammed the gun into his gut. I pulled the trigger, and warmth covered me as his blood gushed out. His strength left him, and I shoved him off, crawling away. Climbing shakily to my feet, I tried ignoring the pounding in my head as I started running to my car again.

"Stop," someone bellowed from behind me.

"Yeah, right," I muttered about fifty feet from my car. My steps faltered when something was tossed from behind me. I watched it roll under my car, and I skidded to a halt, hoping that wasn't what I thought it was. Glancing over my shoulder, I saw a guy backing up, his eyes on the sedan instead of me. Panic tightened my chest, and I stumbled away, running back toward the building.

A loud explosion shook the ground a split second before I was knocked down by the blast. I landed on my stomach, the air rushing from my lungs. I choked out a breath, rolling onto my back, seeing black smoke billowing from my wrecked car. My ears were ringing, making it impossible to hear anything, and I screamed when someone yanked me up, throwing me over a shoulder. I'd lost my gun when the explosion went off, and I couldn't reach my other knife at this angle.

He carried me back inside the building as I pounded on his back. My ribs were searing with pain, but I fought through it, arching my body to wrap an arm around his neck. Grabbing my other wrist once my arm was around his throat, I pulled, cutting off his air. He dropped to his knees, his hold on my thighs disappearing as he tried to displace my arm. When that didn't work, he grasped my hips and flipped me off him backward. I lost my grip and fell to the ground in a heap.

Before I could get back up, he picked me up and threw me into the side of a car. I gritted my teeth, hot pain shooting through my ankle when I landed on it sideways.

"Don't fucking move," he growled, standing in front of me with a pistol aimed at me.

I glared at him, scooting back until I was resting against the car. He had brown hair that fell past his ears, and with his hoodie on, I could only see his hands, which were covered in tattoos. I didn't recognize him at all, and as his hazel eyes bored into me, I wondered who he was with. Joel? The crew? Somehow, I doubted he was from Ridgewood. If they wanted me, Kade and Gray would have come themselves.

"You killed my friends," he grated out.

"You blew up my car," I stated, acting bored. "What now? We wait until the cops come after hearing that explosion?"

He grinned cruelly. "We have some time before that happens."

I swallowed thickly, not showing my panic. He wasn't acting alone if he had connections to pay off the police. I blinked quickly, my mind going hazy. Now that I was sitting still, my battered body was screaming from pain. Looking away from him, I glanced down, seeing a slow growing red stain covering my shirt. Brushing my fingers over it, I cringed, realizing it was my blood. And from the feeling of it, the gash on my stomach was large enough to be concerned about.

"You have any weapons on you?" he asked, not lowering his gun.

I swiped my tongue over my lips. "Why don't you come over here and find out?"

All I had left was a knife, but I wasn't about to pull that out until I had the opportunity to use it on him. He studied me, taking a step closer. I braced myself, seeing the hit coming. Pain exploded across my jaw when he whipped me with the gun, and blood filled my mouth. By the time I was able to focus again, he was already a few feet away from me. Pulling out a burner phone, he tapped a button and put it to his ear.

"Yeah, I have her," he said, his stare not leaving me. "I should have brought more men. Three almost wasn't enough."

Dumbass. He just told me he was the only one left. Good for me; horrible for him. Because I knew he'd fuck up and give me the chance to use my blade. By the way his eyes widened, I was guessing whoever he was talking to was telling him the same thing.

"She's hurt. But alive." He clenched his jaw while listening to whoever was talking. Or yelling, by the sound of it. "It's Milina. I'm sure of it."

My mouth went dry, and my pain disappeared for a moment when I realized he was with Joel's men. That had been my first guess, but now, I was sure. I needed to get the fuck out of here.

"I don't think—fine," he said nervously. He came closer until he was in front of me and crouched down. "He wants to talk to you. Don't fucking try anything."

I'd already slipped my pocketknife from my pocket, and when he reached forward to put the phone to my ear, I lashed out, stabbing him in the neck. His eyes bulged, and he dropped the phone, both hands going to his throat. His breaths were gurgled as the life slowly left him. Grabbing the gun from his hand, I shot him in the head. I attempted to stand but cried out when my ankle gave out.

I sagged against the car, my heart hammering as I heard a voice through the phone. Staring at it for a moment, I grabbed it and put it to my ear.

"Tony? You okay?"

My face paled when I recognized the voice. It wasn't fucking possible. He stopped talking for a moment before he spoke my name.

"Mili?"

"Who knew ghosts could talk?" I hissed, keeping the shock out of my voice.

Liam paused for a moment. "You should have taken longer than a second to check my pulse. Or put a bullet in my head."

My chest heaved as he spoke. I'd thought he died that day at Andy's garage. He'd been alive this whole time. Ice spilled into my veins. Which meant Joel's people knew I'd been in California. That I was alive.

"I'm surprised you didn't come here yourself," I said, feigning hurt. "You thought I wouldn't be able to handle your men?"

"More will be there soon."

I couldn't tell if he was lying or not, but his answer told me one thing. He'd been hurt when his motorcycle crashed. He probably almost did die. And I bet he wasn't fully healed yet, because if he was, he would have come to chase me down himself.

"This whole job was a setup," I muttered.

"We knew someone new had taken on the Sapphire name. After seeing you, I had a feeling. You should have disappeared."

"How'd you know I'd take the job?" I asked, stalling as I tried to figure out what to do.

"I didn't. Actually, this is the third job we sent out over the dark web. You refused the other two." He was calm—too calm. I needed to leave. I tried again to stand but gritted my teeth in pain when my ankle refused to hold my weight.

"You've been working with others," he stated. "That was a dumb move. It made knowing what you've been up to easier."

I froze. Did they know about the crew? Was the crew working with him? Kade and Gray wouldn't give me up, would they? At this point, I had no fucking idea.

"See you soon, Mili," he said quietly before disconnecting the call.

"Fuck," I screamed, throwing the phone to the floor. I dug into my jacket pocket and pulled out my own phone, seeing the screen was shattered. But it was still working. I took a deep breath, finding Caleb's number. "Come on, Caleb. Answer the fucking phone."

It rang and rang before going to voice mail. I ran a hand through my hair, flinching when I felt blood. Hitting my head on the pavement was worse than I thought. And I was losing too much blood. Clenching my jaw, I pressed my free hand against the wound on my stomach. I called Caleb again, snarling in frustration when it went to voice mail again after ringing. I had no one else to call. I had men who worked for me, but they all went through Caleb. I'd never met any of them or had their contact information.

I glanced around, looking at which vehicle would be best to take until I noticed there was something wrong with the tires closest to me. They were fucking slashed.

"No," I whispered, snapping my gaze to the next car. Those tires were cut too. The guys who'd come after me were smart enough to ruin my chance of escape. Even though I knew it was useless, I scanned the last two cars, seeing the same thing.

Giving myself a minute to work up to it, I began scooting away from the car. For a third time, I tried standing, only to collapse again. Tucking the gun into my leggings, I started crawling on the floor, moving toward the back door. Every move I made caused the pain to become nearly overwhelming, but I kept going. I had no doubt that Liam was sending more men, and I didn't stand a fucking chance if I was still here when they showed up.

After what felt like an eternity, I got to the back parking lot. My knees and hands ached from crawling, but I didn't stop until I got to the back fence. I moved slowly, my fear growing when I couldn't find a place wide enough to slip through. Spying a dumpster in the corner of the lot, I made my way there, slipping behind it. I was wedged between the fence and the dumpster uncomfortably but breathed a sigh of relief once I was out of sight. It would be easy enough to hear footsteps before anyone reached me.

I pulled my phone back out and called Caleb again. No answer. I stared at the screen before calling another number. I shouldn't be doing this. I had promised myself I wouldn't fucking involve him.

"Hello?" Rylan's voice came over the speaker, and I bit my lip.

"Hi, Rylan," I said softly.

"Mili?"

"Yeah," I breathed out. "How are you?"

"Uh, I'm good. Are you okay? You sound...different." Concern was in his voice, and I shook my head, wincing from the pain. I must be in bad shape for him to notice something was off over the phone.

"I kinda got myself into a situation." I paused, wishing Caleb would call me back so I didn't have to do this. "I hate to ask, but I need your help."

"Where are you?" he asked instantly.

"A couple of hours from Ridgewood." I hesitated and then rattled off the address of this building. "I need to get out of here before they get here—"

I stopped talking, realizing this was a mistake. If Rylan came when Liam's men did, it would end badly.

"You know what? I'll figure it out," I muttered. "I never should have called."

"Wait," he nearly shouted, knowing I was about to hang up. "Is someone after you? Call the police. They can help."

I laughed hoarsely. "No, they can't. They're either working with the men I'm running from, or they'll arrest me once they see what I did."

"I'll help you," he said quickly. "Stay there, okay?"

"Believe me, if I could leave, I would have," I mumbled, shifting slightly as a sharp piece of fence stabbed me in the back.

"Just stay alive until I get there," he said firmly.

"Don't come alone," I whispered. "You have police you trust? Bring them with you."

"Don't worry, I'll be fine. I need to make a call. Keep your phone close."

I muttered a goodbye and hung up, my stomach knotting. Calling him felt wrong. I had sworn I wouldn't get him killed. I hoped I could keep that promise. I called Caleb again and again, only stopping because my phone battery was getting dangerously close to dead.

Jolts of pain ran through my entire body, and I tried to take note of all my injuries. My ribs were bruised, possibly fractured. The wound on my head wasn't too bad, but I was almost certain I had a slight concussion. My ankle was twisted at best. Maybe broken. My stomach was worrying me most because it was still bleeding. I bit my tongue, slowly lifting my shirt. I couldn't tell where the wound was because there was so much blood. If I didn't get something to stop the bleeding soon, I'd be in trouble. Tugging my shirt back down, I kept my hand pressed against it as I stared at my phone.

Why wasn't Caleb answering? He always had his phone on, especially when I was running jobs. Fear washed through me when the thought of Liam finding him popped into my head. Not possible. They had to create a fake job to find me—no way they found Caleb. At least that's what I'd keep believing.

I stayed still, listening for any movements coming from outside my hiding spot, but the night was silent. I blinked, willing myself to stay awake. But my brain was foggy, and keeping my eyes open was a losing battle. I sank into unconsciousness before jolting awake from the pain. It was a never-ending circle of drifting off and waking back up until I lost track of time. I gripped the gun tightly, hoping I'd be awake if Liam's men found me.

A tear ran down my cheek, and I angrily wiped it away. I would not fucking cry. I would survive this like I did everything else. Or I'd die trying. Death would be better than those men getting a hold of me. Either way, I refused to cry about it. I wouldn't live my possible last moments giving them my tears.

According to the clock on my phone, it had been an hour and a half, and my body was beginning to go numb. Calling Caleb again, I swallowed past the lump in my throat as I prayed that he was okay.

A sudden loud bang had my heart stuttering. If it was Rylan, he would have called first. Craning my neck, I leaned forward until I could see the parking lot. A man with a shaved head and neck tattoos was scanning the area with a gun raised. Goose bumps skated across my skin, and I lifted my handgun, keeping it on him as he crept closer. If he was with Liam, there was no way the guy was alone. I willed him to go the other way, but instead, he came closer, the dumpster catching his attention. I pressed myself back as far as I could go, but it did nothing when the guy poked his head around the corner, meeting my gaze. His eyes widened, and I bared my teeth, aiming my gun at him.

"She's here—"

His yell was cut off when I shot him. I lurched forward, the pain stealing my breath as I climbed over his body as fast as I could. I had seconds before his partners came. My heart thudded as I tried getting to my feet. But my ankle still couldn't hold me, and I tumbled back to the ground. Another bang alerted me to the back door opening again.

"Don't fucking move," a voice shouted. Ignoring it, I went to my knees and raised my gun, but he kicked it out of my hand before grabbing my hair. I couldn't bite back my yelp when he yanked on my hair, throwing me back on the ground.

Another shot rang out, and the guy fell on top of me with half his face gone. His weight kept me plastered to the ground as a hail of bullets flew across the parking lot. I stayed under the dead weight, using his body as a shield. I didn't know how many people were here, but panic clung to me as I wondered whether Rylan was there. I moved my arm across the rough pavement, trying to find a gun or any weapon, but nothing was in reach.

Shots seemed to be coming from everywhere around me, and I could only see one man from where I was lying. He got shot in the chest and fell to the ground. Soon after, the shooting ceased, and I trembled, not knowing who'd won. Or who the fuck was even fighting. The body was pulled off me, and I scrambled away, only to freeze when I saw who was in front of me.

"Kade?" I sputtered out.

"Come on." He reached for me. "We need to get out of here before the cops come."

"Don't fucking touch me," I screeched, stumbling away from him.

"How did you know I was here? Are you working with them? Did you give me up?"

Confusion crossed his face, but I was so out of it, I couldn't tell if it was real or not. "Working with who? We'll talk about it later. We need to fucking leave."

"No," I screamed, losing it. "They knew I was here. There's no way you could have known unless you're working with them."

My breath hitched when someone came up behind me and carefully picked me up, sweeping me into their arms. I flailed, slapping him across the face.

"Rebel, calm down," Gray muttered as he started walking across the parking lot, his hold on me tightening when I struggled. Not that it was doing anything. I was so weak, my hits were nothing anymore.

"Put me down," I cried. "I won't fucking go back. Kill me. Please."

Gray stared at me, pity in his eyes. "We're not working with whoever you're talking about."

Kade appeared next to us. "You can thank the mayor for us showing up."

"Rylan?" Shock coursed through me. "He called you for help?"

"He's out of town. Down south for a business conference. He wouldn't have been able to get here for hours," Kade answered, inspecting me as Gray carried me to their car.

"Bullshit," I hissed out. "He doesn't trust either of you."

"True," Gray mused. "But he seemed to believe that we'd help you."

"I want to talk to him."

Kade opened the back door of the SUV, and Gray set me down on the soft leather. I clamored across the seat, fully intent on leaving the car. Maybe Rylan did call them. But what if he didn't? What if they were really working with Liam and taking me back? I couldn't chance it. I pulled on the door handle, going rigid when it didn't open.

"Unlock the fucking door," I snarled.

"Jesus, how much blood have you lost?" Gray mumbled, sliding into the car next to me. "You're white as a ghost. We need to get you to a doctor."

I pulled my phone out, my nerves smothering me when I saw it was dead. Kade started driving, and I curled away from Gray, my body shaking. I was trapped in this car with men I hoped were here to help me. But if they weren't, it was too late anyway. My vision started going blurry, and I fought to stay focused, but as we got on the highway, I lost myself to darkness.

36

Kade

"Stop staring at her like she's going to bolt," Gray said, coming into the living room. "You heard the doctor. She won't be able to walk without help for a while."

Did it make me a piece of shit that I was glad she wouldn't be able to leave right away? I hated seeing her in pain, but with her laid up, at least I knew she'd be here for a while. Because if she was able, she'd try to leave the second she woke up.

It was a miracle she hadn't broken anything. Her ankle was severely sprained, and the cut in her stomach needed stitches. The doctor guessed she had a concussion from the gash on her head, but that was already looking better. I ground my teeth, my eyes going to her throat. It was red and bruised from whatever had been wrapped around it. The side of her face looked the same, with a small cut on her jaw. The rest of her body was just as battered and bruised from what we saw when we showered her off.

It had been a little more than a day since we brought her back to Ridgewood. Gray and I had barely left her side, even though she'd been sleeping the entire time. I was worried, but the crew doctor assured us that her sleeping was normal.

We both paused when she shifted in her sleep. She was lying on our pull-out couch in the living room, where she'd been since we brought her to our house. She'd been here once before, but she'd only seen the first floor where our study was. Down there was for business. We lived on the second floor, our one oasis from life. A door at the top of the stairs kept the floors separated. There were always members downstairs, even a few bedrooms where they could crash if needed. Crew business didn't happen up here. Not even Vic and Juan had keys to this place.

It was an open concept, and I could still keep an eye on her in the living room as I sat on a stool in the kitchen. The walls were painted a light gray, and all our furniture was black. The stainless-steel appliances were almost brand new. This was the one place I could relax and not worry. We never brought anyone up here.

Except her.

We'd killed the six guys who were after her, and I was regretting not taking the time to look at their ink. We had no idea who they were, although from her reaction when we found her, I was willing to guess it had to do with her past. I'd never seen her as terrified as she was the moment she thought we were taking her to whoever she was running from.

"Did you look at her phone yet?" Gray asked.

I had found her phone on the floorboard of the car a couple of hours ago and plugged it in to charge, hoping something on there could give us answers.

My gaze flicked to the counter where it was charging. "Not yet. I forgot about it."

"Vic and Juan are going to be pissed if they find out she's here," Gray muttered.

"No point in telling them," I responded. "You think she's going to stick around once she's feeling better?"

"You're going to just let her walk away?" Gray asked, arching an eyebrow.

I laughed, shaking my head. "Let her? She'd shoot us if we don't let her go."

A knock at the door interrupted us, and I hopped off the stool. I unlocked it, swinging the door open, my heart seizing when a gun was instantly pressed to my skull. The guy holding the weapon was wearing a black jacket with the hood pulled up. He shoved me back, making enough room to kick the door closed behind him.

"Put it down, man," Gray said quietly from behind me. "You shoot us, and you won't leave this house alive."

I wondered how the fuck he'd gotten past our crew. There were always people downstairs keeping watch. Which was why I didn't have a weapon on me. I never did when I was home. No one ever made it up the stairs that I had to worry about.

"Where is she?" the guy hissed, pushing the gun harder into my forehead.

Keeping my expression blank, I answered, "Who?"

"Don't fucking bullshit me. I know she's here."

"No idea what you're talking about," I murmured. "But if I did, I'd tell you that you knocked on the wrong fucking door."

"She's coming with me," he snapped, rage building in his eyes.

I straightened my spine. "You're not getting out of here alive."

He broke our stare, his gaze going toward the living room. His eyes widened when he saw Mili, and I used his distraction. I grabbed his wrist, lifting his arm to point the gun at the ceiling and punched him across the face. It barely seemed to faze him as he threw a hit of his own. My neck snapped to the side, and I lowered my shoulder, ramming into him.

He tried wrapping an arm around my throat to get me in a chokehold, and I put my knee into his gut. Both our hands were on the gun, fighting for control, when Gray flew past me, knocking the guy into the wall and sending the gun skidding across the floor. They wrestled, and whoever the hell he was, he could fight. But he wasn't winning against both of us. He rolled on top of Gray, and I took that moment to grab him and yank him off, throwing him to the floor.

"Stop." The scream echoed through the room. I glanced up, seeing Mili awake and trying to get off the bed. Her eyes were on the guy, full of worry.

"Mili—"

She cut Gray off. "Don't touch him."

"He came in here ready to shoot us," I grated out.

The guy stayed still, his gaze on us to see if we were going to keep him on the floor. When neither of us moved, he jumped to his feet, waving his hands to show he wasn't going to hurt us. I glared at him, stepping in his way when he went toward Mili.

"That's far enough," I warned, my voice low.

"Kade, let him," Mili said, her voice softening. "He's not here to hurt me. Or you."

"He wanted to take you," Gray said, not an ounce of trust in his gaze as he stared at the guy.

"I'm Caleb," the guy muttered, pushing his hood back to reveal a mess of red hair. "I've heard she's mentioned me."

I bit my tongue almost hard enough to draw blood. "Caleb?"

He ignored me, shouldering past me to get to Mili. I spun around to see him embrace her in a gentle hug. She clung to him, a sob catching in her throat. Fury burned my veins as he stroked her hair. She trusted him. She fucking loved him.

"I'm sorry I didn't answer," he said, his voice thick with emotion. "I lost my phone, and we were an hour from home. By the time I got home to get a new one, your phone was already off. I couldn't track you until it turned back on."

"I thought they got you," she said, her voice trembling. "Fuck. I thought you were dead—or worse."

"I'm fine," he soothed, lifting her fully back onto the bed.

Gray looked just as pissed as I did, and more than a little hurt passed through his eyes as he sat on a stool.

"Want to tell us how the hell you got past our men?" I asked gruffly.

Caleb looked at me, sizing us up as much as we were him. "Don't worry, I didn't kill anyone."

"That's not what I asked," I snapped.

"Shit," Mili gasped when she tried standing again.

"It's not broken," Gray told her. "But you'll need crutches for a couple of weeks."

She finally looked at us now that she seemed convinced that Caleb was okay. "You two brought me back here? Where is here?"

"Ridgewood," Caleb answered before I could, making me scowl. "Their house, I'm guessing."

"Rylan really did call you," she said slowly, as if thinking of the events of yesterday. "Where is he—"

"He was here nearly all night," Gray interrupted with a roll of his eyes. "Left a couple of hours ago. Our house seems to be a revolving door of uninvited guests today."

"Rylan was here?" she asked in shock. "With both of you? In the same room?"

"You act like we can't control ourselves," I muttered. "Not even a hit was thrown."

"Our turn for questions," Gray said, standing up. "Want to tell us who almost killed you?"

Mili pursed her lips, her face going blank. "No."

"We saved you," I growled. "Not him. Not Rylan. You don't think we deserve to know who those guys were? Especially now if we have targets on our backs."

"Did you kill all of them?" she clipped out.

"Yes," Gray answered.

"Then you have nothing to worry about."

"I think," Caleb piped up, "she means to say thank you. For saving her."

The murder in his eyes seemed to have dissipated now that he knew that Gray and I had no intention of hurting her.

A muscle in her bruised jaw flexed, clearly not used to relying on people. "Thank you."

"Who were they, Rebel?" Gray asked, the use of the nickname making Caleb look at him in surprise. "Were they connected to the people who hurt you in the past?"

Those words made Caleb's mouth fall open as he stared at Mili. "You told them about Joel—"

"No," she cut him off sharply. "They heard Rhett talking about him."

Caleb looked between her and us. "I told you not to take them to that job."

I didn't fucking like him. I didn't like how they seemed to have a whole relationship that I couldn't scratch the surface of. Did he know that she'd been here sleeping with not just me, but Gray and Rylan too?

What bothered me most was that I wanted her to look at me like that.

"Joel? Is he the ex-boyfriend?" Gray asked. "He's the one who hurt you?"

Mili took a deep breath, wincing and rubbing her head. "Yes."

"I thought you said he was dead," I said, my hands clenching into fists. I had no idea what he'd done to her, but I knew it was more than enough to warrant death. If he wasn't dead, I'd fix that fucking problem.

"He is," she said quickly. "But he has friends who still want me because of what I did."

"Friends," I repeated. "Was he in this life?"

Her eyes darted to mine. "Yes."

Gray shook his head. "He was in a gang, wasn't he? What gang?"

"It doesn't matter. They broke apart after Joel died," she answered shortly.

"Seems like they still have some ties to send six men after you," I muttered.

"Thank you for helping me," she said softly. "But I handle it on my own now. Caleb and I will leave—"

"Can I eat first?" Caleb asked, standing from the bed. "I've been on the road for the last day."

"If you're going to get food, I might sleep some more." Mili could barely keep her eyes open, and she was already lying down before she finished talking. "Don't leave without me, Caleb."

Both Gray and I were rigid as we listened. I knew she was going to leave, but I wasn't expecting it so soon. My mind was already racing with ways to make her stay, but as I watched her drift off to sleep, I realized it wouldn't happen. She would never stay somewhere she didn't want. She'd do anything to keep her freedom, no matter who got in the way.

Caleb strode into the kitchen, a worried frown on his face. "She's going to be pissed, but I can't take her with me."

My heart skipped a beat. "What?"

"You got some…" Gray trailed off, looking at Caleb's wrist.

I followed his gaze, seeing blood seeping from his wrist. Caleb grumbled under his breath, pulling up his sleeve to reveal a bloodied bandage. He leaned across the island and grabbed a paper towel.

"I guess we aren't the only ones you decided to fight today," Gray muttered.

Caleb glanced at Mili. "I have nowhere safe to take her. They found me. I don't know how the fuck they did, but I barely got away. I didn't lose my phone—it got destroyed when they lit my house on fire."

"You knew him? Joel?" I asked, not having the courage to ask the question I really wanted to know. Like how long he and Mili had been together.

"I knew him," Caleb said slowly. "I'm not telling you anything she doesn't want to share herself."

"You lied to her," Gray said, his eyes narrowing. "Why?"

"Because if I told her I wanted us to separate, she'd refuse to listen."

Neither of us said anything as we stared at Caleb, not sure where the hell he was taking this. He patted his arm, wiping off the blood. His gaze moved to us, as if debating about what to say next.

"She's not well enough for us to be running around the country," he said in a low voice. "She needs to stay in one place until she's healed. And I need to find another place that's safe so I can start tracking them down."

"Them?" I questioned. "How many more are going to come after her?"

"Enough to worry about," Caleb mumbled, running his uninjured hand through his hair. "I need to get all new computers and equipment..."

He trailed off, as if remembering that we were in the room. His jaw tightened, and his face went cold. He was as protective of his secrets as Mili was.

"You work with computers," I said, tilting my head. "You work with her for her Sapphire jobs."

"I work with her on everything. I will do anything for her," he said, his voice going hard. "I will kill anyone who hurts her."

"Seeing as we saved her, we're good." Gray moved to the fridge and pulled out some beers. "We have no plans to hurt her."

"Your security is good here, even though I was able to slip past." He looked around the room. "Can she stay here? At least until she's good enough to travel?"

"She doesn't want to stay," I ground out. "She wants to go with you. We all heard it."

"She'll be fine," Caleb said. "After she gets over the fact that I left—"

"You're not going to tell her you're leaving?" I snapped.

"If I do, she'll try to leave with me."

Well, if he wanted to leave her here while she was pissed at him, I had no issue with that. Gray, on the other hand, was thinking more logically.

"We'll end up like the men she killed at that warehouse if we try to keep her here when she doesn't want to be," Gray muttered.

"You're telling me you two can't handle her?"

Caleb's words brought both shock and confusion, and his amused grin only added to both. *Did he know we'd slept with her? Did he fucking care?*

"What the hell do you want?" Gray asked, crossing his arms.

"Keep her here. Keep her safe. Until I come back."

Gray and I exchanged a glance before I nodded. "Fine."

"Good, it's settled. I'll stay the night and leave in the morning." Caleb leaned across the counter and grabbed his beer before going back to the couch. "But don't forget—you hurt her, and I'll fucking kill you."

"How nice to invite himself to sleep here," I grumbled under my breath before taking a swig of beer.

"Only for a night." Gray leaned on the counter next to me. "But she's staying."

"Better lock up our weapons before she starts using her crutches."

37

Milina

Every muscle ached, and even my skin seemed to radiate pain. I couldn't remember the last time I was this bad off. I'd had bad injuries before, thanks to Joel, but never so much all at once. My head was pounding, and I sucked in a breath when I shifted in bed. In Kade and Gray's house. I couldn't believe they were the ones who'd rescued me. After what I did to them, they could have easily left me for dead.

Feeling someone's breath on the back of my neck, I turned, trying to move as little as possible. I smiled, seeing Caleb's sleeping face. The relief I'd felt when I'd known he was alive was like a weight off my chest. I was terrified I'd never see him again. A noise made me turn back around to look into the kitchen.

Kade was awake, standing at the island. It was different seeing him in such relaxed clothes. He was wearing gray sweats and that was it. His hair was wet, and there were still drops of water on the tattoos covering his bare chest. He was gripping a coffee cup, his glare focused not on me, but on Caleb.

"Hey, Mili."

Surprise jolted through me when I saw Rylan leaning against the wall near the front door. He was dressed in one of his usual suits, and even though he was giving me a small grin, his jaw was tight, and his eyes darted behind me to Caleb.

"Rylan," I breathed out, trying to sit up and grimacing.

He strode across the room, stopping at the side of the bed and crouching until he was eye level with me. He gently brushed hair out of my eyes as he studied the injuries I was sure were covering my face.

"I'm sorry I couldn't come for you myself," he said, keeping his voice quiet. "I was out of town—"

"It's fine," I assured him. In all honesty, I was glad he hadn't been there. It had been a bloodbath, and while Kade and Gray could fight, Rylan could have gotten hurt or killed. "How'd you know Kade and Gray would help me?"

He chuckled. "They were my only options. And even though they're assholes, they seem to have a soft spot for you."

"Not sure that's true," I muttered, my gaze going behind him to Kade. Even as I said the words, I realized that Rylan was right to an extent. They did save me. Protected me. Killed for me. They didn't have to do that.

"Mmm, is that the mayor I've heard so much about?" Caleb's voice was thick from sleep, but the bed moved as he sat up.

Rylan's smile faded, and he glared at Caleb. "That's me. The one she called when she couldn't get a hold of you."

"Apparently, she made the right choice since she's alive," Caleb replied, ignoring the venom in Rylan's words.

I scooted up slowly, the blanket pooling around my waist. Rylan's gaze darted to my body, his stare staying on my chest. I glanced down, wondering if I was bleeding through my bandages. Nope, no blood. But I studied the shirt I was wearing, realizing what he was stuck on. It was a guy's shirt, too large for me. And from the name of a classic rock band, I was guessing it was Gray's. I lifted the blanket a bit more, seeing I was wearing a pair of boxers. The guys must have showered and dressed me after they brought me here.

"Breakfast?" Gray asked as he appeared in the kitchen from the hallway. "I called in an order for donuts and crepes."

"You feed them, and they're never going to leave," Kade grumbled, moving to pour another cup of coffee.

"Caleb and I are leaving today," I stated, glancing at him and frowning when he refused to meet my eyes. "Am I wrong?"

"I have a few things to do first," Caleb said, climbing out of the bed.

"Like what?" I questioned, not enjoying how evasive he was being.

"Want some coffee, Rebel?" Gray asked, taking the pot out of Kade's hands.

My stomach rumbled, and Rylan laughed. "I think she wants food."

I rolled my eyes, ignoring the warmth in my chest. Tension still coated the room, but having them all here was making me feel things. I wasn't sure what it was, but I didn't completely hate it.

The food got here, and we all ate. Caleb stood at the counter with Gray and Kade, whispering things that made me wary. It wasn't like him to keep me out of the loop. Rylan propped himself on the edge of the bed as we both enjoyed the strawberry crepes.

"I have to go to work," Rylan said with a frown. "I'd stay here but—"

"Go," I told him, setting my empty plate down.

"You're going to be here when I come back?"

I bit my lip. "I don't plan on staying, Rylan. I never did."

He sighed, leaning over and brushing a kiss on my forehead. "I'll see you later, Lynx."

I didn't argue with him, even though there was a good chance I'd be gone by the end of the day. I watched him leave, and Caleb came back to sit next to me.

"I don't know why you were so against staying in Ridgewood," Caleb said, loud enough for Kade and Gray to hear. "Even with them making you try to stay, they don't seem that bad."

My stomach flipped when Kade and Gray both stared at me curiously. I hadn't exactly told Caleb everything they'd done to me. If he knew they'd locked a chain around my neck to try and claim me, he would have been on the next plane out here to kill them himself.

"Am I missing something?" Caleb asked when the silence became heavy. "Did they do something more than find you at your apartment?"

No one answered, and I shrugged. "It doesn't matter. They got what they deserved."

Caleb's eyes flashed with suspicion. "What did they do?"

"Nothing, Caleb," I tried pacifying him. "They made up for it by saving me."

"You're protecting them," he said in shock. "They did something bad enough that you knew I'd come, didn't they? And you didn't tell me?"

He gently laid an arm around my shoulders, pulling me close. I leaned into him, ignoring the looks of absolute hostility coming from Kade and Gray.

"Do you trust them?" he muttered in my ear, keeping the words between us.

"To an extent—yes," I answered softly.

He seemed to think for a minute before nodding, as if coming to a decision. "They don't like me touching you. They think you're with me, and they're jealous."

I scoffed. "Don't be ridiculous. They wanted me because the city thought I was theirs."

As if to prove his point, he pulled me until I was as close to him as I could be without sitting on his lap. He was careful, making sure not to make my injuries worse. Kade nearly slammed his coffee cup on the counter, while Gray stood rigidly as his tongue swept over his piercing.

"They want you. They've already proved they'll protect you," he whispered. "And the only reason I'm still breathing is because they know you care about me."

"It doesn't matter," I said stiffly. "We're leaving. They don't need to be involved with our shit any more than they already are."

"Tucker wanted me to tell you that he's thinking about you." Caleb spoke loudly, bringing Kade and Gray back into the conversation.

"Tucker?" Kade asked gruffly. "Please don't tell me another fucking person is coming to our house."

Caleb shook his head. "No, he's on the East Coast, visiting family."

I stared at him. "Why isn't he in Florida?"

"He's staying with his parents for a bit while I'm here with you."

"Who's Tucker?" Gray questioned, not liking that we hadn't included them.

Caleb grinned. "My guy. Boyfriend."

Kade's jaw dropped, and he quickly reined in his surprise while Gray stared at Caleb before huffing out a laugh.

"Boyfriend?" Kade said, his gaze falling on me. "So, you two aren't together?"

"Nope. Never have been," Caleb answered brightly. "She's my family."

I frowned. "You think I'd be messing around with you if I was with someone?"

Neither of them answered, but they both visibly relaxed as Caleb chuckled. "Told you. I think the tension should go away now."

He got off the bed and pulled a phone out of his pocket, handing it to me. Along with something else. He kept my gaze, making sure I knew not to say anything out loud. Under the phone was some type of computer chip.

"I got you a new phone," he said before leaning closer and whispering, "Keep the other thing to yourself for now. I'll tell you about it later."

How the hell was I supposed to hide it from Kade and Gray when I was in their house? Nodding, I leaned back, pretending to readjust my pillow and slipping the small chip into the pillowcase. Why was he giving me this now when we were leaving?

"I have to go," he said, grabbing his shoes. "I'll be back later."

"Wait—where are you going?" I asked, not ready for him to leave my sight yet.

"I need to run a few errands," he said absentmindedly.

"Caleb," I growled. "What aren't you saying?"

"Nothing. Get some rest." He leaned down and gave me a hug. "I'll see you soon, okay?"

Even with my pounding headache, I could tell something was off. Kade and Gray weren't looking at me either, and I sat up, moving to the edge of the bed. I spied crutches across the room but had no way to get to them unless I wanted to crawl.

"Stay in bed, Mili," Caleb ordered, shooting me a grin. "You're going to rip your stitches."

"Tell me where you're going," I snapped.

"I'll be back." With that, he walked out the door, closing it behind him, and I stared at it while Kade moved to lock it.

"Give me the crutches," I demanded, my nails digging into the mattress.

Gray chuckled nervously. "Nope. I think it's best if you can't touch us right now."

His words proved what I'd already guessed. Caleb wasn't fucking coming back. At least not today. And Kade and Gray *knew*. They'd been planning without me. Fear clutched me, knowing there was only one reason Caleb would leave me. He knew something about Joel that he wasn't sharing with me. I gritted my teeth, shooting Kade a scathing glare.

"Give me the crutches," I spat out.

Kade ran a hand through his hair. "Maybe once you calm down."

I let out a frustrated scream. "I'm not staying here."

"You can't even walk right now," Gray said gently. "Take some time to heal. No one will touch you here. You won't have to worry about Joel's men."

I huffed out a breath, leaning back on the bed. Because that was the only thing I could do at the moment. But the second I was good to move, I was leaving.

38

Gray

I walked quietly into the kitchen from the hall, studying Mili as she stared at the wall, clearly deep in thought. It had been days since Caleb left, and she'd been sulking almost the entire time. I'd overheard a few conversations when she called him, and she was just as pissed with him as she was with us. Not being able to leave on her own was driving her crazy. But right now, there was something else troubling her.

"What's on your mind, Rebel?" I asked, making my presence known.

She startled, her head turning toward me. "Where's Kade?"

"Business meeting."

She nodded, going back into her head until I plopped down on the bed next to her. She scowled but made no move to scoot away from me.

"What are you thinking about?" I murmured, my eyes going to her bruises. They'd gotten even darker now, and it made my blood boil knowing what she'd gone through.

She hesitated. "Did you or Kade tell anyone I was working with you?"

I frowned. "No."

"Did Vic or Juan?"

"No." Not that I was aware of anyway. But from the worried tone she had, maybe Kade and I should find out for sure.

"The people after me. They knew I was working with someone," she muttered. "I thought you and Kade gave me up."

She kept my stare, and I realized that was the reason she'd been so petrified when we found her.

"We wouldn't do that," I said in a low voice.

"I'm figuring that out now. If they knew I was working with your crew, they'd already be tearing up Ridgewood looking for me." She settled back against her pillow. "Don't worry, I'll be long gone before they realize I'm here."

"I think we've made it pretty clear that we want you to stay."

"Your necklace proved the opposite," she said bitterly.

"Hey." I gently put my fingers under her chin, turning her face until she was looking at me. "I'm sorry. We did that to push you over the edge and get you to leave town. You were keeping secrets. Juan and Vic didn't trust you. We didn't trust you. It was better for everyone that you left. We didn't realize how badly we fucked up until we saw your face after we did it. And I'm sorry."

Her body was tense as she searched my eyes. "I'm still keeping secrets. That hasn't changed."

"For now."

"For forever," she snapped before her voice softened. "I'm not staying here, Gray. The second I can fucking walk, I'm going after Caleb."

"Well, until then, you're stuck here, so stop complaining."

She grumbled under her breath as I climbed off the couch and walked to my huge shelf of DVDs.

"What are you doing?" she asked.

"We're watching a movie," I answered, pulling out the one I was looking for.

"I don't want to watch a movie."

"Too bad."

I slid the disk into the game console and strode into the kitchen while the previews played. I grabbed snacks and drinks before going back to the bed and dropping them next to her. I took my spot next to her on the mattress, and I could feel her heated glare on the side of my face as I grabbed the remote.

"Give me my crutches," she demanded.

I glanced at them where they were propped against the wall. "Why?"

"Because I'd rather limp around and dig into your lives than watch this with you."

I shot her a grin. "You can do that after the movie."

"Are you enjoying having me at your mercy?" she asked, her voice turning sweet.

I met her gaze. "Maybe."

She raised her hand, dragging her thumb across my lips, making my dick twitch. "Enjoy it then, Gray. But remember—I won't be laid up forever."

"What does that mean?" I asked, amused. "You'll pay us back?"

"Maybe."

"To do that, you'll have to stay in town," I told her, my smile wide.

She rolled her eyes. "What movie is this?"

"*The Breakfast Club*. Have you seen it?"

"No. I've looked at your movie collection." She snagged a chocolate bar from the snack pile. "All the movies are older than me."

"I like classics. Movies. Music." I started the movie. "This is one of my favorites."

I settled next to her, not liking how my stomach was twisting. I was sharing a piece of myself with her and wasn't sure if she'd like it. As the theme song came on, I snuck a glance at her, surprising myself at how much I wanted her to enjoy this with me. She was looking at the screen, so that was something.

She curled up closer to me as the movie played, and I suppressed my grin, seeing that she was watching it intently. Her body relaxed as time went on, and she giggled at a scene before catching herself. The next time she laughed, she didn't even try to hide it. I watched her more than I did the screen. Her laugh was different from the one I'd heard before. It was carefree. Happy. Like she was being herself instead of hiding behind the mask she always wore.

Kade walked in halfway through the movie, and he looked surprised that Mili wasn't throwing a fit about me lying on the bed with her. She barely paid him any attention as she watched the movie. I wasn't sure if she realized she was leaning her weight on me or not, but I stayed still, knowing if I moved, it might jolt her out of the peace she was in. Kade silently sank into the leather chair next to the couch and finished the rest of the movie with us.

When the credits started rolling, she stretched her arms before staring at me.

"For an eighties movie, I guess it wasn't bad," she mumbled.

"Don't lie. You liked it." I grabbed a small bag of chips and opened them.

"Who were you two in high school?" she asked, looking at Kade for the first time since he came home. "You don't strike me as jock types."

"Who do you think?" Kade asked, looking curious.

"Out of the choices in that movie?" She paused, as if having to think about it. "The criminal."

I laughed. "Criminal is such a strong word. I like rebels better."

Her eyes widened when she realized where her nickname had come from. "You think I was a rebel in high school?"

"Were you?" I asked, wondering if she'd open up to us.

She frowned, her stare going past us as she thought of the past. My heart thudded, wondering exactly when her life had turned to hell.

"I used to be the perfect student. Straight As. Played sports. Never even had detention." Her voice became monotone. "Until I met Joel when I was sixteen."

"He went to high school with you?" Kade asked, his eyes darkening.

"He was older than me."

I wanted to ask how much older but had a feeling she'd start shutting down if we pushed too much. Instead, I kept my mouth shut, waiting to see if she'd keep talking.

She cleared her throat. "After that, I dropped out. Got my GED. Under a fake name, but I still count it."

"Where did you grow up?" Kade asked, clearly not on the same page as I was about not pushing her into answering questions.

She stiffened. "The East Coast."

"Your family still there?" My question slipped out before I could stop it. I wanted to know everything about her, and this was the first time she'd ever given us an opening.

"They're dead. My parents. My brothers." Her chin trembled for a split second before she locked it away. "He killed them—Joel did."

Jesus Christ. I bit my tongue to keep calm as Kade sat at the edge of the chair, his elbows on his knees. His hands were clenched into fists, and he opened his mouth before closing it again. Mili scooted to the edge of the bed, staring at the soft cast the crew doctor had put on her ankle. I didn't bother to tell her to stop when she attempted to put weight on it. She winced, cursing under her breath.

"I'm going to need a car when I leave here," she mumbled, telling us the conversation about her past was done.

"Where's your Corvette?" Kade asked gruffly.

"Probably got towed after staying in the hotel parking lot this long. At least I didn't bring it on the job because that car got blown up." Pursing her lips, her gaze darted between us. "Hm, maybe too soon to bring that subject up."

The image of our cars burning flashed in my mind, and I waited for Kade to make some smart remark. But he didn't. He just got up and strode into the kitchen and began pulling pots out. Mili watched him with interest as he pulled an armful of ingredients from the fridge.

"You cook?" she asked, surprise filtering in her voice.

"If he's not in a car, then he's in the kitchen. Cooking is his next favorite thing," I said, earning a glare from Kade.

"I need to shower," she mumbled, looking at me. "Can I have my crutches now?"

My eyes danced in amusement, and I pressed my luck. "If you say please."

"How about I don't stab you for keeping me locked in here?"

I chuckled. "Good enough."

Rolling off the bed, I grabbed the crutches. "Don't forget you can't get your cast wet."

"I know."

The second the crutches were under her arms, she hobbled down the hall to the bathroom. The door slammed shut, and I joined Kade in the kitchen.

"Vic wanted to know where you were today," Kade said as he dumped pasta into the boiling water.

"We need to find out if they told anyone we were working with her," I replied quietly. "She says the people who went after her knew she was partnering with someone."

Kade glanced at me. "I doubt they told anyone."

"Yeah, well, let's make sure before we tell them she's back."

"I don't think we should tell them anything. She made it clear she's running the second she's able to."

"Maybe she'll change her mind," I said, looking down the hall at the bathroom door.

"Doubtful."

39

Milina

"I'm going to kill you," I muttered into the phone as I watched Kade move around the kitchen.

"You're not having fun with your new roommates?" Caleb asked with a chuckle.

"It's been two weeks," I snapped. "I can't believe you left me here. Where are you?"

"Setting things up again. I need a whole new system before I can get back on the web." He turned serious. "They won't find us again, Mili."

"You should have told me what happened. That they found you."

"I did tell you."

I ground my teeth. "After you left me."

"You never would have let me leave without you if you knew they'd found me."

"I'm fine to leave now."

"Really? Should I call Gray or Kade to confirm?" he asked.

I scowled. "I don't need their permission to leave. I can walk out that door whenever the fuck I want."

"Still using the crutches?"

I glanced at my ankle. I'd been trying to put weight on it, and I was finally able to. But the pain wasn't gone yet, even though it wouldn't be much longer until I wasn't limping anymore. And I was still using the crutches to help it heal faster. My stitches were out, and my stomach was pretty much healed besides a bit of soreness. My bruises were a nasty green and yellow color, but they were getting better too. Another week, and I'd be set to leave.

"We need to find Liam." I kept my voice low as I looked at Kade. "He's heading this. If we get rid of him, it all falls apart. He knows how you work, Caleb. He'll keep trying."

"Get rid of him?" Caleb questioned. "You think you could kill him if you found him?"

There was no hesitation. "Yes."

I didn't want to, but I would. He'd had a chance to stop searching for me, and he didn't. I wouldn't go back for anyone, including him.

"Listen, that chip I gave you is so I can get into their computers." He lowered his voice, even though he was on the phone. "Their security is too hard for me to hack remotely without them realizing someone is spying. But if you put that chip in, then I can access it easily. I just need to know when you're doing it. I already have their IP address."

"Why?" I asked, my gut knotting. "You don't trust them?"

"I think Kade and Gray care for you," he said slowly. "And that they'd protect you. But their crew is large. And I don't trust their bosses or anyone else involved. You mentioned they had silent partners, and I think you're right. I want to find out who they are. Especially with Liam knowing you're working with someone."

"I haven't seen their laptops since being here," I said under my breath. "They might be in the office downstairs."

"Figure it out before you leave."

"Are you just trying to get me to stay here longer?"

"You're safe there. But no. They know you. And now they know about me. I want as much information on them as possible."

"Fine. It'll give me something to do anyway. I'm going fucking crazy just sitting here."

"Food's done," Kade said, eyeing me with a slight frown.

"I'll call you later. Stay safe, Caleb."

"See you later, Mili."

After hanging up, I grabbed the crutches and hopped to the island, sitting on the stool. It had taken days to convince them I could come to the kitchen to eat. They wanted me to stay in bed, like I would break if I walked around.

"Caleb okay?" Kade asked, putting a plate of the most delicious looking enchiladas I'd ever seen. Red sauce covered them with cheese on top. Rice was piled on the side, and he set down a bowl of chips.

"He's good. Still won't tell me where he is."

"Probably so you don't try to slip out of here in the dead of the night." He sat down next to me after getting his own plate. "Not that he has to worry. You couldn't step more than a foot out of this house without someone stopping you."

I cocked my head. "You think I couldn't sneak out of here?"

He met my gaze, his lips lifting in a grin. "I dare you to try."

Challenge straightened my spine, and my gaze wandered to the front door. I doubted I'd be able to leave that way, but I hadn't explored the rest of the house yet. Because they hadn't given me a moment alone since I got here.

"You're going to regret saying that when you wake up one day and find me gone."

His confidence faltered a fraction before he turned his attention to his food. I did the same, digging into my rice. It was so fucking delicious.

"Where'd you learn to cook?" I asked the question before I thought about it.

"I taught myself."

"When?"

"When Gray and I took a year off."

I swallowed my rice before asking, "Took a year off from what?"

"This life." He pushed his food around the plate. "Vic and Juan wanted to make sure this was what we wanted."

"They let you choose?" I asked in surprise.

He nodded. "We didn't even last the entire year before coming back. I've been in the crew life since I was thirteen and found out what Juan did. Cars and jobs are what I love."

"Juan," I said slowly. "He's part of your family."

His eyes narrowed. "How did you find that out?"

I grinned, raising an eyebrow. "I wasn't completely sure until you just said that."

A muscle in his jaw clenched. "No one is supposed to know that."

"I guess you'll have to trust me not to say anything." I patted his cheek, and he caught my wrist.

"You should be nicer to the person who feeds you," he murmured.

"How about I just leave, and then you don't have to worry about feeding me?"

His phone went off, breaking the growing tension. He let go of my wrist to check the notification, and he slid off the stool. I watched, frowning when he slipped on a hoodie.

"Where are you going?" I asked.

"On a quick job with Gray."

My heart skipped, and I bit the inside of my cheek. It had been nearly three weeks since I'd been behind the wheel of a car, and I fucking missed it. I knew I had to cool it on jobs with Liam out there, but a small, easy job wouldn't hurt. I jumped off the stool, wincing when I put a bit of weight on my ankle. Kade was almost to the front door, and I grabbed the crutch to go after him.

"Wait. Take me with you."

He spun around, his eyebrow raised. "Go finish your food."

"I can go," I snapped. "I'll stay in the car."

He grabbed his keys off the hook. "No."

"Kade," I growled. "Do not lock me in here."

"Why don't you go call Caleb back so you can finish your whispered conversation?"

I moved closer. "Don't change the subject."

"We'll be back later."

"You leave me alone, and I'll break the door down."

He chuckled. "Good luck."

A tingle ran down my spine, and I lifted my chin, smiling wickedly. "Fine. Go. I'll have fun here."

He paused, gripping the keys tighter in his hand. "Stay out of my bedroom."

"Sure, Kade."

His eyes flashed with warning. "Careful, Mili. You don't want to disrupt this peace we've got going on."

"Oh, I think I do," I purred, teetering on one crutch to run a hand down his chest. "Or you can just take me with you."

The keys clanged to the floor when he snatched my wrist again. "You mess with anything in here while I'm gone and next time, I'll tie you to my bed when I leave."

"You wouldn't."

"Oh, I fucking would." He brushed his lips against my cheek. "And maybe if you're a good girl, I'll even make it enjoyable for you. You seemed to love it the last time I tied your hands."

Heat pooled in my lower stomach even as my anger grew. "You'd try to tie me down when I'm hurt?"

"Don't play that card. Another week, and you'll be good. You think I haven't noticed that you're gaining strength every day?"

I licked my lips. "If you're going to tie me down, better do it before these crutches disappear. Or you might wake up one morning cuffed to your own bed."

"Go sit back down and eat," he said, pulling away from me. "I'm going to be late."

With that, he slipped out the door, and I heard him lock it. I scowled, gripping the crutches and going to the door. The handle twisted but didn't open. I banged on it, realizing immediately that it wasn't a regular door. It had some type of metal in it. Opening it would require a lot of hardware that I didn't have. My curiosity grew as I gazed around the apartment. This was the first time they'd left me alone.

I immediately went for the hallway since I'd spent most of my time in the kitchen and living room. I passed the bathroom, stopping at the next door. It opened easily, and I stood in the doorway, knowing this was Gray's room. It smelled of leather, and his jacket was thrown on a small chair in the corner. His bed was against the back wall and had a metal headboard with horizontal bars. The side walls were lined with more movies than he had in the living room. There were also a bunch of records, which I guessed were probably the classic rock he loved so much. The walls were the same gray as the rest of the house, and I moved toward the large window. It was a straight drop down with nothing to climb. Another way I couldn't leave if I needed to. A smaller door led to a small bathroom with a stand-up shower.

I froze, spying his laptop on his nightstand. I could get the chip and call Caleb right now. I stared at it for a full minute before leaving the room. If they left me alone this time, they'd do it again. I didn't have to do it right away. Going farther down the hall, I stopped at what I guessed was Kade's room, but the door was locked. If I could find something small enough, I could pick the lock. At the end of the hall was one more door, and this one held my interest. Because there was a keypad on the lock. I ran my fingertips over it, wondering what they were hiding. Weapons, maybe. But I had guessed those were downstairs, not up here where they didn't do business.

I hurried back to the kitchen, wanting to finish my food before it got cold. The info Caleb wanted could wait. My ankle wasn't even better yet; I still had time. Once I was feeling better, I'd get Caleb what he wanted and leave. It needed to be soon because I was getting comfortable here. Too comfortable. It was starting to feel like home.

The problem was, it wasn't the house making me feel that way.

40

Rylan

"You were supposed to leave hours ago," Kade grumbled, coming into the kitchen and rubbing his eyes.

"He's been watching her sleep for the past hour," Gray said from the chair. "It's creepy."

"I have not been watching her," I snapped.

"You could go home and sleep," Gray responded. "You shouldn't even be here right now."

The only light in the house was the glow from the TV while a movie played. The volume was quiet so we didn't wake her. She'd fallen asleep hours ago. It was clear that after almost four weeks, she was better, but her body still craved sleep. As if she never got enough. She mentioned before not being able to sleep more than a couple of hours at a time. She seemed to pass out fine here. I wondered if it was because she felt safe.

I bit back my anger that I couldn't be with her as often as Gray and Kade were. They told me about the scene they found her in, and if men were really after her, then she needed to be where she could be protected. Which was here.

She jerked in her sleep, her brow pinching and her lips pressing together. She shifted again, her body going rigid. A small cry broke the silence, and she rolled over, curling up.

"A nightmare," Gray said gruffly, sitting on the edge of the chair. "She had one the night we were in her apartment."

"That fucking asshole wrecked her," Kade growled. "I hope his death was painful."

Before I could continue the conversation, Mili suddenly rolled again, this time screaming like she was in terrible pain. My stomach clenched, and I stepped forward, only for Kade to grab my shoulder.

"Isn't it bad to wake someone when they're having a nightmare?" His eyes darted between me and her.

"I don't give a shit," I snapped, yanking out of his grip.

I already felt guilty enough that I couldn't be there when she'd called for help. I wasn't about to let her get swallowed in more pain, even if it was a nightmare.

I sat at the edge of the bed and gently pulled her into my arms. She flailed, her hand catching the side of my face. Her eyes were squeezed tightly shut, as if it were impossible to open them. She cried out again, and I tugged her closer, realizing she was trembling.

"Mili, wake up," I said, raising my voice. "Wake up."

"No. Don't." She thrashed, and I moved farther onto the bed. "Stop. No!"

Her screams were shrill, and my heart broke, knowing the horror in her past was probably even worse than her nightmares. Gray and Kade were standing at the edge of the bed, looking like they wanted to intervene, but I shook my head.

I shook her. "Mili. It's okay. It's not real. Wake up."

Her eyes finally snapped open, and it took her a few moments to focus on me. She stopped moving, her chest heaving as she gulped in lungfuls of air. Her fingers wrapped around my arm, her nails digging into my skin. She looked behind me, seeing Kade and Gray, and her jaw snapped shut. Her cheeks turned pink as she let go of my arm and rubbed her face.

"I'm fine," she grated out through her hands. "I didn't mean to wake you up."

It was easy to tell that she didn't like looking weak in front of anyone. But I still didn't move.

"Do you want to talk about it—"

"No," she cut Gray off sharply. "I don't remember it anyway."

None of us called her out on her lie. She dropped her hands from her face, frowning when she saw us all still staring at her. She looked a hell of a lot better than she did when she first got here. The bruises were nearly gone, and she was getting around easier. She could leave any day now. Which was why I didn't want to leave. I was worried I'd come to see her, and she'd just be gone.

"Let me stay with you," I murmured. "In case you have another one."

"I don't need your help."

"I can't go home. My house flooded," I said, hearing Gray snicker behind me.

"You're lying," she mumbled.

"Nope. I was going to check into some dingy hotel when I left here."

"You're the mayor. You don't stay at shitty hotels."

"Please, Mili. Let me crash here. You'd be doing me a favor." I grinned when she met my eyes. "Just for tonight."

"Fine."

I glanced over my shoulder at Kade, and he jerked a nod before heading to his room.

"Can you sneak out in the morning?" she mumbled, scooting over to make space for me.

"He hasn't had a problem sneaking out yet," Gray piped in. "He'll be fine."

Unknotting my tie, I pulled it off and tossed it on the chair Gray had been sitting in. I slid under the blankets, and after a moment of hesitation, she lay down next to me. Not close enough to be touching, but I could still feel her body heat.

"You don't have to do this," she said as she yawned.

"Do what? I told you; you're doing me a favor."

"Whatever you say, Rylan."

I stared at the ceiling, listening to her breathing even out as she fell asleep. The days of her being here were numbered, but I couldn't seem to distance myself from her. Especially since the night we'd shared at my office. I fucking wanted her.

And I wasn't the only one. Kade and Gray were hiding her from the crew, which was something new. They were choosing to protect her over the men who'd practically raised them. Because they wanted her too. Between me and them, they obviously had more in common with her. I didn't care.

I'd keep trying to see her until she told me she didn't want me, which hasn't happened yet.

41

Milina

The door closed after Kade and Gray left, and I waited in silence for a few moments before grinning and hopping off the bed. Being able to walk without pain again felt absolutely amazing. No more crutches. Looking down, I twisted my ankle in all possible ways. I jumped a few times, not feeling any tightness in my stomach where my stitches had been. I was fine. It had only taken a damn month.

I was still using my crutches in front of Kade and Gray. If they thought I was good to leave, they wouldn't have left me alone here. My excitement dimmed when I remembered what I planned to do. It almost felt wrong to pry into their secrets now. But Caleb was right. If it wasn't Kade or Gray who'd spilled that we'd been working together, then we needed to find out if someone else in the crew did. It wasn't just my life on the line. It was Caleb's too.

Grabbing my phone and the little chip, I headed down the hall, glancing at the locked door.

"Hey," I said when Caleb answered. "I'm finally alone."

"How much time do you have? It might take a while."

"Enough. They're meeting with Vic and Juan."

He paused. "You okay?"

"Yeah," I clipped out. "Just ready to get this over with and go."

"I'll fly out tomorrow," he said softly. "Unless you want to stay there."

"No. I'm ready. My ankle is good."

"I wasn't talking about your ankle, Mili."

"I was never going to stay here. We all knew that."

"But you want to?"

I sighed, grabbing Gray's laptop and sitting on his bed. "Just tell me what I need to do."

"Open the laptop and put the chip into the slot it fits in."

I did what he told me, and a password screen came up. "I don't know his password."

"You don't need it," he muttered.

I could tell he was concentrating, and I absentmindedly looked around Gray's room, listening to him type away on whatever device he was using. Until I heard a new noise. Chills raced down my spine when the front door closed.

"Fuck. They're back," I muttered under my breath.

"What? No, I need at least twenty more minutes."

"It's fine. Keep working, I'll distract them." I hung up, hearing footsteps getting closer. They'd find me in here any second since I wasn't in the kitchen or living room. I stripped off Gray's shirt and slipped out of my leggings. They'd bought me clothes weeks ago and had brought my stuff from my apartment, yet I still ended up in one of their shirts every day. They were comfy to sleep in—that was what I kept telling myself. Once I was naked, I closed the laptop as far as it would go without it powering off and tilted it toward the wall.

I leaped on the bed, lying on my stomach and resting my face in my hands just as Gray appeared in his doorway. Absolute shock crossed his face, and his eyes raked over my bare body before he took a large step back.

"Nope," he muttered. "Not happening."

I shot him a wicked grin. "What? I was hoping you'd help me test out my ankle. I think it's all better. But a stronger test is in order."

It was my turn to be shocked when he reached forward and pulled his door shut. I scrambled off the bed, tugging at the doorknob. Either he'd locked it or he was holding it from the other side.

"Gray," I shrieked. "Let me out. What the hell are you doing?"

"You're up to something," he shouted through the door. "You take off your clothes and I'm going to end up tied to another fucking chair."

A giggle escaped before I could stop it. "I'm not up to anything."

"Bullshit."

If I could keep up the arguing through the door for another twenty minutes, then this would work out great. I had a feeling that wouldn't happen when I heard the lock twist. I yanked on the door again.

"If you're serious about not planning something, then be laying on the bed when I get back." His footsteps retreated.

"What does that mean?"

There was no answer, and I clicked my tongue as I looked back at the laptop. Fuck. There was no way he wasn't going to notice it open if he came in here and was already suspicious. I scanned the room for a place I could put it out of sight, but his closet was the only choice, and then he'd realize his laptop was gone. That wouldn't go well at all.

"Sorry, Caleb," I muttered, crossing the room and standing near the laptop. I'd give it as long as possible, but when I heard Gray coming back, I was taking it out. I couldn't chance it. They'd try to keep me here even longer if they found out I was snooping. I texted Caleb, letting him know before making sure my phone was locked before I set it down.

Hurried footsteps had me lunging toward the laptop, and I grabbed the chip and shoved it into my leggings that were on the floor, cursing that it didn't have pockets. I folded them, hoping Gray wouldn't pick them up. The door swung open, and Gray's gaze landed on me.

He raised an eyebrow. "You're not on the bed."

"What the hell are those?" I choked out, my eyes on what he was holding.

He smirked, lifting the chains in his hands. "You wanted to test out your ankle. We'll do it my way."

He stepped into his room, kicking the door shut behind him. The chains in his hands were the same ones they had used on me in their study months ago. But this time, there were four instead of just two. He tossed them onto the bed, advancing toward me. He stepped left, and I shuffled to the right. He cocked his head, his eyes dancing with amusement even though a bit of suspicion lingered.

"How long have you been off the crutches?" he asked, lunging to the right, making me go left, farther away from the door.

"I just tried to walk today."

"Hmm," he hummed out. "I feel like that's a lie. You've been holding out on us."

"Maybe I just didn't want to leave," I said, my stomach fluttering as he stalked toward me until I backed into the wall.

"You know, I think my ankle is good," I muttered. "No need to test it out."

"I don't think so." He grabbed my upper arm when I attempted to dart past him. "We can't, in good faith, let you leave until we're positive you're healed."

The whole *we* word had me staring at the closed door. "Where's Kade?"

"Dealing with business."

Before I could answer, he snagged an arm around my waist, pulling me to him. He was being gentler than usual, and a flash of concern hit his eyes as his gaze trailed down my body.

"You're not going to hurt me," I murmured. "I'm back to normal."

"Get on the bed, Rebel."

Raising on my tiptoes, I brushed my lips against his. "Make me."

His eyes darkened, and when I pulled out of his hold, he all but threw me on the mattress. I rolled away, slipping out of his grip when he attempted to keep me on the bed. My muscles flexed, burning with the need to be used for the first time in a month. I was out of practice, and my reflexes were slower than usual, but I wasn't completely useless. Although Gray had a larger chance to get the upper hand, and that made my heart race.

His fingers closed around my ankle, dragging me back to the middle of the mattress. I grinned, not feeling a speck of pain. Flipping onto my back, I used my other foot to try and push him off. He didn't let go, reaching for one of the cuffs as I struggled to free myself. Giving up on getting my ankle from his hold, I sat up and reached for another one of the restraints.

His attempts to cuff my ankle halted when I went for his wrist. He chuckled, blocking my attempt to wrangle the cuff around his arm. He grabbed me above the elbow and yanked hard, making me fall on my stomach.

"You going easy on me?" he asked, pulling my arm behind my back and pressing it against my spine. "Or maybe you're not 100 percent yet."

I wiggled under him uselessly. "Or I just don't want to hurt you."

He leaned over me, his teeth grazing my ear. "What do you want?"

Goose bumps skated along my skin as his mouth drifted to my neck, his lip piercing grazing my skin as he kissed me.

"You," I breathed out. "I want you."

I stiffened, feeling the cuff snap around my wrist. In a quick move, he rolled me onto my back before straddling my waist. My fight against him was feeble at best as he pulled my arm, locking the other end of the chain to his headboard. Now that I was stuck there, he easily cuffed my other wrist, pulling the chain taut as he connected it to the metal frame. I was half resting against the headboard, and he snatched a pillow and moved it behind me so I wasn't on the bars.

On instinct, I jerked my arms, trying to slip the restraints, my pulse speeding up when I knew I was stuck. Gray's heated gaze trailed over my body before he gripped my thighs, spreading my legs apart. Lowering his head, he kissed the inside of my leg, slowly moving upward. Torturously slow. Delicious heat swarmed my lower stomach, and I made a noise of protest when he stopped.

"Do you know how hard it's been not to drag you to my bed since you've been here?" he asked in a low voice.

I raised an eyebrow. "What was stopping you?"

"I'm not the only one who wants you in their bed." He ran his hand up my thigh, stopping just short of my pussy. "It could have made things tense in this house."

"And what changed now?"

His eyes gleamed. "How can I resist such an open invitation?"

A gasp left me when he plunged a finger into me. His thumb brushed my clit, and I squirmed, feeling the pleasure already building.

"Seeing you naked on my bed is something I can't say no to," he murmured, pulling his hand from me. "But as much as I want to bury my face in your soaking pussy, I have to ask—what were you really doing in my room?"

My eyes widened before I caught myself. Tilting my head, I bit my lip. "I think my intention is very fucking clear. So why don't you put your head between my legs like you so desperately want to? Or I'll go have fun all by myself."

His smirk was wicked as he grabbed one of the two chains that were still on the bed. "Go where, Mili? Your ass will stay right there until I'm ready for you to leave. And I'm telling you that it won't be for a while."

My heart pounded as he clicked the cuff around my ankle before he tugged, pulling me as far down onto the bed as my wrist cuffs allowed. He lifted my leg until it was nearly straight in the air, and then he pulled it to the side before he wrapped that chain around a bar on the headboard. He did the same to my other leg, making it impossible for me to close my legs or barely even wiggle. He lay on his stomach, scooting up until his face was right above my pussy.

"What were you doing in here?" he asked again, his voice quiet.

"I was touching myself before you walked in."

"Liar," he rasped. "Don't worry though. We have all the time in the world to get you to tell the truth."

My response was lost when his tongue swept over my clit. My hands clenched into fists as he ravished my pussy. Fuck, it had been too long. Waves of pleasure began washing over me, and the chains clanged against the bars when I arched my back. He brought me to the edge before pulling away.

"Why were you in here?" he asked, pushing a finger inside me.

I glared at him. "Really? You're not going to give me an orgasm until I answer?"

"How bad do you want one?"

"I already told you what I was doing in here."

He tsked. "You're not desperate enough. Let's change that."

He attacked my clit again, his fingers staying inside me as he swirled his tongue, keeping a constant pace that easily had my pussy throbbing around his fingers. Again, he slowed, and I bucked against the cuffs.

"Gray," I shrieked breathlessly. "Please."

"As much as I love hearing you beg for me, that's not what I want."

He started again, bringing me to the edge over and over as I writhed against him. My body pleaded for release, but he only drew me closer each time before stopping. He sucked on my clit, and I screamed, needing just a bit more to get off. But no, he pulled away before that happened.

"I wasn't doing anything," I said, my voice shaking.

"Telling the truth will set you free."

I gasped when he started eating me out again. Every move he made had me going insane.

"Fuck," I breathed out. "This is worse than torture."

He paused what he was doing. "I disagree. I think this is the most delicious torment I've ever inflicted."

He got up, and my jaw clenched as he moved away from me.

Opening his closet, he dug through a small bin before pulling out a couple of items. I watched him, my body begging him to finish what he'd started. He strolled back to the bed with a devious gleam in his eye.

"Ever used a wand?" he asked, holding it up.

I swallowed. "Yes."

The toy he had was long with a large bulb at the end. Technically, they were sold as back massagers, but they gave the best fucking orgasms. My eyes widened when he started unrolling the tape he'd grabbed. He placed the wand to my pussy until the tip of it was pressed firmly against my clit. He began wrapping the tape around my leg and the wand, putting more than enough to keep it in place.

"This tape only sticks to itself," he murmured as he ripped it. "Makes it easier when it doesn't get stuck to skin."

I waited for him to turn it on, my anticipation nearly bursting. I knew how good this toy worked, and I was more than ready for it. But he didn't turn it on. Instead, he grabbed a bandanna, balling it up in his hand.

"Last chance, Rebel. Or I'll leave you here to think about your answer."

"Leave me here?" I squirmed. "You wouldn't."

He chuckled. "I need to shower. But I wouldn't want you to be bored while you wait."

My stomach flipped when he finally reached over and messed with the wand settings. A small vibration hit my clit, and I jerked. Fuck yes. It felt so good. And then it stopped. I scowled, my eyes meeting his.

"Oh, it's set on sporadic right now." He tilted his head. "Can't have you coming yet."

"I'm going to kill you," I muttered, my body on edge from not knowing when the vibrations were going to start again.

"Want to tell me what you were doing now?"

I smirked. "Raiding your drawers to find all your dirty secrets. I guess I should have looked in your closet first since that's where you seem to have your naughty stash."

He looked amused as he got closer and shoved the balled-up bandanna in my mouth. Before I could spit it out, he brought the tape up, wrapping it around my head, covering my mouth until my arguments were nothing but muffled grunts. The toy turned on again, and I bit down on the cloth as my body buzzed from the sensations.

"Enjoy," he said as he headed for his bathroom. "Maybe after, you'll be ready to answer."

He left the door open, and I kept my eyes on him as he undressed before turning on the water. His jeans were near the doorway, and a flash of silver caught my eye as I looked at his keys. Keys that I could use to leave if I needed. My thoughts turned to mush when the vibrations hit again. The glass shower was on the back wall, and I had a clear view of it from the bed. The wand stopped again, and I sagged as much as the cuffs allowed me. Until it turned on again. I struggled to move my pussy away from it, but the tape made sure it didn't move an inch.

I lost track of time and everything else while Gray showered. The toy didn't stay on long enough at all for me to come, and I was going crazy. I fucking needed it.

My legs were nearly shaking as I attempted to get off before vibrations stopped again. My muffled, frustrated scream filled the room when it suddenly halted, leaving me exactly where I'd been for I didn't know how long. Right on the fucking edge. I jerked my arms, straining against the cuffs. Catching movement out of the corner of my eye, I looked toward the bathroom door in time to see Gray lean against the doorway. All he was wearing was a towel wrapped around his waist.

Ink covered most of his chest. His Riot Crew tattoo was sprawled across the left side, and I spotted his bullet scar from when I'd shot him two years ago. A little guilt hung on to me as I tore my eyes from it. His wet hair was down instead of pulled back like it usually was. His tongue flicked his lip ring as he stared at me.

"Ready to talk now?" he murmured, raw lust swirling in his eyes.

I glared at him until there was a knock at the bedroom door. My heart skipped as Kade's voice filled the room.

"Gray, you in there?" he asked gruffly. "Mili isn't in the fucking living room."

My gaze cut back to Gray to see he was still staring at me. His lips tipped up in an amused grin. "Come in."

Surprise shot through me, and my face flushed when Kade swung open the door. He froze midstride, his eyes leaving mine as they moved down to my body. It was then that the wand turned back on, and I cried out through the gag. Sensations racked every inch of me, and I sucked in breaths through my nose as I climbed to the edge again.

"She was in my bed naked when I got home," Gray stated. "Saying she wanted to test that she was all better."

"What was she really doing? Snooping?" Kade asked, his eyes not leaving me.

Their conversation sounded far away as I lost myself to the pleasure the toy was giving me.

"I don't know. She won't tell me," Gray answered. "Not yet anyway. Maybe you can convince her to talk."

They seemed to have a silent conversation as they exchanged a glance, and the tension in the air thickened. It wasn't jealousy or anger. It was all sexual.

"It seems like you proved she's gotten her strength back." Kade strode closer, climbing onto the bed and running a hand up my stretched-out leg. "But I think we should test her stamina."

Before I could process his words, he flicked the button on the wand, and suddenly, the vibrations were nonstop. And strong. It took less than a minute for my body to build to the orgasm that Gray had been depriving me of. My leg muscles burned as they strained against the cuffs. My head fell against the headboard as I came, and I soaked up every wave of pleasure that was racking my body.

But even as the orgasm ebbed, the wand stayed on, building me back up again straight away. My breaths were jagged, and I rocked my hips as I stared at Kade. He was still sitting on the bed in front of me, and he grabbed the back of his shirt, quickly pulling it over his head.

Over his shoulder, I saw Gray, who was watching me just as intently. The towel was gone, and his pierced cock was on full display as he fisted it.

I screamed hoarsely when I came again, this orgasm even stronger than the first. Kade didn't give me a chance to recuperate before he slid two fingers inside me. He pumped them in and out as the wand kept going. I began struggling, my body begging for a break.

"How many do you think you can handle?" Kade asked, his eyes raking over my body. "Because I could watch you like this all fucking night."

Holy fuck. I shook my head before all I could focus on was the sensations exploding through me. Keeping his fingers inside me, he reached over me with his free hand and pulled the tape from my mouth. I pushed out the cloth, sucking in a lungful of air right before my third orgasm hit out of nowhere. My limbs went rigid as I cried out. Kade curled his fingers, hitting my sweet spot, making me jerk.

"Kade," I rasped, my voice gruff. "Fuck. Turn it off."

"What were you doing in Gray's room?"

I couldn't tell which was the worse punishment—Gray's constant edging or Kade's forced orgasms. I breathed a sigh of relief when Kade finally flicked off the toy. He unwrapped the tape that had been holding it in place before tossing the wand onto the mattress next to me. My pussy was still throbbing, and I moaned when he started moving his fingers inside me again. Even as exhausted as my body was, I was still reacting to his touch.

"What were you doing in here?" Kade asked again.

"Nothing. I was bored," I mumbled.

He raised an eyebrow. "Either you were doing something you weren't supposed to, or you want more of this. Which one do you think it is, Gray?"

"I'm thinking a little of both."

Gray's answer had my eyes darting between the two of them. They had some serious self-control, because I was expecting one of them to fuck me by now. My thoughts crumbled when Kade dove down and buried his face between my thighs. My already sensitive clit succumbed to the flicks of his tongue in record time. I twisted in the restraints, having nowhere to fucking go as he brought me another orgasm. My screams echoed through the room as he coaxed me over the edge again.

"Please," I shrieked as my chest heaved. "I can't take another one."

"Mmm, but I'm still hungry." Kade's words shot vibrations through my pussy.

He started again, and Gray came up, running his hand over my collarbone before he rolled my nipple between his fingers. The new touch had my body going even more haywire. Kade's tongue swirled around my clit, his fingers plunging in and out of my pussy. I lost track of time as another orgasm ripped through me. Or maybe it was two. I couldn't tell anymore.

"Fuck," I screamed, coming again. "I can't—"

Gray's lips crashed to mine, cutting off my words. He kissed me, his tongue pushing into my mouth as Kade lured me into another shattering orgasm. My body was trembling, the pleasure too overwhelming to handle anymore. Jerking my head back, I broke the kiss.

"The laptop," I breathed out. "I was trying to figure out the password."

Both halted their movements, and I sagged back, relishing in the reprieve. Kade studied me while Gray's gaze darted to his nightstand, where the computer was.

"I didn't even have a chance to guess what it was before Gray found me." I sucked in a ragged breath when Kade pulled his fingers out of me.

"Now, that wasn't so hard, was it, Rebel?" Gray asked, his lips grazing my neck. "You could have admitted that much sooner, but I think you're enjoying this as much as we are."

My retort was lost when Kade's fingers brushed over my ass before circling around my other hole. I tensed, and he stopped when he saw my reaction.

"Has anyone ever touched you here?" he asked softly.

"Yes," I snapped as my chest tightened. "I didn't like it very much."

He glanced at Gray before meeting my eyes again. "Give us a chance to show you how enjoyable it can be."

I bit my lip, my stomach fluttering. Even though my body was spent, Gray's kisses were already working me back up. He sucked on my nipple, and I closed my eyes, swallowing a moan when his teeth grazed me.

"Don't hurt me," I muttered, giving Kade the answer he wanted.

"The only screaming we want is you begging for more," Gray murmured before focusing on my other breast. "We won't hurt you."

Kade slid his finger over my soaked pussy before he moved it back, slowly pushing it into my back entrance. I was barely aware of what Gray was doing, as I was solely focused on what Kade was doing.

"Relax," Gray ordered gently.

I opened my eyes to see him unlocking the cuffs around my ankles. My legs fell to the bed, and I breathed out a sigh when I stretched my aching muscles. Kade lowered his head back down, lightly brushing his tongue over my pussy as he pushed his finger deeper into my ass. It felt foreign, but not bad. Just different.

He added a second finger, and I held my breath, waiting for the pain to start. But it was just pressure, and it slowly turned into pleasure as he continued to lick my pussy. Gray continued to kiss me, and I shifted, feeling another orgasm build. I watched as Gray freed my wrists from the restraints, and I grabbed onto the bars of the headboard as my body urged Kade to keep going.

Until he stopped.

I frowned but didn't have a chance to argue when Gray suddenly picked me up and moved us to the edge of the bed. He flipped me on top of him, and I was straddling his hips. My body was stiff from not moving for so long, but my muscles relaxed as Gray's hands massaged my skin. He was halfway off the bed, his feet planted on the floor even as he lay on his back. I heard a drawer open, and I glanced over to see Kade pulling out a condom. He held it up, questions in his eyes.

"I want to feel you," Gray murmured gruffly. "If that's what you want."

Jesus, these men had me doing things without question that I would never do before. Even with me not being able to get pregnant, I'd always used condoms. But I didn't want to with them. Instead of answering, I raised myself onto my knees and grabbed Gray's cock. His hands immediately grasped my hips as I guided him to my entrance. My pussy clenched around him as he pushed inside me until I was fully sitting on him. My clit rubbed against his skin, and I jolted from the contact.

I was barely aware of Kade coming up behind me as I rode Gray. And then something cold touched my ass. I glanced over my shoulder, seeing Kade with his pants off and a bottle of lube in his hand. He rubbed more on my asshole before putting the rest on his cock.

"Kade—"

Gray's hand left my hip to grip my chin, pulling my attention back to him. "Breathe, Mili. Focus on me."

He slid his hand down, his fingers rubbing my clit as he stayed still while inside me. Nerves filled me, feeling Kade's cock pressed against my back entrance. He slowly pushed inside me, and my nails dug into Gray's chest.

"You're too big," I choked out. "You're going to fucking break me."

Kade's chest was pressed against my back, and he leaned forward until his mouth was near my ear.

"Only in the best way, Little Hellion."

Pain was mixed with pleasure as he inched farther inside me. My breath was locked in my chest as he stretched me until I thought I couldn't take it anymore. But once he was fully inside me, he began moving. Gray's hands went back to my hips, and he rocked his body, moving in rhythm with Kade, who was kissing and nipping at my neck as they both fucked me.

Hands groped my breasts, and by this point I didn't even know whose hands they were. The pleasure building was different and more overwhelming than I'd ever felt. It came from everywhere at once, making it impossible to focus on anything else. Gray's piercing only enhanced it, and I moaned when one of them started circling my clit again.

I had no control of my own movements as they kept going. Kade thrust over and over, not slowing down as Gray matched his tempo.

"I can't. It's too much," I cried out, my body going tight when my release drew closer.

"Come for us," Gray said gruffly.

Kade's breath tickled my neck. "Let us hear how much you like us both fucking you."

A rough scream tore from my throat as my orgasm hit. It was the most explosive one I'd ever had in my life, and my eyes squeezed shut as the ecstasy engulfed my entire body. Neither of them slowed down, and that only surged on my endless orgasm until I was gasping for breath. Kade grunted, plunging into me one last time before he came. He pulled out, and Gray's fingers dug into my hips as he pounded into me.

"Fuck," he groaned out as he tensed, spilling his release inside me.

I fell on top of him, my body utterly spent. We stayed like that for a while, until he gently wrapped an arm around me and pulled me off him. I fell onto the mattress, knowing I needed to shower but having no energy to fucking move. Hands landed on my back, and I relaxed as Kade massaged my aching muscles. I was nearly half asleep until he whispered in my ear.

"Seven."

I buried my face in my arms. "Seven what?"

"You came seven times."

I pushed out a small laugh. "You almost killed me."

"Next time, I'll get you to ten."

He didn't give me a chance to answer before he pushed off the bed and muttered something about a shower before leaving the room. I glanced at Gray's keys sticking out of his jeans as his arm banded around me, tugging me to his chest. A slither of guilt pushed past my exhaustion, knowing this wasn't going to change anything.

I was still leaving. No matter how much the little voice in my head begged to stay.

42

Milina

There was a knock on the door, and both Kade and Gray shot up from the stools while I watched curiously from the couch. The sexual tension that had bled into the air since last night was nearly tangible. I'd barely talked to them since I left Gray's room. Because anything I said might end up with me back between them while I was naked—again. My body was too sore to have a repeat of last night. But it wasn't just that. I was getting too close. I didn't want to leave anymore, and that was a huge damn problem.

"Yeah," Kade called out through the door. No one had knocked on the door since the day Caleb barged in here. If anyone in the crew needed them, they called.

"You two aren't answering your fucking phones." Vic's anger seeped through his voice, and a chill ran down my spine. "We need to talk. Now."

Gray exchanged a look with Kade before he glanced at me, his jaw ticking. He didn't want to leave me alone after he'd caught me snooping in his room. When Vic banged on the door again, he knew he didn't have a choice. He grabbed his leather jacket off the chair and then caught my chin in his grasp.

"Don't get yourself into trouble again," he murmured.

"Maybe I want back in your bed," I shot back with a grin.

He chuckled. "We'll be back soon."

He and Kade slipped out the door, keeping it half closed so Vic wouldn't spot me. I heard Kade mutter something about going to their office, and I jumped off the bed. Snatching Gray's hoodie from where I'd been lying, I pulled it over my head, keeping the hoodie on to cover my hair. I reached under the mattress, my fingers closing around the keys I'd stolen from Gray's room last night. He'd passed out as soon as Kade had left the room. Although I was surprised he didn't notice they were gone. Then again, he hadn't left the house today.

A shadow of guilt plagued me as I put my shoes on. They'd kept me here. Kept me safe. And here I was, about to spy on them. Yet it still wasn't stopping me. Gray had told me that Vic and Juan hadn't told anyone about me, but I needed to know for sure. Caleb got nothing from the chip because I pulled it out too soon. I could try that again, but the chance of them coming back was too high.

Stopping in front of the door, I tried the first two keys, sucking in a breath when the third one fit. Twisting the lock, I pulled the door open a crack and peeked down the stairs. No one was in sight, and I pulled the hoodie farther around my face before slowly making my way down the steps. My stomach tightened when I saw the first floor was crawling with crew members. None paid attention to me though. Apparently, since I was already in the front door, then if I was here, I belonged, like everyone else.

Keeping my back straight and my steps purposeful, like I knew what I was doing, I wandered through the hall, trying to get my bearings. This must be the back of the house, and seeing as I'd only been in their office at the front, nothing looked familiar. I kept my eyes down, not meeting anyone's gaze as I made my way to the foyer. I turned down the shorter hall, their office finally in my sights.

The door was closed, and I peered down the hall, my pulse spiking when someone walked by. He kept going, and I pretended to walk past the study, spinning around when the man was gone. I stared at the door, biting my lip before pressing my ear to it. Not a sound came through, and I frowned. Fuck. Gently laying my hand on the knob, I hesitated for a second before twisting it. The odds of them seeing the door crack open were more than possible, but it was a chance I was taking. With the door open an inch, voices finally drifted out, and I tensed, ready to bolt if I had to.

"We know she's here," Vic stated, not sounding happy about it at all.

"Who?" Gray asked.

"The girl. Mili. Sapphire. Whatever you want to call her." Juan joined the conversation. "Now we know why you've been spending so much time at home."

My heart stuttered, and I leaned closer.

"Who told you that?" Kade asked gruffly.

"Someone reached out," Vic answered.

There was a pause before Kade's voice filled the room. "Someone?"

"If you're going to keep secrets, I don't feel obliged to share it with you," Vic snapped.

"We've been learning about her," Gray piped up. "That's what you wanted, wasn't it? You wanted her under your thumb. We couldn't do that until we learned her weaknesses."

Vic scoffed. "And why didn't you tell us?"

"Because she needed to think we were protecting her," Kade said, his voice hard.

Every cell in my body was on fire, and my chest was so tight that it literally hurt. They were lying. They had to be fucking lying. Because if they weren't, then everything for the last month—or even since I came to Ridgewood—had been a lie. I had begun to trust them. To depend on them. They wouldn't do this to me.

"Well," Juan drawled, "what have you found out?"

"She cares for someone. And he helps run her Sapphire jobs." Gray's voice was louder than all, which meant he was closest to the door. But I inched closer, looking through the crack to see them all surrounding one of the desks, with none of them focused on me. "We get him, and she'll do whatever we say."

Over my dead body would they fucking touch Caleb. Anger had my chest heaving, and I was seeing red. What was worse was the hurt that had me paralyzed.

"Good," Vic muttered. "You think she'll keep opening up?"

"Yes," Kade answered. "As long as she trusts us."

"Then keep doing it and report back to us."

Silently closing the door again, I rushed down the hall, just aware enough not to bump into anyone. I needed to get back upstairs before they realized I'd eavesdropped.

One chance. I'd give them one chance to tell me their words were lies. But I was going to have a backup plan ready just in case. My phone was already at my ear as I stumbled back to the second floor. I locked the door behind me before racing to Gray's bedroom.

"Hey, Mili."

"Rylan." I scanned Gray's room before crouching down and tossing the keys under his bed as if he accidentally dropped them there. "How do you feel about Kade and Gray?"

He paused. "What?"

"Do you still want them to pay for their crimes? Or has your heart changed since you've spent so much time with them in the last month?"

"I deal with them for you," he said softly. "I've stopped going after them because I can see you care—"

"That's the thing," I cut him off, "I don't care. I'm done with them. And I want them gone."

"Gone? Like you're going to, um, kill them?"

"Nope. That's too easy." I made my way back to the living room so I could keep an eye on the front door. "I want to help you take them down."

"How?"

"I have access and info about two warehouses full of stolen merchandise you can tie them to." I hesitated for a moment. "And I have a gun with Kade's prints that will match a murder from two years ago during a robbery of a Rolls-Royce."

I'd kept the gun I'd taken from him that night after all this time. It was in a storage locker only hours from here. I never thought I'd use it, but here I was.

"You're going to snitch?" Shock was evident in his voice, but there was anger there too.

I switched the phone to my other ear. "You think I'm going against some kind of code? Even if I was, why would you care?"

"I don't," he grumbled. "Sometimes I forget I'm on the right side of the law. Growing up on the north side...the one thing ingrained was to never go to the cops. And I never thought it would be coming from you."

"Yeah, well, all rules are out the fucking window when they decide to try and use me."

"Use you?"

"I don't have time to explain. I can get what you need to arrest them," I said quickly. "And it'll stick. But I need you to do it tonight so I can leave without them trying to follow. Can you do that?"

There was silence, and I bounced my leg. "Rylan?"

"Yeah, Mili, I can do that," he said softly. "Are you sure this is what you want?"

I ignored his question. "Only tell people you know aren't dirty. They can't get tipped off about it. I'll text you when I'm ready."

My heart thudded unevenly when Kade and Gray walked through the door a half hour after I talked to Rylan. I resisted the urge to jump off the stool and confront them right there. Kade saw me first, and he gave me a small grin before heading to the fridge. Gray was more subdued, but neither said a word. Taking a deep breath, I forced myself to remain calm.

"What did Vic and Juan want?" I asked, casually stirring my straw around in my glass.

"They wanted to go over details about a new job," Kade answered, popping the top off his beer.

Before he was finished talking, numbness began climbing through me. And I welcomed it with open arms. It was a hell of a lot better than dealing with the emotions of knowing they lied to me.

"They still don't know I'm here?" I asked, giving them one last chance.

"We told you that we wouldn't tell anyone, Rebel." Gray fell into the leather chair. "They won't have any idea until you want them to know."

Rage slid through me, keeping me on the stool. How stupid had I been to let them play me? I opened my phone and texted Rylan.

Mili: Do it now.

Setting my phone down, I finished my drink, trying to keep my anger under control. My hands shook, and I jumped up, acting like I wanted more water.

"What if they do find out I'm here?" I stared at Kade as he glanced at Gray.

"We'd help you leave town," he answered, questions in his eyes. "What's with all the questions?"

"I just want to make sure it's safe to stay here. I don't trust Vic and Juan."

"You'll be fine here." Gray nodded at me. "Let's watch a movie."

I fell onto the pull-out bed and wrapped my arms around my legs, attempting to stay relaxed when Kade sat next to me. I wouldn't even look at him. If I did, I was scared they'd see the truth in my eyes.

Because I was so close to losing it that I wasn't sure I'd be able to keep it under control.

Gray started the movie, and I peeked glances at my phone, watching the minutes tick by. Twenty minutes into the movie, I didn't even know what it was about. A nervous sweat covered the back of my neck, and I was positive they could both feel the tension radiating off me. Another half hour went by, and I began wondering if Rylan was going to back out.

Until both Kade's and Gray's phones started ringing. A second later, a deafening pounding shook the front door.

"Open up. Police."

Kade scrambled off the bed, and Gray shot up from the chair, his eyes bulging. Kade grabbed me, yanking me to my feet.

"Go to the bedrooms," he told me as the pounding continued.

"They're cops," I snapped. "You think they aren't going to check the rooms?"

"There's another way out—"

Before he could finish, we all ducked and covered our heads when a boom exploded, loud enough to make my ears ring. Smoke billowed in from the blown-out door as men rushed into the house. They had SWAT gear on and their guns raised. There were at least seven of them, and the last to walk in was Rylan.

"On the floor," one of the cops bellowed.

They didn't give Kade or Gray a chance to follow the order before one of them grabbed Gray, bringing him to the floor. He didn't resist, keeping his arms on his head. Kade was shoved into the wall by two officers, and he tried pushing them off until they forced his hands behind his back, handcuffing his wrists.

I raised my arms above my head, letting fear fill my gaze. The cops looked at me, but Rylan cleared his throat and shook his head. They left me alone, yanking Gray up from the floor after he was cuffed and slamming him into the wall next to Kade.

"You better tell us what the fuck the charges are, Mayor," Kade spat out once he caught sight of Rylan. "You slimy son of a bitch."

Not having to pretend anymore, my face went cold as I stepped closer to Kade and Gray. Both seemed surprised that I wasn't in handcuffs with them. Gray's eyes darted between Rylan and me, and he let out a hollow laugh.

"You're protecting her. Was this the plan all along? We invite you into our fucking house, and you turn on us?"

"This wasn't his plan." I slid my hand into Kade's hair, jerking his head until he was looking at me. "It was mine."

Kade's jaw went slack from shock until he realized I'd betrayed him. Pure rage darkened his eyes as he tried pulling out of my hold.

"Mili?" Gray forced out hoarsely. "You did this?"

"Next time you want to lie to me," I murmured as venom filled my voice, "remember that a woman always fucking knows."

They began shouting when the police tugged them to the doorway. My heart pounded, knowing the crew would now be my enemies once they found out. Kade gave me one last glance before he was shoved down the stairs, the hurt in his eyes making my stomach lurch. They started this. I had to fucking remember that.

"You okay?" Rylan asked quietly.

"I am now," I stated, picking up my bag and grabbing my phone. "I need to go."

"Come back to my house. Just for a bit so we can talk."

"I need to get the hell out of this city before Vic and Juan realize it was me who turned in Kade and Gray."

"You will. I'll even get you a car. Please, Mili," he urged, pulling me into his arms. "I know that after this, you're really not coming back. Give me five minutes with you."

"All right. Five minutes."

43

Milina

We were only two streets away from Kade and Gray's house when Rylan pulled into a driveway. My nerves had only gotten worse since we got in the car. I gave it less than an hour before Kade and Gray got word out that this was all me. I needed to get as far away from Ridgewood as I could. I'd already texted Caleb to tell me where he was, and I was waiting for him to respond.

"You okay?" Rylan asked as he took the keys out of the ignition.

"Perfect," I muttered. "Thank you, Rylan."

"You know I've been trying to take them down for years. It's you I should be thanking."

"It won't bring down the whole crew."

"No…but it's a start."

"I really should go—"

"Come inside first. I'll give you some food for the road."

I chuckled. "You don't want me to come in for food."

"I just want to talk."

"Only for a few minutes." I got out of his car and followed him through the garage.

He opened the door for me, and I stepped into a hall. He flipped on the lights before leading me down the wide hallway until it branched out into a large living room. From the pristine white couch to the glass table with nothing on it, this house looked like it was staged to sell.

"I'm going to take a guess that you don't spend a lot of time here," I muttered.

"No, I'm usually at my office." He gently took the backpack off my shoulder and set it on the couch before pulling me into his arms.

"I thought you liked them," he said, searching my eyes. "What did they do to you?"

I frowned. "They lied. Their bosses know I'm here and they want me. And when I asked them about it, they didn't come clean."

Something seemed to be on the tip of his tongue, but he only shook his head, pulling me with him to another room. The house was one floor, and the hallway seemed to connect all the rooms. We stopped in what looked like a small library. One wall had floor-to-ceiling shelves of books, and I glanced at a couple of titles, wondering if we had the same taste, but from what I saw, it was all nonfiction biographies.

We stopped in front of an oversized chair, and Rylan sat down first before tugging me onto his lap. A lump grew in my throat, knowing what he was about to say.

"I'm leaving. Nothing you can say will change that," I said quietly.

He ran a finger down my cheek. "I know. You'll be safer that way anyway."

"The crew might retaliate against you," I said with a frown.

"Don't worry about me. I can handle it."

With those words, he kissed me, his hand going to the back of my head. I opened my mouth, his tongue clashing with mine. I let myself forget about the world for the next few minutes as I kissed him. Until my phone vibrated in my pocket. Pulling away, I saw it was Caleb.

"I have to take this." I climbed off him.

He stood when I did. "I'll go get that food I promised you."

Watching him leave the room, I answered the call. "Hey."

"Why are you leaving?" he asked immediately. "Did they do something?"

"You could say that," I mumbled. "Where are you? I'm leaving in a few minutes. Once I get a car."

"Are you okay—"

"I'm fine," I interrupted. "Where are you?"

"Nevada."

"Not too far. I should be there by morning."

"I'll text you the address." He paused. "Are you coming by yourself?"

"Yes," I clipped out. "I'll call you later."

"Wait. I got back on the dark web. There's a new name popping up."

I stared out the window into the darkness. "Name?"

"Yeah. I've seen it before, but it was never an issue until now."

"Does it have to do with Joel?"

He sighed. "I don't know. I don't think so. But it has to do with you."

My shoulders tensed. "How?"

"I just tracked his online movements, and he's been searching about you. Sapphire. Jobs. Identity. People who know you." The keys on his computer clacked in the background. "He's been at it for months, and I don't know how the fuck I missed it."

"Who is he?"

"I've tried finding his real name, but he knows what he's doing. I only know his screen name."

I leaned against the glass. "What is it?"

"The Chameleon."

"Chameleon?" I whispered, frozen in place.

My heart stopped, and I tried to stop the images rushing into my head. It wasn't fucking possible. That name could mean things to a lot of people. Yet my night with Rylan wouldn't stop playing on repeat. When my fingers brushed his chest tattoo. His chameleon tattoo. No. He wasn't a part of my world. He was the good guy. The man who'd put his life on the line for me.

"What's wrong?" Caleb asked. "Do you know who he is?"

"Mili, you ready?"

I spun around, my stomach dropping as Rylan stepped through the archway and back into the library. Did he hear me? Was it him? It couldn't be. But why was dread claiming me as I looked at him now?

"I have to go," I muttered.

"Wait. What happened—"

I hung up, sliding my phone back into my pocket. Forcing a grin, I glanced at the small bag in his hands. "Thanks for the food."

"Of course." His smile was the same as always, except maybe a little sad. "Everything okay?"

"Yeah, it was just Caleb."

"Did he tell you where he is?"

I swallowed. "Yes. He's back in Florida."

I shifted, panic clawing me when I realized I didn't have my bag. Which had my gun in it. He'd taken it off and then brought me to another room. Was that on purpose? I shuffled forward, moving to take the bag from his hand, but he pulled back. My eyes snapped to his.

"Are you okay?" he questioned.

"No. My nerves are fried. I need to leave."

Again, I went for the bag, and this time he dropped it and snatched my wrist. My breath hitched, my suspicion full-blown now.

"I heard you," he murmured, his gaze locked with mine.

"Heard what?"

My heart was pounding in my ears, and I decided it was time to end the charade. Him grabbing me only meant one fucking thing.

"Tell me, Rylan. What does your tattoo really mean?" I asked, my voice almost catching.

Regret flashed in his eyes, but it didn't mean a thing to me now. He'd been playing me for months. I ripped my arm from his grasp, backing up until I was far away from him. Unfortunately, that meant the doorway too since he was standing in front of it.

"Let me explain," he said slowly, his body tensing.

"Please fucking do," I snapped.

"Not here. We need to go somewhere—"

"Hell no. I'm leaving."

I advanced toward him, making it very clear I had every intention of getting past him one way or another. Even with being laid up for a month, I was still deadly. I could handle him.

"I can't let you leave," he said in a low voice. "Not now. You were never supposed to find out."

I didn't even try to ask what he meant. I could do that another time when I wasn't trying to run from a city. He wouldn't be hard to find. And Caleb could do more research on him before I made a move.

"You're more than welcome to try and fucking stop me." My grin was full of hatred. "I won't even need a gun."

He lunged first, surprising me. I ducked to the side, swinging my fist toward his face, but he blocked it with his forearm.

"I'm not going to hurt you," he grunted, failing to block my next hit.

Too late for that. These three men had caused my heart more pain than I'd ever experienced. We moved around the room with him blocking my hits and me trying to land one good enough to give me a second to run. No matter which way I went, he never let me near the doorway.

"Get off me," I snarled when he grabbed my arm. I moved to hit the inside of his elbow, but he kicked out, sweeping my feet out from under me. I crashed to the floor, and I tried scrambling away before he could get on top of me. I slammed my foot into his kidney, and he groaned, but it didn't slow him down. Fuck, he was strong. Much stronger than I thought. And he knew how to fight. It seemed he had as many secrets as I did.

I got back to my feet, only for him to get his arms around my waist, sending us both onto the chair. I landed on my stomach, my knees hitting the hard floor. He got one arm behind my back, practically sitting on top of me while he reached for the other.

"You fucking asshole," I screeched, attempting to stand. But with his weight smothering me, that was impossible.

Something soft wrapped around my wrists, and I writhed, trying to get free. My face was nearly shoved into the cushions, and he didn't let up until whatever he tied was tight. I twisted my wrists, knowing I could free myself, but not right away. I'd have to work through the damn knot. He finally climbed off me, pulling me with him.

"I told you. I'm not going to hurt you." He didn't look me in the eye as he kept a tight hold on my arm and pulled me out of the library. His tie was missing, telling me what was around my wrists. "But we need to go somewhere so you'll understand."

"Let go, Rylan. Please." My voice trembled, and I worked my way up to real tears as I swallowed my anger. If he really didn't want to hurt me, then maybe I could play on his emotions.

He glanced at me, shaking his head. "Nice try, Mili. But no matter how hard you try to act, that anger toward me is deep in your eyes."

My tears stopped, and my glare turned into loathing. "I fucking trusted you."

His jaw clenched. "I know. That was the whole point."

I didn't respond, letting him lead me down the hall. If I put up a fight, he'd only pick me up and make it harder for me to work on the knot. He walked a little behind me, making it easy to tell if I was going to attack. I just had to wait until he messed up. One second of him distracted was all I needed. We got to the end of the hall, and he stopped in front of a locked door. Keeping my chest pressed against the wall, he quickly unlocked it before placing me back in front of him.

My stomach tightened when all I saw was a set of stairs leading to a basement. "Where are you taking me?"

"You'll see when we get there."

"Not good enough." I moved to try and rush him, but he saw it coming, and he leaned down, throwing me over his shoulder. My screams did nothing as he carried me down the stairs. I craned my neck, seeing nothing but a long tunnel. A few lights made a dim pathway, and I flailed my legs until his arms tightened around my thighs. I subtly moved my fingers, trying to reach the knot as he walked farther into the tunnel.

44

Kade

I leaned against the counter, staring at my phone, waiting for the damn call.

"How long do you think it'll take her to find out we aren't behind bars?" Gray asked, watching crew members put a tarp over our doorway until we could get a new door.

"Not long," I muttered.

"She might come back to finish what she started." Gray sounded almost wishful about that.

"She's smart enough not to," I grated out. "She's as good as dead if she does. Vic and Juan want her even more now that she turned on us."

"When we got her arrested, she said it was boring." He chuckled. "Never would have guessed she'd do the same fucking thing."

"But she did do it," I snapped. "She fucked us over. And she did it instead of killing us because she thought it would be worse on us. She *hates* us."

Gray's smile fell, and his eyes went cold. "I know that, Kade. Thank you for reminding me."

One of the guys came up to the counter. "That's as good as we can get it until your new door gets here."

I nodded. "Make sure everyone stays clear of the stairs. Actually, keep everyone in the front of the house down there."

The guys left, letting the tarp fall into place. It was going to be fucking annoying not to have privacy for the next day or two. But that wasn't what was on my mind. She was, like always.

"Has he called yet?" Gray asked.

"No."

"You think—" He stopped talking and turned toward the hall. "Did you hear that?"

"Hear what?"

I straightened up, hearing it too. It almost sounded like...a woman screaming. Gray and I looked at each other before racing to the end of the hallway. The noise was louder now, and I hurriedly typed in the code, unlocking the door. Gray's shoulder hit mine when I pulled it open. My heart stuttered as I stared into the room.

"What the fuck?" Gray muttered in shock.

Rylan closed the closet door, turning to face us. But it wasn't him that was the surprise. It was the girl on his shoulder who was screaming bloody murder and thrashing like crazy. Rylan's jaw was clenched as he walked past us.

"What the hell are you doing here?" I hissed. "And with her?"

Rylan didn't answer, striding into the living room and dumping Mili onto the leather chair next to the couch. It was only then that I realized her hands were tied. I raised an eyebrow, wondering how hard it had been for him to do that. From his red, splotchy cheek, I was guessing she'd put up a fight.

"You fucking asshole..." she trailed off when her gaze landed on

Gray and me. Her eyes darted around the room, growing wide when she realized she was back in our house. "What the hell?"

All three of us stood in front of her, and Rylan pushed her back down when she tried getting off the chair. She scowled, glaring at him as she leaned back.

I turned toward Rylan. "Why the fuck is she here? You were supposed to make sure she left town."

Rylan scrubbed a hand down his face. "Caleb found my name on the web. She knows."

"Shit," Gray mumbled.

"What's going on?" Mili growled, her eyes trailing over each of us. "Did you—did you plan this together? Are you working with Rylan?"

We stayed silent, and I crossed my arms, my stomach twisting painfully. She was never supposed to find out. Rylan was going to make sure she left town, and that was supposed to be it. If Vic and Juan knew she was here, there were going to be huge fucking problems.

"Since none of you want to answer me, then let me leave," she snapped.

"Yes," I said quietly. "We're working with him."

"The whole arresting thing was what? An act?" she shrieked, staring at Rylan.

"Yeah. But he wasn't supposed to blow our door off," Gray said, trying to lighten the mood.

"How long? Tell me how long the three of you have been working together," she demanded.

"Forever," I stated simply.

She frowned in confusion. "What?"

Gray shrugged. "He's part of the crew. Always has been."

Her lips parted. "No. That's not possible. He has no affiliation—"

"That was the point," Rylan cut her off. "We never went our separate ways like I told you. We just let the public think we did."

Her chest heaved as she took in that information, still looking at us like we were lying. I crouched down, and she pressed into the cushions to get away from me. Her distrust radiated from her every pore.

"How do you think we knew everything?" I asked softly. "The night you were at the dive bar with that biker. Who did you tell where you were? When we were in Roseville and we snuck in the hotel room without you noticing? How did you think we did that? Because we knew what you were doing."

"We knew when to go to your apartment because you told Rylan you'd leave in the morning, not at night," Gray added, clearly wanting her to know everything now that it was out. "We didn't just get lucky."

Her nostrils flared. "Fuck you. Fuck all of you."

"You were supposed to leave," I snapped. "Ry called us the second after you told him your plan to fuck us over—"

"Ry?" she asked sharply. "He's not just a member of the crew, is he? You're all friends."

She was spot on. The three of us were best friends. The tunnel he'd brought her through led between our houses. He lived here and had the other home for show.

"How did you find my apartment?" she asked snidely. "I know I didn't give you a chance to put a tracker on any of my things."

I shook my head. "No. At least you didn't with Gray or me. You didn't trust us enough. But Rylan? You opened up more to him."

She snapped her head toward him. "You did it? When?"

Rylan hesitated. "The first time I kissed you. I put it in your bag."

She huffed out a laugh. "Holy shit. You all outplayed me."

"It started out that way, yes." Rylan put his hand on the armrest. "It changed though. Because I started to care for you. We all did—"

"Save it," she snarled. "I don't believe anything that comes out of your fucking mouth."

The truth in her words ripped me apart. She would never fucking forgive us. And I was fine with that if she was out of this city and safe. But I could see it in her eyes. She wasn't about to just leave. She wanted sweet vengeance now that she knew Rylan was with us. But if she stayed here, she'd be in trouble. Vic and Juan wanted her to pay for what she'd tried to do to us.

"What now?" she sneered.

"Seeing as we don't have a door, you'll stay at Rylan's until we can figure it out," I answered, seeing her go rigid.

"I'm not staying here," she hissed.

"You are for now." I held her stare, not wavering. She knew Rylan's other identity. If she and Caleb picked it apart, then they could take down the entire crew. Plus, I was sure if we freed her now, I'd have to worry about waking up with a gun to my head.

"Fuck," I muttered, reaching for her. She twisted away from me as I slid her phone out of her pocket. "Caleb's going to track her."

She glared daggers at me while I slid the SIM card out and shut down the phone. "He'll find me anyway."

"Let's hope by then we can come to some kind of agreement that doesn't end with you trying to kill us," Gray muttered.

"I never should have come here," she muttered, staring at the ceiling. "I should have just planned the Panther job alone."

Her words weren't for us. She was thinking out loud as we all watched her. My phone vibrated, and I strode to the counter, seeing Vic's name flashing on the screen. I walked down the hall, answering it.

"Yeah," I clipped out.

"Come to the club. We need to meet," Vic demanded.

"Now?"

"Yes, now. Both you and Gray...and bring her."

My blood went cold. "She's not here."

"No more fucking lies," he roared. "I have men coming now. She's coming whether you want her to or not. And then we need to talk to you and Gray about what loyalty is."

"We live for the crew," I snapped. "She'll work with us. You can't kill her."

"Get here now."

He hung up on me, and I stared at the phone for a moment before racing back to the living room. I caught Rylan's sleeve, dragging him into the hall.

"Ry, take her back to your house now—"

Noises came from the front of the house, and I peeked around the corner. Six guys suddenly appeared, pushing the tarp to the side. They looked nervous, but once they saw Mili, one of them started typing away on his phone. Shit. I pushed Rylan farther back, giving him a silent warning to stay out of sight. Only a select few in the crew knew about him. Keeping it a secret was why it worked so well.

"We have orders to bring her to the club," one of them said, lifting his chin.

"Fuck that. I'm not going." Mili cried in protest when I pulled her up. I moved to untie her wrists, only to find she'd already gotten herself free. I raised an eyebrow, and she shrugged before shaking out her arms.

"We really don't have a choice right now," I breathed in her ear. "Either Gray and I go with you, or those men are going to take you without us."

"Aren't you their bosses?"

"They take orders from us. But Vic and Juan's say goes over ours. They're here on their orders. Not ours."

"I won't go."

"They're not going to hurt you." I held her upper arm, leading her toward the door.

"They can't hurt me any more than the three of you already have," she muttered.

One of the men moved to take her from me, and I shoved him aside. "I got her."

"Let's get this over with," Gray mumbled as he followed us down the stairs.

45

Milina

I was still reeling after learning about Rylan. And I was kicking myself for not seeing it. But thinking back, I couldn't remember one time I was even suspicious of them working together. They were good. More than good. I gritted my teeth, shifting in the middle seat and accidently brushing against Kade. I was stuck between him and Gray in the back seat while two men were in the front. The short ride had been silent, and my stomach knotted with nerves when we parked behind the club.

Vic and Juan would want my head after all this. Kade promised they wouldn't hurt me, but I couldn't take his word on that. Or anything else. I was done trusting them or anyone else besides Caleb. If I got out of here alive, I was never coming back.

"Come on, Rebel," Gray said in a low voice, grabbing my arm lightly.

Holding my head high, I shook off his hand and climbed out of the car. My eyes darted around the alley, looking for a chance to bolt. But the men who brought us joined with four others, and they were all sporting weapons of some sort. I didn't stand a fucking chance. We climbed the stairs, and Kade opened the door, going in first with me behind him.

My heart raced when Vic and Juan both turned their attention to me. They were pissed, and their anger was all on me. Sapphire or not, they wanted to take their revenge out on me. Kade and Gray both angled themselves in front of me, a move none of the men in here missed. My eyes wandered from the bar to the couches before going to the one-way glass. This room was where my adventure in Ridgewood had started. I guessed it was poetic if this was where it ended.

But I wasn't about to go quietly. I sure as hell wasn't going to hide behind a wall of muscle. I was Sapphire. Strong. Deadly. And not a fucking coward. Letting my gaze settle on dangerous, I pushed past Kade and Gray, ignoring their protests. Striding to the bar, I poured myself a drink and moved toward the glass, surprise filtering through when I saw that the club was empty. They'd shut it down for this meeting.

"Mili. We have things to discuss," Vic said gruffly.

"We do," I purred, turning and giving him a lethal smile. "I don't enjoy being summoned."

"You don't call the shots anymore," Juan snapped. "You tried ruining us."

"No, I was playing. If I actually tried, you wouldn't be standing here right now."

Kade and Gray were watching with frowns on their faces, neither of them liking that I was across the room from them. My gaze flicked to the door near me that went down to the club. As of right now, that was my way out since the other door was blocked by about six men. I wondered if it was unlocked.

"As much as we need to talk about this, we need to wait." Vic's words made my attention go back to the bar. "We're having a business meeting."

"You think I'm going to work with you now?" I asked, trying to ignore my growing anxiety. "Who are you meeting with?"

"Someone who is interested in working a job with Sapphire," Juan answered.

I straightened up, fear washing through me. "You told someone I've been working with you?"

"Someone reached out to us," Vic answered, watching me carefully.

I inched back toward the door. "Do they know I'm here?"

Gray whispered something in Kade's ear, and I watched, my panic growing when Gray disappeared behind the door marked *Private*. Juan glanced at him before focusing back on me. Apparently, whatever Gray was doing wasn't out of the ordinary.

"Do they know I'm here?" I asked louder, making Vic scowl.

"I told them it was a possibility," Vic answered. "You want to make up for what you did to Kade and Gray, then you'll work the jobs we want. Understand?"

"What's his name?" I asked, my voice getting shrill.

"It doesn't matter. You'll do it." Vic stirred his drink, nodding at his men, who strode across the room, cutting off my exit plan.

"What's his fucking name?" I screamed.

Kade's eyes grew wide, but I ignored him, stalking to the bar. The tension thickened when I got within a foot of Juan and Vic.

"Who?" I spat out.

Vic studied me, shaking his head to the men who I was sure were closing ranks behind me. "They haven't given names."

"They've given something," I hissed. "You wouldn't meet with them without knowing something."

"You're not running this," Juan said gruffly. "It doesn't matter who the fuck it is—"

Snaking my arm around him, I grabbed an empty beer bottle, smashing the neck of it against the counter. Juan moved to get a hold of my arm, but I pressed the jagged glass against his neck before he had a chance. Vic went rigid, and Juan stayed absolutely still as he glared at me.

"Mili," Kade said from behind me. "Put it down. We'll talk about this."

"We were talking," I said, tilting my head. "But no one here is saying the things I want to hear."

"You're dead if you hurt me," Juan snapped, a vein above his eye bulging.

"You never planned for me to survive this anyway. At least with this, I'll take one of you with me." I pressed the glass into his skin harder. "Give me a fucking name."

"You won't do it," Vic sneered.

"Fucking try me," I told him, my voice calm. I wasn't scared to die. I'd expected it when I walked into this room.

"A symbol," Juan grated out. "That's all they gave us."

"What was it?"

"A skull. With snakes going through its eyes," Juan answered, nearly flinching when my body jerked.

"No," I breathed out, my breath locking in my chest.

I staggered back, making Juan sag against the counter. Hands grabbed my arms and spun me around until I was looking into Kade's eyes.

"Mili, what's wrong?" he asked quietly.

"What did you do?" I shrieked.

"What? Nothing—"

"You brought them here," I screamed, losing all sense of calm as my panic took over.

Kade tried wrapping his arms around me, tugging me farther away from the bar. I let him, running my hand over his clothes until I found what I was looking for. It wasn't a gun, but the folding knife I pulled from his pocket was better than nothing. I flicked it open and swung it, giving Kade one warning to let me go.

He released me, concern swirling in his gaze. "We'll talk about this—"

"There's nothing to talk about," I hissed, my voice shaking. "You brought them here. I'm fucking dead."

"Who?" Vic asked.

I didn't answer, stumbling back until I hit the couch. They all watched me but made no move to grab me as I held the knife tightly. There were too many men in here for me to fight my way through when they had guns and I didn't. Gray came out of the other room, readjusting his hoodie, stopping in his tracks as he looked past me.

"I told you that I'd find you, Mili."

The voice came from behind me, and my body locked up. Panic flooded through me as I whirled around. New men were now pouring in through the door. But it was the one who was already inside the room, staring at me, who made fear flood me.

"Liam," I choked out, taking a step back.

His eyes bored into mine before I broke the stare, my eyes darting around to find some sort of escape.

"There's no way out," he murmured as if we were the only two in the room. "Not anymore."

"I won't go," I cried out hoarsely. "I'll die in this room before that happens."

"You know him?" Vic asked sharply. "What is this?"

"This is exactly what we wanted," Liam said, keeping his eyes on me. "Don't worry. You'll be paid handsomely for turning her over."

"The fuck she's leaving," Gray snarled from behind me.

I didn't dare look behind me, and I straightened my stance when Liam stepped toward me. My heart was beating painfully, taking note that there were at least five men with him. A couple I recognized while the rest were new faces.

"Come on, Mili," he coaxed quietly. "You fight, and this will end badly."

"This wasn't what we talked about," Vic said gruffly. "She works with us."

"We'd love to work with your crew in the future. If Mili's working with you, then you must be good," Liam praised, trying to keep the peace. "But right now, she needs to come with me."

"Fuck you," I hissed, my fear swallowing me. "I'm not going."

"You are," he stated. "One way or another."

He came at me, and I raised the blade to go for his throat. He easily avoided my attack, his hand lashing out to try and grab my wrist. I yanked my arm back, keeping a grip on the knife. I swung at him, slashing his arm. His grunt was the only sign that I'd gotten him. He fell back for a moment, and I saw his men raising their guns and aiming behind us. If I were to turn around, I was sure the crew was doing the same thing. They had no idea what the hell they'd gotten themselves into.

I stayed light on my feet as I watched Liam's body to see which way he was going to move. Doubt clouded my thoughts. I could defend myself against him for only so long. Liam was the one who taught me to fight. I'd kept up with it after I escaped, but he still knew my moves more than anyone. And he was better than me. Plus the men he brought with him—I was so fucked.

"Don't do this," I pleaded, trying to keep my words quiet. "Please, Liam."

He shook his head. "It's too late."

He lunged at me again, this time successfully getting a hold of my wrist. Before he even tried prying the knife from my hand, he snapped a handcuff around my wrist, tightening it until it pinched my skin. I punched him across the face with my left hand, bringing my knee up to his stomach. He yanked me to the side, making my neck snap painfully. There was shuffling in the room, but all I was focused on was Liam as he went for my other arm.

"No," I screeched, feeling the metal close around my wrist. Liam's face was stone cold as he locked the handcuff. He took the knife from me, closing it and tossing it behind me.

"Let her go," Kade growled from behind me.

Liam spun me around, kicking the back of my legs until I fell to my knees. I stared down at my cuffed hands, my head swimming. I had a wire in my bra I could use to free myself, but I doubted Liam would give me a chance to move for it. He kept a hand on my shoulder to keep me from getting back up, and I finally raised my head. Gray and Kade both had guns aimed at Liam, while the rest of their men were focused on the men behind us. Vic and Juan were still near the bar, both had weapons out too.

"What the hell is going on?" Vic hissed, his eyes falling on me. "You told us you wanted to work with her."

"We've been looking for her for a long time," Liam murmured, his fingers digging into my shoulder.

"Why?" Kade snapped, meeting my gaze.

There was a noise behind me, and all eyes went behind me before a new voice rang out.

"Because she needs to come home."

46

Milina

Fear shot down my spine, and my mouth went dry when the voice from my nightmares echoed through the room. My heart seized, terror sinking into my bones. Even if Liam's hand wasn't on me, I couldn't move if I tried. Someone came up beside me, and I squeezed my eyes shut, praying this wasn't fucking real life. Fingers grasped my chin, yanking my head up, forcing me to confront my own personal hell.

"Open your eyes, Lina. Do you know how long I've waited for this moment?"

I didn't listen, not having the courage to look at him. I should have let the crew kill me. It would have been better than this because now I knew I'd survive the night. Trapped in a life that was worse than death. I cried out as pain exploded across my jaw when he hit me. Shouting filled the room, but I was only focused on the hand that grabbed my face again.

"Open your fucking eyes," he growled. "You know I don't like asking twice."

I swallowed thickly, forcing my eyes open. He came into focus, and I choked down my sob when I met his gaze. It had been nearly six years since I'd seen him, but he looked almost the same. His hair had a few silver strands throughout the brown, but it was still long on one side. New tattoos crawled up his neck, but his cruel smirk was the same as all those years ago. His eyes blazed with both anger and smugness as I stared at him.

"Still so beautiful." He released my face, running his fingers down the cheek he'd just hit. "But you've changed. You've got an attitude... and fight. I don't fucking like it."

"Joel, I'm sorry," I breathed out hoarsely. "I never should have done it—"

"Done what?" he asked, acting genuinely curious. "Tried burning down my fucking empire before trapping me in a hellhole of a prison? Everyone thought I was dead. But don't worry, I'm fixing it. And now you're back where you belong."

"I betrayed you. Just kill me." I bit back my whimper when his hold on my face turned painful.

"Oh no," he murmured. "You know I could never do that, Lina. You're mine."

"You need to leave our club," Kade spoke up, his voice nearly shaking with rage. I couldn't see him past Joel, but no one in the room was moving. Guns were still raised in a standoff that I knew the crew had no chance at winning.

"We're leaving," Joel answered, his eyes gleaming dangerously as he hauled me to my feet.

"Not with her." Gray stepped closer, making everyone shift with tension.

Joel laughed, shooting ice down my spine. "Oh right. Liam, make sure these men get the money—"

"We don't want your money," Kade snapped. "We have a deal with her to work a job. It's not finished yet."

"I'll work with you," Joel said, annoyance crawling into his voice.

"We don't know who the fuck you are," Gray said as he crept even closer.

Joel watched him curiously. "I thought you wanted to work with Sapphire."

My chest tightened, the world I'd built in the last five years shattering under me. I stumbled when Joel yanked me in front of him. Gray's jaw clenched as he watched, his hand tightening on his gun.

"Mmm," Joel hummed out. "You've fooled all of them, Lina. What a naughty little liar you are."

"Lying about what?" Vic asked stiffly.

"She didn't just fuck me over. She stole from me." Joel's fingers stayed wrapped around my arm. "My money. My name."

The air in here seemed stifling as everyone stared at me. Kade and Gray had questions in their gazes, and I looked back at the floor, refusing to let them see my face. My eyes brimmed with tears, and I sucked in a breath, forcing them away.

"She locked me away and then took the Sapphire name," Joel murmured. "As if she didn't know my men would figure it out."

"You were Sapphire?" Juan asked, shock in his voice.

Joel's nails dug into my arm. "I *am* fucking Sapphire. I'm not dead. And now I get to reclaim what she took."

I could feel Kade's and Gray's stares, but I kept my gaze on my cuffed wrists. Caleb was right. I never should have started working as Sapphire. But I couldn't stop myself once I started. It made me strong. The power. The jobs. I craved it—needed it.

"I don't give a shit who she is or isn't," Gray growled. "You're not taking her."

"If it's not about working with her, then it's something else..." He trailed off, and my stomach plummeted, knowing what he was going to ask next. "It's more than just business. Were you fucking him?"

He twisted me around, fisting my hair until he could study my face. "I know that's not possible."

A lump grew in my throat. "Joel—"

"What self-respecting man would touch a woman who is clearly owned by someone else?" His hand slipped under my shirt, and I cringed as he dragged his fingers over my lower back.

Gray was now close enough that he could almost reach out and touch me, but he stayed still as Joel lifted my shirt, a snarl vibrating his chest when he saw my tattoo.

"You covered my artwork," he said, his voice full of venom. "Why? So you could whore out while I was gone? Did you really think I wouldn't come back?"

"I'd rather die than be yours again," I exploded, unable to take it anymore. I was struggling to breathe, suffocating from the life I couldn't escape.

He raised his arm to hit me, but another hand grabbed me, pulling me from Joel. I slammed into Gray's chest, his arm going around my waist. I froze when Joel pulled his gun out, pressing it against Gray's forehead.

"You don't touch what's mine." Joel's eyes filled with threat.

"You heard her—she doesn't want to be yours," Gray shot back.

"Gray, let go," I said under my breath, knowing Joel would shoot him in a heartbeat.

"She'll always be mine." Joel looked at me. "Sapphire wasn't the only name she took."

"What are you talking about?" Kade snapped, and I heard his steps halt when Joel's finger went to the trigger.

"As my wife, she has my last name."

Gray's heart raced against my back, and I bit my tongue as they heard all of my secrets. In name, I was Joel's. I'd gotten married at nineteen. Not because I wanted it. But I went along with it because by then I was already stuck with him and I saw no escape. What did it matter if he forced me to marry him when he'd already had me trapped anyway?

"Now, let her go so we can leave," Joel demanded.

"This is our city. Our club. And now you're threatening my men," Vic roared from somewhere behind me. "Put the gun down, or you and your men won't leave alive."

As Joel responded to Vic, Gray leaned down, his lips brushing my ear.

"You survived him," he whispered. "I see you shutting down. Don't. You're strong. You have a voice now. Use it, Rebel. Don't fucking let him take that from you again. You won't leave with him."

Joel's eyes dropped to my face, scowling when he saw how close Gray was to me. Fear paralyzed me as I stood there. Joel had ingrained in me that I was weak. Nothing but an object to him. And I'd believed that for years until I snapped. Was I strong enough to finally fight back? Or just stupid now that the devil was staring me in the face? I failed at escaping him. And if I thought life was bad before, I knew it would only be worse now.

But as I watched Joel, I came to a decision. I couldn't stand by and do nothing because every instinct screamed that he was about to pull the trigger. I ripped out of Gray's grip, my cuffed hands grabbing Joel's wrist and pushing his arm up so the gun was pointing at the ceiling. The shock in his eyes terrified and satisfied me at the same time. I'd never fought back against him.

"That was a mistake," he spat out, trying to shake off my grip.

"Wait. Joel, I'll go with you." I let my voice tremble while I let go of his arm to grab the collar of his shirt. "I'm sorry."

Before he responded, I smashed my head into his face. He choked out a curse, his eyes watering as blood gushed from his nose. I threw my knee into his balls before going for his gun again. It only took a second to wrestle it from his grip, and a rush shot through me, knowing I could finish him right now. My gut twisted because I wouldn't. There was a reason he was still alive. Why I sent him to prison instead of killing him. Gritting my teeth, I kicked his ankle out from under him before ducking when shots rang out.

"No one fucking shoot her," Joel bellowed through his pain. "She's mine to deal with."

I crawled away, climbing to my feet and seeing Liam out of the corner of my eye. I raised my gun, and he must have realized my zero hesitation because he launched himself behind the couch when I shot at him. I ran toward the door, shooting anyone who tried to grab me. I didn't know whether they were Joel's men or part of the crew—and I didn't care. I was getting out.

I made it to the door and bounded down the stairs, taking two and three at a time. Someone was at my back, but I didn't take the time to see who it was. I raced through the empty club, still hearing shots from above. I slammed into the doors, my breath hitching when I found them locked.

Someone ran into me, and I raised my gun until I saw Gray. I looked behind him, my heart lurching when Joel's men came from the stairwell. But that wasn't the reason panic had a hold on me.

"Kade—"

"He's fine," Gray ground out. "Don't worry about him. Get out of here, Mili. And don't fucking look back."

He opened his hand, revealing a set of keys. I looked over his shoulder, my warning catching in my throat when one of the men raised his pistol and shot. Gray stumbled into me when it hit him in the back. His eyes widened as his breath left him.

"No!" I screamed. "Gray. You're okay. I'll get you out."

I aimed, shooting the guy in the heart, not sparing him another glance while I focused on Gray. He fell to his knees, and I grabbed under his arm with my hands still cuffed, trying to lift him back up. I could barely hold his weight, and he shook his head, groaning.

"Go, Mili," he demanded, his voice laced with pain. Raising his arm, he grabbed my wrist and pressed the keys into my palm. "There's a car down the street. Go left when you get out the doors."

"I'm not leaving you," I cried, my body shaking. "This is my fault."

"Go," he nearly yelled, shoving me off him as he fell back to his knees. "Run. And don't look back."

"No—"

One of the men got closer, and I shot him in the shoulder before aiming again and getting him in the head. I was only using one hand since the keys were in my other. Having the cuffs on made it even more difficult. There were two more, but they halted, hearing Joel yelling upstairs. When they turned to go back toward the stairs, I fumbled with the keys, finding the one that fit the lock. The door swung open, and I moved to grab Gray again, but he pushed me away.

"Leave," he grated out. "I know you'll get out. I need to find Kade."

My stomach sank, not having the heart to tell him that he wasn't moving after the bullet he took. He was lying on his back, and I went to roll him over to see the wound, but he shoved me again.

"I'm not running to leave you here to die," I screamed, trying to make him see sense.

"You're running to survive," he told me as he jerked a nod to the open door. "Go."

I raised my eyes to see Joel, his murderous gaze set on me. My stomach dropped, and I gripped the gun tighter as some of his men appeared behind him.

"I'm sorry," I choked out, squeezing Gray's hand. "I never should have come to Ridgewood—"

"Don't fucking say that," he growled. "You heard what Kade said. It was fate, Mili."

Tears flowed, and I shook my head. "No—"

"Come here, Lina," Joel sang out, striding across the bar floor as if he had all the time in the world. "You really don't want to upset me any more than you already have."

Gray let go of my hand, meeting my eyes. "Go, Rebel."

Choking back a sob, I scrambled to my feet and raced out the door. I turned left, hitting the alarm on the set of keys Gray had given me. I kept hitting the button as I ran until the car started beeping when I was halfway down the block. Footsteps were clamoring behind me, and I ran to the car, jumping into the driver seat. It was a red Mustang, and I shifted it into gear as I flew down the road. Headlights were behind me, proving Joel's men had seen me get into the car.

I whipped around a corner, trying to remember any good side streets I could disappear on. I doubted Joel had changed his taste in cars over the years, and that meant whatever he and his men were driving probably outmatched even this Mustang. I needed to lose them before they gained on me.

I glanced at the gas gauge, cursing when I saw it had under a quarter of a tank. But that was a problem for later. Pressing down on the pedal, I pushed the car, barely slowing when I took another turn. I fishtailed, quickly getting back under control as I got to an open stretch of road. Headlights blinded me in my rearview mirror, and my grip tightened on the wheel. My wrists were raw and aching from the cuffs, but I pushed that away as I decided which way to go.

The car jerked when one of the two vehicles chasing me hit my back bumper. I swerved over the line as I tried to stay steady. With the speed I was going, they only needed one good hit to send me off the road. But Joel didn't want me dead, so he wouldn't do that. I shifted gears again, the pedal on the floor as I shot forward. A Porsche flew past me, and I bit my tongue, staring at the car that would beat mine in any fucking race. I shifted the wheel, moving to the other side of the road, but it did the same, keeping me behind it.

"Fuck," I muttered, attempting to get past it again. I saw a side road coming up, and I braked hard, my seat belt locking as I turned the corner. The road was narrow, and I was driving right along the highway. Headlights followed behind me, and I screamed when another car suddenly pulled beside me from another street. I glanced over, seeing Liam in the driver seat once we went under a streetlight. He matched my speed, staying inches from the Mustang. The road was barely big enough for us to be side by side, and buildings lined the street, making it impossible for me to widen the distance between us.

The other car stayed behind me, and I grinned when I saw a wide intersection coming up. The second the road got larger, I moved away from him while keeping the same speed. He had to know what I was planning, but he didn't accelerate or brake. Bracing myself, I jerked the wheel to the right, slamming into his car. My head hit the seat, making my teeth slam together, and I spun around, stopping in time to see his car hit a pole. The other car screeched to a halt next to me, and I barely glanced at it. It was some type of sedan that I could lose the second I hit open road.

Which was what I planned to do next.

I stepped on the gas, going back the way I came. The sedan followed, and I veered onto the entrance ramp of the highway. I dodged cars, staying in the fast lane of the three-lane road. Weaving in and out of the midnight traffic, I hoped there were no cops out. I'd run, but there was no promise I'd get away. Soon, the headlights that were following me disappeared, and I finally let out a long breath. I didn't slow down, not wanting to chance that they were still close enough to see my taillights.

I unclenched my fingers, which were stiff from gripping the wheel, and slowed to a speed that wouldn't be considered a felony if I got caught. My eyes darted between the road and the rearview mirror as I drove, and even though I was almost positive I'd lost them, I was still a ball of nerves.

Gray's face flashed in my mind, and I swallowed thickly, scared to even wonder if he was alive. Or Kade. What if they were both dead because of me? At first, I'd thought they were part of the reason that Joel had found me. But Gray helped me leave. He wouldn't have done that if he'd been in on the planning, would he? Or maybe they were, and then changed their minds. I didn't fucking know. All I knew was that I didn't want them dead, even if there was a possibility that they'd betrayed me.

My harrowing thoughts were interrupted when, a half hour later, the gas light turned on. I frowned, knowing I had less than fifty miles until the car died. I had no money on me. No phone. Nothing. I hadn't even stopped to take off the handcuffs yet. I drove another twenty minutes before getting off the highway and going into a city I'd never been in before. I passed the gas stations, tapping my fingers on the wheel. There were cameras everywhere. It would be stupid to steal gas. I'd just have to switch out cars.

I drove around the city until finally finding the beach. A few scattered cars were parked, and I glanced toward the sand, seeing people swimming and partying near a bonfire. Their laughs drifted through the open window, and it made my jealousy soar. A life of fun was something I hadn't had in a long fucking time. I circled around again, seeing a truck parked away from the other cars. Anticipation spread through me when I realized the windows were down. Parking far enough away, I slipped my hands into my shirt, pulling the wire from my bra. Once I picked the handcuff locks, I rubbed my sore wrists before taking the time to slide the wire back into place. I hopped out and locked the car, scanning the huge beach parking lot.

I stayed back, watching and making sure I was alone before walking briskly to the driver-side door. Going on my tiptoes, I reached through the window, hitting the unlock button to find out it wasn't locked. I frowned, wondering if the person who owned it was drunk. Who kept their windows down?

I climbed in, looking around before focusing on the interior. I blew out a frustrated breath, seeing it was a push button start. No key needed. I wouldn't be able to hot-wire this without tools. Newer vehicles made it a lot more difficult to boost if I didn't have the key. I turned, looking in the back seat for a toolbox. There was a small duffel bag, but it only had clothes in it. Reaching across the center console, I opened the glove box, freezing when my gaze landed on a handgun. I shot up, peering through the windshield. Maybe the guy didn't leave his truck unlocked because he was drunk. Maybe he left it because he knew people wouldn't fuck with his car.

I pursed my lips, debating for a quick second before grabbing the gun and putting it in my waistband. I pushed papers aside, seeing if there was anything else. Lifting the center console cover, I found ten dollars, and I snatched that too, shoving it in my bra. If I couldn't take the truck, at least I could use the money to gas up the Mustang until I found another car.

Pushing the door open, I jumped out, and my breath hitched when I got slammed into the side panel. I went for the gun, but the person grabbed my arm, shoving it into the truck door and holding it there.

"What the hell were you doing in my truck?"

I raised my head, looking at the guy who had me pinned. His hair was a dark brown and a bit longer on the top than the sides. He was wearing a tank top, and his arms were covered in ink. He looked more confused than angry as he took me in. My gaze went over his shoulder, seeing a blond guy staring at me.

I laughed lightly, shaking my head. "I got into the wrong car. I might have had too much to drink."

"If that were true, then what were you reaching for?"

"My phone."

His hand released my arm, and I stayed still when his eyes trailed down my face. I tilted my head to the side, but he'd already seen the bloody lip that Joel had given me.

"Are you running from someone?" he asked, his voice softer.

"Her wrists are cut up too," the blond guy muttered.

"I—I got into a fight with my ex, and he wasn't happy I was leaving him," I mumbled, surprisingly telling the truth.

A third guy appeared out of the darkness, and when he came under the light, I tensed. He had a tattoo on his neck that I recognized. They were in a gang. For the life of me, I couldn't remember the name, but I did not need to be around anyone in the life right now. Not when I had Joel after me, and possibly the crew. I didn't know who their allies were.

"I'm fine," I stuttered out. "I just want to go home."

"You live around here?" the guy in front of me asked.

"I have family that I can walk to. I'm sorry about touching your truck."

He released me, stepping away. My heart pounded, and I shuffled back, only for the blond to get in my way.

"I'll drive you," he said, his voice gentle.

"Thanks, but I'm good."

I began walking away, hearing the truck door open. Upping my speed, I began jogging, needing to get back to the Mustang before they realized I'd stolen from them.

"She took my fucking gun," the guy roared from behind me.

Fuck me. I bolted forward, full-blown running now. They chased after me, and I made it to the Mustang, only to be slammed into it. I reached behind me, grabbing the gun before he could get my arms. Raising it, I jammed it into the blond guy's chest, making his eyes bulge.

"Get the fuck back," I snarled.

"Who are you?" he asked.

"I don't want trouble," I stated, hearing one of the others chuckle. "I'll give the gun back. Just let me leave."

"Not until we know who you are," the guy grated out, staying still as I kept the gun on him.

"I'm no one. I'll leave your city."

My mouth went dry when something pressed against the side of my skull. Out of the corner of my eye, I could see the neck tattoo guy standing next to me with his arm up. His own gun stayed on me as the blond ripped the weapon from my hand. My jaw clenched when the guy kept his gun on me while grabbing my arm and pulling me away from the car.

"Make it easier on yourself and tell us what you're doing here," the blond guy said as they forced me to walk back toward the other vehicles.

"Nothing. I got in a bit of trouble, and I needed a car."

The brown-haired guy walked next to me. "You were going to steal my truck?"

I shrugged. "I didn't."

"You with a gang or MC?" he asked tightly.

"No."

The other guy scoffed. "Then why did you react to my tattoo? You spying on us?"

"Holy shit. No. I had no fucking idea whose truck that was."

"Sorry if we don't take your word for it," the blond guy said as we stopped behind a small car.

"She might have tats," one of the others said.

"Touch me, and there're going to be problems," I hissed, my pulse spiking.

They all exchanged a look before the trunk lid popped open. I began struggling, realizing what they planned on doing.

"Don't you fucking dare," I screamed when two of them picked me up and pushed me into the trunk.

"We just have to make sure you're not here to hurt us, and we'll let you go," the brown-haired guy said. He seemed to be the one in charge.

"I'm not. I don't know who the hell you are."

"We'll find that out."

All three of them stared at me for a moment, and I thought maybe they'd changed their minds. Until the lid slammed down on me, and muffled words came through the trunk.

"Welcome to Suncrest."

TO BE CONTINUED...

Author's Note

I am so excited to be sharing this story with all of you! I fell in love with the characters so much, and can't wait to finish their happily ever after in the next book. Thank you all for taking the time to read Runner, and I hope you enjoyed it! I would like to thank all my friends for helping this book become a reality. My friend, Jo, who made the amazing cover, putting a face to my story. To all my alpha readers who helped the story along as I wrote it, I appreciate you all so much! And of course, to my editor, Sax, and my proofreader, Beth. Thank you so much for making the story as good as it can be! And a huge thank you to all my readers. You all are the reason I keep writing my stories!

Until next time,
Kay Riley

ABOUT THE AUTHOR

Kay Riley writes dark contemporary romance. She loves writing feisty, strong heroines, and keeps things interesting with unexpected twists. Kay grew up in the Midwest but has lived in some amazing places, including Japan.

When she's not writing, she is spending time with her husband and kids. She loves cats, coffee, reading, and her guilty pleasure is watching reality shows.

You can follow Kay on social media to keep up with her newest stories.

ALSO BY KAY RILEY

SUNCREST BAY SERIES:

FATEFUL SECRETS

TREACHEROUS TRUTHS

RUTHLESS ENEMIES

HEIRS OF BRAIDWOOD

BURIED BETRAYAL

DEVIOUS DESIRES

RECKLESS REDEMPTION

STAND-ALONE:

RUBY REVENGE

SAPPHIRE DUET

RUNNER

ENDGAME

LITTLE HAVEN SERIES

TAINTED DECEPTION

TAINTED DESIRE

SHADOWS OF WAR SERIES

BITE OF SIN

Made in United States
Orlando, FL
01 April 2025